Hello, Stranger

RACHEL MARKS

PENGUIN BOOKS

PENGUIN BOOKS

UK | USA | Canada | Ireland | Australia
India | New Zealand | South Africa

Penguin Books is part of the Penguin Random House group of companies
whose addresses can be found at global.penguinrandomhouse.com.

First published by Penguin Michael Joseph 2022
Published in Penguin Books 2024

001

Typeset by Jouve (UK), Milton Keynes
Printed and bound in Great Britain by Clays Ltd, Elcograf S.p.A.

The authorized representative in the EEA is Penguin Random House Ireland,
Morrison Chambers, 32 Nassau Street, Dublin D02 YH68

A CIP catalogue record for this book is available from the British Library

ISBN: 978–1–405–94903–3

www.greenpenguin.co.uk

MIX
Paper | Supporting
responsible forestry
FSC® C018179

Penguin Random House is committed to a
sustainable future for our business, our readers
and our planet. This book is made from Forest
Stewardship Council® certified paper.

To Carl, for being my rock, and
Coco, my miracle in so many ways.

The Day of the Break-Up

LUCY

'You know this has to happen, don't you? That there's no alternative.'

We are lying in bed eating croissants, sharing the same tray – leaning towards each other so as not to spill crumbs on the quilt – our foreheads nearly touching, and in many ways it feels just like any other Sunday morning. Radio 2 is blaring out from the kitchen – we spend our lives with Jamie turning it off and me turning it back on – him enjoying the silence and me needing background noise. He has covered my croissant in Nutella, just how I like it, neither too little nor too much, and drowned his in jam so that it constantly spills out the sides and runs down his fingers. Normally, once he's finished, I'll grab his hands playfully and start to lick the jam off and he'll try to push me away with his legs, until we inevitably end up back under the covers.

But I don't think that will happen today. Because today I am leaving our relationship, the best relationship I've ever had in my life, knowing that it will be the relationship I will compare all others against. That one day I will walk down the aisle and there will be another man standing at the end waiting for me and amidst the joy I will feel a flutter catch in my chest as I picture Jamie at the altar and wonder *what if?*

'There's not no alternative. The alternative is that we don't split up.'

We're talking about it in the way we might discuss a story in the paper or on the evening news, both starting by calmly presenting our argument, using well-thought-out examples to back ourselves up, listening to each other's point of view whilst knowing we are never going to agree. I'm a complete nightmare for backing down – we both know that – and he loves me anyway for which I love *him* immensely. I know that this conversation will probably go the same way as all our others do – with me storming off in frustration that he won't accept that I'm right and then, when he needs space, me following him around not understanding why he can't *just see* my side. But at the moment all is reasonable and calm.

'So we don't split up and you spend your life regretting it, resenting me . . .' I can hear the emotion filtering its way into my voice and take a deep breath, trying to remain measured so that he knows that I'm not just jumping on some spur-of-the-moment worry and blowing it out of proportion. That I've thought this through for the past two months or so – well, in many ways, since the moment I met him and realized how amazing he was. I've tried it every which way in my head, listed all possibilities, all outcomes, and I know that there is no other option.

'If I'm making the decision then I'd never resent you. That wouldn't be fair.'

I push the tray on to his lap and stand up, putting on the joggers and T-shirt that I left on the floor beside the

4

bed when I took them off last night. He hates that I scatter my clothes around the bedroom floor, spending his life picking them up and dumping them in one huge pile, as if that's somehow making the room tidy.

'You wouldn't do it on purpose. Resentment isn't something you *choose*, or something that you can choose *not* to feel. It creeps up on you slowly and eats into you until it eats the love too.'

'Like a monster? Or a moth?' A hint of a smile creeps across Jamie's lips and I know exactly what he's doing – trying to remind me of all the wonderful things about him so that I change my mind and stay. But I don't need reminding. And I can't allow myself to soften.

'You're not taking me seriously.'

His face falls suddenly. 'I am. I just don't want you to be right on this occasion.'

I want to sit back on the bed, to take his face in my hands and kiss him.

'What if I promise to let you be right about everything else for the rest of our lives and you just let me have this one thing?' he continues, looking up at me with his big brown eyes, his hair a beautiful mess, as it always is after he's woken up, and I wish I *could* let him be right about this. I wish with all my heart that he *was* right, but I know that if I climb back into that bed with him and pretend that everything is going to be OK, it's going to ruin both our lives.

'I'm going to move in with Amy for a bit. You keep the house for now and, when you're ready, I'll help you to sell it.'

'Lucy.'

'It's for the best.'

'So why does it feel like the worst day of my life?'

He looks so sad and I wish that he'd just shout at me, storm off into his man cave (the bathroom) and slam the door. Why does he have to be so bloody adorable? How am I supposed to leave him when he's like this? I try to think of something I can say to provoke him. But at the same time, deep down I know this isn't just another argument. There will be no make-up sex. And I don't want our last 'moment' to be us screaming at each other.

'It's going to be OK. I know it is.'

I say it as much for myself as for him. Because the longer I stand here, the less sure I am that it's true.

JAMIE

As Lucy stands there telling me that we can't be together, talking about moving out and selling the house as if we're discussing our weekend plans, it occurs to me that she is the most beautiful woman I've ever seen or will ever see in my entire life. Her light blonde hair has the perfect amount of kink; her big blue eyes are so full of raw emotion, whatever emotion it is that she happens to be feeling – rage, sorrow, concern, excitement – her eyes are always brimming with it. She can never disguise it – well, not to me anyway. She is the type of person who feels passionate about everything – a woman being depicted chauvinistically in a perfume advert; the fact that next door's cat should be trained not to shit in our garden; the man who should've stood up for the pregnant woman on the bus. My mum once said, 'Doesn't it get annoying sometimes, having to be the water to her fire?' And yes, sometimes when her intolerance for injustice is directed towards me, when I am the one supposedly at fault, it makes me want to punch a wall or run to the end of the garden and scream because she is so infuriatingly stubborn and will never ever see my point of view. But at the same time, in my eyes she is never more beautiful than when she's taking on the world, trying to right it one tiny injustice at a time.

'It's going to feel shit for a while,' she continues. 'For a long while, I expect. But one day you'll meet someone else who is perfect for you in every way, and I want you to pick up the phone and call me and say "thank you".'

She smiles now, just a tiny one, but it's the first she's given me since this conversation began and I want to jump on it, to water it and help it grow.

'What if I sink into a pit of despair, get a drug habit, lose my job, become homeless, don't even have a phone to call you with, what then?'

For a moment I think she's going to sit down beside me, and my heart starts to race because I know that if she does, I'll be able to convince her to stay. That we'll end up back in bed, making love until we ache. But as she starts packing things into a bag, I realize that I've actually done the opposite, that my being nice has convinced her even more that she's doing the right thing. Perhaps I should just start screaming at her.

'I'll come and get more of my stuff in the week whilst you're at work.'

'You don't have to avoid me, you know?'

She shakes her head and I'm scared she's about to start crying. 'I do.'

I know exactly what she means, that seeing each other and not being together would be too hard. But the thought of not seeing her, of days waking up to an empty bed – the bed we shared – of eating breakfast and not fighting over the milk, of going to work without her silly messages to get me through the day, of coming home and not tripping over the shoes that she *always* leaves on the mat despite the fact we have a shoe rack right beside the door, of not arguing over what to watch on the television, of the day ending, and the next one starting, the cycle complete and her not being there for any of it, it feels impossible.

'OK. Well, just hold on to your key. In case you forget anything.'

She continues packing and I force myself to get up and into the shower. I don't think I can bear to watch her gathering up her things, stuffing them into bags in that haphazard way she always does.

The water is cleansing, the gentle rhythm of it falling on to my head, my shoulders. It was the same when Dad died, and when Thomas died . . . It was the little things that got me through – the fact you still had to brush your teeth, to eat, to shit – and the way that if you just kept doing them the hours passed and life continued. I wash my hair. I'm lucky – aged thirty-three and it's still thick, dark, but then Dad's was at forty-six when he died. That was the other thing – trying to be grateful for the little things, to find tiny amounts of joy where I could.

I finish washing and dry myself with a towel, putting it neatly on the radiator in case Lucy wants to use it later. But then I realize she won't be here later and that thought alone makes me want to curl up into a ball on the bathroom floor. I can still hear her through the en-suite door, shutting drawers and zipping bags. I brush my teeth and go back into the bedroom to get some boxers out of the drawer.

It should be vaguely comical, me walking around the

bedroom naked with my todger swinging from side to side (or jiggling might be a better word – I'm not *that* well-endowed) or if not comical then awkward, but it just feels normal. And that makes me feel even more sad.

I get dressed in jeans and a T-shirt and then take our tray down to the kitchen, where I wash up our breakfast stuff along with the mugs from last night's hot chocolate, the moment the dreaded conversation began. Well, it began a long time ago really. Lucy leaving is not a surprise, but it still feels like my body is going through the process of shock. I never actually thought she'd do it. I thought we'd just continue having some form of this conversation for the next ten years until one of us miraculously had a change of heart.

I don't empty the dishwasher even though it's full (Lucy's job), but I do take out the bins (my job) and put on the kettle for a second coffee, automatically calling up to Lucy to ask if she wants one.

'No, it's OK. I'll have one at Amy's,' she shouts down.

Amy is Lucy's sister. They're polar opposites but best friends. Amy manages the lives of her husband and two young children with the efficiency of an army sergeant (rather than a painting or a photograph, they have the family rota as the focal point of their kitchen wall), so the fact that she's agreed to Lucy coming, like a whirlwind, into her ordered home shows just how desperate Lucy must be to get away from me.

As I'm drying up the things on the draining board and putting them into the cupboard, I hear Lucy's footsteps on the stairs. They're always heavy, despite the fact she's so slim. I wonder if she's going to try to just sneak out without saying goodbye, and if she does whether I'm going to let her. Putting down the tea-towel, I listen carefully, imagining her grabbing her coat off the rack and putting on her trainers – silver, muddy. And then suddenly she's standing at the kitchen door and I'm staring at her like an idiot.

Neither of us speaks and I try to think of something brilliant to say, a beautiful parting speech, a line she will remember for the rest of her life, but instead I just say, 'How did we get from croissants to this?', and actually it's more poignant than I mean it to be because I was talking about this morning, but in fact for our first date, we met for breakfast and she was surprised that I ordered a croissant instead of a full English 'like all other blokes'. At the time, I'd wondered if it made her see me as less 'manly' and if so, whether that was off-putting to her, but she agreed to a second date so, either way, it clearly wasn't a deal-breaker.

I wonder if I should ask her now what she thought that day. It suddenly feels like there are so many questions I should've asked her over the past year – like when one of your grandparents is on their death bed and you feel this panicked rush to find out who they were when they were younger, what they liked to do at school, how many times they'd been in love, how they decided on their career. All these questions that just didn't seem important when they were still very much alive.

Lucy doesn't respond – just gives me a sort of

half-smile, but a smile that has absolutely no joy in it. An ironic smile, in fact, because it's full of deep and utter sadness. And then she comes over and gives me a hug and a tiny kiss on the cheek and I never want to let her go, but I know I have to. Because the absolute tragedy of all this is that she might be right.

We release each other and she goes back through the lounge towards the hallway, me following, and I suddenly notice her goldfish staring out forlornly from its bowl (the one I've always argued is too small but Lucy insists is 'just right'), wondering why it's being abandoned. Well, it's probably not wondering that – I suspect I'm projecting – but that's how it appears to me.

'What about Sharky?'

Lucy looks over at her fish. 'You keep him. He likes it here.'

I should probably argue that I never really wanted a pet, particularly one as useless as a goldfish, but stupidly I find a sort of comfort in Lucy leaving a tiny part of herself here so I say, 'OK.'

When we reach the hallway, Lucy picks up four rucksacks full of her stuff, shoving one on each shoulder and then picking up the other two in her hands.

'Let me help you.' I go to reach for a bag but she shakes her head and moves away.

'I need to just go.'

I nod slowly. And then the really, really shit bit is when she leaves, actually walks out of the door, the door we argued over which colour to paint for several days after moving in. She wanted some radical bright shade and I thought it had to fit in with the others along the row. We compromised with a sort of beachy blue, despite the fact we live nowhere near the sea. And then I'm left on my own, in a house that's far too big for just me and with a blank day where my only plan was to spend it with Lucy.

I go back upstairs to torture myself with an empty bedroom, a wardrobe devoid of her things, and that's when I spot it, sparkling on the bedside table like an abandoned glitter ball. The ring I spent so many hours agonizing over. And it hits me that she's never coming back.

Before

LUCY

I'm up at 9 a.m. on a Saturday, which is unheard of. I normally spend the first few hours of the day lounging in bed, looking at stuff on my phone, reading a bit, maybe drifting back off for another twenty minutes. But today I have a date. With someone called Jamie. He's a friend of a friend of a friend – we met briefly on a night out. He gave me his number, and we've been messaging back and forth for a few weeks. Just silly stuff – lamenting how bored we are at work, being British and musing on the weather, exchanging witty comments about current news stories.

When he first suggested breakfast for our first date, I really wasn't sure. I am not a morning person. *At all.* Sometimes it feels like I've got split personality disorder – I'm one person when I wake up and a totally different person once it gets past twelve o'clock. I also worried he was trying to be a bit quirky – one of those blokes who is always trying to be 'off the wall' to disguise the fact that really he's a vacuous shell with nothing inside. But then he said it was so that if he liked me, we could continue the date into the day, and if he didn't like me he still had time to fit in another date before bedtime, and I liked that he was laying his cards out on the table, albeit disguised with humour. And besides, there's less pressure to a morning date, less formality than, say, dinner. In the evening there is always the inevitable question of whether or not you'll end up going home together, which always mars the rest of the evening for me because I never sleep with someone on a first date. Well, not any more, anyway. And it always pisses me off to watch a man try to pretend he's OK with that – that he doesn't want to come home with me either – when clearly that's all he's been thinking about since the moment he left home wearing his 'lucky pants'.

I look through my wardrobe and try to decide what to wear. It's April – bright, warm but not hot. Not quite summer dress weather. I could go jeans and a T-shirt but it feels a bit boring. Despite being concerned about him wanting to come over as 'quirky', embarrassingly I want him to think that *I* am – not annoyingly quirky but different enough to stand out from the crowd. *Alternative*. I opt for denim dungarees and a long-sleeved top, finished off with a chunky colourful necklace, then spend the entire walk there (as I keep catching glimpses of myself in shop windows) worrying that I look like a carpenter, or a painter and decorator. I think sometimes women want to *think* men like girls who wear dungarees and flip-flops when the reality is men want to see us in something ultra-feminine and a little bit revealing, like a short skirt and heels. Oh well, it's done now. There's not time to turn back and get changed (I'm already ten minutes late – don't think I've ever been on time for anything in my life) and, besides, I don't own anything like that anyway.

When I reach the café, Jamie is already inside, sitting in a booth looking at his phone. I wonder whether he's messaging me right at this moment to find out if I'm still coming or, worse, if he's messaging someone else – if I genuinely am just one date in a line-up of many. He didn't seem like that sort of bloke when we met, but you never really know. As the door slams closed, he looks up, his face breaking into a smile as soon as he sees me. He's as gorgeous as I remember, dressed casually in jeans and a white T-shirt, but he doesn't look like a dick. Often hot men are dicks – it's one of life's simple truths. But Jamie has the kind of eyes that make you think he would be nice to your mum. It's probably ridiculous to think that you can decipher that information just from someone's eyes, but that's how I feel as I view him from across the café.

As I reach the booth, he doesn't stand up to give me a hug or a kiss on the cheek, so I sit down opposite him, worrying for a moment that perhaps he's not as impressed as I am by what he sees, that he's thinking, *I thought she worked in a bookshop, not doing manual labour. Who wears dungarees?* But then he makes a joke about hurrying up and ordering so he can get on with his next date, and I don't think he'd say that if he really was about to bail on me. Unless he's a sadist, of course, which I guess is possible.

We go to the counter and he orders a croissant whilst I peruse the array of cakes and the breakfast menu on the wall, feeling mildly annoyed because a croissant is exactly what I want to order and now it looks like I'm copying him to show how much we've got in common or something embarrassing like that. But if I don't order one then I'll have to watch him eating his and spend the morning feeling resentful when he's not actually done anything wrong. (I love my food. Ordering the wrong thing can ruin a whole day.) So I order a croissant too, and he doesn't comment on it. He offers to pay – I decline – and then the lady behind the counter gives us a little pot of jam. I have to ask for Nutella (like I always do in these places) and, with a look of disapproval, she goes into the back, then comes out with a great big family-sized tub and plonks it on my tray.

Back at the table, Jamie watches me spreading Nutella on to my croissant as if I'm a particular specimen of human he's not encountered before. 'Nutella, hey?'

'What is it with people and my choice of breakfast spread? Have you never heard of pain au chocolat? It's basically the same thing.'

'So why didn't you just order a pain au chocolat? They had a big pile of them.'

I finish spreading my croissant and then lick the knife. 'Well, because it's not exactly the same. The chocolate in pain au chocolat is bitter. I like it sweeter. Is that a problem?'

Jamie smiles and holds up his hands. 'Not at all. Well, not to me anyway. The woman behind the counter didn't look too impressed.'

'I know! Miserable cow. It's not like I asked her to go and cook me something especially or to go out on the farm and get me a freshly laid egg.'

Jamie laughs, scraping the last of the jam from around his pot and spreading it on his croissant.

'Aren't men supposed to eat a full English for breakfast anyway?' I continue. 'I've never met a man who orders a croissant.'

'Well, I'm not like other men.'

'Isn't that what all men say?'

We tuck into our croissants and I notice that he uses a sticky part of his to pick up the dropped flakes of pastry off the plate like I always do. I'm not saying it's a sign that we're meant to be or anything, just an observation.

'So tell me a bit more about yourself. You work in a bookshop . . . ?'

'It's a temporary thing. I want to be a writer really.' *Why does that always sound so pretentious?* 'I mean, I'm trying to write a novel but I've only written a few chapters and they're crap so . . .'

I trail off, wishing I'd never started. Being an author has been a dream of mine ever since I was little but every time I sit down to write it feels pointless and indulgent. Plus when I showed my ex, Jude, my opening chapters he screwed up his face and mumbled, 'It's OK,' dragging out the 'ay'. Unsurprisingly, I've not written any more since.

'If you write, you're already a writer, surely? Anyway, what's it about?'

'Oh, it's nothing impressive. Boy meets girl, boy breaks girl's heart, standard sort of thing.'

'Why don't you switch it up? Why doesn't *she* break *his* heart?'

'I want it to be realistic. How many guys do you know who've got their heart broken by a girl?'

Jamie sits up straighter in his chair, suddenly animated. 'Plenty.'

'Have you ever had *yours* broken?'

'Of course I've been hurt by girls.'

'But I mean really had it smashed apart, battered into tiny little pieces through no fault of your own?'

'Well, no, not exactly, but . . .'

'See! Proving my point right there. It's different for men.'

Jamie wipes his fingers on a serviette. 'Well, you seem like the kind of girl who could break a man's heart.'

It's cheesy and it should send me running for the hills because it sounds like one of those typical rehearsed lines blokes whip out to get in your pants, but somehow coming from Jamie it feels genuine and I can't help but be flattered that he thinks I've got that capability. I mean, I'm not sure it's necessarily a good thing to be the type of person who breaks hearts. Possibly, I should be offended. But I'm not.

'I'm sorry,' Jamie says, his cheeks colouring. 'That was not a first-date thing to say, was it? Can you just erase that from your consciousness?'

I wipe my hand across my forehead. 'Gone.' I open a sachet of sugar and pour half into my coffee. 'So you work in event management?'

'It sounds fancier than it is. It's mostly corporate events. Boring stuff. It's my mate's company. He needed some help a little while back and I wasn't really enjoying my marketing job so I decided to give it a go. It's not bad as jobs go, but nowhere near as cool as being a writer.'

'To be fair, right now I just work in a bookshop.'

'Well, that's a cool job as well.'

He's possibly trying a little too hard but it doesn't come over as fake. In fact, he just seems like a decent, honest bloke, which means I'm probably going to discover he's got some hideous, unforgivable secret that makes me doubt, not for the first time, whether I actually have the capability to read a person. But, for now, the date is going well and I'm hoping he's going to suggest we make a day of it.

It's like he reads my mind because he says, 'Are you doing anything after this?'

'No plans until this evening.'

I don't really have any plans this evening either, but I need some kind of get-out clause if the date turns sour and besides, I don't want to be *too* available.

'Ah, so that's when you're meeting your full-English-breakfast-eating, rugby-playing hulk of a man?'

'He's a footballer, but close.'

Jamie smiles, and it's the kind of smile I can imagine looking at when we're both in our eighties and still thinking it's the most gorgeous smile I've ever seen, which is not a good thing to be thinking on a first date. *Play it cool.*

'I didn't really see you as a WAG.'

'Why not? I can be very glam when I want to be, thank you very much.'

'I'm sure you can, but trust me, I meant it as a compliment, not that I didn't think you could be glamorous.'

I lower my eyes. 'So what are we going to do today?'

'Oh, I didn't mean I wanted to spend the day with *you*. I was just being polite asking about your plans.'

I slap Jamie's hand and he laughs.

'Argh,' he continues. 'You're putting the pressure on me now to think of some kind of unusual, exciting way to spend the day.'

I look out the window. 'It's a nice day. We could get a picnic from Tesco, walk along by the canal?'

As I say it, I worry it makes me sound really boring, but then a look of relief washes across Jamie's face. 'Sounds perfect. Let's go.'

JAMIE

It seems Lucy is quite passionate about what we buy for our picnic. So far, sausage rolls (*what? Cold?*), Scotch eggs (*all sorts of wrong*) and Dairylea dunkers (*are we children?*) have been refused, so I've decided to take a step back and let her choose. After the total car crash that was the 'you seem like the kind of girl who could break a man's heart' comment I plucked from the list of worst things to say on a first date earlier, I'm not taking any chances. Because Lucy is *incredible*. She's the sort of stunning that makes you feel like the whole world is looking at you and thinking, *What the hell is she doing with him?* I mean, she actually *is* the type of girl who could break a man's heart. I expect she's broken plenty. I picture her as some kind of assassin, walking around destroying men with just one look. When she turned up in *dungarees*, I lost all strength in my legs and couldn't stand up. I've had a girl-in-dungarees fantasy for as long as I can remember but I've never met anyone with the confidence to actually wear them. And she's a *writer*. Doesn't every man want to end up as some hot girl's muse?

'How about a tub of coronation chicken, a baguette and some crisps?' Lucy suggests after much deliberation.

'Perfect.'

And it is perfect. I once made a picnic for a girl who

moaned that I'd bought cider and packaged sandwiches instead of prosecco and an assortment of salads, cheeses and cold meats. I knew then that that relationship was doomed.

I carry the basket and Lucy gets all the things we need, adding a bag of double chocolate chip cookies and two cans of Coke (diet for her and, at my request, full sugar for me) and then we scan it through, paying half each at Lucy's insistence, and take our carrier bag of goodies on our walk along the canal. A lot of the path is single file, so I keep having to turn around to hear what Lucy is saying – and then as I'm doing so I nearly smash head-first into a guy on a bike coming the other way, apologizing profusely as he just about saves himself from toppling into the canal. Lucy giggles, but I wonder if it's in a kind of embarrassed is-this-guy-Mr-Bean-or-something? way and wish, not for the first time, that I was a bit more suave. I'm glad when the path opens up and we can walk along side by side.

The sun is shining – it's warmed up since this morning – and it makes being here with Lucy feel even more perfect. As we walk, she does most of the talking, but I don't mind. I'm just glad to be out with her in person. The weeks of messaging have been exhausting, constantly having to think of some sort of clever or witty repartee. I'm funny-ish in person but WhatsApp is not where I shine. And Lucy seems to be able to create brilliantly hilarious messages within seconds.

Today, she tells me about her sister, Amy, who is five years older than her and has two children – Otto, three, and Lauren, six – who she 'loves as if they were her own', then about the bookshop and the two women she works with, Mandy and Tilda – the three musketeers as she calls them. She talks about how she spends at least half the year travelling (there doesn't seem to be many places she *hasn't* been to), and then she gets distracted, becoming incensed as she spots two beer cans thrown in the grass at the side of the path. With a shake of her head, she picks them up then deposits them in the bin that we soon pass.

'How many steps was it? Ten? Twenty max? God, people are so lazy.'

I try not to smile because I don't want her to think I'm not taking her seriously. I just love how animated she is. And the whole time she's talking, I want to stop her and kiss her, but at the same time, I could listen to her talking all day. Normally, I have a tendency to drift off when having a conversation with someone, but with Lucy, I'm fully focused on every word. Suddenly she stops mid-sentence, pushes her hair out of her eyes and says, 'Enough about me. Tell me more about you.'

The pressure feels intense – trying to think of something interesting to tell her about myself, when suddenly my whole life, everything about me, feels insignificant and dull. 'What do you want to know?'

'I don't know. Do you live on your own? Any siblings? Any deep dark secrets?'

I smile. 'No deep dark secrets. I live with the mate who owns the events business. I don't have any siblings.'

27

For a strange moment, despite never normally telling anyone about what happened, I have a desire to tell her about Thomas, but then I realize that would just be really weird on a first date and push the thought aside.

'I bet you're a Mummy's boy then? Only child and all that.'

I always think when girls ask you questions about your relationship with your mum, it's a test. *Is he close enough to his mum to suggest he respects women but not so close that I'll always be overshadowed, that he'll always have to get his mum's approval about everything?* It's a hard balance to strike so I decide to just be honest.

'No. I mean I love her, of course. She's my mum. But we're not as close as I'd like us to be.'

I don't really remember what things were like before, but when Mum lost Thomas, she withdrew into herself. I get it now but at the time I felt like she blamed me somehow or that I wasn't enough on my own, like she needed another child to make her happy. So we drifted apart whilst Dad and I got closer. And maybe it wasn't just Thomas. I'm not sure Mum and I ever had that much in common. I never really felt that she 'got' me; I always felt like a disappointment because I didn't do better at school, didn't want to take up an instrument, do my Duke of Edinburgh or any of the other prestigious extra-curricular activities she tried to encourage me to pursue, whereas Dad always made me feel like he was the proudest man in the world to call me his son. When Dad and I were together, we never stopped laughing. We were always having some adventure or another – camping, climbing, skateboarding, making dens, carving swords – whereas Mum preferred to keep her clothes clean, her things tidy. She always got annoyed with Dad when he took me climbing over rocks that jutted out into the sea to look for crabs or let me help with campfires. When I was older, Dad explained that it was because what happened with Thomas made her risk-averse, but as a child I just felt like she didn't want me to have fun.

'Me neither,' Lucy says. 'I'm not sure I've ever quite fit the image Mum has of what a daughter should be like. Amy does, she fits it to a tee, but me not so much.'

'Why's that?'

'Amy went to university, she's a lawyer. She settled down, had the big fancy wedding, impressive house, two obviously gifted kids. I work in a bookshop, no degree. Instead I've "wasted" my time travelling and live in a tiny little place on my own.'

'I don't think time spent travelling is a waste.'

'I agree. I don't see the time I've spent seeing the world as a waste. I've met all sorts of fascinating people and seen the most beautiful things. But Mum just thinks I've got nothing to show for my life. I think if I'd gone either the career route or the "mother hen" route, she would've been happier, but as I've done neither . . .'

'I can relate to that. I'm not sure I've ever quite lived up to my mum's expectations.'

'What about your dad? I'm a Daddy's girl through and through. Winds Mum up a treat.'

'Yeah, I was really close to my dad too, but he died when I was sixteen.'

'Oh, I'm sorry. That's tough.'

I focus on the path then kick a stone and it splashes into the canal with a plop. 'Sorry, this isn't really light and airy first-date sort of chat, is it?'

'It's OK. I've never been great at the whole small talk thing anyway.' Lucy nods her head towards a picnic table in the near-distance. 'Want to stop for lunch?'

'You must have read my mind.'

We head over to the table, sitting next to each other on the one side. Lucy takes the food out of the plastic bag, one item at a time, then rips the baguette in half, opens it up and uses a plastic fork to stuff it full of coronation chicken.

'There you go,' she says, holding the baguette out towards me.

'It's OK, you have it. I can make my own.'

'Don't be silly, I insist. Plus I've saved more of the filling for mine.'

'And there I was thinking you were just being kind.' I take the baguette off her and take a big bite. 'Delicious. I can add excellent culinary skills to the pros on my mental pros and cons list.'

Lucy narrows her eyes. 'You have a pros and cons list about me?'

'Oh yeah, I make one about all my dates. Helps me decide whether to go on a second date with them or not.'

'Well, technically we're kind of on a second date already, aren't we? Breakfast being our first one.'

'I suppose we are.'

Lucy finishes making her own baguette and then puts the fork on the table. 'Well, I'm glad you decided to go on a second date with me, despite, I'm sure, a long list of cons.'

'Me too.'

I always get a gut feeling within about twenty minutes of a date as to whether or not it's a goer and right now my gut is telling me that I want to see Lucy again and again, as many times as she'll let me. And it's bloody *terrifying*.

We finish our baguettes, the conversation between us stalling for a while as we eat, and then Lucy opens the packet of cookies.

'Right, there are four. So do we stuff our faces now or do you want to take one home with you?'

'Unless we save one each for next time?' I offer. 'You could look after them for us.'

I should probably play it cool – women seem to secretly like the chase – but I like her too much to not show her that I'm interested.

'So there's going to be a next time, is there?' She looks up at me from under her hair. She's got this cute little blonde bob with a straight fringe that just covers her eyebrows.

'I was hoping so.'

'OK, deal. I'll save you a cookie for next time.'

Get in.

I put on my best 'not bothered' expression as she hands me a cookie.

'Think we might be about to witness a duck-choking

incident,' I say, nodding towards a group of ducks battling over a whole slice of bread, the toddler who was feeding them clearly getting bored of breaking the bread into little pieces.

Lucy smiles. 'Do you know what? Once I was feeding the ducks with Lauren and this guy actually came over and snatched the loaf of bread out of my hand and started shouting at me for poisoning them.'

'Seriously? What did you do?'

'I told him ducks had survived for thousands of years being fed bread, snatched the loaf back and continued to feed them. He just stood there staring at me like I'd threatened him with a crowbar or something despite the fact *he* had started on *me*. People sometimes.'

I laugh. 'I get the sense it wouldn't be wise to get into an argument with you.'

Lucy sits back. 'I just stand up for what I believe in, that's all.'

'It wasn't a criticism. I always say it's better to care than not to care.'

Lucy raises an eyebrow. 'You really always say that?'

'Well, no, I've never said it before in my life, but I like someone who's passionate about what they believe in.'

'Yeah, that's what all blokes say until they actually have to put up with me.' Then she puts her hand on my arm and, ridiculously, it causes what can only be described as flutters in my stomach. 'Don't worry. I'm actually not that bad.'

I nod, momentarily lost for words, and then she holds eye contact with me for a little longer than is natural and

I wonder if I should kiss her, whether she'd like the show of confidence or be totally put off by too-much-too-soon. But before I can make a decision she starts putting our rubbish back into the plastic bag and stands up and I'm glad I didn't go for it because she clearly wasn't feeling the same way.

'Shall we head back?'

I want to say, *no, let's stay here all day*, but instead I stand up too and we walk back along the canal. This time, when we get to the narrow bit, I make sure I stand behind her to avoid any more accidents. And then we reach town again, and I wish I could somehow make the path longer.

'Right, I'm parked at Cheapside,' she says, pushing her hair off her face.

'I'm this way.' I point in the opposite direction.

'Thanks for a nice day.'

'You too.' We stand there awkwardly for a few moments. I hate the end of a date. There's always the whole question of 'do we kiss or don't we?' hanging in the air. Eventually, I kiss her demurely on the cheek and then we stand there a bit longer, as if neither of us wants to be the first to turn and leave. But then, predictably, she's the one that does.

'What's the best before date on those cookies?' I call out. 'Surely it's got to be less than a week?'

Lucy turns back, a smile filling her face. 'I think they should still be all right by next Saturday. If you're not doing anything then?'

'Obviously I'll have to double-check my ridiculously

busy social calendar but the cookies were pretty good. I wouldn't want them to get past their best.'

'Of course not. Well, I guess I'll wait for you to get in touch once you've checked your schedule then.'

I take my phone out of my pocket. 'Oh, miraculously it looks like next Saturday is free.'

'Fancy that. See you next Saturday then.'

'Look forward to it. The cookies, I mean.'

'Obviously.' Lucy smiles and then she turns back around and continues to walk to her car, me standing there like an idiot just watching her go. And then the best thing happens – she turns around for one more sneaky look – and if anyone is watching me head back to my car, I bet I look like a bloody lamb skipping down the road.

LUCY

Jamie messaged me the evening of our first date. In fact, it wasn't even quite the evening, more late afternoon. And, stupidly, I decided to ignore it. *For three days.* What is it in the female psyche that, despite hating it when a man is emotionally unavailable (like Jude was), feels nervous when a man seems too keen? Or maybe it's just me.

Anyway, in the end I managed to squash the part of my brain determined to turn me into a cat-obsessed spinster long enough to message him back and he suggested we meet at the cinema. At first I thought it was a slightly odd suggestion, rather than the typical drinks or dinner, and as I walk into the foyer, it feels a bit like regressing to my early teenage years when the cinema was the only place I was allowed to go after dark (Dad making sure he dropped me off and picked me up as soon as the film had ended). But there's something oddly nostalgic about the smell of popcorn that hits me as I walk in.

It's not long before I spot Jamie, who looks effortlessly handsome in a short-sleeved denim shirt and jeans, and I try to ignore the fact that I have butterflies in my stomach when I see him (I really *am* regressing to my teenage years).

'Double denim, hey? Very few can carry it off.'

Jamie runs his hands down his shirt. 'I'm probably one of the many, then.'

We agreed via WhatsApp to watch a thriller. It seemed like fairly neutral ground for an early date, the other options being a soppy tearjerker, a political biopic or some gruesome horror. But as we sit down, late (my fault, of course), we seem to be the only people in the cinema so I'm not convinced it's going to be an award-winner of a film.

'Feels like a zombie apocalypse,' Jamie says, looking around as we search for our seats, not that it really matters where we sit.

'Well, at least we've got cookies.'

'If I get really desperate, I'll just have to eat you.' As soon as he's said it, Jamie goes bright red. 'I didn't mean it like that.'

I laugh, find our row and sit down, Jamie sitting beside me. And then the lights go down and suddenly I wish that someone else was in the cinema with us because I feel this weird sort of tension between us – the only two people here, alone in the dark.

Despite the fact it's empty, as the trailers start, we still follow the rules of not talking, clearly conditioned from years of cinema-going. Both of us focus our eyes on the screen and then Jamie says, 'Shall we move a bit further back? I think my neck is about to snap.'

'Go on then. I didn't want to say anything, but I was getting double vision being so close.'

Jamie stands up and starts heading up the steps.

'Shall we go in the posh seats at the very back?' I say over his shoulder.

'But they're more expensive. We're not allowed.'

I nudge Jamie in the back. 'Live a little.'

He turns around and rolls his eyes and then we go and sit in the more comfortable leather seats at the back of the cinema. The film starts so we settle down and start to watch it. And after a while, I feel his hand on top of mine, creeping over gradually like a spider, and without looking at each other, we entwine our fingers and it feels like I'm twelve again when holding hands seemed like the naughtiest and most exciting thing in the world.

We stay like this all through the first third of the film, until I lean towards Jamie and whisper in his ear. 'Do you think it's time for cookies?'

'OK, but why are you whispering?' he whispers back.

'I don't know. Is this better?' I shout at the top of my voice and he covers my mouth.

'Careful, they might throw us out.'

I reach into my bag and pull out the cookies, handing him one and taking the other for myself. 'Food not bought on the premises. We're breaking all sorts of rules tonight.'

He laughs and then takes a bite. Once he's finished his mouthful he leans towards me again, so close I can feel his breath on my neck. 'The film's a bit shit, isn't it?'

It really is. There's this serial killer on the loose but the police response is so farcical it's impossible to take it seriously. They easily could have caught him a dozen times already.

'I'm so glad you said that. I was worried you were sitting there really enjoying it. It would've made me question your suitability.'

'Wow. Bit brutal, isn't it? Don't like the same films – big black mark.'

'You don't have to like the same films, but this one? Come on. I like my men with a morsel of intelligence.'

'That rules me out then.'

I tuck into my cookie and look around us at the empty cinema. 'Remember when you were younger and you'd always sit in the back row so you could spend the film secretly snogging?'

Jamie gives me this look. It starts as a sort of shy smile then turns into something more intense and I don't know what the hell is wrong with me because I've *never* kissed a man first *in my entire life* – the thought of making the first move is mortifying to me – but I find myself leaning towards him and kissing him. We've both got half-eaten cookies in our hands and possibly bits of cookie still in our mouths (he definitely tastes of chocolate) so it's probably not the perfect time to kiss him, but as I do, despite myself, I feel my stomach flip over like I'm on a big-drop rollercoaster.

When we stop and both draw back, he raises his eyebrows. 'Well, that was unexpected.'

And because I'm completely horrified that I just pounced on him, I act like it never happened, staring straight ahead at the screen. Until, after a few minutes, Jamie leans over, putting his hand on my face, and, gently manoeuvring it towards him, this time he kisses me, and soon we're passionately making out in the back row like school kids. And then, in a very surreal moment, we both stop, sit back in our chairs and watch the film again, as if we barely even know each other, and I find myself starting to giggle. Before long, it becomes something more akin to hysterics, taking over my whole body. And as my chair begins to shake, Jamie looks over at me and starts laughing too until we're both sitting in an empty cinema watching the shittest film ever with tears of laughter in our eyes.

'Come on, let's go and get a drink.' Jamie takes my hand in his and pulls me up and I grab my jacket and bag and we head out into the blinding light of the foyer. Once outside, we both separate to put on our jackets, but then we find each other's hands again.

'The Retreat?' Jamie asks.

'Sure. It'll take me back to my youth. We spent a lot of time in there back in the day pretending to be eighteen and getting very, very drunk.'

'So you grew up here?'

'Yep, Stroud born and bred. I'm guessing you didn't?'

I'd already noticed that he has a slight northern accent, not strong, but distinctive enough to tell he isn't from the area. Plus, Stroud's a pretty small town. I probably would've come across him if he'd grown up here.

'I'm from Chester. My mum moved here when I was about twenty because of work so when I finished uni in Bristol, it made sense to move back in with her for a bit.'

'And now you live with your mate? Is it as bad as I imagine, two lads living in an apartment together?'

He laughs. 'At our age, we've gained basic hygiene skills. And we can both cook moderately well. You might be surprised.'

We enter The Retreat. There are no tables free so we have no choice but to prop up the bar.

'Right. What do you want?' Jamie takes out his wallet.

'Oh, it's OK. I'll get my own drink.'

Sometimes I wish I didn't feel the need to be such a feminist. It'd certainly save me a lot of money. But there's always been a part of me that feels like not paying my fair share is suggesting that I *need* a man. And I don't. My life is perfectly full without one. Well, full-ish. Coming home to an empty house can feel a bit shit sometimes. And yes, it would occasionally be nice to have someone other than Sharky (my goldfish) to talk to – he doesn't have a great deal to offer in terms of conversation – but I don't *need* a man.

'I want to buy you one.'

'OK, but I'll get the next round.'

'If you insist.'

'I do.'

'So what do you want?'

'Well, they do this shot called a Squashed Frog. It's disgusting, but it's an unwritten rule that you have to order it if you drink in here.'

'Can I change my mind and suggest another pub?'

I shake my head and secure eye contact with the barman. 'Two Squashed Frogs, please.'

'OK. Coming right up.' The barman looks as if he's

stifling a smile. He's only about eighteen. I expect the sight of two 'old' people doing shots is amusing to him.

'I'm more of a pint kind of guy, I have to be honest.'

'Well, for tonight, we're breaking the rules.'

Jamie reluctantly agrees, but when the drinks arrive, his face falls. In his defence, it does look like an amphibian has died in the glass. I'm not exactly sure what's in it, but there's definitely sambuca, advocaat possibly, and some type of curdled green alcoholic beverage.

'After three.' I pick up my glass and Jamie eventually follows. 'One, two, three.'

We both down the shots and slam them down on the bar, Jamie's face screwed up like a child eating broccoli.

'See, it wasn't that bad, was it? Same again?'

Jamie holds up his empty glass and looks at it as if he's resigned himself to his fate. 'Why not?'

I tap him on the leg. 'That's the spirit.'

JAMIE

We're in the pub and Lucy's making me drink these hideous shots that look like and have the texture of snot. And yet it's the happiest I've felt for quite some time. Maybe the alcohol helps, giving me that warm fuzzy glow you only really get when you're drunk or watching a Richard Curtis film, or maybe it's the fact that she kissed me earlier. *She* kissed *me*. But, either way, I don't want the night to end.

Lucy orders another round and then puts her hands on her hips. 'OK, truth or dare.'

I hate truth or dare. The lads always used to play it at uni and whenever anyone suggested it, I felt my insides recoil as they are doing right now. And even this doesn't put me off this girl. I really am in trouble.

'Really not a truth or dare person. I always just go truth to avoid having to do a dare.'

Lucy smiles. 'Funny, I always go dare.'

'Maybe you have more juicy secrets to conceal than I do.'

'Maybe. I think perhaps I'd just rather run down the street exposing my breasts than expose my soul.'

Her cheeks pinken slightly, and it's nice to see her vulnerable side.

'Well, if that's the kind of dare we're talking about, perhaps I do want to play.'

The barman puts two more shots down in front of us and we do them automatically now, without a countdown.

'Truth be told, I was actually just suggesting the game so I could find out all the answers to the questions people want to ask on an early date but are too afraid to.'

'Go ahead. No game needed.'

I sound more confident than I feel.

'OK. How many people have you slept with?'

Why do women *always* want to know the answer to this question? And is there a right answer? If you go too low, do they think you're a bit weird, that you'll be shit in bed? Obviously too high is not a good thing. But what is the happy medium? Five? Ten? Fifty?

'And you have to be totally honest or something bad will happen to you,' Lucy adds, as if she can see the cogs of my brain working.

'Something bad?'

'Yeah, a curse or something, like seven years' bad luck. You'll end up going into the toilets later and smashing a mirror.'

'OK.' I mentally go through the women I've slept with and count them on my fingers.

'You don't know without counting?'

'I'm just making sure. I don't want seven years' bad luck, do I?'

There was the girl I lost my virginity to, aged seventeen – Kelly. I'd love to say she was my first love, that it was an amazing experience, but the truth is it was an embarrassingly short fumble in an upstairs bedroom at a house party. Then there were Emma, Kate and Alice at university. (Emma was a freshers' thing – not exactly a one-night stand, more a two-night stand. Kate and Alice were nine-month and twenty-month relationships respectively.) Then there was my longest, most serious relationship to date, with Anna, who I lived with, both of us wasting four years playing it safe despite us both knowing deep down that the love wasn't there. Or at least not the spark. I think we *did* love each other, but in the way you might love a dog. Actually, looking at Instagram, some people *really* love their dogs. The fire just wasn't there. It wasn't right. And since then, a year later, there's only been Holly, who I went on a few dates with but neither of us were really into it and it just fizzled out.

'Six. I think that's OK?'

Lucy nods, but her expression doesn't give anything away. 'Six is respectable.'

'You?'

'You're the one in the hot seat, I'm afraid. Like I said, I'll take the dare every time.'

I get an immediate sinking feeling. I don't even know why. Because I'm scared she's keeping things from me that would make me see her in a different light? If she told me she'd slept with a thousand blokes, would it mean I didn't like her any more? That I couldn't see a future with her? Where do these arbitrary rules even come from?

'OK then, next question.'

'Longest relationship?' she asks.

'Four years.'

'Ever been married?'

'No.'

'Engaged?'

'No.'

'Got any kids?'

'*No*,' I say emphatically. 'I think I would've told you that bit of information.'

Lucy smiles. 'Just checking.'

'So why did your last long-term relationship end?'

'We realized we didn't really love each other, not in the way you should if you're going to spend your life with someone. That it was a relationship of convenience, I guess.'

'Did she end it or did you?'

'I think she raised the question and then it was a joint decision.'

'So you would've just stayed with her if she hadn't raised it? Carried on settling?'

It's a good question. Would I have done? I know I would've said something eventually, but if I'm totally honest I may well have wasted another few years, which is not something I'm proud of.

'It was a joint decision.'

She narrows her eyes but then seemingly accepts my answer because she moves on to her next question. 'Doggy or missionary?'

I don't respond straight away and Lucy puts her hand on my arm. 'Don't worry. I'm only joking. You don't have to answer that.'

'So, come on, at least tell me something about your-self? Last serious relationship?'

I know so little about her and I feel like I want to know everything.

'The last thing I want to talk about is that arsehole.'

The barman starts cleaning the bar in a clear signal that he wants us to leave and I look around, surprised to see we're the only ones left in the pub.

'I think it might be time to leave,' I say, subtly nodding my head towards the barman who is looking grumpier by the second.

'Saved by the bell.'

I smile and we grab our jackets and wander down to the taxi rank. Lucy links her arm through mine to steady herself, although I'm not exactly stable. When we get there, we pause, and I get the sense that neither of us wants the night to end.

'You can come back to mine for a few more drinks if you want?' Lucy asks. 'I can't offer you the delights of a squashed frog but I've got a bottle of vodka and some lemonade.'

I try to bite back the beaming smile forcing its way on to my face at the thought of more time with Lucy. 'Yeah, sure. Sounds good.'

When we get to Lucy's front door, it's just beginning to rain as she struggles to get her key in the lock. I fumble with the torch on my phone to help her and, just before we get really wet, she successfully opens the door. Once inside, she turns on the light to reveal her lounge and it's exactly how I expected it to be. Bright abstract art on the walls, a large dramatic clock above the fireplace, geometric print cushions on the sofa. It's small and messy (multiple mugs, magazines, books and random stuff on all the surfaces) but the epitome of stylish. Of course it is. You only have to look at Lucy to know she's going to live somewhere like this. I'm now really glad she didn't come to my place.

'I'll get us a drink. You relax on the sofa.'

Lucy leaves me in the lounge and I'm drawn to a big photo collage on the wall. It's full of pictures of Lucy in a variety of amazing locations. A few I recognize: the Leaning Tower of Pisa, the Statue of Liberty, the Taj Mahal, and others that are more obscure. There's Lucy abseiling, rafting with a group of tanned, toned people, giving the thumbs up from what looks to be the top of a very stormy mountain with a different group dressed head to toe in ski gear. There's one guy who features in both shots with his arm around her and I wonder if he's the ex she didn't want to talk about earlier. Of course he looks like a model.

I hear Lucy coming back through from the kitchen and quickly launch myself in the direction of the sofa so she doesn't think I'm being nosy, but being drunk I sort of fall on to it and Lucy laughs.

'Nice place,' I say, trying to regain my composure as Lucy sits down beside me.

'Thanks. My mum always says I've got too much junk cluttering up the place, but I like it. Reminds me of all the amazing places I've been.'

'Looks like you've been to a *lot*.'

Lucy smiles. 'Yeah, I guess. Still so many more places I want to go though. Do you travel?'

A lot of my friends had a gap year when we finished school but I went straight to university and then directly into the world of work. But I don't want Lucy to think I'm unadventurous. 'Not as much as I'd like to.'

She seems satisfied with this and takes a large swig of her drink so I do the same before putting it back on the coffee table. And then we sit there slightly awkwardly, just looking at each other, and because I'm feeling quite drunk and she looks so beautiful, I lean forwards and kiss her, listening to the rain lashing against the window. It's not long before her hands slip under my top and mine under hers but then suddenly she pulls away and I worry that I've come on too strong even though I'm sure it was her hands that started wandering first.

'I'm wasted,' she says, running her hand through her hair. 'Would it be really rude to just go to bed? I'm sorry. I know I was the one who invited *you* back.'

I feel suddenly awkward, like I shouldn't have come. 'No, not at all. I'm pretty whacked too. I'll call a taxi.'

Lucy shakes her head. 'You can stay if you don't mind the fact I'm going to be asleep soon.'

As confused as I am about the mixed signals, there's no way I'm going to say no to spending the night with her even without the sex. To be honest, as much as I fancy her, I'm probably too drunk to put in a decent performance anyway. But I do wonder why she suddenly put a stop to things when she seemed so keen at first.

48

'Not at all. Sure you don't mind me messing up your sofa though?'

'My sofa's not very comfortable so you can sleep in my bed if you want? Boxers on though.' She looks to the floor as she says it, so much shyer than she was in the pub, and I'm curious as to where that earlier confidence came from and what's really underneath. I feel like I want to look after her, despite the fact I can already tell that the thought of me thinking she needed to be 'looked after' would be abhorrent to her.

'Of course.' I draw two lines across my chest with my finger. 'It'll just be nice to wake up and see you in the morning.'

It'll just be nice to wake up and see you in the morning? Shoot me now.

Lucy smiles and holds out her hand. 'Follow me then.'

We go up the narrow staircase that leads to a small hallway and I follow Lucy through a door to her bedroom. It's as stylish as the lounge, her bed covered in cushions like they are in magazines. There are quite a few clothes scattered on the floor though and Lucy quickly starts picking them up and shoving them on top of her laundry basket.

'I'm just going to get myself sorted for bed. Feel free to move the cushions – just throw them on the floor in the corner – and make yourself comfortable.'

She goes into the en suite, gathering what looks to be some pyjamas on the way. While she's in the bathroom, I remove the cushions from the bed and put them in a pile in the corner. Then I take off my clothes, leaving my boxers on, and fold them, placing them neatly on the floor beside me, and quickly slip under the covers before Lucy emerges. And when she does, I expect my eyes look like they've been propped up on matchsticks because as much as I try to play it cool, she looks amazing. She's wearing these little shorts and a vest top (and I'm fairly sure no bra – what the hell is she trying to do to me?) and without her make-up she looks even more beautiful than she does with it on, and it feels like I'm getting a glimpse of the real, authentic Lucy. Like I've got some kind of special pass.

She switches on her bedside lamp then turns off the main light and climbs into bed beside me. And for a while we just lie there, both on our backs staring at the ceiling, making sure neither of us touch.

'Are you happy for me to turn the light out?' she asks – again, that shyness that there was no sign of in the pub, and I find the thought of peeling back all her layers so appealing.

'Sure.'

She leans over and switches it off and then turns on to her side so that she is facing away from me. And somehow the dark (and probably the numerous shots) gives me the confidence to move towards her and wrap my arm around her, and I'm relieved when she snuggles in to me and takes my hand in hers. I have to be honest, it's hard to control my natural urges – I'm only human – but I'd die if she were to feel a certain part of my anatomy poking into her (like a horny teenage boy), so I take a deep breath and try to focus on something boring like algebra or counting sheep.

'You OK there?' Lucy asks, probably reacting to my intake of breath.

'Yeah, fine. You?'

'Yeah, I'm good,' she giggles, pulling the cover higher up over her shoulder. 'Night night. See you in the morning.'

'Night.' I want to say more but I'm not quite sure what to say and then I just come out with, 'You know, I like sleeping with you. As in, sleeping beside you.'

It's a bit bumbling as I trip over some of the words, and I wonder if I should've just kept my mouth shut, but then Lucy lightly rubs her fingers up and down my hand. 'I like sleeping beside you too.'

My face feels like it's being stretched into a wide clown-smile and I pull Lucy in even closer, relax my head on to the pillow and start stroking her hair, more content than I've felt in a very long time.

The Day of the Break-Up

JAMIE

I pick Lucy's engagement ring up off the bedside table and put it on my little finger, twirling it around, the blue stone glowing every time it hits the light. I hate that she left it. Not just because it shows me how serious she is about this whole splitting up thing but because I wanted her to keep it regardless. What the hell does she expect me to do with it? Take it back? Sell it? *Give it to someone else?*

For a moment, I wonder if I should drive over to Amy's house – get down on one knee on her doorstep with the ring in my hand and ask Lucy to marry me again. In my head, it would be exceptionally romantic and she'd leap into my arms crying and Amy, Dave and the kids would cheer in the background and we'd all have champagne and celebrate being one big happy family. But I know that in reality Lucy would look at me as if I was an orphaned child that she was unable to take in. And I'd end up walking back down the drive with my tail between my legs, feeling even worse than I do now, if that's possible. And anyway, what if she's right? What if I *can't* ever get over what happened between us? What am I going to do, spend my life subconsciously punishing her for it? What if we *are* better off going our separate ways?

So instead I climb into bed, *our* bed, shuffling over to her side and breathing in the smell of her hair serum, which lingers on her pillow. I can still just about feel her warmth on the sheets from where she lay this morning. And I think it's this that I'll miss the most. Lying in bed with Lucy. Not the sex, although of course I'll miss that. But just stroking her hair until she falls asleep. I remember she told me once that no other bloke had done that for her. That they'd moaned it made their arm ache or they were too tired. And I remember wondering why because I loved just lying with her like that, sensing how it calmed her, feeling her relax beneath my fingers.

I take the ring off. Suddenly it feels intensely important that Lucy has it. Getting up and finding an envelope, I slip the ring inside and then find a scrap of paper and write her a message, adding it to the envelope and then sealing it. I rush downstairs and grab my shoes from the rack, wishing Lucy was here to take the piss out of me for putting them there so neatly.

As I get in the car and start driving, I wonder what I'll do if Lucy comes to the door. And the truth is that I don't know. Hand her the envelope and walk away? Take her in my arms? But if I did that, how would I ever let her go?

When I get to Amy's, the first thing I notice is that Lucy's car isn't on the drive, so I look up and down the road in case she chose to park it elsewhere but there's no sign of it anywhere. And I suddenly have this horrible thought that perhaps she never had any intention of going to Amy's. What if she's been lying to me? What if she's gone somewhere else? I shake it away, hoping I'm just being irrational, and head towards the front door, each step feeling like a mile.

Looking through the windows, there's no sign of Amy or the kids, so I quickly post the envelope through the letterbox then hurry back down the drive to the car. I sit there for a moment, checking to see if anyone comes to the door, but it remains closed so I start the engine and head home.

Before

LUCY

Jamie and I have now been on nine (ten if you count the first one as two) dates. April has bled into May and the weather has been so amazing that it's felt like a sort of fairytale summer romance. We've had a picnic in a field of bluebells, a day trip to the beach where we built sandcastles, rode on donkeys and ate ice cream like children, and spent many an hour in various beer gardens drinking shandy and chatting until it gets dark. And today we are going paddle boarding at South Cerney lakes. Jamie said he's never been before so I thought I'd give him a lesson.

He's due to pick me up in about fifteen minutes and I still can't decide which bloody underwear to put on so I'm currently standing in a black lacy matching bra and knickers from M & S staring at myself in the mirror and despairing that it's just so *boring*. I go through this rigmarole before every one of our dates just in case things go in that direction, but so far I've always paused things at the critical point. And Jamie's so lovely that he acts like he didn't even think that's where things were going and just spends the night holding me. But he must be getting frustrated with me – *I'm* frustrated with me – I really want to have sex with him, but I just want things to be different to how they were with Jude. Effing Jude.

I examine myself again, wondering if I should change back into my one and only set of sexy red underwear, which is currently lying on top of my cover, having changed out of it and back into the black set multiple times. I don't want it to look like I'm trying too hard, like I've put fancy underwear on especially, having planned to sleep with him all along, but at the same time I fear that in making him wait I've inadvertently built the anticipation and I don't want him to be disappointed.

The doorbell rings. Great, he's early. Why can't he be like me and perpetually late for everything? I quickly pull on some skinny jeans and a T-shirt and shove my red underwear in the drawer, feeling momentarily sad that I didn't have the guts to go for it. And then I go to the door, opening it as nonchalantly as I can (can you open a door nonchalantly?). Jamie is standing there in a Gulf Stream T-shirt and shorts, holding out a bottle of rosé (he clearly listened when I said it was the only wine I could tolerate – my palette still several years behind my actual age).

'For later? I thought we could get take-out? Unless you have other plans in which case you can enjoy the wine without me.'

I take the wine and kiss him on the cheek, feeling the familiar flutter in my stomach I always get when I'm around him. 'Sounds good. The take-out with you, I mean.'

'Good. You look beautiful as ever, by the way.'

I touch my loose-fitting T-shirt. 'Hardly.'

'Just accept the compliment, will you?'

I smile. 'Sorry. You look very handsome too.' Jamie does a little bow. 'Right, let me just get my stuff. One sec.'

I leave Jamie in the hall and run to get my things, shoving a rash vest, bikini top, some swim shorts and a towel into a bag and searching yet again for my ever-elusive keys. Not on the coffee table or the fireplace. Not on the kitchen worktop. I run upstairs. Not obvious in the bedroom. I hurry back downstairs and just as I'm about to have a toddler-esque temper tantrum I notice my key fob, a photo of one my favourite places in New Zealand, poking out from down the side of the sofa cushion. I grab it and return to Jamie, a little flustered and sweaty.

'Keys playing hide and seek again?'

I punch him in the arm.

'I could buy you a hook to put them on, you know? I never lose mine any more.'

'Well, bully for you. Let's see how smug you are when you're tumbling head-first into the water.'

Jamie laughs and we head out to his car. As we drive, Tracey Chapman's 'Fast Car' comes on the radio and I sing at the top of my voice, Jamie looking over at me with an amused expression.

'What? It's a great song.'

'I know it is. I'm just jealous I can't sing as well as you.'

'Go on, give me a line.'

Jamie shakes his head. 'My music teacher once told me I was the most tone-deaf student she'd ever had.'

I can't help but laugh. 'I'm sure you're not that bad. Go on. For me.'

Jamie takes a deep breath and then he belts out a line of the song, completely out of tune, and it's so unlike him that it takes me by surprise.

'Blimey. She was right. Horrible.'

'Told you.'

'They could use your voice to torture prisoners.'

'All right, all right. Don't rub it in.'

When we arrive at the lakes, we go into separate changing rooms. I'm already in my bikini top and swim shorts drifting around the path outside when Jamie emerges in full wetsuit.

'You do realize it's twenty-six degrees today, don't you?'

'Not in the water, it's not.'

I smile. 'So are you ready to put those abs to good use?'

He puts his hands on his hips like Ronaldo before taking a free kick. 'I was born ready.'

'Come on then.' I take his hand and lead him to the reception where we check in and collect our life jackets and then a young lad leads us to the paddleboards and hands us both an oar.

'Just stay away from the sailing boats in the middle of the lake and put your hand up if you need any help. Have fun.'

Jamie looks a little panicked as the lad pushes the paddleboards out into the water for us without any further information, so I demonstrate how to climb on and stand up. Jamie copies me but almost immediately falls off and splashes into the water, emerging with pondweed hooked on to his ear.

The lad laughs and wanders off and I hide my smile with my hand. 'You'll get the hang of it.'

Jamie pulls the pondweed off his ear, shaking his fingers to release it back into the water. 'Let's hope so, hey.'

He climbs back on to his board and we start to paddle around the outside of the lake, Jamie looking decidedly wobbly.

'It really feels like being in the Stockholm Archipelago,' I say, surveying the landscape. It's so beautiful and calm. The rich blue sky, the surrounding green of the trees, the gentle breeze on our faces.

'I've never been to Sweden. In fact, I've not done any of Scandinavia.'

'Oh, you should. It's stunning. I always joke with my parents that there must be some Scandinavian blood in me somewhere because it always feels like going home.'

'Maybe you can take me sometime.'

'Yeah, I'd like that. I've got a friend called Stina who lives out there and she's always asking me to go and stay with her. I'm sure she'd be happy for you to come too.'

'Sounds good.'

We paddle a bit further, Jamie annoyingly seeming to have got the hang of it suddenly as he overtakes me, glancing back and giving me a mocking wave.

'Look, you're a natural now.'

I look around to see where the voice came from and find it belongs to a toned, tanned woman probably in her early forties, smiling widely at Jamie as she paddles beside us. She must have seen him fall over earlier.

'Ah, thank you,' Jamie replies, looking a little uncomfortable with the attention. It's no wonder he gets attention though. He *is* gorgeous. 'I've got a good teacher.'

He winks at me, and I don't know why but for some reason I lose my balance and go flying into the water, my board turning over with a dramatic splash. Jamie's admirer laughs and paddles off, her stability ridiculing me as she does.

I clamber back on then rub the water out of my eyes. 'Stupid woman created a riptide and made me fall.'

Jamie stifles a smile. 'Oh, that's what it was.'

'Yes, that is what it was, thank you.'

'I'm clearly such a natural it didn't affect me.'

I give Jamie a pretend-glare. 'If we could just make it around the rest of the lake without you getting chatted up, that would be great.'

'I'll try my best to be less irresistible.'

'You're not that irresistible.'

'Is that so?' Jamie raises an eyebrow. 'You hate it that I'm faster than you, don't you?'

'You are not faster than me. I'm just taking it easy. It's not a race.'

'Of course, you're right.'

'I'm always right. Remember that.'

Jamie smiles and then we both paddle off, me increasing my speed to make sure I keep up with him this time.

Back at home, we order pizza and share it on the sofa with large glasses of rosé. After all the exercise earlier, I'm already feeling a bit drunk. And as we finish eating,

I feel the same nervousness and tension I always feel at this point of the evening. The terrible contradiction between wanting to rip Jamie's clothes off and being ter-rified of being that vulnerable again.

'You know, I really miss you when I'm not with you.' Jamie finishes the last of his wine and then puts his glass on the coffee table.

I keep wondering when he's going to stop saying sweet things like this, when he'll reach the point where he feels he's done the hard work and that I'm his, that he no longer needs to make an effort. Maybe once I've slept with him? Or when we make it official? I've presumed neither of us is seeing anyone else, but we've not actu-ally talked about it or put a label on it. It seems a bit stupid asking someone to be your 'boyfriend' when you're twenty-eight, but I suddenly wonder if I should've done or whether I should be worried that he hasn't asked me.

'Sorry, is that a bit intense?'

I realize that, being deep in thought, I haven't responded.

'No, not at all.'

I don't say I miss him too, even though I do and I'm fairly sure by the look on his face that he was hoping I might.

'Do you want any more wine?' he asks, getting up and collecting our glasses.

'Yeah, OK. And don't worry, I can do that.'

'It's not a problem.'

He goes into the kitchen and I can hear him opening

the fridge to pour us more wine. It's weird listening to him moving freely around my space, touching my things. I'm not used to having another body here and I'm surprised how much I like it. The only time Jude really came over was at the end of the night when he wanted sex. He was never very fond of cosy nights in.

Jamie comes back with fresh glasses of wine and hands one to me. Then he points to my notebook on the coffee table, which has 'Careful or you'll end up in my novel' on the front. 'So that's where the genius happens, is it?'

'Oh, I don't know about that.'

Jamie reaches over and pulls my legs over his. 'Can I read it? Your novel, I mean.'

An image of Jude's disapproving face as his eyes scanned my words lodges in my head. 'It's really not very good.'

'I don't care. I'd just really like to read it.'

Maybe it's the wine lowering my inhibitions, but there's a little part of me that wants to share it with him and to know what he thinks, whether it's any good or whether I should just give up.

'I don't know. It feels a bit like standing in front of someone naked.'

'Well, you're welcome to do that too.'

I push him in the chest and then reach under the sofa and pull out my laptop, scrolling down to find the Word document and opening it. I haven't had the heart to look at it since I showed it to Jude.

'Please be honest, though. Don't just say you like it to please me.'

'Of course.'

I feel sick as he reads and have to cover my eyes with a cushion, but when I peek out, he is smiling in the right places. It's only five chapters long but it feels like he's reading for hours.

When he finishes, he closes the laptop, puts it back under the sofa and looks at me with an earnest expression. 'It's brilliant. Honestly.' Then he grips on to my knees. 'You have to finish it, Luce. It's funny and raw and insightful. It would be a tragedy for no one else to read it.'

There's such sincerity in his eyes and the relief makes me feel like I might cry. I hadn't realized how utterly terrified I was of being knocked down again. I lean towards him and kiss him. And I'm not sure what it is, maybe the intensity of sharing my words with him, maybe his perfect response, so different from Jude's, but soon our hands are running under each other's clothes and whereas normally this is the point I shut things down, I don't this time. I pull his T-shirt over his head and he stops kissing me for a moment and appears to ask me with his eyes whether I'm thinking what he thinks I'm thinking so I try to give him a look that says yes and we begin moving towards the bedroom, attached. When we get to the stairs, we stop kissing and I take his hand and lead him up to my room, trying to push any fears aside.

When we get to the bed, he gently removes my T-shirt and I slip my jeans off wondering what he thinks of my choice of underwear, whether he's even really aware of it, as he starts to remove my bra, struggling as all men do with the clasp. And this tiny moment of hesitation is all it takes to stop me in my tracks, and as much as I don't want to be, I'm back with Jude, him telling me he's head over heels in love with me when we're in bed and then refusing to acknowledge me as his girlfriend in front of his friends.

I stop kissing Jamie, his hands on my waist, and he pulls back, his eyes suddenly full of concern. 'Are you OK?'

I open my mouth, ready to say, 'of course', but I don't want to pretend with Jamie. I don't want this to become another sexual experience that makes me feel more distant rather than closer to the person I share it with.

'I'm sorry.' I sit down on the bed and reach for my T-shirt, pulling it on. Jamie sits beside me in his boxers. He is so handsome, not too muscly but perfectly toned, his skin a light tan, a smattering of dark hair on his chest and running down his tummy in a line, like ants.

'Is it too fast? I'm sorry. I'd never force you into something you don't want. You do know that, don't you?'

I let out a deep sigh. 'It's not that. I did want it. I *do* want it. I'm sorry. You're probably thinking I'm a right head case, aren't you?'

Jamie shakes his head and rests his hand lightly on my cheek. 'I think you're beautiful.'

I look into his lovely eyes and part of me wants to just start kissing him again, to forget this little freak-out and have sex with him as planned. But it feels tainted now, thoughts of Jude in the back of my head, and I don't want anything with Jamie to feel tainted. I suddenly feel the need to be alone, and yet I don't want Jamie to leave. Why am I such a mess?

'I'm going to go and do the washing-up. I've got Netflix on my laptop. Find us a good film to watch.'

Jamie stands up and pulls on his jeans. 'No, I'll do the washing-up. You find the film. I'll be back in five.'

Before I have the chance to protest, he's out the room and heading downstairs, and it's exactly what I need, and I love how he seems to instinctively know that. And now that he's left the room and the tension has dissipated, I find myself longing for him to come back.

JAMIE

I find some washing-up liquid in the cupboard and squirt it into the bowl of hot water I've run, swirling the suds with my hand. I know there must be more to this whole freaking out every time we start to get more physical, but I also sense that she's not yet ready to tell me and I don't want to force her.

I wash our wine glasses and a pile of things she's left on the side and then put them on the drying rack. Then I pour us both a glass of water. There's a photo of her and her sister on the windowsill along with a brightly coloured Shaun the Sheep ornament. Whereas Lucy is blonde, her sister has dark hair. They're both very pretty, sharing the same warm smile and sparkle in their eyes. For a second, it makes me wonder what Thomas would've looked like now, whether he would've looked like me. Mum took some photos of him when he was born, finding a strange comfort in looking at them in the months after his death, but I hated it. His blue skin, his expressionless face.

I take the glasses upstairs and find Lucy in bed, her laptop on her knee.

'If you want me to go home, that's perfectly fine by the way.'

Lucy pats the bed beside her. 'Get your jeans off and get in.'

I smile, remove my jeans and climb in beside her. 'So, what film have you found for us?'

'*Good Will Hunting*. It's a classic. Have you seen it?'

'Seriously?'

'What? Please don't tell me you hate it or our relationship will be hanging in the balance.' It's a relief to have her mocking me again, the earlier awkwardness gone.

'It's my favourite ever film.'

Lucy rolls her eyes. 'Come off it. You're just trying to win brownie points.'

I draw two lines across my heart.

'Well, maybe we're meant to be after all.'

'Was it ever in doubt?' I shuffle back, leaning against the headboard. 'And when you said about our "relationship"?'

'Yeah. What?'

'Well, I've been meaning to ask you but it felt a bit like being back at secondary school . . .'

'What is it?'

'Do you want to be my girlfriend?' The word sounds stupid coming out of my thirty-three-year-old mouth, but I want her to know that I'm serious about her. That there is no one else.

'I'd love to be.' She wriggles down so that her head is on the pillow and lifts up the cover. 'Come on over here then, boyfriend. I promise I won't bite.'

I move towards her and squeeze my arm beneath her as she rests her head on my chest. Pulling the laptop on to my knees, I press play on the film and, as we watch, I stroke her hair, laughing when she starts shouting at Will for pushing Minnie Driver's character away.

'It's so obvious he loves her really,' she says, incensed.

'How many times have you seen this film?'

'I don't know, about twenty. Why?'

'You're very animated.'

Lucy pinches my nipple hard.

'Ow, that hurt.'

'Serves you right. There's nothing wrong with being passionate about stuff, you know?'

'I know. I like it.'

We watch the rest of the film, her openly blubbing in the tear-jerking places while I try to disguise my watery eyes, and when it's finished, she sits up, takes the laptop off my knees, closes it and puts it under the bed. Then she turns on her side so that she's facing me, and I follow suit, turning on to mine to meet her eyes.

'Thank you,' she says.

'For what?'

'For not being a dick.'

'I get the feeling that's one of the best compliments I'm ever going to get from you.'

Lucy smiles. 'Maybe.'

'So do you want to go to sleep?'

She shakes her head and then she starts kissing me and running her nails up and down my thigh. 'I actually had something else in mind.'

'Are you sure?'

She nods and then reaches down and slides her hand into my boxers and any sense of self-control I had vanishes and I pull off her T-shirt and, after that, there's no more hesitation from either of us. And without a doubt it's the best sex I've ever had in my life. When you put a girl on a pedestal like I have with Lucy, the first time can be scary. The fear that it won't live up to expectations. Yours. Hers. But it exceeds mine and when it's over I want to tell her that I love her, but I know that it's too soon, that it would sound stupid, a post-coital-induced heightening of emotions. And maybe that is all it is. But I'm not so sure. Because I've never felt like this before. Not after sex, not during. This intense feeling that this is the person I've been waiting for all my life.

In the morning, I wake up first, taking the time to just watch Lucy sleeping for a while before getting up and going downstairs to make her a coffee and some toast. I cover it in Nutella and make a piece for myself, eating it quickly before going back upstairs. When I get to her bedroom, I'm pleased to see that she's stirred. Slipping on her T-shirt, she sits up in bed.

'Thank you. You don't always have to make me breakfast, you know? I can do it for you sometimes.'

I climb back into bed beside her. 'I like doing it.'

She finds my thigh under the cover and gives it a squeeze. 'Well, thank you. You're an excellent boyfriend.'

I smile as she tucks into her toast and I wonder if I should bring up last night, check that she's OK with everything that happened after she originally halted things between us.

'I had a great night,' I say, testing the water and going

in gently so Lucy has the choice whether or not she wants to open up to me about what happened.

'Me too.'

'You're sure that it was OK? That it was what you wanted?'

She looks a little shy and I hope that it's not too much, but then she says, 'I'm sorry that I've been so weird about it all this time. I bet you've been wondering what's wrong with me.'

I shake my head. 'I just worried I was doing something wrong.'

'Not at all. You've been amazing. It's just, with my ex, I think the sex masked a lot of our issues. He'd turn up late but barely ever stay, hated going to see my family, never wanted to commit to anything . . . sorry, do you really want to hear this?'

'I want to know everything about you.'

She puts her hand on top of mine. 'I just wanted things to be different with you. Not all about the physical, I mean. I wanted us to really get to know each other first without sex confusing things. Wanted to know that you liked me for more than just my mind-blowing performance in the bedroom.'

I smile. 'Well, it's definitely about more than the physical to me. And you can always tell me if you don't want to do it. You don't need an excuse.'

She sips her coffee and then puts it on the bedside table next to her empty toast plate. 'And can I tell you when I *do* want to do it?' She wiggles her eyebrows suggestively.

'Absolutely.'

Then she kisses me and we make love for the second time and it's just as amazing as the first. And I realize that there's definitely no hope for me now. I am well and truly smitten.

LUCY

When Jamie first suggested a long weekend away, I reckon he was thinking more Cornwall or Devon, as he looked quite shocked when I suggested an activity week-end in Andalusia. But I'm getting itchy feet not having been anywhere new for a while, and we've been together three and a half months now, so it feels like a suitable time for our first holiday abroad. And so here we are, staying in an eco farmhouse I found in the Cabo de Gata Nature Reserve. Sometimes I worry that one day Jamie will wake up resenting the fact he always ends up going along with my ideas and tell me to sod off, but I hope I'm wrong.

We're in the middle of nowhere, so quiet you can hear the birds in the trees, the crickets in the grass. It's owned by a Spanish couple in their early sixties, Gabriella and Santiago, who greeted us with hugs and kisses on our cheeks and showed us to our small rustic room in their ramshackle farmhouse. As part of the accommodation package, they will be cooking all our meals – so they told us to take some time to explore and that supper would be ready for eight.

We dumped our suitcases and now I've dragged Jamie out to have a walk around the grounds. We wander through the olive groves, the heat blistering, and then end up at what is supposed to be the swimming pool but looks more like a big barrel filled with slightly stagnant water, a barrage of insects gathered around the edges.

'Fancy a dip?' I tease.

Jamie raises an eyebrow. 'Do you think we should've had some jabs before we came here?'

'Where's your adventurous spirit?' I grab his hand. 'Now, do you want to go and christen that bed before going down for dinner?'

'Oh, well, if you insist.'

We go back to our room and Jamie pulls me on to the very squeaky bed, both of us laughing as we strip off. There's no air conditioning, just a very weak ceiling fan (it's probably solar powered or something), so by the end we're both sweating buckets. The shower looks a little questionable but it's that or a quick dip in the pool, so we take it in turns to brave the shower. Jamie valiantly takes the first slot to test it – it's very much only luke-warm but we're both so hot we don't mind – then we get dressed and go down to dinner.

It's still gorgeously warm even though the sun's almost set, and the view is beautiful; the mountains in the background, and the farmhouse surrounded by olive groves as far as the eye can see. It's the kind of place that gives you that sense of inner calm of being somewhere stunning, completely unspoilt by humans. Everything is communal – one big happy eco family – and the other party staying here are already sitting at the large table set out on the terrace. It's a family of four, and the parents introduce themselves – Katie (Mum), Sam (Dad) – and then introduce their daughters, Betty (eldest) and Lilly (youngest), and we tell them our names in turn. The girls look to have a similar age gap to my sister's kids but are perhaps a little bit younger, maybe two and five. They're a little New Age; Mum and Dad are white but both have dreadlocks, Dad's wearing a tie-dye T-shirt, his facial hair unruly. I imagine they've never shopped in Primark, that they've loudly boycotted McDonald's, that the girls have never in their lives been allowed a plastic toy. I've met a lot of people like them while travelling and have always felt they looked down on me for shopping on the high street or eating standard meat from the supermarket or basically being an integral cog in the capitalist machine as they see it. But, so far, this family seems very open and welcoming.

After a few minutes of talking about where we're from (unsurprisingly they are from Brighton), Gabriella and Santiago come out with dish after dish of amazing food – paella, a variety of fish dishes, salads, a range of exotic breads. It all smells divine and everyone around the table fills their plates – Katie putting a bit of each dish on to plates for the girls – and we all tuck in. The kids try all the different foods without a fuss, and I can't help thinking of Otto and Lauren, the faces they would pull at the food being served up to them.

'I can't believe they're happy to eat all that. It's amazing. My niece and nephew wouldn't go near any of it.'

Katie puts her hand on each girl's head in turn. 'Oh yeah, they've always been good eaters. We travel a lot so I guess they're used to trying new things. We've never given them much choice to be honest. Horrible parents that we are.' She laughs.

'No, I think it's amazing.'

'I was a total nightmare,' Jamie chips in. 'Mum said I'd live on beans on toast and even then it had to be a certain brand of white bread.'

'You might have a problem with your kids then,' Santiago jokes. 'They say things like that can run in families. Our daughter was a fussy eater too, used to drive me mad. Took after her mother.' He shoots a look at his wife. 'Gabriella would barely eat anything until she met me and I taught her the joys of good food and excellent wine.'

Gabriella puts her hand on her husband's arm. 'Changed me for the better.'

Santiago makes sure our glasses stay topped up the entire evening (I've never liked red wine before but Jamie convinced me to try a glass, and it's the best I've ever tasted), and he and Gabriella tell us stories about life at the farmhouse and unusual guests they've had over the years, like the ones who refused to eat as a group and insisted all meals were left outside their room, and the man who came with three different women, all staying in the same room together. And we spend the night laughing, soaking in the warmth and the comfort of sitting out under the stars in a beautiful spot, with new people who we actually like, sated by the gorgeous food and wine.

Once it's getting late, the two little girls (who have been impeccably behaved, colouring in their activity books and answering Gabriella's questions politely) start to look tired and lie down, each one resting their head on one of their parents' knees. Jamie looks over at them with an unexpected tenderness and I feel a niggle of fear that makes me realize how much I like him.

'Right, I suppose we should call it a night,' Katie says, and I feel a strangely acute sense of sadness at this perfect night coming to an end.

'Oh, stay out a little longer. Just one more glass.'

Katie looks at her empty glass and then at her husband, who gives her a look that says, 'Come on, time's up.' And she picks up the youngest girl, who flops her head on to her shoulder, and shakes her head. 'I'd love to but they'll be total miseries in the morning if we don't get them off to bed.'

I look for the resentment that being encumbered with two children is curtailing her fun, but there isn't any, just a deep sense of contentment.

'Yeah, I remember when Elena was that age,' Gabriella chips in. 'Always needed her beauty sleep. Mind you, she still does at thirty-two or she's a total monster.' She goes over to each girl in turn and gently pats their heads. 'Sleep tight, beautiful girls.' Then she looks up at Katie. 'In fact, she's coming over tomorrow. She has a daughter, Maya, who must be about the same age as Lilly. If you're around at all in the afternoon, I bet she'd love to play with your girls.'

'That sounds amazing. Thank you.'

They exchange warm smiles before Katie and Sam

carry their girls to their room, and I try to shrug off a familiar sense of isolation.

'Perhaps we should get some sleep too,' Jamie says. 'You've got a busy day planned for us tomorrow, haven't you, Luce?'

'Oh, what are you up to?' Santiago says. 'Do I need to make breakfast early for you? We usually have it about nine.'

'We're going rafting, but not until eleven so breakfast at nine will be fine.'

'Great. Well, we'll leave you both to sleep.' Then the two of them start gathering up all the plates and dishes.

'Let us help,' Jamie says, but they won't have any of it, almost pushing us off the terrace. 'No, go. Enjoy being young lovers.'

We both smile, but as we walk back to our bedroom, I can't help feeling annoyed, and even though I know the true cause of my sensitivity has nothing to do with Jamie ending the night early, I snap, 'I didn't want to go to bed yet.'

'Come on. You'll thank me for it in the morning.' Jamie puts his arm round my waist and guides me towards our room as if I'm unable to walk on my own, which isn't far from the truth, but it feels patronizing and I find the next words coming out of my mouth without being able to stop them.

'Jude and I would've stayed out until the early hours. He always knew where to find the party.'

I don't know why I say it or what's wrong with me. Yes, we used to party on the beach until the sun was

rising, Jude always managing to infiltrate the most interesting groups, or dancing the night away in foreign clubs,
always being the last to leave. But he also made me work
for every ounce of his affection like it was some kind of
game.

Jamie removes his arm from around my waist, stead-
ies me and then moves away. 'Well, I'm sorry I'm such a
bore.'

Before I have the chance to respond, he walks off
ahead, leaving me to stumble my way back on my own.
When I reach our room, Jamie is already in bed, lying on
his side turned away towards the wall. And I realize it's
our first fight.

I climb into bed beside him, feeling horribly drunk
and knowing that I should just leave things until the
morning, when I've sobered up and won't say something
I might regret, but I just can't leave it be.

'So you're just going to go to sleep, are you?' I say,
expecting a battle and getting in my defensive line first.

Jamie sighs and turns to face me. 'I'm sorry for walking off. I was just hurt.'

I pause. It's so unexpected to have a man apologize.
With Jude, it was always me that had to say sorry, even
when I wasn't in the wrong.

'It's OK. It's my fault. I was just having a great night
and I didn't want it to end.'

'Well, I'm sorry that I didn't realize that. That I ended
the night before you wanted to.'

I put my hand on his cheek. 'I didn't mean what I said,
about Jude.'

'He probably *was* a lot more exciting than me. I'm not exactly a party animal if that's what you're looking for?'

'Not at all. I was just being a drunken dick. Promise me you won't give it another thought?'

Jamie nods but I can see in his eyes that he's still concerned and wish I could just go back and not say what I said.

'Seriously, you're everything that Jude wasn't.'

Jamie raises his eyebrows. 'I'll take that as a compliment, I guess.'

'It's definitely a compliment.'

Finally, he smiles and then pulls me towards him and I turn round so that we're spooning, Jamie's arms like a protective barrier wrapped around me.

JAMIE

After an amazing continental breakfast (I'm going to be two stone heavier by the time we get home), we start on our itinerary for the day – rafting, followed by horse riding and then a mountain climb. The most energy I usually expend during my holidays is the walk from the swimming pool to the hotel bar, so being on holiday with Lucy feels more like being at a boot camp and I'm slightly nervous at my ability to keep up. I'm learning that she is one big ball of energy that never seems to get used up, like she's permanently attached to a battery charger, whereas while I'm not unfit – in fact, I like to think I'm in fairly good shape – I *do* have a limit. Still, I'm determined to show Lucy that, like Jude, I *can* be adventurous and exciting, so I pretend that I'm not already exhausted just reading the plan for the day.

We get to the water sports centre and meet the rafting instructor, who introduces us to the couple that we're going to be sharing a dinghy with. They're one of those action-man couples – both a mass of muscle and sinew, both perfectly tanned, model good looks. I expect they do triathlons weekly, eat ten eggs a day. When they start talking, I'm glad to discover that they speak very little English, so we don't have to engage in conversation, as I'm sure they'd only put me to shame with the adventures they've had. Before we set off, we're given a safety talk and then we have to put on our life jackets and climb into the 'boat'.

'Scared?' Lucy asks, a twinkle in her eye.

'Nope. Perfectly relaxed,' I lie.

She laughs and our instructor climbs in, hands us each an oar and then sits at the front. When we start out, it's very calm and, I have to admit, stunning. We meander through caverns, the movement of the raft creating a much-needed breeze in the sweltering heat. But just as I'm beginning to relax, I see it coming up in front of us: an eye-watering drop, the water spraying out in all directions.

'So this is our first drop,' the instructor announces, shouting to be heard over the powerful roar of the water. 'Think of it as a bit of a test run before we get to the proper falls. Keep your oars in, but if we get a bit stuck in the current at the bottom then follow my lead for which side to row.'

'A test run?' I can't stop the question from popping out.

Lucy leans over and kisses me, a huge mocking grin plastered across her face. 'Trust me, it's exhilarating. You'll love it.'

She'd mentioned that she'd been rafting in Norway a year or so ago and how much she'd loved it. It hadn't bothered me at the time, but now I suddenly remember the photo on her wall of the group of them in the boat, and I wonder whether the guy with his arm around her was Jude. I bet *he* wasn't shitting his pants.

As we get closer to the drop, I hold on tight to the ropes around the edge of the raft, the fabric cutting into my skin, and notice that old action-couple don't even hold on, just sit back as if they're lounging on a hammock somewhere with a margarita. Then suddenly we're falling and Lucy's right, it's exhilarating, and when we get to the bottom, we all have to move to the left of the boat and push with our oars to get out of the rip and then we're back in calmer waters, but slightly faster than before, floating through large expanses and then little streams. And when I see the next drop in the distance, I'm no longer scared, I'm willing the boat on, excited for the adrenaline rush.

There are a couple of hairy moments – when the raft tips up a bit too far and we all fall to the other side, and when we're nearly flooded by a huge wave of water splashing over us – but the whole time I feel a smile fixed on my face. When I glance at Lucy, she looks exactly the same, and I wonder what I've been doing with the rest of my life because I've *never* felt this alive or happy. It's like I've been sleepwalking for the past goodness knows how many years and Lucy's finally woken me up.

Afterwards, we get sandwiches from the reception area and sit on a bench overlooking the water to eat them, the sun beating down on us.

'Ready for horse riding? Hopefully a bit less daunting than the rafting,' Lucy says, before taking a bite of her sandwich.

'I'm actually quite scared of horses.'

'Seriously?'

'Well, no, not really scared. But they can be quite unpredictable, you know? And their eyes freak me out a bit. They always look a little sinister.'

'Horses are beautiful.'

I shake my head. 'That's what people say, but take a proper look in their eyes. Always plotting, I reckon.'

Lucy laughs. 'So did you enjoy it in the end? The rafting?'

'Honestly? I loved it. You were right. It's one of the best things I've ever done. Thank you. I think this is my favourite holiday ever.'

Lucy smiles and takes another bite of her sandwich, and I worry that she's avoiding having to say it back, that she's feeling awkward that perhaps this isn't her best holiday ever and combined with what she said last night about Jude always being able to find the party, I can't help feeling a little insecure.

'Did you travel a lot with Jude?'

Lucy looks to the floor. 'I was just really drunk last night. You honestly have nothing to worry about.'

'Often the truth comes out when we're drunk though, doesn't it?'

'No. Only crap comes out of my mouth when I'm drunk. Now if you want to know my *true* feelings . . .'

Her face breaks into a cheeky smile and then she leans towards me and kisses me, gently at first but then becoming more passionate. When we finally break apart, I can't stop myself from smiling too, my insecurities melting away. And looking at Lucy, I suddenly realize that I am definitely madly, deeply, overwhelmingly in love with her. And I wonder if I should tell her here and now, but then she looks at her watch.

'Come on, we better get to the stables. Our creepy-looking horses will be waiting for us.'

I grab our sandwich wrappers and throw them in the nearby bin. 'OK then. Let's go.'

The horse riding is actually scarier than the rafting. My horse definitely gives me this look when I climb on that says, 'Who do you think you are, assuming you can just sit on me whilst I carry you in this heat?', and the whole journey he keeps raising his head and rearing up on his hind legs as if he's trying to shake me off, or venturing away from the rest of the pack, as if he's on a mission to get me lost somewhere and dump me in the blistering heat. Lucy thinks it's hilarious, of course, that I'm the one lumbered with the rebellious horse, and she can't stop laughing when we get back to the ranch.

'They can sense your lack of trust, you know? It's like dogs, they know if you don't like them.'

'I'm not convinced. I think it was just bitter to have me riding on its back rather than you.'

'Well, I do have a softer bum.'

By the time we get to the last activity of the day, worrying I'm on the verge of a coronary, I manage to persuade Lucy to just climb halfway up the mountain, promising we can try to make it all the way to the top tomorrow, and we head back to the farmhouse for a dip in the less than enticing pool. After our swim, we have sex, sleepily as I don't have much left in my locker, and then we have a quick nap before dinner.

When we wake up, Lucy gets in the shower and I nip down to Santiago and Gabriella to ask them if they'd mind if we took our dinner somewhere just the two of us. At first, I reckon they think I'm going to propose because Gabriella gets quite misty-eyed, so I feel a bit stupid when I say I just want to tell Lucy that I love her, like we are two teenagers rather than grown adults. They both look overjoyed though and say they'll help set me up a little candlelit table among the olive groves. They hurry me back to our room so as 'not to ruin the surprise' and say to leave it to them, so I run back and, luckily, Lucy is still in the shower.

As she gets out, I don't want her to notice I'm slightly out of breath and pink-cheeked so I climb straight into the shower after her. She's used all the semi-warm water so I stand there shivering, the freezing water making my head hurt as I wash my hair, and then climb out as soon as I've got the shampoo out.

Lucy has put on a cute little summer dress, bright yellow, and she looks beautiful, her skin glowing from the endless sun of today. When she sees me, a towel wrapped around my waist, she smiles – and I know that I'm doing the right thing telling her that I love her, because I do, more than I've ever loved anyone. I must stand there looking stupid because she says, 'What?'

'Nothing.'

'Get ready then. I'm starving and seriously looking forward to some more of that amazing food. If Santiago wasn't married, I might've run off with him with those cooking skills.'

I laugh and then go to get ready myself, putting on some smart khaki shorts and a white linen shirt and spraying myself with aftershave.

'Right. Let's get going.' I hold out my hand and Lucy takes it.

You can smell the heat in the air as we get outside and I guide Lucy towards the olive groves.

'Where are we going? You do realize I'm starving, don't you? And that I'm prone to getting hangry?'

I smile but continue to lead her to the destination I agreed with Santiago and Gabriella. I'm starting to feel nervous but then I see the little table, a large candle in the centre, and tealights in jars surrounding it in a circle, and I know that it's perfect.

Lucy must suddenly spot it too because she says, 'What is this? What's going on?'

'I wanted to make tonight a little bit more romantic. I hope you don't mind missing out on eating with the others?'

Lucy pauses, surveying the set-up and then securing eye contact with me, and I can't be sure but I think there are tears in her eyes. Then she looks away. 'Are you cooking?'

'No, Santiago is still doing the cooking.'

'Phew.' Lucy wipes her brow dramatically and we continue walking towards the circle of candles. They've left a path to walk through so we do, and then I pull out Lucy's chair and she does a little curtsy. Before sitting down, she lifts up on her tiptoes and kisses my cheek. 'Thank you. It's perfect.'

I try not to show how chuffed I am as I sit opposite her and within seconds (as if one of them was hiding in the olive bushes and spying on us) Santiago arrives with some wine and Gabriella follows with a range of appetizers – olives, bread and oils, squidgy cherry tomatoes – and then they both wink at me and leave us alone.

'So what's all this in aid of?' Lucy asks, sampling each dish in turn.

'I just . . .' The words seem to be stuck, so I swallow and then start again. 'I know I'm maybe not the most adventurous man in the world, the most exciting . . .'

'Seriously, Jamie. Not this again,' Lucy interrupts.

'Hang on, let me finish. I'm not saying I'm not a huge catch.'

Lucy smiles.

'But being with you has made me realize how empty my life has been, how I've basically been drifting.' I take a deep breath. 'What I'm trying to say is that I love you, more than I've ever loved anyone.' I pause, but she doesn't respond so I feel I have to continue. 'I'm sorry, is that too much? I know we haven't been together all that long.'

I suddenly worry she might be about to run off through the olive groves, leaving me sitting here alone. But then she shakes her head slowly. 'It's not too much.'

I wait for her to say she loves me too, but she doesn't,

and I try not to feel too despondent. Maybe she's just not ready to say it back yet.

'It's really beautiful,' she says, before popping an olive into her mouth.

'Santiago and Gabriella set it up.'

'Well, it's very romantic. And this food . . . God, I'm going to be the size of a house by the time we leave here.' Lucy holds her tummy, which is practically non-existent.

'Tell me about it. Although I reckon we've burnt quite a few calories today.'

'Yeah, sorry. I know it was quite intense. I'll go a bit easier on you tomorrow.'

I shake my head. 'I had a great day. Thank you.'

'Followed by the perfect evening,' Lucy says smoothly.

'If Carlsberg did holidays . . .'

Lucy laughs, mopping up the last of the chilli oil with some bread. 'Maybe we should start our own business? Holiday planners extraordinaire.'

'I'm not sure I'd manage to get any work done if I worked with you.'

Under the table, Lucy slips off her flip-flop and starts running her foot up my leg. 'True. That could be a problem.'

Suddenly, Santiago appears. 'Appetizers OK?'

'Perfect. Thanks,' I mumble, a little flustered.

'Fabulous. Thank you.' Lucy looks up at Santiago, giving him her full attention.

He takes our plates away and then Gabriella appears with our mains. They're such a well-oiled machine, I can see how they've made the business a success. It's not tapas like it was last night, but steak and a huge pile of chips, the steak looking perfectly cooked.

'Wow, this looks amazing. Thank you so much,' I say, putting my hand gently on Gabriella's arm as she sets our plates down in front of us. 'And thank you for going to the trouble of bringing it along here. I do appreciate it.'

'No problem at all.' Gabriella places a hand on my shoulder. 'We're always happy to support a bit of romance.'

I notice Lucy's cheeks pinken, Gabriella leaving us to it. The food is delicious. It tastes as good as it looks, and Lucy and I are both quiet whilst we tuck in.

Then I place my knife and fork down on my plate and lean back in my chair. 'So, what *have* you got planned for us tomorrow? Deep sea diving? Jumping out of a plane?'

'Not quite. I suppose we need to actually climb that mountain. Then a bit of canoeing maybe? But it's your holiday as much as mine. I don't have to make all the decisions.'

'I don't mind you making the decisions.'

'But I wouldn't think any less of you if you did. Feel free to tell me to stop being a bossy cow. I won't like you any less.'

I get the sense that she wants me to be more assertive, that actually she might be saying she'd like me *more* if I was. But I'm not being submissive for fear of annoying her, I just like the things she's suggesting. I like how she's widening what I hadn't realized had become quite a narrow life that I was leading.

'Don't worry. If I don't like something, I'll tell you. If you piss me off, I'll make sure you know about it.'

Lucy raises an eyebrow. 'I think I'd quite like that.'

'Is that so?' I nod in the direction of our room. 'Fancy giving dessert a miss tonight?'

'Missing Santiago's dessert? Is your head on straight?'

I laugh. 'I'll take that as a no.'

'Why don't we ask for it to take away though?' Lucy suggests, reaching out to put her hand on my arm.

'Won't it look a bit obvious what we're going to do?'

'Oh, I plan on being very loud. There'll be no mistaking what we're doing.'

Lucy gives me this look and then Santiago appears to take our plates and I have to refocus.

'Best steak I've ever had,' I say, looking up.

'Ah, thank you very much. That's very kind of you to say.'

'It really was amazing, but I don't suppose we could have our desserts to go?' Lucy asks. 'I'm so full I could do with a little lie-down first.'

She puts her hand on her stomach and Santiago bites back a smile. 'Of course. How about I drop them outside your room later?'

'Perfect. Thank you.'

Once Santiago is out of view, we practically run back to our room, removing each other's clothes as soon as we get through the door and throwing them on the floor before entwining ourselves on the bed.

Afterwards, we lie naked on top of the duvet for a

while and then Lucy slips on her underwear. 'Do you think our dessert might have been delivered by now?'

She goes to the door, opens it, and comes back with two plates with slices of chocolate cheesecake on, along with dessert forks. Bringing them over to the bed, she climbs back in and we sit up against the headboard, pulling the white sheet up over our legs.

'Naked cheesecake eating. Feels very decadent,' I joke.

'You know *you* make *me* happy,' Lucy says, ignoring my comment as if she didn't even hear me.

'Good.'

'And I love you too.'

She doesn't look at me as she says it, her eyes focused firmly on her cheesecake, but I can't stop a huge beaming smile from appearing on my face. When I lean over to kiss her on the cheek, she brings her shoulder up to her face and then starts tucking into her dessert and I can tell that she needs me not to make a fuss of what she said, to almost pretend it never happened.

'You know, with cheesecake like this, even *I'm* tempted to run off with him.'

Lucy laughs and puts her hand on my leg under the covers, and I get the sense she's saying, 'Thank you for understanding my need to play this down.' So I smile at her to say, 'You're welcome.'

The Day of the Break-Up

LUCY

I don't go straight to Amy's. I can't face it yet. I know she'll be the wonderful supportive sister that she is – make me a cup of tea, hug me, tell me everything's going to be OK – but if someone is nice to me right now, I'm going to break down in tears. So instead, after driving around aimlessly for a while, I go to Coffee #1 where I choose the richest, most calorific-looking slice of cheesecake and a mocha (with the hope of drowning myself in chocolate) and search for a table. After a minute or so, a lady stands up and offers me her table and even that small act of kindness has me on the edge of a humiliating public crying fit.

Tucking into my food, a slight nausea in my stomach, I wonder what Jamie's doing, if he found the ring on the bedside table, if he threw it across the room or perhaps carefully put it away, saving it for someone more deserving. Will I always do this? Sit and wonder what Jamie's doing? I know it's only been fifty-three minutes since I walked out of our home and I should probably cut myself some slack, allow myself time to grieve, but I feel this awful panic that this feeling of immense emptiness will never go away.

I look at my phone, noticing a little green circle in the corner of my WhatsApp icon and click on it, trying not to get too excited. It's probably just a new message on one of the many group chats I'm part of, people swapping stories of amazing places they've been to or planning exotic meet-ups, but when I click on it, it *is* from Jamie and I feel my chest tighten – even though I know it's stupid, that him messaging me isn't going to change anything, but I just miss him. Already. I miss him so much.

What you doing? x

I wonder if I should say something witty, or whether that would seem insensitive. Maybe I should be very cold, formal, so he knows there's no changing my mind. In the end, I just go for honest.

Drowning my sorrows in cheesecake x

Much the same here, except ice cream. You left a whole tub of Ben & Jerry's in the freezer.

To think of our life only a few days ago, when I brought home Ben & Jerry's from Tesco for us to share in front of some crap on the TV, it makes me so very sad.

I was planning on collecting that with the rest of my belongings, you know? In fact, it was the top of my list.

Sorry. I'll buy some more and leave it for you.

It's OK. I bet it's not as good as my cheesecake anyway.

I tuck in, feeling slightly sick from the chocolate overload and watching the three dots as Jamie types.

Remember that cheesecake Santiago made for us? God, it was good.

I smile, but my heart aches at the memory. The night Jamie told me he loved me. The way I was so bloody coy about saying it back. And now I wish I'd shouted it at him, smothered him with affection. I wonder if this is his intention, to make me think of that night, or whether he's just innocently reminiscing.

Best. Cheesecake. Ever.

There's a pause and then a message comes through.

What if I never find cheesecake that good again?

I take a deep breath, trying to keep my resolve while wanting to run out of the café and all the way home.

You will x

He doesn't respond and I feel like I have so much more to say but I'm not sure how to say it. I type a message and then delete it and then type it again.

I am sorry about what happened. All of it.

I can see that he's typing again and feel a strange nervousness about what his response might be.

I know. Me too x

Before

LUCY

I don't know what to wear. It's stupid. I'm sure Jamie's mum is not going to judge who I am as a person by the clothes on my back, but it feels disproportionately important to choose the right outfit. I can hear Jamie downstairs – I greeted him in my dressing gown and then told him I wanted to get ready on my own and that he had to wait in the lounge. He probably thinks I'm totally crazy, but I just can't bear the pressure of him being here whilst I try on different outfits, wondering what he's really thinking and if he's just being polite.

I pull on an A-line black skirt and floral blouse and look in the mirror, immediately letting out a long, pained breath. I look like I'm dressed for a work experience interview, like I'm playing at being an adult. I slip my clothes off, leaving them on the floor, and then try on the navy dress I've put out on the bed. Urgh. Far too formal. Why don't I have any decent clothes? I take off the dress and throw it across the room, accidentally knocking a glass of water off my bedside table and spilling it all over everything. Getting more irritable by the second, I put my dressing gown back on, run downstairs, past Jamie and into the kitchen to get some kitchen towel.

'You OK?' he calls and I can hear it in his voice – the fact he thinks I'm insane.

'I'm fine,' I say curtly, avoiding eye contact and running back past him and upstairs to the bedroom. I quickly dab the carpet, cursing myself as I wipe the water off all the books, magazines and paperwork I have piled up underneath my bedside table.

As I'm cleaning, I hear the door open and look up to see Jamie with a bemused expression on his face. 'You sure you're OK?'

I drop the kitchen roll and it unravels across the floor, and it feels like the moment to admit defeat. 'No, not really.'

He comes over and puts his arm around me. 'It's taking you a long time to get ready. You're not nervous, are you?'

I screw up my face. 'No.' Then my shoulders fall. 'Maybe. I just want her to think I'm pretty, and nice, and better than all your exes.'

Jamie smiles, taking my hand to pull me up. 'I'm sure she's going to love you.' Then he wraps his arms around my waist. 'But even if she didn't, it wouldn't change anything. I'd still feel exactly the same way about you as I do now.'

I know he means it in a reassuring way, and I'm touched that his mum's opinion wouldn't colour his own. But it matters to *me*. I'm not typically liked by partners' mums. I don't know why. I just don't seem to fit the desired daughter-in-law mould. To be fair, even *my* mum's not particularly impressed with me, so I can't exactly expect anyone else's to be. But I want her to be impressed, for her to tell Jamie he's made an excellent choice and that he should hold on tight to me.

'Thanks.'

He lets me go and wanders over to my wardrobe. 'Come on then. Show me what you've got. I'll choose something.'

I raise my eyebrows then open my wardrobe door, slightly embarrassed by the total lack of order to my clothes. Jamie starts leafing through my stuff, pulling out a pair of skinny black jeans and my favourite T-shirt – the one I got from Urban Outfitters years ago. It's big and baggy, and not at all smart, but it always makes me feel great when I'm wearing it. He places the clothes on the bed. 'How about this? This is you, right?'

I'm so touched that he knows me so well and yet I find myself sighing and slump on the bed while Jamie sits down next to me. 'But I was trying not to be me. Well, to be a better version of me.'

Jamie puts his hand on my thigh. 'You're pretty perfect just as you are.'

I rest my head on his shoulder. 'Thank you, but I know you're just saying that because that's the sort of sweet thing a boyfriend should say at this moment.'

'So it's just a line?'

'Well, no, I suppose I am pretty perfect.'

'There you go then.' He stands up and passes me the T-shirt. 'Come on, we're going to be late. Time to get ready.'

'Close your eyes then.'

'Really? Are we still at that stage of our relationship?'

'Well, we don't want you getting overexcited, do we?'

'Fair point.' Jamie sits on the bed, leaning up against the headboard with his feet up. 'Eyes are now firmly closed.'

I look at him, thinking for a moment how handsome he is, even with his beautiful big brown eyes closed, and then quickly get dressed. I've already done my hair and make-up and actually feel pretty happy when I look at myself in the mirror. Jamie's made a good choice with the outfit. But I'm still nervous and it makes me realize how much I like him. The fact that I'm desperate to impress his mum scares me. And 'scared me' usually ends up acting like a bit of a dick.

'OK, you can open your eyes now.'

Jamie opens his eyes one at a time and a huge smile floods his face. 'Gorgeous. Right, let's go. My mum hates it when I'm late for things.'

I'm quiet on the journey there, letting Jamie waffle on about this huge dinner dance he had to organize for work where the bosses demanded eight-course meals and spent thousands per head. It's not that what he's saying isn't interesting, but I struggle to focus, the nerves sitting right in the centre of my stomach.

When we pull up on the driveway, the house is exactly how I expected it to be. Large, detached, wisteria covering the walls. The front garden is very ordered, rows of pot plants lining the path to the door, well-cared-for hanging baskets next to the windows, the hedges neatly trimmed. I imagine Jamie's mum to be very sensible, tidy, confident but slightly reserved, as if she likes to keep herself to herself. I'm not sure I can accurately gauge all that from the outside of her house, but when she opens the door, dressed in a long floral skirt, a white T-shirt and a pearl necklace, her face set in a smile that somehow lacks any real warmth, it seems like a fair evaluation.

'Hi, Mum.' Jamie kisses his mum on the cheek and then holds his hand out to me and I realize that I'm standing back almost hiding behind him. 'This is Lucy. Lucy, this is my mum, Sandra.'

I step forward (or perhaps Jamie pulls me) and I'm not sure whether to follow his lead and kiss his mum on the cheek, or hug her, or shake her hand, and it all gets in a bit of a muddle and I end up giving her an awkward kind of bumped cheek greeting. 'It's nice to meet you, Sandra.'

She looks at me like she's not sure what to make of the clumsy oaf standing in front of her. 'You too, Lucy. Come in. I've just made some tea.'

I already know without seeing it that the tea will be served in a teapot with matching china, a plate of home-made cakes and scones to the side.

I'm right and have to stifle a smile when we enter Sandra's living room to see a very pretty floral teapot on the central coffee table with matching dainty teacups and saucers. I'm a little thrown by the biscuit choice, however. Jaffa Cakes. Far more down to earth than I expected. I feel myself relax slightly.

We sit down on Sandra's sofa, Jamie and I together while she sits on an armchair opposite us. Her living room is show-home tidy. I dread to think what she'd make of my place. It's a bit dated, the walls painted magnolia, ornate vases on the fireplace alongside gold photo frames. There's a school photograph of Jamie, probably aged about fourteen, his wavy hair parted into curtains with some kind of heavy gel.

Sandra pours me a cup of tea and hands it over. 'Help yourself to biscuits,' she says, leaving them on the table.

And as much as I'd love a Jaffa Cake or two, I don't feel I can reach out and take one so instead I just eye them longingly. Luckily, Jamie knows me well enough to grab me a couple before tucking in himself. I gently squeeze his thigh as a thank you, noticing that his mum's eyes follow my hand, and I suddenly fear that she's deemed it inappropriate.

'So tell me all about yourself, Lucy. What is it you do? Where do you live?'

'I work in a bookshop. And I live in Rodborough.'

'A bookshop? Oh, how lovely.'

I don't think I imagine the condescending tone and it immediately gets my back up. Of course I'm not good enough for Jamie in Sandra's eyes. I was stupid to think I ever had a chance of convincing her. 'I think people focus too much on careers these days, on money. I'd rather see things, travel, you know?'

I'm not really devoid of ambition. Although I'd never admit it to anyone, I *do* take my job seriously and I'd also love to make something of my writing one day, however unlikely that may be. I just hate always being judged on my job, my lack of degree, the clothes I wear.

'Well, yes, I guess . . .'

'Lucy's writing a novel, aren't you?' Jamie interjects, reaching out and taking my hand. And I know he thinks he's being supportive, but it feels as if he's reinforcing the idea that it's not good enough to 'just' work in a bookshop.

'Sort of. Playing around with an idea, but I doubt I'll ever finish it.'

'Of course you will. It's going to be a bestseller, I just know it.'

Sandra offers a strained smile, a reflection of how I feel myself. 'So what's your novel about?'

'Oh, it's total low-brow trash.'

'Stop putting yourself down. It is not,' Jamie chips in.

'I'm not saying there's anything wrong with it. We don't all want to read, or write, a Booker prize-winner.'

My tone is unnecessarily spiky. Both Jamie and his mum look uncomfortable and I know I'm making a fool of myself, so I brush the crumbs off my jeans and stand up. 'I'm sorry, but can you tell me where the bathroom is?'

'Of course.' Sandra shows me through to the corridor, pointing to the bathroom at the end. 'It's just down there.'

I smile and slip past her, trying to stop myself from running towards the bathroom door. When I get inside, I close the toilet seat and sit on top. Why am I behaving like this? I can just imagine them sitting there in the lounge, Sandra asking Jamie why the hell he's with me, telling him to get rid of me as soon as possible. And she'd be justified. I'm being an idiot. And why? Because I'm *scared* I'm not what Sandra would want for her son? I don't even know her. I stand up, take a look in the mirror, wipe away a little rogue eyeliner underneath my eyes and take a deep breath. After flushing the toilet so it looks as if I really did need to go, I wash my hands through force of habit and slowly walk back to the lounge, where Jamie and his mum are discussing her plans for the garden and Jamie is offering to help with the heavy lifting and carrying.

As I walk in, he tries to catch my eye and I get the sense he's asking, 'What the hell is going on?', but I just turn towards his mum.

'You have a beautiful house, Sandra,' I say, trying to make amends.

'Oh, thank you. It feels a bit big for little old me sometimes, but I can't imagine living anywhere else now.' Sandra's eyes appear momentarily wistful, before she takes a sip of her tea and seems to paint on a brave face. 'I was just telling Jamie that the summer house I've been planning for months is arriving next week. Would you like to see the plans?'

'I'd love to.'

'Come on then. Jamie, you can stay here if you want. I know I've bored you enough with them already.' I get the sense she's trying to get me on my own.

'I don't mind. Luce?'

'Don't worry, I won't bite. Come on, Lucy.'

Anxiously, I follow Sandra through to the kitchen. Again, although it's not exactly my cup of tea décor wise, it's very grand and there's not a thing out of place. Sandra picks up a brochure off the kitchen table, flicking through and showing me the summer house she's having, which I make a big fuss of, and then she leads me through the bifolding doors out to the garden. It's lovely. A bit neater than I'd have it, all very tidy flower beds, shrubs and flowers in rows, but still very pretty.

'It's going to go over there. I figure I can sit in there and read my book, maybe try my hand at a bit of painting. I've always wanted to give it a go, but never got round to it, but what better time than now, hey?'

Behind the confident woman who opened the door, I can see that there is someone far more fragile and it endears her to me. 'Sounds great. It'd be the perfect place to read and paint. I'd love a place like this. My garden is smaller than a postage stamp.'

'Well, maybe you and Jamie could get a place together one day.'

I look at the ground. 'Yeah, maybe.'

'He's totally smitten with you, by the way. I probably shouldn't say anything, but I haven't seen him like this before. I think he finds it hard to open up sometimes, after losing his dad and . . .' She pauses and a shadow seems to fall across her face. 'I'd hate to see him get hurt.'

I realize it's a warning and actually quite like the fact she's so protective of her son. I wish my mum had my back more often. When she meets Jamie, she'll probably tell him to run a mile.

'I really like him too. He's a very special man. You must be very proud.'

Sandra continues to walk me around the garden, stopping every few steps to show me her flowers. 'Yes, well, of course I am.' We get to the end of our circuit of the garden. 'Right, shall we go back inside? I expect you two have got things to be getting back to.'

I sense a hidden sadness in Sandra and don't feel we should just leave. 'Actually, perhaps we could take you out for lunch?'

Sandra waves away my comment with her hand, 'Oh no, don't worry about me. I've got plenty to be getting on with here.' We head inside. 'But I've got lots of food in if you did want me to make something for you? It'd just be sandwiches and a salad, though.'

'Sounds great.'

We go back into the lounge, where Jamie has demolished the entire plate of Jaffa Cakes.

'Lucy suggested we have some lunch. If you don't need to be anywhere?'

Jamie narrows his eyes at me and then turns to his mum. 'Sounds good. As long as you don't need to get back, Lucy?'

I shake my head. 'I'd love to stay.'

'OK, great.' Jamie smiles at me. 'Mum makes the best brie and bacon sandwiches, don't you, Mum?'

'Well, they're nothing to write home about.'

'Rubbish. Just you wait, Lucy. You'll be asking to come here every Saturday.'

Sandra laughs. 'Don't expect this kind of treatment

every weekend.' But I can tell that really she'd love for this to become a regular thing, and caught up in her bravado, I see a little bit of myself.

'So, Mum clearly loved you,' Jamie says in the car on the way home, as we start the dissection of the day. 'What did she say to you in the garden? Nothing too embarrassing, I hope.'

'I think she was just trying to suss out whether I'm going to break your heart.'

'Oh, God, why? What did she say?'

'Nothing. Just being a protective mum, as all good mums should be.'

Jamie raises his eyebrows. 'She's never really seemed that protective to me. Generally happy to just let me get on with things.'

'I'm not sure. I think she cares a lot more than she lets on.'

'Takes one to know one, hey?' Jamie teases and I reach over the gear stick and hit him in the side.

'I'm sorry that I was a bit snappy. About the writing.'

'It's OK. I didn't mean to upset you.'

I shake my head. 'I was being stupid. Sometimes I feel a bit . . . I don't know. It's my own deep-seated issues.' I say the last bit in air quotes.

Jamie reaches over and puts his hand on my knee. 'Well, I like that you cared. That you were worried about what to wear and stuff. Made it feel like it mattered to you.'

My phone buzzes in my pocket and I pull it out. 'Of course it mattered.'

When I look at my phone, my heart starts to race. It's from Jude.

'Everything OK?' Jamie asks and I realize I must have gone quiet.

'Oh yeah, just my mum, hassling me about when she's finally going to get to meet you. She's obsessed.'

Jamie laughs and I turn my phone screen well away from him, open the message and read what it says.

I'm home. I miss you. Can we meet? X

JAMIE

A week after Lucy met my mum (who rang later that evening to tell me Lucy was 'very pretty' and 'seemed lovely' but in true Mum style had to drop in that she did wonder whether we were 'on the same page'), we are going to meet Lucy's family. It's a far more exuberant affair than last week, as her mum, dad, sister, sister's husband and their two children are going to be there. Lucy has prepared me that they're quite loud and outspoken and I can't pretend I'm not a little bit nervous.

But as soon as we go into her sister's house, her dad greets me warmly, embracing me in a manly hug and welcoming me in, leading me straight to the fridge to get me a beer. It makes me feel embarrassed about when Lucy came to Mum's. How staid it must have all felt. The matching china, the polite, slightly awkward conversation over a cup of tea. And then I feel bad for feeling embarrassed because Mum's the only family I've got and she's always supported me, even if we're not as close as I might like.

The house is modern, immaculate. It looks like one of the properties that would be featured in *Livingetc* – all clean lines and light airy spaces. It's hard to believe that two children live here. There are no visible toys, muddles. You'd think Lucy was the one with kids, the state her place is usually in. But actually the mess is growing on me. After Mum being so clinically clean and tidy, telling me off for every crumb I dropped on the floor, there's something comfortingly homely about it, although I'm not sure I'd say that if I lived with her.

Looking through the patio doors to the garden, I can see the rest of the family outside, the kids playing Swing-ball, the adults sat around a table drinking wine.

Lucy's dad hands me an ice-cold beer. 'Here you go, son. Ready to join the crazies in the garden? Please ignore Lucy's mother. She's wonderful but a little bit insane, isn't she, Luce?'

'Just a little bit.'

'Don't worry, I'll look after you.' Lucy's dad puts his arm around my shoulder and guides me out into the garden.

As soon as I walk through the door, Lucy's mum runs over, her hands flapping excitedly in front of her, and then she draws me into a tight hug and kisses me on the cheek. 'Oh, it's so lovely to meet you, Jamie. Sit down, sit down,' she says, patting a chair next to the one she'd been sitting in. 'I want to know all about you. Lucy's always so bloody cagey.'

I smile, trying not to look hurt that Lucy hasn't said much to her mum about me. 'Lovely to meet you too, Mrs Maddison.'

'Oh, please call me Lyn. Mrs Maddison makes me sound about a hundred and three.'

I sit down as instructed and Lucy goes over and picks Otto up, spinning him round, and then she puts her arm around Lauren before grabbing her bat and taking her place in Swingball, Lauren taking it good-naturedly.

'So Lucy says you work in event management?'

'Yeah, it's my best mate's business. It's not bad as jobs go.'

'Sounds great. And do you live on your own?'

'No, I live with Matt, the guy I work with. It's not ideal, I guess, but I'm not sure I'd be very good at living alone. I like the company.'

'Absolutely, I'm with you. I don't know why Lucy likes it so much. Always has been an odd girl.'

'I can hear you, Mum,' Lucy calls over.

'A bit of peace and quiet sounds great to me,' Lucy's sister chips in, then she holds out her hand for me to shake. 'I'm Amy by the way. And this is Dave. Nice to meet you.'

Dave stands up and shakes my hand too. 'Nice to meet you, buddy.'

'Maybe you could move in with Lucy,' Lyn says, reverting back to our previous conversation.

'Mum,' Amy chastises, reaching over and slapping her mum on the hand.

'Well, she has her big birthday coming up in a year and a half,' she says to Amy and then she calls out to Lucy, 'I can hear your biological clock ticking from here.' Lucy rolls her eyes then leaves the kids to play and comes over, grabbing more wine off the table and pulling up a chair.

'Not everyone's desperate to spend their days changing nappies and wiping snotty noses,' Lucy teases and then turns to her sister. 'No offence, Sis. Otto and Lauren are exceptions to the rule, of course, but that's because I get to give them back.'

Amy waves her hand. 'No offence taken. You're right, they're a nightmare.' She smiles and looks over at her children and it's obvious how much she adores them, how she wouldn't change her position for the world.

'You'd love it, Luce,' her mum continues. 'And look at Jamie here, you'd make beautiful children.'

Lucy's dad comes over, takes his wife's wine glass and tops it up. 'Stop scaring him off, you,' he says, giving her a pretend menacing look.

In the past, this sort of conversation would've brought me out in hives. At one point Anna started talking about getting married and I felt this odd sense of doom in my gut. I'm not sure she ever really felt passionate about marrying *me*. It was more that she was getting to an age where getting married seemed to be the done thing and I was the person she happened to be in a relationship with at the time. But it's funny – with Lucy, it doesn't feel scary. If anything, it feels exciting.

Lauren and Otto run over, both stealing handfuls of crisps off the table. 'Come here, you troublemakers. Come and meet Aunty Lucy's boyfriend, Jamie.'

Lyn grabs Otto, who climbs up on to her knee whilst his sister shyly leans into her mum's side.

'Impressive Swingball skills, you two.'

'I'm the best,' says Otto.

'He's not,' Lauren whispers, shaking her head at the ridiculousness of her younger brother.

'Well, I'm better than both of you,' Lucy teases.

'How about I take on Aunty Lucy? Show her who the real best is?' I ask the kids, who both nod emphatically.

Lucy holds out her hand for me to pull her up. 'Come on then, Andy Murray.'

We play a very competitive game of Swingball, Otto blatantly cheering on his aunty whereas Lauren is a bit more subtle in her allegiance. Obviously taught to be polite to visitors, she watches on intently, unable to stop a small 'yes' coming out of her mouth when her aunty gets the rope towards the top.

Lucy is just about to win and I see the glee all over her face, she's almost dancing, but then I take a huge swipe and whack the ball round to her side and she misses it for two whole rotations, taking the rope back down towards the middle.

'So, we're playing rough, are we?' Lucy bends her knees and bounces from side to side like Emma Raducanu waiting for her opponent to serve.

I hit the ball towards her and she whacks it so hard, the bat flies out of her hand and nearly hits Otto on the head, but he ducks just in time.

'Watch out for my children, Luce,' Dave shouts over. 'I know it would mean they were quieter but I do quite like them with their heads on.'

Lucy is undeterred. In fact, she looks more determined than ever, retrieving her bat and smashing the ball back round to me. This time, it's *my* head she nearly takes off, as the ball goes high and flies towards my face.

'What is it with you and heads?' I say, out of breath.

Lucy laughs but keeps on playing, her shots getting more violent each time, the kids giggling on the grass beside us. The rope is nearly at the top, it's my big chance to save it, but I scuff my shot and Lucy punishes me by sending the ball flying back round towards me and the rope reaches the top.

'Woo hoo!' She drops her bat to the floor and jumps up, as if she's just won Wimbledon. Then the kids fly over, Otto leaping into her arms and Lauren wrapping herself around Lucy's leg. And I can't help the stabbing jealousy of what Lucy has – all this love, this 'proper' family, all of which was stolen from me.

'You OK? Losing knocked the wind out of you?'

As Lucy speaks, I realize that my face must have fallen so I paint on a smile and turn to the kids.

'Right, which one of you wants to take me on next?'

Both children shout, 'Me!', so I take it in turns to play a game with them both, letting them win, of course, whilst Lucy goes back to sit with her family and drink more rosé. I can hear them talking in hushed voices and wonder what sort of assessment I'm getting, whether I've passed the test.

Lucy's dad and Dave start up the barbecue, my first one of the year, and it smells great. We sit and drink whilst the food cooks. The sun is shining, it's a perfect temperature, and everyone is in great spirits. Lucy's right. Her family are all outspoken – well, particularly the women. The men seem happy to sit back and watch, chipping in the odd witticism but ultimately allowing the women in their lives to take the lead. I join in when I can, hoping I don't say anything that puts a black mark against my name, that I can be accepted into this wonderful bubble.

When the food's ready, the kids eat theirs on a picnic blanket on the lawn and us adults sit at the table. We drink and stuff our faces and laugh; a perfect afternoon.

'So, Jamie, what do you think? Want to run a mile?' Lucy's dad asks, tapping me gently on the back.

I shake my head. 'Quite the opposite.'

Lyn winks at me. 'See, told you he's a keeper.'

I smile, hoping she's referring to their quiet chat earlier and that I've been given a good review.

'To be honest, it's been just me and my mum for a long time. My dad passed away when I was sixteen so this is perfect.'

Lyn puts her hand on my knee. It's weird – she's more tactile with me than my own mum is, and it makes me a little sad. 'I'm sorry to hear about your dad.'

I shrug. 'It's OK. It was a long time ago.' Not that the pain gets any easier. In fact, I think maybe it gets worse as time passes, but I suppose you just learn to live with it better. Most of the time, anyway.

'Doesn't get any easier though, does it?' Lyn says, as if reading my mind. 'Still miss my mum and dad as if it were yesterday, and it's coming on ten years.'

'Well, it definitely helps, to be part of this.'

'You're welcome any time. You're part of the tribe now.'

'Poor you,' Dave jokes and Amy punches him in the arm.

Then the kids run over demanding pudding and Lyn goes inside, the two of them attached to her either side. Soon after, they come out with huge bowls of ice cream, topped with marshmallows, sprinkles and chocolate sauce.

'Where's mine?' Lucy asks, dipping her finger into Otto's ice cream before he swipes it away, protesting loudly.

'You've got tiramisu. Is that OK, your majesty?' Lyn says, putting down a tray with a huge bowl of home-made tiramisu and a pile of dishes.

'Ah, thanks, Mum. You did my favourite.'

Lyn puts her hand on Lucy's shoulder. 'See, I'm not such an evil dragon after all.'

Lucy looks up at her mum and gives her a genuinely warm smile. 'Still a dragon, but not totally evil.'

Then Lyn serves up and we all tuck in, silence descending on the table as we enjoy the delicious food.

LUCY

It's an empty Sunday at the beginning of August and Jamie and I are sitting on my sofa reading our books, my head in his lap as he strokes my hair, but my mind keeps wandering and I'm not taking any of it in.

After Jude's text a couple of weeks ago, I've been feeling strangely unsettled. Of course I haven't replied – there's no way I want to open that door again – but I can't help feeling this distinct yearning for adventure.

'Let's just drive towards the water. Have some lunch, a nice walk,' I say, closing my book and sitting up.

'What water?'

'I don't know. I'll just look for blue on the map.'

'You can't just drive with no destination.'

'The journey is the destination or whatever the saying is.'

Jamie rolls his eyes. 'At least let me pack a picnic then. In case we end up stranded somewhere.'

'Well, if you must.'

Jamie goes into the kitchen and I follow him through as he starts rifling through the fridge to find something suitable for sandwiches.

'You know, if you ordered things by type, it'd be much easier. A meat shelf, a veg shelf . . .'

'Ah, but this way it's more exciting. You put your hand

in and you never know what you're going to pull out. Sometimes I find amazing things I never even knew I had.'

Jamie laughs. 'Like this?' He pulls out a yoghurt that looks like it's about to explode and studies the lid. 'March the twenty-ninth. Just a few months past its best, then.'

I take it off him and throw it in the bin. 'We can't all be as perfect as you.'

'True.' He finds some pâté I'd forgotten I'd bought the other day, checks the sell by date and then starts spreading it on to some bread, adding sliced tomato and then wrapping the sandwiches in cling film.

I grab a large packet of crisps out the cupboard and a bar of Dairy Milk and add it to the sandwiches, which Jamie then puts in his bag.

'Right, can we go now, please?'

'I still think we should google where to go.'

I grab Jamie's hand and pull him towards the front door. 'We live in one of the most beautiful parts of the country. Trust me, we can't go wrong.'

Heading towards the 'blue' on the map serves us well and we end up at a campsite near Symonds Yat where we drop the car and follow the signs down towards the river. After a pretty walk through the trees, we reach a little cut-through and end up on a deserted shingle beach at the edge of the River Wye. It's stunning and the weather this year continues to be amazing, the sky such a brilliant blue that it feels like being abroad.

'I didn't bring my trunks.'

'Well, that's very unprepared of you,' I tease. 'There's

no one here, though, so you can swim in your pants. Come on, I'll race you.'

I start stripping off my clothes, throw them on to the beach and then run into the river, yelping as the sharp stones that make up the riverbed dig into the soles of my feet and the cold water cramps my legs. When I look back, Jamie's stripped down to his boxers and is running in after me.

'Ow. It's like standing on broken glass,' he shouts.

I've reached the point where it's deep enough to swim now and I launch into the current and let it carry me further down the river.

'Just throw yourself off up there and it'll take you to me.'

Jamie struggles over some rocks that make a pathway into the middle of the river and then jumps into the current. 'Woo hoo,' he yells as he lies on his back and floats, at speed, towards me. Once he gets here, he puts his feet down, grabs me by the waist and lifts me up into the air. 'God, I love you.'

When he lowers me back down, I kiss him. 'I love you, too.'

We frolic in the water, swimming against the current until we tire and splashing each other when we're back on level ground. But after a while, I notice Jamie's lips turning blue. 'Shall we go and get warm?'

Jamie nods, his teeth chattering.

'Plus, I'm starving,' I add.

We struggle back over the stones and throw ourselves on our blanket.

'See, you're glad I brought a picnic now, aren't you? We're literally in the middle of nowhere.'

'I would've hunted out some chocolate to survive. I have this special sense.'

'Chocolate sense?'

'Yeah. It's my superpower.'

Jamie takes the sandwiches he made out of his bag and we sit and eat, drying off almost immediately in the heat of the sun.

'The weather this year has been amazing, hasn't it?' I say before taking another bite of my sandwich.

'Everything about this year has been amazing.'

I kiss Jamie on the cheek. 'It's been pretty good, I suppose.'

Once we've finished our sandwiches, I get out the bar of chocolate, which has melted, getting it all over my fingers, which I then wipe on Jamie's chest.

'We could use it as body paint,' he teases.

I stick out my tongue.

'Sexy,' he says.

'I thought so.' Then I bite off a bit more chocolate before wrapping it back up and putting it in the bag. 'Right. I'm going for another swim. You coming?'

Jamie stretches back on our blanket. 'No, I think I'll just lie here and watch you for a while.'

'Perv.'

I run over the stones, eeking at the pain, and then charge into the water, looking back and smiling at Jamie as I do.

JAMIE

Whilst Lucy has a swim, I google places to stay nearby and find this shepherd's hut that looks amazing. Secluded. Stunning view over fields. Hot tub. I go off behind the trees, pretending to have a wee, and instead ring the owner, not holding out much hope that it'll be available. But after several rings, a man answers and it turns out I'm in luck. There's a gap in the schedule tonight, and if I don't mind it only having a cursory clean then it's mine. I cheekily ask him to throw in a bottle of champagne, which he does at an additional cost, and I text Matt to ask him if it's OK to have tomorrow off (I know he'll be cool about it and it's Lucy's day off anyway). When I get back to the beach, I spot Lucy in the water, floating on her back. She's so stunning. Sometimes I struggle to believe she's mine.

I swim out to meet her and she drapes her arms around my neck and kisses me. We spend the afternoon swimming and reading and then we go for a walk along the banks of the river before heading back up to the car as the sun begins to set. I don't tell her about the shepherd's hut and instead just start driving in that direction.

'Aren't we supposed to be going the other way?' Lucy

asks when she finally notices we're going in the opposite direction to home.

'I'm not ready for the day to end yet.'

Lucy raises an eyebrow.

'You're not the only one that can be spontaneous, you know?'

She laughs and then settles back into her seat, seemingly happy to wait for my surprise. I quickly stop at the garage on the way, smuggling some burgers, burger buns and ketchup into the boot before continuing on our journey.

When we pull up at the shepherd's hut, it's on its own overlooking a large area of fields and I'm really chuffed with how beautiful it is.

'Welcome to our bed for the night.'

Lucy's face breaks into a huge smile. 'Oh, it's amazing.' She rushes out the car and around the hut, suddenly spotting the hot tub. 'You do realize it's my life's ambition to have a hot tub in the garden? Once I have a garden that's bigger than a hot tub, of course.'

'Living the dream.'

Lucy comes over and kisses me. 'Thank you. This is really lovely. But I thought you had work tomorrow?'

'I just booked the day off.'

'Well, you *are* full of surprises today.'

I find the key box and type in the code the bloke gave me and then release the key, using it to let us in. In a bucket of ice on the side is a bottle of champagne with two flutes next to it and a tray full of candles.

'Right, let me just get my useful box out the boot.'

'Useful box?'

'Yeah, it's got everything you could need.'

'I've got to see this.'

I get the box out of the car and bring it over, grabbing a lighter out of it and lighting the candles then putting them around the edge of the hot tub. I pour us both a glass of champagne and bring them out.

'Cheers,' I say, giving one to Lucy and then clanking mine against it.

Lucy takes a sip and then goes back to my box, pulling out all my things in turn. 'A compass?'

'Very useful if you get lost without phone reception.'

'Clean pants?'

'You'll be wanting to borrow those in the morning.'

'Wire wool?'

'Are we getting in this hot tub or not?'

Lucy strips down to her bra and knickers and then climbs in so I follow her and we lay our heads back on the edge of the hot tub.

'Look at the stars,' Lucy says. 'They're so clear.'

I point up at the sky. 'That one there is Hercules. And that one that looks like an upside-down flag is Ursa Minor.'

'How do you know all this?'

'My dad taught me. We used to spend a lot of time camping.'

Lucy snuggles up next to me, resting her head on my chest, and I put my arm around her.

'Your dad sounds like he was a really cool guy.'

'He was the best. I know people often say that after

someone's died. You listen to their eulogies and think, are you describing the same person I knew, because a lot of the time he was a bit of a dick, but with Dad, everything they said was completely true. When people would stop me in the street to tell me what a great bloke he was, or send me messages telling me how he'd improved their life in some way, I always knew they were being completely honest because he just really was *that* guy.'

'I wish I'd had the chance to meet him.'

'Oh, he would've loved you. Would've told me he'd beat the shit out of me if I messed this up.'

Lucy laughs. 'I think my dad feels the same way about you.'

'You know, your dad reminds me of mine a little bit. I'm not sure what it is. The way he lets your mum take the lead, maybe.'

'Yeah, he's always been like that. I used to think he was scared of her but then I realized that he actually loves her fiery side. I mean, I'm sure it annoys the hell out of him sometimes too, but I really don't think he'd change her.'

'My dad too. Always put Mum on this pedestal. He used to say, "Respect women, son, for they are definitely the fairer sex in all ways."'

'Clever man.'

I smile. 'Yeah, he was.'

'It must be rare these days. Two people who aren't from broken homes, the product of successful marriages.'

'Yeah, I suppose you're right. Although it feels like my home was pretty broken in a lot of ways ...' I wonder whether I should tell her about Thomas, but it's been such an amazing day, I don't want to bring the mood down. And besides, it's not something I find easy to share with people. The only person I've ever told is Matt and that took me several years. I don't know why. Sometimes it feels a bit pathetic, to be so gutted about something that happened when I was a kid, so full of grief over someone I never even met. 'But yeah, it's nice to see that marriages can work, that people can be happy together.' I look at my fingers. 'I'm starting to look like a prune. Shall we build a fire?'

'We can try.'

I grab a towel out of the car (another thing I always keep in there) and pat myself dry before handing it to Lucy to wrap around herself. After gathering some small strips of wood from the wood store, I get some steel wool and a battery out of my box, touching them together to create a flame. 'Not so silly now, is it?'

'That's actually pretty cool.'

I'm secretly pleased to have impressed her but try not to show it as she grabs the battery from me, takes some more steel wool out the box and has a go herself.

I add some more wood to the fire as Lucy strips off her wet underwear and puts her clothes back on. I do the same and we sit down by the fledgling fire.

'You know what I'm going to say, don't you?'

'You're hungry?'

'Starving.'

I get up and head to the car, getting out the burgers I bought at the garage and bringing them back to Lucy. 'Mr Organized strikes again.'

'Just get cooking, will you?'

Cooking burgers on an open fire is actually much harder than anticipated and they're quite charred by the time we eat them, but Lucy doesn't seem to care, devouring them with the same gusto she does all her food. I tuck in too, suddenly starving.

When we finish, Lucy leans over and kisses me. 'Thank you again for this.'

'No problem. But you do realize you just transferred the ketchup from the end of your nose on to mine?'

I wipe my face and Lucy kisses me again, this time rubbing our noses together on purpose. Then she takes her phone out, holding it out in front of us for a selfie, both of us giggling like school kids as she captures the perfect end to a perfect day.

The Day of the Break-Up

JAMIE

I sit on the sofa staring at Lucy's goldfish bowl, the empty tub of Ben & Jerry's I consumed earlier discarded on the coffee table. Sharky swims up to the glass and eyes me woefully.

'Bit rubbish without her, isn't it, buddy?'

I'm sure he nods and I wish I could pick him up out of the water and give him a hug, but I'm not sure he'd appreciate the whole not being able to breathe thing. So instead, I get up and go over to his bowl, giving the glass a stroke, and as I do, a picture on our photo wall catches my eye. I remember when we put it up, the hour-long debate we had about it. I wanted all the photos in a row, identical frames, same distance apart, carefully measured, not just done by eye as Lucy suggested. She wanted them 'random', different coloured frames, a range of sizes, all higgledy-piggledy. She won, of course, stealing the spirit level off me and using it as a sword whenever I tried to straighten any of them.

I find myself smiling as I look at the photo of us from our night in the shepherd's hut, Lucy's tongue appearing oddly gigantic as it licks ketchup off my face. I remember we didn't get to sleep until about 3 a.m. We spent ages by the campfire and then eventually went into the shepherd's hut, finishing off the champagne and cuddling up in bed, the wood burner glowing in the corner. We didn't even have sex that night, just stayed awake chatting. We talked about everything (or so I thought) – our childhoods, our school days, her travels, my work, ideas for her novel, things we still wanted to achieve. I still wonder why she didn't tell me the truth then. But I suppose I didn't tell her about Thomas either. I wonder if things would've been different if we had both opened up. Whether it would've saved some of the heartache, but I'm not sure.

Looking at the photo now, it's odd. We look so naïve. Like children before they realize that the world contains wars and disease and poverty and horrible people who do really shitty things. God, how I wish that we could go back there. That we could go back and stay in that moment for the rest of our lives. Perfectly happy in a way I never knew existed before I met Lucy. But you can't go back. You can't un-know. So instead I take my phone out of my pocket, gutted to see there are no further messages from Lucy even though I only checked it five minutes ago. What am I expecting her to say anyway? That she got the note and she's coming home?

I sit and stare at the screen, hoping it might contain something, *anything*, to make me feel better. But no amount of Twitter or Insta or shopping for bargains on Amazon daily deals is going to take away this gnawing, agonizing emptiness.

So, to my surprise, I find myself messaging Mum. It's weird, but through all this stuff with Lucy we've become so much closer. At least that's one positive, I guess. I start to type, realizing I have no idea what to say, so I keep it short and to the point, hoping she can fill in the blanks.

Lucy's gone x

Before

LUCY

'You know you really don't have to come.'

'Don't be silly, I want to.'

'You want to come to a seven-year-old girl's birthday party?'

'Sure. Jelly, ice cream, birthday cake, balloons . . . what's not to like?'

'Amy's hired one of those awful children's entertainers – puppets, cringey jokes, balloon modelling where the balloons make that awful squeaky noise like fingernails on a blackboard.'

'Do you not want me to come or something?'

'Of course I want you to come if you want to. I just don't want you to feel obliged.'

'I don't. I love kids. It'll be the highlight of my week.'

I feel my heart sink slightly, the niggling fear I've started feeling when I'm around Jamie. That it's too good to be true. That I'll end up hurting him, or him me.

'OK. I'll see you later then. I could pick you up so you can at least have a beer to help get you through it.'

'Sounds like you're the one who's going to need a drink. What time does it start?'

'One.'

'OK, I'll pick you up in about an hour. Can I come in fancy dress?'

'No.'

'Spoilsport.'

'See you later.'

I wrap a present for Lauren – a set of 'proper' acrylic paints, some oil pastels, some watercolour brush pens and a pad of thick artist's paper. She reminds me of myself a little bit, the way I was with writing when I was little. I was always making up stories, creating mini books. My parents could lose me for hours as I sat in my room writing. And I see that in Lauren but with art, the way she's fully content when she's creating, and I want to encourage that in her.

Ironically, I spend the next forty minutes or so sitting on the sofa with my laptop on my knee trying to write. Since Jamie said it wasn't total shit, I've been trying my best to finish my novel but I keep getting distracted and, a measly two hundred words later, I hear a knock at the door. When I open it, I'm faced with the vision of Jamie in full Spider-Man costume, mask and all, and I can't help but smile. I pull off his mask to see that he's grinning widely underneath too.

'Sorry, I couldn't resist.'

I put my hands on his face and kiss him. 'You actually look pretty hot. If we had more time, I might have to take you upstairs.'

'There's always afterwards.'

'I look forward to it.' I grab my keys. 'Let me just get the present. One sec.' I run upstairs and retrieve the present off the bed and then we go out to Jamie's car where there is a gift wrapped in colourful balloon wrapping paper on the passenger seat. I pick it up so I can sit down and then put it on the back seat with mine, trying not to show how touched I am.

'I wasn't sure what to get so I just nipped out and got her a cuddly toy,' Jamie says, a look of concern on his face. 'Then I've spent the whole journey over here thinking it's probably too young. Do seven-year-olds still like cuddly toys? Sorry, I don't have a lot of children in my social circle.'

I feel an ache in my chest – not only did he bother to go out and get Lauren something, he's also spent time worrying about whether it's right. Jude wouldn't have even come to the party, let alone considered bringing a present. Yet another reason I know I'm doing the right thing not texting him back.

'She *loves* cuddly toys. She has them all lined up along the end of her bed and then she has this rota for which one gets to sleep with her every night.'

'That's adorable.'

'I know.'

'Do you think she'll mind adding another one on to her rota? It won't mess it up?'

'She'll be over the moon.' I reach over and put my hand on his thigh. The material of the costume feels horrible and I feel myself smiling again. 'Thanks for getting her something. You really didn't have to.'

'You can't go to a kid's party without a present. That's the whole point of having a party, isn't it?'

'You could've shared mine. I wrote your name on the card anyway.'

'From Lucy and Jamie?'

'Yeah. What? It's no big deal.'

Jamie bites back a smile, but I can tell he knows it *is* a big thing for me. 'Thank you. And I'm sorry, I didn't put you on my card so now it'll look like I'm extra nice because I got two things.'

'Always have to come out on top, don't you?'

When we arrive, no one hears the doorbell so I try the door handle and it opens. Heading towards the kitchen, the patio doors open to the garden, I can see that it's typical kid's party hell, overly excited children tearing around the place, balloons being smashed into faces, vacuous bubblegum pop blaring out of the stereo. I love Lauren and Otto with a passion that surprised even me, but I hate going to their birthday parties. It was OK when they were really little and Amy just did a family thing. Then it was basically just an excuse to eat cake and relive the childhood joy of jelly and ice cream, but now she insists we come along to their parties with their friends and I hate every second. Children who are no relation to you are just irritating. Call me a monster but it's true. They moan and whine and tell tales on each other all the time. And they're just *so* loud. Why do they have to be so loud? One of Lauren's friends in particular, Beatrice, gets right on my wick. She's one of those girls I always hoped Lauren would never become (and thankfully she hasn't). Bossy, know-it-all, her parents think she can do no wrong and their adoration has obviously fed into her own inflated self-view. I mean, she's only seven so I shouldn't be too harsh on her, but I can just see her in ten years' time, captain of the hockey team, head girl, lording it over everyone else.

Suddenly, Amy comes rushing past from upstairs holding bandages and antiseptic cream, and I can hear someone screaming in the garden as if they've severed a limb.

'Beatrice fell off the climbing frame and has a slight graze on her knee.' Amy rolls her eyes and I smile. 'Wow, Jamie. I am loving the fancy dress. Wait till Otto sees you.' She laughs and then she rushes outside and I can hear her putting on her fake 'oh, it's so terrible, you poor thing' sympathetic voice, knowing I'd never have it in me to keep up the pretence.

'I'm guessing Beatrice likes a bit of drama,' Jamie says.

'Worst child ever.' I go to the fridge, take out a half-empty bottle of wine, fetch a wine glass from the cupboard and pour myself a very generous measure. Then I take out a bottle of lager and hand it and a bottle opener to Jamie.

'Bit harsh, isn't it?'

I know he's only joking, but I wonder if a part of him thinks less of me. And it scares me, because I like being on a pedestal in his eyes.

'Oh, I just see Lauren in her shadow a lot of the time and it annoys me. Lauren should never feel like that. She's the shining star amongst those kids.'

Jamie comes over and wraps his arms around my waist. 'Said by a wonderfully loyal aunty.' Then he kisses me on the cheek. 'It's very endearing. I can just imagine you with your kids having playground brawls with the other mums.'

I smile weakly and steer us outside to join all the others.

Outside, Jamie gives my mum a warm hug and my dad slaps him on the shoulder. I can tell how much they like him. My parents are fairly transparent. I sense them staring at me, silently telling me with their eyes, 'Don't fuck this one up.'

Dave is hiding behind the barbecue, using the pretence of cooking the sausages to avoid having to get involved with the kids, fair play to him. I wander over to him and he holds up his beer and clinks it against my wine glass.

'Favourite time of the year,' he says, a wry smile on his face.

'I like the barbecue shield. Can I be sous chef?'

'Of course. Then I can blame you when Amy shouts at me for burning the sausages.'

'Deal.'

'He seems like a good bloke.' Dave tilts his head towards Jamie, who is laughing away with my mum like they're best friends. 'Better than that Jude twat, that's for sure.'

'Well, that's not saying much really, is it?'

'Seriously though. He seems good for you, in my humble opinion anyway, which is probably worth bugger all. And that Spider-Man costume – that's going to score him major points with the kids.'

I smile, but it's forced.

'What is it?' Dave asks, clearly sensing my reservation. He's actually quite a sensitive bloke. When Amy first got with him, I thought he lacked emotional depth. But the more I got to know him, the more I realized he was just a little more reserved than my family (not difficult) and

I've grown fond of him over the years. An honorary big brother.

'It's nothing.'

'He's not one of those blokes that charms the pants off everyone in public but then acts like a dick when you're at home, is he?'

'Like Jude?' I smile.

Dave shakes his head. 'He never fooled me.'

'No, Jamie is equally lovely when it's just us.'

'So what's the problem?'

'Me. As always.'

'Ah,' Dave says slowly. 'The kid thing?'

I nod solemnly and Dave puts his arm around my shoulder.

'There's nothing wrong with not wanting children.'

I watch Jamie cavorting around the garden with a kid on each arm. 'Try telling everyone else that.'

Jamie frees himself of the two hanging off his arms and starts chasing the other children around the lawn, all of them giggling and running over to him and sticking their tongues out before quickly darting off before he can catch them. Otto grips on to his leg so he picks him up and carries him around whilst he chases the others, Otto clearly thrilled to be Spider-Man's helper. Amy needn't have bothered with a children's entertainer for after the food, as Jamie seems to have it covered. Once they've finished tag, he lies out on the grass as if he's exhausted and all the kids start climbing on top of him.

Suddenly, Mum is beside me and I already know what she's come over to say.

'Look at him. He's amazing with them.'

'Mum.'

Mum gives me this look, the picture of innocence, but we both know she has a hidden agenda. 'I'm just saying, look at how he lights up around them, and them around him.'

It's true. He looks as happy as I've ever seen him, and it appears a hundred percent genuine.

'Good for him.'

'Come on, Dave. Tell her. You wouldn't be without them, would you? I bet you worried a bit about losing your freedom at the start, didn't you?'

This is not a new conversation and Dave gives me a slyly conspiratorial look. 'Of course I wouldn't be without them. But that doesn't mean it's right for everyone.'

Mum waves Dave's words away. 'Change is never easy. It's bloody scary in fact. But often it turns out to be the best thing in the world.'

I take a deep breath. 'And what if it's not, Mum? What if you hate every second of it and ruin your kids' lives in the process?'

'That wouldn't happen. Tell her, Dave. You'd never regret having a child, would you?'

Dave looks like he's not sure what to say, wanting to support me but slightly scared of upsetting Mum.

'Don't answer that, Dave.'

Mum goes to carry on lecturing me, but I walk inside to get the hot dog rolls and ketchup, picking up the pile of animal paper plates and taking them outside to Dave. Luckily, Mum's gone back to the others, helping to unravel the cling film off bowls of carrot sticks, celery and pepper that none of the kids will touch, and filling large bowls with crisps, which will be demolished in seconds.

'I'm sorry. I did try to stick up for you,' Dave says, filling the first roll with a sausage.

'Don't be silly. It's fine. I know nobody understands where I'm coming from, not even Amy. I'm sure she sits in bed at night musing over what's wrong with me.'

Dave raises an eyebrow and I know that I'm right.

'Maybe there is something fundamentally wrong with me,' I continue. 'Like I was born missing the procreation gene or something. But it's me. And everyone's just going to have to learn to accept it, or at least live with it, because trust me, if anyone could've changed my mind over the years, it would've been me. God knows I've tried.'

'Life's too short, Luce. Follow your heart. Do what makes you happy. And you never know, Jamie might be happy to do things your way. I mean, I love the kids, but stress-free holidays, weekends just sitting having an uninterrupted lunch at a nice pub, a life full of adventure – it's not exactly unappealing.'

I force a smile. 'Thanks, Dave.'

'Right, we need to be more like a factory line now and speed up, OK? We're going to have a total rampage of kids in a minute otherwise.'

'OK. Let's do this.'

After the kids have stuffed themselves (I managed to get one measly hot dog, a single Wotsit from the bottom of the bowl which turned out to be a bit soggy so had possibly been in a child's mouth already and spat out, and a plethora of vegetables), it's time for the revealing of the cake and for everyone to sing 'Happy Birthday'.

Amy is amazing at birthday cakes. She has never bought one and her creations could rival even the most upmarket bakery. Every year she has a different theme, usually set by the kids. This year, it's animal themed because Lauren has recently shown a real interest in animals, poring over books and demanding lots of visits to the zoo. Amy has decorated the edge of the cake with long grass made out of shards of icing and then on the top she's made a tiger and an elaborate tree with a monkey hanging off one of the branches. When Lauren sees it, her face lights up, rightly so, and she looks at her mum with a sense of awe. Then we all start singing and Dave holds up his phone and records Lauren blowing out her candles whilst everyone else claps eight times, chanting out the numbers from one to seven and adding 'one for luck'. Jamie stands close to me and puts his arm gently around my waist and when I look at him he has that warm fuzzy look that people always have at these moments and I'm sure he's picturing watching his daughter blow out the candles on her cake one day. And I know that I should feel envious of Amy. That this joyously happy scene should give me a stirring sensation in my gut, a sense of longing, and for the thousandth time, I wonder why, even when I'm with someone as wonderful as Jamie, it doesn't.

JAMIE

The kids disperse one by one, sent off with a party bag and some cake. I'm actually quite envious. Party bags were always the best bit about a party. Getting home and discovering what plastic tat you had to play with.

'Wow, that's better,' Lucy says, leaning back in a chair. 'I can finally hear myself think.'

'They all loved you,' Lucy's mum says, tapping me on the shoulder. 'The Spider-Man costume was an inspired move.'

'Yeah, I'm a bit hot though.' I undo the Velcro and slip the top part of the costume down so it hangs at my waist and reveals my T-shirt. 'Ah, that's better.'

'Are you going?' Otto asks, peering up at me with his big blue eyes. I look over to Lucy.

'We can stay for a little bit, OK?' she says, reaching over and ruffling Otto's hair.

I sit down with the others and Otto clambers up to sit on my knee and at first I'm not sure what to do but then I put my arms around him and rest my chin on his hair.

Lucy glances over but then she quickly stands up. 'Come on, birthday girl. Let's go and get your presents.'

She takes Lauren inside and they come out with the gifts Lucy and I bought.

'This one's from Jamie.'

Lauren gives me a shy smile and then takes the present. Ripping off the paper, she reveals the teddy bear I chose and immediately draws it into a tight hug, her face so full of genuine joy that I feel a bit emotional.

'What do you say to Jamie, Lauren?' Amy puts the bowls she was collecting down on the table and touches Lauren lightly on the head.

'Thank you, Jamie,' Lauren says, still tightly clutching the teddy bear.

'You're very welcome. You can add him or her to your rota.'

'I'm going to put him on tonight's. He can share with Lamby.'

'Wow, that is a prized spot,' Dave says. 'He must be special.'

Lauren squeezes the bear. 'He is.'

I quickly try to pull myself together. 'I'm glad you like him.'

Lucy picks up her present and gives it to Lauren. 'And this one's from me.'

Lauren still doesn't let go of the teddy, putting him under one arm so that her hands are free to open Lucy's gift. As soon as she sees the art materials, it's obvious how excited she is and I can see how happy it makes Lucy, which just makes me love her all the more.

'Can we do some painting now? Will you stay and help me?' Lauren looks up at Lucy with such a pleading expression I can't imagine she'll be able to say no.

Lucy smiles. 'Of course. Let's go and get some water and some of your brushes. Because you're better at art than most adults, I thought it was time you had a set of proper grown-up paints.'

You can see the pride on Lauren's face as Lucy takes her hand and they go and get the things they need. When they get back outside, Lucy sits with Lauren and they both paint and I do 'Row, Row the Boat' with Otto a thousand times. And there's no other way to explain it; it just feels right.

When we get back to Lucy's, I don't get out the car.

'Aren't you staying tonight?'

'I'd love to but I promised Matt I'd cook tonight. And I currently have no clean clothes for work tomorrow.'

Spending most of my time at Lucy's is amazing, but I feel bad for not pulling my weight at home. Besides, Matt and I used to take it in turns to cook, but I haven't done it for ages so I promised him this morning that I'd make my 'famous' spaghetti bolognaise tonight. I reckon every man has his signature dish – the one meal he thinks he can make relatively well, the one he always makes for a first date – and spaghetti bolognaise is mine.

'Lucky Matt.'

'I'll cook it for you one night this week if you want?'

'I've got a few things to do this week and I'm having drinks with the girls from work on Wednesday, but Thursday would be good if you're around? It can help sort out my hangover.'

I can't help it – although it's stupid, I feel a sinking in my stomach at the thought of not seeing Lucy for a few days. 'OK. Sounds good.'

'Well, thanks for coming to the party.'

'Not a problem. I loved it. You know you're amazing with Lauren and Otto?'

Lucy shrugs, looking uncomfortable with the compliment. 'I don't know. I probably let them have far too much sugar and get away with murder, but that's what an aunty is for, isn't it?'

'Well, I think you're amazing and they clearly adore you.'

'Thanks.' Lucy looks at me and the usual mocking sparkle in her eyes is replaced with something far more earnest. 'Sometimes I think you're far too good for me.'

'Only sometimes?'

Then almost immediately the wry smile is back. 'Oh yeah, a lot of the time I think you're lucky to have me. Definitely punching.'

I smile. 'That I am.'

Matt and I eat our spaghetti bolognaise on trays in front of the TV, accompanying it with a bottle of beer each rather than what would be the much better suited wine.

'You've done it again, mate,' Matt says, holding up his bottle. 'I'd definitely shag you if you produced this on a first date.'

I laugh.

'So how was the kid's birthday party? As hellish as I imagine?'

I shake my head. 'It was actually really good fun. The Spider-Man costume seemed to go down well. The kids loved it. So did Lucy, I think.'

Matt laughs. 'I'll have to try it with Mia.'

'I reckon you've got more of the Clark Kent about you. Maybe get a Superman one.'

'Ooh yeah, then Mia could be Lois Lane. I always had a bit of a thing for Teri Hatcher when I was younger.'

We both tuck into our food, wrapping the spaghetti round our forks multiple times and still not managing to eat it without it unravelling and splattering.

We look at each other, tomato sauce dripping down our chins, and laugh. 'Good job this isn't a first date.'

Matt wipes his face with the back of his hand. 'So how's it going with Lucy anyway? Still head over heels?'

'Honestly, don't take the piss, but I looked at her today, looked at her sister's family, and I thought, this is it. This is exactly what I want. What I've been missing all this time.'

'Woah, mate. That's great.'

'It is. But it's terrifying. I always knew I wanted a family, you know, especially after losing Thomas, and Dad.' I can feel myself getting choked up so I cough to clear my throat. 'But I've never met anyone who I could actually see it happening with. It's been less than five months, though, so I probably sound totally insane.'

Matt shakes his head. 'You don't sound insane to me. Just sounds like she's the one.'

I'm so glad I've got Matt. I spent many years hanging out with blokes whose only mission in life was to make you feel smaller than them. Everything that was said was front. Life was always a competition. And God forbid you acknowledged that you had a beating heart inside your chest. But with Matt, I can be totally open and I know he won't take the piss or that, if he does, it's only warm-hearted banter.

'Thanks, buddy.'

'In fact, talking of "the one", I had something I wanted to discuss with you.' Matt looks a little nervous and I'm suddenly slightly worried about what he's going to say. 'I asked Mia to move in with me.'

I look at him as if I don't really understand how this is news. She practically lives with us anyway. In fact, this is one of the first nights she hasn't been here in weeks. But then the penny drops.

'You want me to move out?'

Matt shrugs, looking uncomfortable. 'You're my best mate and there's no way I'm going to leave you homeless. But Mia wants a fresh start. For us to get a place of our own. So we've started having a look and we've found this great little cottage in Bisley. I said I needed to talk to you first. I mean, it's tiny, but worse comes to worse you could live there with us for a bit. Until you find something of your own.'

I smile at Matt. I can see the anguish this is causing him. His concern that my perception will be that he's putting 'hoes before bros'.

'It's fine. I'll find somewhere else. I'm happy for you, buddy.'

The relief is palpable on Matt's face. 'Thanks, mate.' Then he scrapes the last of the sauce off his plate and puts the tray on the side table. 'You could always move in with Lucy?'

I picture being with her every night, waking up to her every morning, and it's definitely an image I like. But I'm not sure she'd feel the same.

'Nah, she's very protective about her place. I know she'd feel like I was intruding.'

'So why don't you ask her to get somewhere together? A fresh start like we're doing?'

I open my mouth to object, but then I realize that it's a great idea. A chance to show her how serious I am. To properly start our life together.

'You don't think it's too soon?'

'No way. When you know, you know, right?'

I spend the evening thinking about what Matt said. Although I'm nervous about Lucy's reaction, I know that I want to live with her. As I iron my clothes for work, I start imagining it. Going and choosing somewhere together. Deciding on décor, painting, putting up shelves. With Anna, domesticity often felt boring, stifling almost, like the life was being drained out of me, but with Lucy it seems like an exciting adventure. Once I've hung up my clothes, I start searching on Right move for places in the local area in our price range. I've got a fair bit of savings from when I sold the place I shared with Anna, so combined with the money we'd get from selling Lucy's place, we should have enough for a decent deposit, and the money I waste on paying Matt rent each month could easily go towards quite a big mortgage. We could get somewhere really amazing. A forever home. A dining room where we could host dinner parties. A proper garden that one day could be used for football and trampolines and sandpits. It's crazy but I feel almost giddy with excitement at the prospect. I just hope Lucy feels the same way.

LUCY

'Thank you so much for Lauren's presents. She carried on painting all evening. I had to tear her away at bedtime. And she loved the teddy bear. Did Jamie choose that himself?'

'Uh huh.' I finish my mouthful so that I can speak properly. I'm on the phone to Amy on my lunch break, sitting outside Starbucks with a baguette and a frappé. It's a gorgeous late August day. The kind of day I really resent being stuck inside the shop because I know that autumn is just around the corner. 'I didn't even tell him to get her anything. He just turned up with it.'

'God, he's actually perfect, isn't he?'

I nod, even though she can't see me. 'I worry he's too perfect.'

'What do you mean? You're not worried he's going to turn out like Jerk Jude, are you? Jamie seems very different. Very genuine.'

I consciously don't tell her that Jude messaged me a month or so ago, as I know she'll only give me a lecture about not falling under his spell again. If I'm totally honest, there have been a few times I've been tempted to text back, like after Lauren's party, but I know deep down no good would come of it.

'Jerk Jude? That's a new one. And, no, I know Jamie

isn't like Jude. He is genuine. But sometimes I do feel like Jude understood me. That we were kindred spirits of sorts.'

I know as soon as I've said it that Amy is going to explode. 'Kindred spirits? Jude is an arsehole. *You* are amazing. You are not kindred spirits with that man.'

I use my free hand to guide the straw into my mouth and take a large sip of my frappé. 'I don't know. I just think Jamie's probably looking for someone more like you. Someone *normal*.'

Amy is quiet for a while and I wonder what she's thinking, if secretly she agrees with me. 'You *are* normal.'

'He was amazing with the kids, wasn't he? He seemed in his element.'

'Yeah,' Amy says solemnly and I know she knows what I'm getting at. 'Lauren and Otto adore him, especially Otto since he turned up in that costume. Poor Dave pales in comparison.'

'Bless him.' I take another sip of my drink. 'I think maybe we need to have "the chat". So he can decide if he still wants to be with me or not.'

'Well, maybe . . .' I can hear in her voice that she's treading carefully and I'm fairly sure I know what's coming. 'I don't know . . . perhaps you'll feel differently after a while with Jamie? I mean, maybe it's just that you've not been with the right person in the past?'

I sigh. 'It's not that.'

'You could just wait and see how things go.' There's a sense of optimism in her voice. I know that she'd love for me to have kids. For Lauren and Otto to have cousins to play with, for her to be an aunty. 'I mean, you don't need to make any life-changing decisions right now. See how you feel in a year or so, once you've been together longer.'

'I'm not going to change my mind, Amz. I know you don't get it, but like you've always been sure you wanted kids, I've always been sure I don't.'

'OK. But I still don't think there's any point in ruining a great relationship now when none of us know what the future will hold anyway. Perhaps he's infertile? Perhaps one of you will be hit by a car tomorrow?'

'Thanks.' I laugh and hear Amy start laughing too.

'Sorry, that was an awful thing to say. I guess I just mean that this is the happiest I've seen you in a long time. Jamie treats you like you deserve to be treated and I don't want you to ruin that because you're scared about how he or you might feel one day in the future when you don't even know what's going to happen. Does that make sense?'

'Yeah, you're probably right.'

'I'm always right. That's all part of being a big sister.'

I gather all my things together. 'Suppose I better get back to work. See you soon, yeah?'

'Of course.'

When the phone goes dead, I get up and throw my rubbish in the bin and walk back to work – the familiar ache of never really being understood hitting me right in the chest.

*

It's drinks out with the girls from work tonight. We're an eclectic little threesome. There's Tilda – just turned twenty, engaged to her childhood boyfriend. She's quirky – pink hair, homemade clothing, nose ring – and a total sweetheart. Mandy is in her early fifties, with two grown-up sons who are away at university. Her husband earns tons of money but is always away on business so she works in the shop for the company really. She's read *everything* and never stops talking about books. And then there's me.

We sit in one of the bars in town sharing a cool, crisp bottle of rosé between us and we're all at that lovely merry stage when any daily defences have been dropped and the conversation becomes all the more interesting. Somehow, we've got on to the topic of Jamie, who popped into the shop at the end of the day just to give me a kiss and to tell me he loved me, the soppy bastard.

'He is *gorgeous*,' Mandy says. 'You lucky thing. I bet he's a rocket between the sheets.'

'Mandy!' Tilda says, blushing. 'You can't say things like that about someone else's boyfriend.'

'Why not? Lucy doesn't mind, do you, darling?' She puts her hand on my arm and I shake my head. 'Got to get your kicks where you can at my age.'

I laugh. 'By picturing my boyfriend in bed?'

'You should be flattered we all want to sleep with him.'

'Who says I want to sleep with him?' Tilda says before taking a sip of her wine. Of the three of us, she's the most reserved and I can sense that some of the stuff Mandy comes out with makes her feel uncomfortable.

'Oh, come on. I saw you get all bashful when you spoke to him.'

Tilda looks like she wants the floor to open up and swallow her whole. 'I did not.' Then she turns to me. 'Not that he's not fit. He is. But I haven't thought about him . . . well, like that, you know?'

I smile. 'Don't worry, I know you haven't. It's only Mandy here who can't keep her mind out the gutter.'

'I spend a lot of time on my own.' Mandy laughs and downs her glass of wine before refilling it to the top. 'Anyway, please tell me he's a dick so I don't have to come round to your house and kill you in a jealous rage.'

'I'm sorry. He's not a dick.'

'Urgh. So not fair.'

'I'm really happy for you, Lucy. You deserve someone lovely,' Tilda says, and it feels a little bit patronizing coming from a twenty-year-old, but I can tell how sincere she is.

'What about you? I can't believe it's the wedding at the weekend. Are you prepared?'

'Oh yes,' Mandy chips in. 'I *love* a wedding. Can't wait. I bet your dress is stunning.'

Tilda's not the sort of girl to share photos of her dress or her cake. In fact, she doesn't even mention the wedding unless we bring it up, but I can tell by the look on her face that she's excited.

'I think everything's ready. Mum's been helping me out a lot.'

'And you're sure that Aaron is the one? Not having any last-minute doubts?' Mandy is obsessed with the fact Tilda is so young, that she's never dated anyone other than Aaron, and she's always questioning Tilda about it.

'I'm sure.' Tilda looks over at me for back-up.

'You seem perfect together,' I say. 'I think you're lucky to have met "the one" at such a young age. Beats the years of dating and getting it wrong.'

'Ooh, I don't know. I quite enjoyed getting it wrong,' Mandy jokes and we all laugh.

I hold up our empty bottle. 'Right, my round. Same again?'

They both nod and I go up to the bar. There's only one person working so I wait for them to serve the woman in front of me, perching myself on a barstool whilst I wait. I'm reading the drinks offers chalked up behind the bar so I don't notice him at first – but then I feel a hand on my back and turn to see him standing right next to me. Jude. He looks gorgeous, his long dark hair tied up, his skin tanned after his recent exotic adventure. And I can't help it – I feel a ripple of excitement. He's always had that effect on me, from the moment I first spoke to him on a beach in Bali to the last time I saw him – before he rang me to dump me. I hate it. But it's there.

'Hey there, stranger,' he says, leaning in to kiss me on the cheek, the smell of his aftershave coming with him.

'What are you doing here?'

'It's really great to see you, you know? You're looking stunning as always.'

Forever the charmer.

'You're not.'

He smiles. 'You know I can always tell when you're lying. You get this certain look in your eyes.'

'Shame I can't say the same about you. It would've been useful to know when you were lying.'

Jude runs his hand up my back and I want to slap his arm away but I don't. 'Come on, don't be like that.' Then he brings his mouth close to my ear. 'I've really missed you, you know?'

'I haven't missed you.'

Jude points at my eyes. 'See, you're lying again.'

As much as I don't want to, I find myself smiling, idiot that I am.

'That's better. That's the Lucy I love so much.'

Love so much? Then why did you leave me and tear me in two?

'Let me buy you a drink,' Jude says as the barman heads towards us.

'I'm buying a bottle to share with my friends.' I point to the table and notice Mandy glancing over at me with an apologetic look and I narrow my eyes at her and then turn back to Jude. 'Aren't you meeting someone anyway? I'm guessing you didn't come here to sit and drink alone?'

Jude looks at me with a serious expression. 'I came here to see you.'

'What? What do you mean? How did you know I was going to be here?'

'Since you didn't reply to my message I came into the shop to see you. You were on your lunch break. I managed to get it out of Mandy where you were going tonight.'

So that's why she was looking at me apologetically.

'Well, I'm sure she made it clear I didn't want to see you. You shouldn't be coming to where I work anyway.'

'I'm allowed to buy books, you know.'

'Did you? Buy a book?'

Jude puts his hand on the top of my arm. 'Come on, Luce, what else could I do?'

'Leave me alone?'

'Don't be like that. One drink. For old times' sake.'

I want to tell him to sod off, to walk back to my friends with my head held high, but I'm not sure if it's because I'm drunk or because of my earlier chat with Amy – but I find myself wanting to talk to him. And yet I don't want to give him the satisfaction.

'I have nothing to say to you.'

'One quick drink then I promise if you tell me you never want to speak to me again, I'll leave you alone, never contact you again.'

'You promise? One drink, and no more messages, no more showing up at work?'

Jude draws two lines across his heart.

'OK, but it will be *very* quick, and then I'm going back to the girls.'

'Deal. Glass of rosé?'

'Sure.'

We both order our drinks and then I take the bottle over to the others.

'I'm so sorry, Lucy,' Mandy says, clearly flustered. 'He said he wanted to invite you out for dinner tonight so I told him that you weren't interested, that we were going out ourselves, and he guessed it would be here and I wasn't good enough at hiding it on my face that he was right.'

'It's OK. It's not your fault. Anyway, he's promised me if I have one drink with him, he'll leave me alone.'

'Are you sure that's a good idea?' Tilda asks, her face etched with concern.

'It's fine. Don't worry, I'll make it quick.'

Neither Mandy nor Tilda look convinced, but they reluctantly wave me off and start pouring themselves more wine as I head back to Jude, a nervousness in my tummy that irritates me.

When I get to the bar, he pats the barstool next to his, and although I hate doing anything he asks me to, I take a seat.

He holds up his pint glass and I grudgingly chink my wine glass on it. 'To soul mates,' he says.

'To mistakes,' I retort and he laughs.

'So how have you been? Been to any amazing places recently?'

'I just did an activity weekend in Andalusia. Rafting. Mountain climbing. It was stunning.'

'Oh cool. I just got back from South America – you *have* to go to Bolivia. It was epic. You'd have loved it. The people were amazing.'

I nod and take a sip of wine, trying to ignore the feeling of envy in my stomach.

'Remember that time in Bali when we gate-crashed that party on the beach?' Jude continues.

I nod in a non-committal way, knowing where this conversation is going.

Jude leans towards me, putting his arm around my waist. 'And remember afterwards, in that cove?'

I push him back on to his own stool. 'Can we talk about something else?'

I can't deny that the sex we had that night was exhilarating. It was frantic and exciting and I felt like the sexiest girl on earth. Jude had a way of making me feel that way at the start. Well, a lot of the time really. But then there were also all the times he made me feel worthless.

'So did you go on your own? To Andalusia?'

'No, with my boyfriend.'

'Boyfriend, hey? Nothing serious, I hope.'

'Why do you care?'

'Why do you think?'

'Because even though you don't want me, you don't want anyone else to have me?'

Jude shakes his head. 'You don't really think I'm like that, do you?'

'Who cares what I think? You left me, remember, Jude? Standing on my own with an estate agent outside the apartment we were supposed to be buying together.' I hear the emotion in my voice making it sound strained and hate that he's witness to it.

'I'm sorry. I was stupid. I freaked out. I'm sorry.'

I shrug. 'It doesn't matter now anyway, does it?'

'It does matter. Because I'm still in love with you.'

I'm well aware that Jude could charm the birds out of the trees; that this is probably just another one of his lines. But he actually looks really genuine and I feel a strange mixture of emotions in my chest.

'It's serious,' I say, making sure my wall stays firmly in place, and then I drink a large amount of my wine to empty my glass so that I can leave.

'It won't last.'

I shake my head and let out a long, pained breath. 'And why's that, Jude?'

'Because we're destined to be together, you and me. Two peas in a pod. We'll find our way back to each other in the end.'

'No, we won't. Look, I should get back to my friends.'

Jude reaches out for my hand but I keep it close to my side. 'Just a bit longer.'

I sigh. 'Why, Jude? What's the point?'

'Because I miss you.' He runs his hand through his hair, pushing the bits that have escaped back behind his ears. 'I'm going to India in a few months. Come with me. You could see Aanya again. You can't really tell me you want to settle down in boring suburbia.'

'You know nothing about Jamie, about our relationship.'

'You're right. I'm sorry. It's just I desperately want you back. Losing you was the biggest mistake I've made in my life,' he says, his voice pleading. 'I'm so sorry, Luce. I never should've let you go.'

'Not managed to find someone else you can manipulate so easily, hey?'

'Don't say that. I don't want to manipulate you. I love you. You're the only girl I've ever met who wants the same things as me.'

I put my glass on the bar, trying not to let his words seep in. 'Night, Jude.'

'I'll do anything to change your mind. To show you I'd never let you down again.'

'You won't change my mind.'

Before he can say anything else, I climb down off the barstool and head back to the girls, making sure I don't look back and trying to ignore the seeds of doubt he's managed to plant in my head.

JAMIE

Lucy lies on the sofa whilst I cook, or try to, as I search her kitchen for all the things I need. There's no sense of order to her drawers and cupboards and it makes me smile how she manages to get anything done in such chaos. I finally find a garlic crusher at the back of one of the cupboards and continue preparing my meal. It smells great and I'm starving, but at the same time I feel a bit sick at the thought of asking Lucy to move in with me. What if she laughs in my face? What if it scares her off? But then I keep telling myself: why wait, when I know how sure I am about her?

'Have you got everything you need?' Lucy calls through.

'Yes, you just relax, my hungover princess.'

I finish cooking and find a candle on the side and light it with the gas hob. I put the candle on the table and then serve up and go to the doorway to the lounge.

'Madam, dinner is served.' I bow and Lucy smiles and then forces herself up off the sofa and comes through to the kitchen.

'Looks amazing,' she says sleepily. 'Thank you.'

We sit down to eat and I lead in with something casual. 'Good day at work?'

She nods, her mouth full of spaghetti. When she's

finished swallowing, she says, 'It was pretty quiet today. Maybe the hot weather put people off. I know I'd rather not have been stuck inside.'

'Me too. Feels like a waste, doesn't it?' I hold up the wine bottle. 'Hair of the dog?'

'Oh, go on then.'

I pour us both large glasses, taking a gulp to steady my nerves. 'So, anyway, Matt and his girlfriend have decided to move in together.' I stop, wishing I hadn't started in this way. I don't want Lucy to think me wanting to move in with her is just a matter of convenience. 'Well, it got me thinking and . . .'

'You want to stay here for a bit?'

'Not exactly. I was actually wondering if you wanted to move in together? Get a place of our own?'

The expression on Lucy's face is not the one I hoped for. She just looks uncomfortable, like she's trying to find a way out of the situation that causes the least upset for me. 'Wow, I wasn't expecting that. I mean, it's quite soon, isn't it?'

It's like a knife to the chest, all the excitement I've been feeling the past few days smashed to smithereens. 'I'm sorry. I just thought . . .' I stop, feeling stupid for thinking we were on the same page. 'Never mind, you're right. It's too soon.'

Lucy reaches her hand over and puts it on top of mine but it feels patronizing. 'I'm not saying a definite no. I'm just a bit shocked. I mean, it's not even quite been five months. Most men will barely commit to a regular date night in that time.' She laughs but I don't feel like joining in. 'Plus, I'm an absolute nightmare to live with. I'm messy and moody and unreasonable . . .'

'It's OK. You don't need to make excuses. I'm a big boy.'

'Well, not that big,' Lucy jokes and I smile, but it's an effort. 'The food's delicious by the way,' she continues, clearly attempting to change the subject. Not that I have any desire to continue it. I'm humiliated enough as it is.

'Thanks.'

We both concentrate on our food for a while, neither of us seemingly knowing what to say, until Lucy decides to raise the topic again.

'You know how much I love this place. I worked really hard to get it.'

It almost feels like she's mad at me for suggesting she give it up and we find somewhere new.

'Yeah, I know. It's fine. Don't worry. It was just an idea.'

'You're welcome to move in here for a bit though. I'm not going to put you out on the streets.'

'It's OK. I'm sure I can find somewhere to rent pretty easily. And Matt said I can move in with them for a bit if I'm stuck.'

She doesn't argue and it confirms for me how she's feeling. And I realize I haven't got it in me to hang around tonight.

'I'll just tidy up and then I'm going to get back. I'm not even the one that went out last night but I'm exhausted. Maybe I'm going down with something.'

Lucy nods. 'Leave all this. You cooked for me. That means I do the washing-up.'

'OK. Thanks. I hope you feel better tomorrow.' I don't feel like kissing her but I'm aware it would look weird if I didn't, so I give her a kiss on the cheek.

She starts collecting the plates and puts them beside the sink, turning the tap on to run a bowl of hot water, so I head towards the door.

Before I leave the room, she turns to face me. 'You don't have to go, you know.' I can't tell if she's saying it out of pity or whether she doesn't actually want me to leave.

'Thanks, but like I said, I'm pretty tired. I'll see you soon though, OK?'

'OK. Sleep tight.'

I leave the room and go through to the hallway to put on my shoes. As I'm doing it, I hope she'll appear in the doorway, telling me she's changed her mind and that she was just being silly, feeling a bit scared, but she doesn't and I can hear the clinking of her starting the washing-up, so I just leave.

When I get home, Matt and Mia are cuddled up on the sofa watching some sort of serial killer documentary. Noticing me coming in, Matt grabs the remote and presses pause.

'How did it go?' he asks.

'Oh yeah, you were going to ask Lucy to move in with you, weren't you?' Mia chips in, looking excited.

'She said no.'

Matt drops his eyes, looking almost guilty. 'Oh. I'm sorry, mate.' He glances at Mia and then back at me. 'But like you said, she does really love her place. It might just take her a while to get her head around moving some-where new.'

I shrug. 'I think it was just too much too soon. I prob-ably should've waited.'

Mia shakes her head. 'Don't you go blaming yourself, Jamie. There's nothing wrong with putting your feelings on the table. It's lovely that you want to make that sort of commitment.'

'Thanks. Shame she doesn't feel the same way.'

'Maybe she's just been hurt in the past,' Mia offers.

'I think her ex was a bit of an asshole.'

'Well, there you go then, probably just scared.' I know she's trying to make me feel better so I give her a warm smile.

'Thanks, guys.'

'Well, you are more than welcome to rent the spare room in our new place for a while,' Matt says.

'Yeah, of course,' Mia adds.

I appreciate their kindness, but I know they want to start a new chapter in their lives and there's no way I'm going to intrude on that. 'No, I'll rent somewhere else. It's fine. I'm sick of being a third wheel all the time any-way,' I joke.

'I'm not sure our relationship will work without you, to be honest,' Mia says. 'We might run out of things to say to each other.'

Matt laughs and I smile. They're such a solid couple that I know their future holds only a deep contentment, and I'm so glad they've found each other, even if right now it only highlights to me what I don't have.

'I think you'll manage. Right, I'm going to go and waste a few hours on social media.'

'Sure you don't want to join us? We're only about fifteen minutes in.'

'It's OK. Thanks, though, guys. And thanks for the chat.'

'Anytime,' Matt says and Mia blows me a kiss.

When I get into my room, I power up my laptop and look at various film reviews, an article about whether weight training or cardio is better for you (not that I do much of either), and then absent-mindedly browse Twitter. I pick up my phone to text Lucy but then put it back on my bedside table. What is there to say? And she hasn't contacted me, even though I'm sure she could tell I was upset. It's funny how one minute you can feel on top of the world, life full of hope and possibility, and the next minute everything just feels flat.

LUCY

I haven't spoken to Jamie since he asked me to move in with him last night. I know it sounds silly – it's only two o'clock the following day – but it's the longest we've been without any communication since we got together, and it feels odd. I know I need to be the one to contact him – I could tell how hurt he was when I didn't jump at the suggestion of buying a place together – I'm just not sure what to say. My head's all over the place. In the end, I decide to send him something silly, a photo of a dog wearing a cow onesie that I spotted on the way to work. After a few minutes I check my phone and there's a picture of his face beside the message, so I know that he's seen it, but no reply.

I sort the books on the display table at the front of the shop. It looks fine as it is but it's quiet and, to be honest, I need something to take my mind off stuff. I colour co-ordinate the piles of books and am pleased when I move away and two customers go straight to my display, picking up books and perusing the blurbs.

'Are you OK there? Looking for any recommendations?' I ask one of them, a man in his fifties.

'Actually, yes. I'm looking for some new crime. I've read all the usual suspects.'

I pick up a few new crime debuts that have been

widely recommended and hand them to him. 'Some great new crime writers here to discover.'

I talk him through what each book is about, giving him a good ten minutes of my time and expertise, and then he gets out his phone and looks up the prices of the books on Amazon, quite openly in front of me.

'I'll have a think about them. Thanks for your help.' And then he walks off, probably pressing 'add to basket' as he does.

'More sales for our favourite competitor?' Mandy says, walking over.

'I think they should send me some kind of reward.'

Just before I approach another customer, a delivery guy walks in with the hugest bunch of flowers I've ever seen. If Tilda had been in today, I would've presumed they were for her (Aaron is often making romantic gestures), but she's not, so Mandy and I eye each other suspiciously. Then the delivery guy says my name and I feel my cheeks blush as I take the obscene bouquet from him.

'Ridiculously hot and utterly romantic? How is that even fair?' Mandy says, shaking her head before going to the till to serve someone.

I smile and take the little card out of the flowers, touched that Jamie has reached out to me when really it should be the other way around and relieved that I haven't ruined everything between us. But when I see the name at the bottom, I'm shocked. They're not from Jamie. They're from Jude.

Please meet me for a quick drink after work today. Six p.m. at Curio. I really need to tell you something.

I tuck the card into my pocket, pretending to Mandy it was just a soppy note from Jamie, and then take the flowers to the stockroom, wondering what I'm going to do about meeting Jude. A huge part of me says, 'no way', but there's a tiny (very stupid) part of me that wants to hear what he has to say.

The day trickles its way towards half-five and I'm relieved when we can finally shut up shop and I can go home. Except, being the idiot that I am, I don't walk straight to my car like I should do. Maybe it's because I still haven't had a reply from Jamie, I don't know, but I take a detour via Curio Lounge and, sure enough, Jude is sitting in the window seat, looking out. When he sees me carrying his bunch of flowers, a huge smile fills his face and I know I'm going to have to go in and join him, if only to tell him to leave me alone once and for all.

When I've got inside, I notice he's already bought a drink for me and his presumptuousness irritates me. Trust Jude to be that cocky to buy a drink for me even though he had no idea whether I was going to turn up or not. Plus it's exactly what I would've ordered at this time of day – a strawberry and lime cider (we lived on it in Sweden) – and *that* irritates me even more.

He must be expecting this response because when I sit down on the chair opposite him, he says, 'I bought you a drink just in case. I hoped maybe if I bought it, it'd be a good omen and you'd arrive. And it worked.'

'I'm only coming to tell you that I'm not interested and to give you these back.' I try to hand him the bunch of flowers but he moves his hand away.

'They're for you. I don't want them.'

I put them on the floor under the table. 'Look, what have you got to say that's so pressing anyway, Jude?'

'First, I'm truly sorry. The way I ended it was really shit. To not turn up to the apartment ... well, it was unforgivable.'

'You're right. It was.'

We'd made plans to go for a second viewing of this apartment we were interested in. It was amazing. Top floor. Modern. Spacious. Jude had inherited a fairly large sum of money from his grandma so we could put a big deposit down to make the monthly payments manageable on our sporadic wages. We planned to rent it out whenever we went travelling so that we could use the money to pay the mortgage each month. I was so excited about seeing the apartment again and, while I was at work, I'd texted Jude a couple of times to remind him we were meeting there at six. He hadn't replied, but he was a bit hit and miss with his phone so I wasn't overly concerned, but then when I arrived to meet the estate agent and he wasn't there, I started to feel nervous. I was late (as usual), the estate agent standing outside the apartment block looking around. I went up to him, hoping maybe Jude had gone inside already, but he informed me that Jude hadn't turned up yet. I checked my phone again to see if I had any messages to explain why he was late, but there was nothing. We waited for about fifteen minutes and then I decided to go up and look on my own, pretending to the estate agent that I'd received a text from Jude to say he'd been caught up at work.

I still remember how I felt walking around the apartment – the desperate sinking feeling in my stomach. The life that I'd pictured disappearing before my eyes. I kept trying to tell myself Jude would have a reasonable excuse for his no-show, but I knew that he'd got cold feet. On reflection, I can see he'd been a bit off for weeks, ever since our conversations about the apartment had become more serious and considered, looking at figures and deliberating over what furniture to buy. He'd been fine when it was just a romantic vision, but the reality had made him twitchy.

He didn't call me until about eight that night and I knew as soon as I heard his voice that my fears were well founded and that he was about to call things off. He pinned it all on me, of course. Said he'd thought I was more of a free spirit, that he worried we were too different, that my wanting to live with him felt too intense and stifling for him. I begged and pleaded, said we could forget the whole 'moving in' thing and just stay as we were, but he wasn't having any of it. I cried for weeks, found it hard to go out for months, but slowly, very slowly, I started to heal. Which makes me wonder what the hell I'm doing back here.

'I'll never hurt you again, I promise. I'll make sure you have the best, most exciting life you can ever imagine. We can even move in together if that'll make you happy.'

The way he makes it sound like he'd be doing me a favour makes me long to see Jamie.

'You splitting up with me was the best thing that ever could've happened. So please just leave me alone.'

'You don't really mean that. You're not thinking straight.'

One of Jude's regular tactics – to label me as a psycho, neurotic, unhinged; to make me question myself until I'm no longer sure if I'm right. *You're being too emotional, controlling, possessive. You don't respect my need to be free.*

'No, you're wrong, Jude. This *is* me thinking straight.'

'All right, all right, don't get arsey. I remember that temper well. Remember how I used to shag it out of you.'

He wiggles his eyebrows and it sends me flying back. Yes, the sex was amazing, but he never made me feel valued, always made me feel like I wasn't really good enough for him. Whereas *Jamie* . . .

I bite my lip to stop myself from crying.

'Please don't call me again. I mean it, Jude.' I leave the flowers under the table, ignore Jude's protests and walk out. And as soon as I reach my car, that's when the tears *do* come, big fat sobs that make my whole body convulse as I rest my head on the steering wheel. And just as I'm about to start the car, I get a reply from Jamie.

I'm sorry if I came on too strong with the whole moving in thing. Can we just go back to how we were? x

I drive straight to Amy's house, practically running up the path and banging on the door. When Amy opens it, she immediately senses that I'm in a state, as she draws me into a hug then ushers me in.

'What's going on?'

'I'm sorry to just turn up like this. Is it OK?'

'Of course it is. You know that. Besides, the kids are out on play dates and Dave is working late so you have my full attention. Do you want a cup of tea? Something stronger?'

'Tea sounds perfect.' I sit on the stool at the breakfast bar whilst Amy puts the kettle on. There's always something reassuring about someone making you a cup of tea – I'm not sure what it is, but I immediately feel more relaxed.

'So what's up?'

I prop my head up on my elbow. 'I've messed everything up, as usual. What the hell is wrong with me?'

'Oh, Luce. Is it Jamie?'

'Sort of.' I let out a pained breath. 'I just met Jude for a drink.'

'What? Why? I thought he was in Outer Mongolia or somewhere.' Amy doesn't even try to disguise how dismayed she is with me.

'South America. Anyway, he got home a month or so ago. He messaged me.'

Amy raises her eyebrows.

'Before you get cross with me, I ignored it. But then I bumped into him the other night at the pub and we got chatting for a bit.' I run my hands through my hair. 'He was going on about how we were kindred spirits and weren't destined for suburbia and . . . well, then Jamie asked me to sell up and buy a place together and I freaked out and said it was too soon.' I shake my head. 'I'm a total dick.'

Amy puts a cup of tea down in front of me and then

sits opposite me at the breakfast bar and wraps her hands around her own mug. 'You're not a total dick.'

'You're a terrible liar.'

Amy smiles. 'I'm not lying. But I do think you really need to take some time to consider what it is you want. Before someone gets hurt.'

'Jamie, you mean? Before I hurt Jamie.'

Amy shrugs. 'And yourself.'

I sigh. 'But it's not a simple thing, is it? I want Jamie. But I don't want to give up the adventures. I don't want to "settle down". I want him to come with me, or if he can't sometimes because of work, I want him to support my need to.'

'So tell him that.'

'And what about the whole family thing?'

'If you're adamant you don't want one, then you need to tell him that too.'

'But what if then he doesn't want me? What if he leaves?'

Amy sighs, her eyes full of a painful truth. 'What's the alternative, Luce? Keep running so that you never have to face the *possibility* of him hurting you? So you hurt him first? Keep holding stuff back from him?'

I chew my bottom lip. 'You're right. I know you're right. I'll talk to him. Tell him the truth.'

'Good girl.' She stands up and goes over to the cupboard, pulling out a box of biscuits and bringing them over. 'Now, this is what we really need right now.'

When I get back, I park my car on the road, struggling to find a space as usual, and then head up the path towards my front door. And just as I get there I see a bunch of flowers on the doorstep, some simple wild-flowers. And they're so much more 'me' than the ones Jude sent me and it's as much as I can do to stop myself from bursting into tears again.

I bend down and pick up the card.

Sorry again. I love you, Jamie x

I message him straight away, hoping it's not too late.

You have nothing to be sorry for. Do you still want to come to the wedding with me tomorrow? x

Of course. Pick you up at 12? x

Relief washes over me as I go inside and sort out my outfit for the wedding. I know I'm going to have to tell Jamie everything – about Jude, about why I had reservations about moving in with him, the whole not wanting a family thing – I just have to hope he'll still want me when I do.

We arrive a little bit late to Tilda's wedding (I left the present on the side and Jamie had to race us back for me to pick it up) but we manage to get into the church before she starts her journey down the aisle, finding a space to sit down at the end of one of the pews near the back. I don't think we're technically on the right side, but I'm not sure it really matters.

The church looks beautiful, the ends of the pews adorned with flowers, candles in all the alcoves, greenery wrapped around the pillars. I'm not one of those women who has pictured my wedding since childhood, but the more weddings I attend, the more I get an idea of how I would like mine to be. I wouldn't want it too fancy, just classic and pretty. Same for my dress, although I'd like something a little bit quirky. I imagine Jamie standing at the front of the church, where Aaron is now – I'd want him to be blown away.

'It looks amazing, doesn't it?' he says now, scanning the whole church. And I love that he's the kind of guy that notices things like that and comments on it.

'It's beautiful.'

I rest my head on his shoulder and he puts his arm around me. And it feels so safe and relaxed. The one time Jude accompanied me to a wedding there was this awkward underlying tension. He kept making little comments about how 'boring' it was, and how 'predictable', like he was determined that I know we would *never* be getting married so there was no point ever bringing it up. He was purposefully unaffectionate, as if he was scared that if he showed me that he in any way cared I'd be hassling him to propose the minute we got home. But Jamie's not like that at all.

All at once, the organ pipes up and a hush descends on the building as everyone stands and Tilda and her dad appear at the entrance to the church. She's wearing an amazing simple slimline silk dress, a single flower in her hair. Her dad looks as proud as punch, and tears form in my eyes as I imagine *my* dad on my wedding day, if I'm lucky enough to have one. And then, whilst everyone else's eyes remain glued to the bride, I look at Aaron. I always love to watch the groom at this point in the ceremony, the first moment he lays eyes on his wife-to-be in her wedding dress. Aaron doesn't disappoint, his face breaking into a beaming smile as he lifts his hand to wipe a tear from under his eye. I'm so happy for Tilda to have found someone who so clearly adores her. Like Mandy, I was a bit sceptical at first when she said she'd been with him since she was thirteen, and getting married at twenty seems so young, but seeing the look on their faces as they turn towards each other, I'm genuinely quite envious of her – to be so sure of what she wants at her age.

Jamie holds my hand for the whole service and when it's time to sing the hymns, he belts them out, whereas Jude used to stand beside me staring at his phone and not even joining in. When they say their vows, I look over at Jamie, who is fully focused on Aaron and Tilda and smiling warmly. And I know I've got a good one here, and I realize I really do have to be honest with him – to stop hiding. Because I *do* want this to last. If all goes well, I want it to be us standing at the front of the church making our promises to each other one day. And we can't do that until he knows exactly who I am and all that being with me entails.

After the service, we go outside and throw confetti over the happy couple, before the crowd disperses and we all go to our cars to drive to the reception venue – a gorgeous country house hotel about three miles down the road.

'I love weddings, don't you?' Jamie says, as he's driving.

I can't help but laugh.

'What?'

'Just you. Are you even real?'

'What do you mean? Are men not supposed to like weddings then?'

'Maybe the free booze and food, but not normally the service, no.'

Jamie shrugs. 'I didn't realize I was so odd. I just love seeing all the families coming together, everyone so happy. Sorry, I guess I'm a sap.'

I put my hand on Jamie's thigh. 'Don't apologize. It's lovely.'

When we arrive at the hotel, we're greeted by a waiter who hands us both a glass of champagne, followed by a waitress carrying a tray of canapés. I don't know what it is about weddings, but despite the fact I always make sure I eat before, I'm always starving. I grab some kind of smoked salmon thing and a mini tartlet and Jamie takes a chicken skewer.

'I made a bad choice there,' I say, peering at his much larger piece of food.

'You got two things.'

'I'm still not sure they're as big as yours, even combined.'

'Swap?' Jamie holds out the skewer.

I survey my two choices and decide to stick with them. 'No, it's OK, but thank you. That's true love, that is.'

'Sharing my chicken skewer with you?'

'Yeah. Again, not many men would be so kind.'

'You've clearly not been with the right men.'

I kiss him on the cheek. 'You're right. I haven't.'

We make our way through the guests, mostly faces I don't recognize until we see Mandy and her husband, Mark. It's always a huge relief to find someone you know at a wedding. I find weddings where you don't know anyone drag – you end up drinking far too much and peaking by four o'clock. Jamie chats away happily to Mark whilst Mandy and I cover the usual topics of how amazing Tilda looks and how delicious the food is and how we already feel drunk with the endless supply of champagne. But it really is a lovely day; the room is awash with smiles and laughter. And it continues all through dinner, everyone getting on and enjoying themselves. I blub my way through the speeches (they've always been my Achilles heel) and imagine what my dad would say. I know he'll have me in total pieces, soppy bugger that he is.

And then it's the first dance. Tilda and Aaron have chosen 'I'm Kissing You' by Des'ree and it's actually a really beautiful and poignant moment. Sometimes I find the first dance a bit cheesy, but it feels like being in *Romeo and Juliet* (although hopefully with a happier ending) and when the crowd is invited to join them, I take Jamie's hand and pull him on to the dance floor, and I'm not sure why but as we dance, I feel like crying. I'm not sure if it's happiness or fear, but I just feel overwhelmed.

'What's up?' he asks, stopping for a moment.

'Can we go somewhere and talk?'

'Yeah, sure.' I can see the fear in Jamie's eyes and I want to reassure him that it's nothing bad, but maybe that's not true. Maybe what I have to tell him will be the worst thing ever in his eyes.

I leave the dance floor with Jamie following behind, weaving our way through the canoodling couples until we're outside. I find a bench overlooking the vast lawn and sit down, Jamie sitting beside me, his eyes questioning.

'What is it? Is everything OK?'

'I don't know. It's just . . . being here, seeing them . . .'

'It makes you realize you don't want that with me?' Jamie interjects and he looks so sad, so scared, that it just makes me love him all the more.

'No. God, no. It makes me realize that I do.'

Jamie's face breaks into a smile, the sense of relief clear in the way his shoulders drop, his neck and jaw looking less tense. 'Is that what you wanted to tell me? You looked so scared, as if you were about to break my heart.'

'I worry I might be.'

Jamie looks concerned again and I realize the roller-coaster of emotions I'm putting him through and how I just need to bite the bullet and tell the truth. 'Just tell me what's wrong, Lucy. This relationship's never going to work if we're not honest with each other.'

'I saw Jude.'

'Oh.' He looks like I just punched him in the stomach then he nods slowly. 'So that's why you didn't want to move in with me? It all makes sense now.'

'No, no, well, not in the way you think.'

'That's reassuring.'

I wish I knew how to explain, but I know anything I say is going to hurt him. 'I bumped into him when I was out with the girls and then he sent me flowers at work so I met up with him yesterday to tell him to leave me alone.'

Jamie stares me right in the eye. 'So what do you mean, not in the way I think?'

I take a deep breath and let it out slowly. 'Jude's a total dick, let me just say that first. But he knows the real me and he doesn't judge me. He actually likes me better for it.'

As soon as I've said it, I wish I hadn't. I'm not even sure where it came from, it's certainly not what I planned to say, but I suddenly realize that it's true, that maybe that's a huge element of what's always drawn me to him.

Jamie stands up. 'I'm going to go. Please apologize to Tilda and Aaron for me. Say I felt ill or something.'

I grab on to his hand. 'Please don't go. I'm sorry. Let me explain.'

'Explain what, Luce? How Jude is the only one who really knows you? How our whole relationship is built on pretence? I've tried my hardest to get to know you. I've opened up my heart to you, asked you to move in with me, but you seem determined to keep me at arm's length and I'm too old to waste any more time.'

It's a side to Jamie I've not really seen and, in a strange way, I'm actually glad that he's standing up to me. 'I'm sorry I said I didn't want to live with you. I do.'

'So why did you say no? What do you mean, Jude knows the real you? Just be straight with me, Lucy.'

'I don't want children.'

Jamie stares at me blankly so I feel I have to continue.

'And I can tell that you do. And I'm scared that that means you won't want me any more.'

It's such a relief to have it out and yet, when Jamie just stands there not saying anything, I'm terrified that I'm right.

JAMIE

At first I'm not sure what to say. Does she mean she's not ready for kids? Or that she never wants them? Is this really what's been holding her back from moving in with me? I sit down again, and after a few seconds, she says, 'So, are you going to say something?'

'Um, I'm not sure what to say. So do you mean you never want kids?'

Lucy looks at her feet and nods. 'I'm sorry.'

'You don't need to apologize to me. But how come? I mean, how can you be so sure?'

'I don't know. I just don't. I've never had that desire that most women have. I've never felt broody, or empty without one.'

I nod, but the truth is I don't really understand. 'Maybe you're just not ready for any of those feelings yet? You're only in your twenties. It doesn't necessarily mean they'll never come.'

Lucy sighs, as if she thinks I'm utterly stupid and that I'll never understand anything. 'That's what everyone always says.'

'Well, maybe they're right. I mean, I didn't necessarily know I wanted kids a few years ago.' It's a lie. I've always known I want children. But maybe a huge part of that is losing Thomas. I'm sure there are tons of people in the world who can't see themselves ever wanting children and then suddenly they hit a certain age and the desire kicks in.

Lucy sighs. 'When people say they want kids, no one ever says, "Are you sure you won't change your mind?", do they? Because that's the norm. But I know how I feel. Call me selfish, but I don't want to have to consider a child when I'm planning my next adventure. I don't want my days filled with kids' TV or play dates or school plays. I see how happy it all makes my sister but it's not for me.'

I nod, even though I love the sound of all that stuff. I want to teach my child to ride a bike, to comfort them when they have a bad dream, to share my favourite films with them. But I also know that I love Lucy, that she's the person I want to end up with. And despite what she's saying, I can't help feeling that one day she *might* change her mind. Priorities change. People change.

'I love the thought of a life of adventures with you.'

'Even if it means no children?'

It all feels so hypothetical. I can't really take it seriously. 'Yeah, I guess.'

I can see that my answer's not enough for her, but I'm not sure what to say.

'Look, it's a lot to take in, I know. Take your time to think about it, OK?'

'OK. I mean, it doesn't change how I feel about you though. And anyway, what's all this got to do with Jude? I don't really get it.'

Lucy sighs. 'He didn't want kids either, so when he found out that I felt the same, he was overjoyed. And it's the first time I've ever really felt accepted. It's hard to explain when you're not a woman, what it's like. The expectation. The disgust, even. So many times you're made to feel like a monster.'

'Of course you're not a monster.'

'You'd be surprised what most people think.'

I think about Jude, about how she clearly thinks they're better suited. 'Well, maybe you should just go back to him. You already said he's more exciting than me. You could spend your lives travelling the world and doing crazy things I'm too terrified to attempt.'

Lucy takes my hand. 'I don't want Jude. I want you.'

It's such a relief and yet I don't feel as happy as I should.

'Look, I know it probably seems a bit intense,' she continues. 'And I wasn't going to say anything for a while because things have been going so great between us, but when you asked me to move in with you, I realized that I don't want to waste your time, or mine. I don't want to wake up in a couple of years heartbroken because you've decided you can't accept what I have to offer. That's why I'm telling you now. So you can make an informed choice.'

I'm so glad that my fears were unfounded, that actually she does feel the same way about me as I do about her. She *does* see this as something long lasting. But can I just agree to never having children?

When I don't respond, Lucy says, 'I'm sorry. I expect I'm not quite what you signed up for, hey?'

I shake my head. 'Not at all. I mean, there's no rule book saying people have to want children, is there?'

'I'm guessing you do want them? I mean, if I hadn't just dropped this bombshell on you?'

Yes, passionately.

'I don't know. I guess I always thought I would have kids. But maybe you're right, maybe it was just because that's what people do. I'm not sure I've ever really examined it.'

I hope she can't see that I'm lying.

'You're great with kids though,' she says.

'Other people's maybe. That doesn't mean I'd be any good with my own.'

'I think you would.'

It feels like she's trying to persuade me to split up with her, and I want to say, 'Stop, I don't want to be pushed away from you,' but I guess she just wants me to be sure.

'Look,' Lucy continues, 'just think about it. I'm not saying "let's get engaged" or anything. Things might not work out between us anyway. I just think, if we're going to buy a place together, and I'd really like to, it's only right that you know what you're committing to.' Then she stands up, seemingly to signal that the conversation is over. 'Right, shall we go back and enjoy this wedding?'

'Yeah, sure,' I say, trying to focus on the positives. If there's one thing I've learnt over the years it's that the only surety you have is 'right now', and right now I have an amazing woman who loves me, who I fiercely love back, and I'm determined to enjoy the evening.

We take each other's hands and make our way back to the dance floor. The music is an eclectic mix, from the latest pop songs to old classics like 'Come On Eileen' but we dance to them all, forming a circle with Mandy and Mark, and another couple that were on our table (I've forgotten their names already), until we're hot and sweaty.

'Drink?' Lucy asks.

I wipe my forehead. 'Absolutely.'

I buy Lucy a vodka and Coke and I get myself a beer, then I sit down on a chair at the edge of the room and Lucy sits on my knee.

'Well, that burnt off some of that sticky toffee pudding,' I say.

'I know something that'll burn off some more,' Lucy whispers into my ear. After the alcohol, and the warm glow you get from spending the evening on the dance floor at a wedding, the slightly sombre mood from earlier seems to have passed and we're both in high spirits.

'Well, it'd be a shame to waste that luxurious-looking hotel bed.'

We dropped our bags off earlier, not having any time to really explore the room because Lucy had made us late as usual. But we did both notice the huge fancy bed.

'Want to go up now?' she asks.

'You sure you don't want to stay and dance with your friends?'

Lucy shakes her head. 'Let's go and say our goodbyes.'

'OK.'

We down our drinks and put our glasses back on the bar then go and say goodbye to Mandy and Mark before hunting down Tilda and Aaron.

'We're going to call it a night. But it was a perfect wedding,' Lucy shouts above the music.

'Thank you so much for coming. And it was lovely to properly meet you, Jamie,' Tilda says, smiling widely at me.

'You too. You look stunning.' I kiss her on the cheek and then shake hands with Aaron. 'Congratulations, mate. It's been a great day.'

'Thanks. It was nice to meet you.'

Then we sneak off the dance floor and head up to our hotel room. We're both quite drunk and it takes Lucy a while to find the key card, hidden at the bottom of her handbag.

'Got it. Right, how does this work?' She waves it across the handle and I take it off her and push it into the slot. When I remove it, the little light turns green and I open the door, gesturing for Lucy to go in before me.

'Ever the gentleman.'

'You won't be saying that in a minute when I'm tearing your clothes off.'

This makes Lucy laugh and she starts kissing me frantically and pulling at my clothes. And somehow we manage to get naked and fumble our way to the bed, where I throw her down and climb on top of her. We must be right above the disco because the music is almost as clear up here as it was on the dance floor.

'Looks like we've got a soundtrack.'

Lucy smiles then grabs hold of my buttocks and pulls me towards her. Afterwards, we lie there as the music slows, obviously entering the end of the set – the romantic section.

'If you still want me to, I'll put my house on the

market first thing Monday morning,' Lucy says, looking up at me shyly.

'You don't have to. I know how much you love it. And I don't blame you for being cautious. It's OK. You don't have to do it to prove something to me.'

'I'm not doing it to prove anything to you. I'm doing it because I'm sure about you. And I want us to get the perfect place and make a million memories there.'

It's an offer I can't turn down.

'In that case, let's do it.'

I kiss her and then mouth the words to the song floating up through the floor, telling Lucy about our groovy kind of love. And she laughs until the music stops – then everybody cheers.

The Day of the Break-Up

LUCY

Everything on the walk back to the car reminds me of Jamie. The café where we had our first date, The Retreat – where we drank squashed frogs and I realized how much I *really* liked him. Even places like Greggs take on a strange romantic sort of melancholy – the way we'd always get a cheese and bean slice when we came into town, the feel of Jamie's hand in mine as we walked these cobbled streets together so many times. It's the sort of thing that used to send a shiver of fear down my spine – the 'boring everyday' – and yet with Jamie it never felt boring, and I guess that's how I knew how much I loved him. Even hanging out the washing whilst he sat in the garden reading his book, or sitting at the dining table watching him cook the dinner, I felt content.

Passing all the places we'd frequent together, I have a sudden desire to move away for good, far away from all these memories. It feels like the only way I'm going to survive this, but I know in reality I couldn't leave my family. That, as much as I love visiting different countries, immersing myself in different cultures, getting caught in storms that make English weather seem utterly bland, I will always reach that point where I need to come home. And Stroud is my home. It's the sort of place people always return to, no matter how far and wide they travel away from it. And in a strange, nonsensical way, I don't want to be far away from Jamie, however much it hurts having him near and not being with him.

I walk through the park back to the car and am sure I recognize the person sitting on the bench ahead of me drinking a coffee. There are not that many people with pink hair, although in Stroud there's probably far more than the national average.

When I get nearer, Tilda looks up and smiles. 'Hey you. What you up to?' Then she must read my sombre facial expression because she pats the bench. 'You look like you need a chat.'

I sit down beside her. 'I left him.'

She puts her hand on top of mine. 'Oh, Luce. Do I need to ask why?'

I shake my head. She's the only person I've told about what happened, so I'm really glad it's her I've bumped into as it feels like I don't have to explain, that she will understand.

'And how are you feeling? Again, I probably don't really need to ask.'

I take a deep breath. 'A big part of me feels like I'll never get over this. That I've just said goodbye to the love of my life.'

Tilda nods. 'And the other part?'

I look down at my left hand, a slightly paler line of skin on the ring finger. 'Relieved that I don't have to feel guilty all the time.'

Tilda doesn't say anything, just squeezes my hand, and I rest my head on her shoulder until I feel ready to stand.

When I get to the car, I climb in, checking my phone again to see if there are any more messages from Jamie. There aren't, so I start the engine and set off towards Amy's, singing along to the cheesy pop on Heart in an attempt to cheer myself up.

But then Phil Collins comes on and, as I'm singing, the words catch in my throat as I suddenly remember Jamie mouthing it to me, lying in a bed ten times more luxurious than our own, when the world felt so full of hope. And I wonder what the hell I'm doing, why I'm heading to Amy's, when really I should be heading home.

Before

LUCY

I can't help but feel a little sad as the estate agent walks around the house, taking photos and checking measurements. But I'm sure that Jamie is what I want, and I know that we're going to be really happy in our new home. After work tomorrow, we're going to look at this place we've found and I'm really excited. It looks amazing in the photographs. It's in Chalford (my favourite village), has three bedrooms and the garden . . . wow. It's huge and it's even got a stream running along the bottom. *A stream.* I'm just hoping there's no catch. It's amazing what a good photographer can achieve. Talking of which, I wonder if the guy in my house is performing miracles, making the tiny rooms appear more spacious with a clever camera angle.

'Nearly done,' he calls from the courtyard garden. There's no way he can make *that* appear spacious. There's barely room to swing a cat, as my dad would say. Although I'm not sure why anyone would ever want to swing a cat.

'No problem. Can I make you a cup of tea or coffee?'

'No, I'm fine, thanks.'

When he finishes, he comes in and we sit at the dining room table, him opening his folder.

'So, I think we're looking at about two hundred

thousand. I've got these comparable properties for you to see how I've come to the valuation.'

He hands over the details and I take a quick look, but I'm confident with his decision. I'll make about ten thousand on it if it sells for near the asking price, and I just want to get it sold, before any doubts or anxieties halt me in my tracks.

'Sounds good to me.'

He looks surprised, as if he's used to a battle. 'OK, great. Well, I think I should be able to sell it pretty quickly. We're far enough away from Christmas and there's always quite a high demand for this sort of property with lots of character features.'

'Great. I mean, I've loved it here.'

'Yeah, I think it's a great place for a single person or a couple pre-kids.'

I feel myself bristle. 'Or a couple who don't want children?'

The estate agent looks taken aback and I realize my tone was possibly more aggressive than I intended it to be. 'Well, yes, of course. Anyway, I think I've got everything I need. I'll call you as soon as we have any viewings.'

'Thanks.'

I lead him to the door, see him out and then ring Jamie.

'Are you OK?' he asks on answering. He sounds out of breath like he's just got back from a run.

'I'm good. Just had the estate agent round. Should be on the market by tomorrow morning.'

'That's great,' Jamie says, but he doesn't sound like he thinks it's great.

'Is everything OK?'

'Of course. I mean, yeah, it's nothing. Sorry. Long day at work. I only just got in.'

'Do you want me to call you back a different time?'

'No, no, of course not. Wait a second, let me just get a beer and then I'll take the phone into my room.'

I listen to the clinking and the hissing of Jamie getting a beer out of the fridge and removing the top off the bottle.

'Right, I'm sorted now.'

'So are we still on for going to see that house tomorrow?'

'Of course. Can't wait.'

'So why do you sound like you're putting on your enthusiasm?'

I feel a sudden wave of panic. That Jamie's having second thoughts about wanting to commit to anything with me after my 'don't want kids' confession at the wedding.

'I'm not, it's just . . .' I hear Jamie let out a long breath. 'I feel bad about you selling your place. I know how much you love it. We can just go for somewhere cheaper, you know? It doesn't matter.'

I feel instantly relieved. 'Don't be silly. The place we're viewing looks amazing. A proper garden! We can have barbecues, dig a vegetable patch. There's room for a hot tub. And views that we can gaze on when we're sipping our champagne amongst the bubbles. It even has a walk-in wardrobe for God's sake. I won't have to vacuum pack my summer wardrobe in winter and vice versa in summer. We can have a proper size dining table and have dinner parties . . .'

Jamie laughs. 'You've clearly thought this through.'

'Absolutely. You don't need to worry. I'm sure about selling the house.'

'Good. I'm glad.'

The woman that shows us round is one of those really annoying estate agents who treats you like you're stupid and that you can't, in fact, see the obvious damp on the walls (*it's just the shadow – amazing the tricks the light can play, isn't it?*) or realize that the kitchen needs to be completely ripped out and replaced (*nothing a lick of paint can't fix*). Luckily for her, we love it despite any flaws it might have, and can see its huge potential. The kitchen/diner is open plan and big enough for a lovely wooden dining table (like the one this family have got) plus room for tons of cupboard space so that I can actually access my pans without them all getting wedged in the pan drawer, preventing it from opening. The lounge has a feature fireplace with a wood burner (another essential) and – the jewel in the crown – the large garden with its stunning views out over the valley.

'Imagine how amazing it'll be without the trampoline. Perfect spot for my hot tub,' I say, as we peruse the outdoor space.

The estate agent smiles. 'I agree. I don't know why anyone has these nasty trampolines. They're such an eyesore. I'm just glad they weren't really a thing when my kids were growing up. Anyway, do you want to have a look upstairs now?'

I look at Jamie, who is staring into the distance. 'Jamie?'

He shakes his body as if he's just woken up. 'Yeah, thanks.'

The estate agent leads us upstairs and we walk into the second bedroom, kitted out with toys and unicorn bedding and kid's drawings framed on the wall.

'Good size,' Jamie says before quickly moving on.

Next we go to the master bedroom, which shares the garden's amazing views, and then the estate agent, rather reluctantly it appears, leads us to the third 'bedroom', which definitely had the clever camera angle treatment in the photographs.

'Now as you can see they're using it as a snug, but I think it would make a gorgeous nursery.' She looks at me and smiles, clearly trying to tap into my maternal instinct to disguise the fact there's no way you could fit a bed in here. I lower my eyes, and the estate agent clearly picks up on a 'vibe' as her face flushes. She probably thinks I'm infertile and that she's just made a huge faux pas.

'It's not actually big enough to be classed as a bed-room though, is it?' Jamie says, breaking the awkward silence.

'Oh yes, it's been measured and you could fit a single bed just there.' She points to the one wall, where even if you could just about fit a bed, you'd struggle to get in and out of it.

'I think it's pushing the trade descriptions act a little bit,' Jamie says, turning around to leave the room.

'Would you like to see the garden again?' the estate agent asks, a little desperately, as she leads us back downstairs.

'No, I think we're good, thanks. Unless you want to?' Jamie turns to me and I shake my head then he addresses the estate agent again. 'Thanks for showing us around. We've got another viewing after this and then we'll be in touch if that's OK?'

We haven't got another viewing and it's pushing six o'clock so I'm sure the estate agent can tell Jamie's lying, but I expect she's used to the games that are played with property purchases.

'Of course. But I really think this place will be snapped up soon, so I wouldn't leave it too long if you like it.'

I try not to smile as I watch the two of them making their moves against each other like a game of chess and then she shows us out and we wander back to Jamie's car, which is parked down the road. The estate agent drives past and we wave her off with a smile.

As soon as we're in the car, I turn to Jamie excitedly. 'You love it, yeah? We're going to put an offer in?'

Jamie reaches into his pocket for his car keys, puts them in the ignition and starts the car. 'Well, yeah. I think the price is a bit high though. I mean, that third bedroom is definitely not a bedroom. Legally, I'm not sure they can call it a three-bedroom property.'

'But we don't need a third bedroom, do we?'

'Yeah, I know that we don't need it.' It's probably just

me projecting my own insecurities but his tone seems a little 'off'. 'But it will have affected the asking price. A two-bedroom property could be as much as forty grand less.'

I nod. I know that it's good to think about all of these things practically. Jamie is probably a very important yin to my yang. But right now I just want us to be excited and 'carried away'. You only buy your first house together once, and I want it to feel magical.

Jamie reaches over and puts his hand on my thigh. 'I'm sorry. I'm being a killjoy. I'll ring her first thing in the morning and put an offer in.'

'Can't we do it tonight?'

'I think it'd be better to wait. We don't want to seem too keen. And are you happy for me to go in fifty grand below the asking price because of the bedroom?'

'Well, I don't want to lose it. And we should have the money if mine sells for close to the price it's on for.'

'I know. But I don't want to be ripped off. And we could do with some money left over to sort out the damp problems and buy a new kitchen, which it desperately needs.'

'OK. I'll trust your judgement with this one.'

'Thanks. And don't worry, if it looks like we're going to lose it, I'll quickly go in with something a bit higher.'

When we arrive outside my house, Jamie switches off the engine but remains seated.

'Aren't you coming in? You're welcome to stay over.'

'Oh, thanks, but I've got a ton of work on. We're organizing this big event for the weekend and Matt and

I really need to sit down together and plan the logistics tonight.'

'Oh right, OK. Maybe tomorrow then?'

Jamie looks at the floor awkwardly. 'I actually promised Mum I'd go there for dinner after work. I'm trying to make an effort to see her more regularly.'

I notice that he doesn't invite me to join him. It's strange, but I sense the tide has changed, the balance of power. I find there's always this moment in a relationship, the moment that I surrender, that I allow someone in, lower my defences, that suddenly it feels like I lose the power battle, that I'm terrifyingly vulnerable. And today it feels that way more than ever, like Jamie is pulling away, but I'm not sure if I'm just imagining it.

'But how about the next day?' he continues. 'Hopefully we'll have our offer accepted on the house and we can go out and celebrate?'

Maybe I *am* just imagining it.

'Yeah. That sounds good.'

He leans across the handbrake and kisses me, but it's more friendly than brimming with passion and I wonder if I should grab his face, kiss him back hard, but it feels a little desperate.

'Night then.'

I leave him and go inside, telling myself that gripping on to something tightly doesn't mean it won't slip through your fingers if it's really meant to.

JAMIE

We sit around Mum's dining table and it reminds me of when I was younger, after Dad died, when this table suddenly felt too big – as if the size of it was mocking us both. I wondered if Mum might buy a new one when she moved here rather than transporting this cumbersome thing all that way, but she didn't. In fact, she brought all the old furniture with her. And I get it – that leaving the house she shared with Dad was hard enough; to get rid of the stuff in it was a step too far.

Tucking into Mum's delicious spaghetti bolognaise (I learnt from the best), I wonder how to broach the subject that's never far from my mind. Mum and I don't really do heart-to-hearts, but at the same time I don't know who else to talk to. If Dad were here, I would've spoken to him. I could talk to him about anything – the shame I experienced after my first wet dream, the girl at school that I had a huge crush on, the lads I never really fit in with. He never looked embarrassed at anything I had to say, never judged or lectured. God, I miss him. Some days it's just a dull ache, but others, like today, it's like a parasite.

'Lucy has put her place on the market and we're looking to buy somewhere together.'

'Oh, that's great news, Jamie. I'm really happy for

you.' There's always a formality in Mum's tone. Sometimes I wish she'd just give me a huge bear hug like Dad would've done. 'I could tell you were serious about her when you came over together. So how does Matt feel about this development?'

'He's moving in with Mia. It was that that kind of spurred me on, I suppose.'

'Well, there's definitely more of a spark between you than there was with Anna.'

I'm surprised that she's picked up on that. Maybe she knows me better than I give her credit for.

'Oh, yeah. I feel totally different than I did with Anna.' I eat a mouthful of spaghetti. 'We've found a place we really like in Chalford. She wanted me to put an offer on it today.'

'But you didn't?'

'It's not worth the asking price.'

Mum nods slowly. 'So what's the real reason you're not sure about it?' She smiles and again, it feels like I've underestimated her in the past – her ability to read me. And I suddenly feel sad for all the years we've wasted not really being that close.

I smile too, acknowledging that she's caught me out. 'Lucy told me she doesn't want kids.'

Her reaction is much the same as mine was to start with – what's the big deal? 'Oh, well, she's still pretty young. The maternal drive doesn't kick in for everyone straight away. You've still got plenty of time for all that.'

I shake my head. 'She says she's sure she'll never want

them. That she wants us to travel instead. She seems fairly certain.'

'Well, maybe she's wise. I mean, having a child is a wonderful thing, but it also changes your entire life and it's full of heartache and guilt and regret.'

It hurts to hear her talk about motherhood in this way – that I've unwittingly caused her so much pain. Although I'm sure in part she's talking about Thomas.

'But would Dad have been enough for you? If he'd not wanted children, would you still have married him?'

Mum nods and although I appreciate her honesty, it's an odd feeling. To think that she would've chosen not to have me if that's what my dad had wanted. 'Now you're here, of course I'd never change things. But if your dad had said he didn't want children, I would've still married him. That said, I'm not sure I'm as natural a mum as I think you would be a dad. You're more like your father.'

I feel tears threatening and work hard to hold them back.

'If he'd had to choose,' she continues, 'between you and me, I mean, he would've chosen you, I think. Nothing made him happier than being a father.'

I struggle to swallow my food. 'So what do I do?'

Mum laughs. 'I hope you didn't come here to ask me that.'

I shrug.

'I can't answer that for you, son. Depends how much you want a child. And how much you love her, I guess. Could you be happy, just the two of you, do you think?'

'I know that I love her. That she makes me happy. But I *have* always wanted a child. And after what happened with Dad and well . . .'

'Thomas?'

It feels odd to hear her say his name. We never talk about what happened.

I nod. 'I guess I'm just scared of life always feeling that little bit empty, of there always being that hole . . .'

The words catch in my throat so I have to stop talking, and when I look up at Mum, there are tears in her eyes too, which just makes it even harder not to cry myself.

I still remember the day Dad died as if it were yesterday. I was at school and, at the time, I was so mad at Mum for not calling me, for waiting until I'd got home. She said it wouldn't have made a difference. He'd had a huge heart attack. There was no time for goodbye. But I couldn't bear the thought that I'd been messing around with Bunsen burners in my science lesson, me and my mates giggling when our teacher got stressed because we were all setting fire to our pencils, our ties. I'd been acting like a dick, I'd been laughing, when my dad had been fighting for his last breath.

I didn't fall apart. Not in the way everyone expected me to. It was a couple of months before my GCSEs so all my teachers thought I was destined to fail – they pushed for an extension so as not to waste all the hard work I'd put in over the two years. But I didn't want it. I told them I'd be fine taking my exams, and I was. I felt bad about that for years. About the run of As I got when my dad had just died. Now I see it was my coping mechanism, to focus on the revision, to shut out what had happened, to pretend that life could carry on as normal. But rather than it getting easier, as grief is supposed to, time being the great healer and all that, for me it just got harder. The gap that Dad left just kept growing until I felt like I was more holes than solid pieces.

Maybe that was why I stayed with Anna for so long; because I'd given up on ever feeling whole again, or even close to it. Of ever feeling the kind of happiness I used to feel sitting next to Dad, fishing at the lake, him telling me about his childhood or teaching me the strengths and weaknesses of all the Superheroes or trying to scare the life out of me with ghost stories. He was always such a brilliant storyteller. Mum used to mock him – 'not another one of your convoluted stories' – but I loved all the little details he put in, the way he could make anything come alive. He gave me my first beer on one of our many fishing trips, and I remember him laughing when I winced. He taught me how to make a fire using the sun and a magnifying glass, the names of the birds that woke us up in the morning, explained to me what lived in all the different shaped holes that we passed in the woods. We whittled sticks to make spears, played baseball with branches that had broken off the trees and fallen apples. Even when I hit fifteen and all my mates mocked me for still wanting to spend a lot of my weekends with my dad rather than being out drinking with them, I didn't care. Because that's when I was at my happiest.

It feels like my life ever since has been spent trying to find that again. And now I have it with Lucy – or at least something close to it. But that's been tainted now, somehow, and I think that's what I hate the most; that I can't find my way back to that heady feeling I used to feel when I was with her.

'Talk to her, love,' Mum says, placing her hand on top of mine. 'People do all sorts of things for the person they love. Maybe she'll come round if you tell her what it means to you.'

'And if she doesn't?'

'Then I guess you need to decide whether she's worth sacrificing a family for.'

It feels like *Sophie's Choice* – I either lose Lucy, who is most definitely the love of my life, or I say goodbye to the chance of ever having a family of my own. It's tricky, because the one idea feels ethereal, some distant vision of how I expected my life to turn out. Whereas the other is right here, right now, flesh and bone. This person that I have come to depend on. And, truth be told, I'm still hoping that she'll change her mind one day. But what if she doesn't? It wouldn't be fair to turn around in however many years and break her heart over something she has been completely honest with me about.

'I think maybe I thought having a family of my own one day might finally fill the hole, you know?'

'I guess it's hard to know until it happens.'

'I know. You're right. Either way it's a leap of faith.' I finish my food and put my cutlery down on the plate. 'Thanks, Mum.'

She smiles. 'I know I'm not as good as your dad was with matters of the heart, but I am always here. I hope you know that. I might not have the best advice to give but I will listen.'

'I think you've done a great job with the advice.'

'I wish I could tell you what to do, love, but that wouldn't be fair. Or right.'

I nod, knowing that she's right but still wanting someone to just make the decision for me.

'I do know that you light up when you're around her though.'

I smile, stand up and collect our plates, taking them to the dishwasher and putting them in. It's so empty, just a single cup and plate, and it makes me sad for Mum, living all alone way before her time, and although I'm tired, I suddenly want to stay a little longer.

'Fancy a film night?'

Mum is unable to hide the shock on her face. 'You're not going to inflict one of those terrible DVDs you and your dad used to watch on me, are you?'

We go in to the lounge and I scan through our family DVD collection. So many memories in that box alone. It's weird how simple possessions can hold so much emotional weight. I hold up *Indiana Jones* – it was always the only film Mum would tolerate because she had a crush on Harrison Ford.

'Good choice,' she says, biting her lip.

And for once she doesn't automatically sit down on the other sofa. She sits beside me, and we watch the film, and I can almost feel Dad beside us, chatting away with his running commentary that always used to drive Mum mad.

LUCY

I never thought that domesticity would be something I could feel this excited about. But I've already had an offer on my place (only two grand below the asking price), and we're just waiting to find out if our offer on the new house has been accepted, and it feels like a huge adventure.

I can hear my phone ringing in another room so I hunt around for it (why can't I just put it somewhere I can easily find it?), eventually locating it on the side in the bathroom. It's Mum.

'You've sold the house. You guys are really moving in together,' she screams as soon as I answer the phone.

I can't help but smile at her enthusiasm, even though I can already predict the direction this conversation is going to go in. 'We are.'

'I'm so happy for you. Your dad and I really love Jamie, you know? Perfect son-in-law material.'

I laugh. 'Don't go buying a hat just yet, but you're right, he is.'

'We're so glad you're finally settling down.'

'I'm only twenty-eight, Mum.'

'Well, I was married with a two-year-old and you in my tummy by then.'

'Really? You've never told me.'

I can just imagine Mum rolling her eyes. 'Yes, ha ha.

Anyway, what I mean is that we are glad that you've finally found someone who looks after you, who makes you happy. After the heartache, I mean – before you get all uppity about it.'

I feel myself soften. 'Thank you. I'm glad too.'

'So when do we get to see the new place? The pictures online look amazing. That garden.'

'I know. Lovely, isn't it?'

'Perfect size. Plenty of room for entertaining even with the trampoline in it.'

'Well, we won't be having a trampoline, of course.'

'Maybe not now.'

I lean my head back on the sofa. Why does it always come to this? I always pretend (to others, to myself even) that Mum's opinion doesn't bother me, but secretly I'm always waiting for her to turn around and say she's proud of me. That maybe she can't relate, but that she respects me, my life choices. But it feels like I will always disappoint, like because of my choices she will always love Amy more.

'Let's not have this conversation, Mum. It's a day to celebrate, yes?'

'Do you want to die alone?'

It's always her trump card. 'Seriously, Mum. Is that all you've got? How about, "Do you realize your life has no purpose?" If we were religious perhaps you could try the "You're going against God's will." Or just the simple, "Are you a cold-hearted monster?"'

'Stop it, Lucy. You know that's not what I'm saying. But if you had kids then you would understand how I feel. It's a mother's job to protect their children, to ensure they are happy and content before you leave this world.'

'Mum.'

'I won't be here forever, darling. And I want to know you have your own family around to care for you. I don't want you to wake up in ten years regretting a decision you made when you were too young to really understand the consequences.'

'So now I'm too young? I thought I was getting old?'

'Don't twist my words.'

'I'm not.'

'Look, I rang you to offer our congratulations, not to fall out with you.'

'So just be happy for me, Mum. Please.' I can hear my dad in the background, probably telling her to go easy on me.

'I am happy for you. But you can't be mad at me for caring about you. For not being able to sit back and watch you make a catastrophic mistake.'

I suck in a deep breath and let it out noisily. 'Bye, Mum.'

'Just give our love to Jamie, will you?'

If it didn't hurt so much, it'd almost be funny that Jamie has taken on the role of the hero and I the villain.

'Will do.'

I put down the phone, pour myself a glass of rosé and go upstairs to put my best dress on. We're taking Lauren and Otto to the cinema tonight so that Amy and Dave can have a rare night out together, and I'm entirely overdressed, but I'm determined not to let my mum ruin my celebratory mood. I don't often look in the mirror and like what I see, but this evening I'm looking pretty good. I'm going to go out with my gorgeous boyfriend who loves me for me and have fun with my wonderful niece and nephew. So I brush my mum's disappointment off – before it has time to infiltrate my bones.

We get our tickets and then take the kids to the pick and mix counter.

'Right, go and get yourselves a bag each.'

'Mummy makes us share,' Lauren says, too honest for her own good.

'Ah, but tonight we're celebrating Aunty Lucy selling her house, so it's allowed,' I say, my hands on her shoulders.

Lauren smiles but looks a bit nervous, but Otto jumps right in, grabbing a bag and starting to fill it with multiple forms of sugar. Jamie goes with them, discussing the merits of the different sweets and putting in a few chocolate mice for us, and soon their bags are full.

'Right. Slushies as well?' Jamie says. 'We are celebrating after all.'

The kids start jiggling with excitement.

'Yes, please,' Otto says and I imagine how proud Amy would be of their manners. They're great kids. She's done an amazing job with them.

In the waiting area, there's a cardboard cut-out of the brightly coloured monsters from the film we're going to see, the type where the faces are removed, so after we've got our drinks, Jamie hurries over and puts his face in one of the holes, sticking his tongue out and going cross-eyed.

Otto giggles. 'Uncle Jamie looks silly.'

I look at him now moving along to the next monster and giving that one a cross face. 'Yes, he is very silly, isn't he?'

'Come on, you lot. Come and be the other monsters.'

The children run over, Lauren just tall enough to be the smallest monster, and Jamie lifts Otto up to one of the others and they both try to copy the face Jamie did, tongues stuck out and eyebrows hilariously wiggly as they try and fail to go cross-eyed. I take a photo and send it to Amy.

'Come on then, crazy kids. Let's go and see this film.'

The film is very juvenile, lots of slapstick humour, but the kids laugh so hard that it makes us laugh too. At the mildly scary bit, Lauren climbs into my lap and Otto into Jamie's and I use Lauren's hands to cover my eyes and Jamie stands Otto on his knees to use as a human shield.

'Don't be scared,' Otto says, sitting back down on Jamie's knee and putting his hand on his cheek. 'I'll 'tect you.'

Jamie pauses and then kisses the top of Otto's head with a tenderness that makes my heart hurt a little bit.

The children stay on our laps for the rest of the film and demolish their sweets (I keep stealing them out of Lauren's bag, her playfully slapping me away). And then the film finishes and we walk back to the car, Lauren telling us all her favourite bits and Otto stumbling along sleepily holding Jamie's hand. Halfway there, Jamie picks him up and carries him, Otto's head resting on Jamie's shoulder.

Back at the house, we let ourselves in and take them straight up to bed, since Amy and Dave won't be back until late. It takes about forty minutes to get them into their pyjamas and to brush their teeth because they want to show us all their new things – Otto getting a new lease of life now he's home – and neither of us have the heart to say no.

In bed, they can't stop talking about the film.

'It was funny when the monster did a poo in the dog basket,' Otto says, giggling.

'Yes, it *was* funny, wasn't it?' I say, stroking his hair.

'Once Daddy did a poo and it was *so* big it blocked the toilet,' Otto continues, using his hands to show us how big the poo was (the size of an anaconda, apparently).

Jamie and I laugh.

'You're not supposed to tell them things like that,' Lauren says, shaking her head in dismay like she's twenty-seven rather than seven.

'Don't worry, we won't tell him,' Jamie says, putting his fingers to his lips. Otto smiles, putting his fingers to his lips too.

'Right, you two. Sleepy time. We'll just be downstairs if you need us.'

We give them both kisses and cuddles then turn their nightlight on and the big light off and go downstairs.

'Beer?' I offer, getting a bottle of rosé out of the fridge and pouring myself a glass.

'Yeah, thanks.'

I grab him a bottle, open it and pass it to him and we sit on the sofa and browse the TV menu.

'So have you heard any more about our offer?' I ask Jamie. 'They're taking a long time thinking about it.'

'Oh, I haven't made it yet.' Jamie doesn't meet my eye, taking a swig of beer from his bottle.

'I thought you were going to do it straight away.'

'I've just been working out the figures. And work's been manic. I've not had a chance.'

I nod. He presses play on some crime drama as if to signal that that is the end of the conversation, and I try my hardest not to read too much into it.

Later in bed I stare at Jamie's muscular back, wondering if he's asleep, wondering how long I can continue to pretend that there's nothing bothering me.

'Why haven't you put in an offer on the house?' I say to the back of his head.

'I told you,' he says sleepily. 'I've been really busy at work and trying to look at the figures in more detail, to make sure we go in with the right price.'

I know there's more to it than that and that I need to find a way to bring up what's been worrying me.

'I fell out with my mum earlier.'

'Oh, how come?'

'She was trying to scare me into changing my mind about having kids. Asking if I wanted to die alone.'

I laugh, but Jamie doesn't. Instead, he takes a deep breath.

'Do you ever wonder, with the kid thing, that perhaps

if you and your mum had a better relationship, you might feel differently about it?'

I know he'd never have said something like that to my face and it feels like he's slapped me.

'No, I don't.'

I expect him to react to my curt reply by turning over and apologizing, but he stays still.

'But you clearly do?' I push.

He turns to face me now and I get the sense that he's trying to soften what he has to say. 'Our relationships with our parents can be responsible for a lot of things, you know?'

'And since when have you been a psychologist? You and your mum barely even look at each other, so what effect has that had on you?'

Jamie sighs and turns his back to me again. 'Let's just talk about this when you're feeling calmer.'

It's so patronizing and I'm so annoyed that I can't stop myself from sitting up and leaning over him so he has no choice but to look at me. 'No, let's talk about it now.'

He lies on his back, looking up at the ceiling wearily. 'I shouldn't have said anything. I didn't mean to upset you. But, yes, maybe my relationship with Mum has affected me in ways I don't understand.'

'But you know bugger all about mine and my mum's relationship.'

'Fine. Forget I even said anything. Let's just go to sleep.'

'Oh yeah, I can just go to sleep now that I know you're lying there thinking I'm a freak. Emotionally scarred from my relationship with my mother.'

'That's not what I'm saying. It's not what I think.'

'So what do you think, Jamie? Because it's obvious you've not been open with me since the wedding. I knew you'd been acting off but I kept telling myself it was just me being worried after letting my guard down. I should've trusted my instincts.'

'I've not been *off* with you. I've just been thinking, I guess.'

'Because you're not really sure about me?'

For the first time tonight, Jamie looks me in the eye and I'm surprised to see it's not defensiveness on his face, but a sort of anger. 'No, Luce. It's not that I'm not sure about you. I love you. I think I've made that pretty clear. But is it easy for me to say goodbye to the chance of ever having children? No. I'm sorry, but it's not.'

'So why don't you just leave me then? Find someone better, someone who wants the same as you?' I ask, tears threatening.

Jamie puts his hand on my cheek, his thumb softly stroking it. 'Because I know there's no one better than you. That's the problem. I've waited my whole life to find someone who makes me feel the way you do, so I'm fairly certain there would never be anyone who came close.'

'Only fairly certain?'

Jamie smiles.

'So what do we do, then? How do we get past this?'

'Well, what if . . .' Jamie pauses and I know that what he has to say is going to be something hurtful, because I can see how reticent he is to spit it out. 'Couldn't you reconsider it, for me? Think of what an amazing time we had with Lauren and Otto tonight.'

'That's not fair, Jamie. You can't guilt-trip me into having a child.'

'But you can guilt-trip me into *not* having one?'

I toss the covers off and search for some joggers and a T-shirt amongst the pile of clothes on my floor. Putting them on, I expect Jamie to apologize, to beg me to come back to bed, but he doesn't. He just turns away from me and pulls the cover up over his shoulders. So I storm out, slamming the door to make a point, and head down to the sofa, where I toss and turn for about thirty minutes, cold with only a thin throw to cover me. When I know there's no way I'm going to sleep, I stomp back up the stairs, ready to reignite the argument with Jamie, but when I open the bedroom door, I can hear him snoring and it drives me mad that he can just go to sleep. I'm tempted to throw something at him to wake him up, but instead I force myself to go back downstairs to the sofa.

I lie awake for hours, going over and over the argument in my head, thinking about what I *should* have said. It's probably about three in the morning by the time I finally drift off.

I wake up feeling groggy, noticing that it's very quiet. And when I go upstairs, Jamie has gone, the bed neatly made, despite the fact it's at least an hour earlier than he usually leaves for work.

Amy pours me a glass of wine and we take our drinks outside and sit on the patio.

'So, calmly, tell me what's happened.'

I called in sick to work this morning, feeling awful from the lack of sleep and the argument with Jamie, and when I arrived at Amy's, I stormed through the front door and demanded alcohol despite the fact it was only eleven o'clock. She didn't ask any questions, quickly rooting a bottle of rosé out.

'Jamie and I had a huge fight. Well, it wasn't even really a fight. He quite calmly told me that I'm broken and that perhaps I should examine why I don't want a baby. That maybe it's something to do with my 'fractured' relationship with Mum.'

Amy nods slowly, but rather than reassuring me that he's being completely unreasonable, she says, 'Have you ever examined it?'

'Have *you*?' I don't mean to shout it but I'm so sick of constantly being treated like there's something wrong with me. 'Have you ever examined why you *do* want them so much?'

Amy looks at her feet and shakes her head. 'No. I'm sorry.'

I take a deep breath. 'It's OK. I'm sorry for shouting.' I take a large sip of my wine. 'And for your information, not that I should have to explain . . .' I smile and Amy gives me an apologetic smile back. 'Yes, I've examined it. I feel like I've spent my entire life examining it. And it has nothing to do with my childhood or my relationship with Mum or Dad or you. I'm not emotionally scarred. I just don't have it in me. I don't feel broody when I see a baby. I don't feel an ache at the thought of not seeing my child graduate or get married. I feel an ache at the thought of not seeing the world and I don't want to compromise on that. I don't want to wait until my kids are grown up before I travel and I don't want to take them with me. I want to go to art galleries at the weekend, not kids' parties.'

Amy looks at me as if she thinks I'm missing something vital, like someone working through a maths problem but missing a critical step.

'You think I'm a selfish cow, don't you? That I'm immature and one day I'll grow up and regret it. That I'll curse present-day me.'

'No. It's not selfish. And I get it. You do have to make some huge sacrifices for kids and you're right, it's a totally different lifestyle. Travelling isn't the same and weekends aren't the same, but what about all the good bits? The rewarding stuff? Have you thought about that too? What you'd be missing out on?'

I nod. 'Sometimes I look at Lauren and Otto, the way they look at you, how much they love you, and I think how amazing it would be to be loved like that.' I feel tears catching in my throat and Amy reaches over and takes hold of my hand. 'But I know I would spend a lot of my time resenting them. And wouldn't that be more selfish? To have a child just to have someone who loved me that much, even though I don't want so much of what goes along with it?'

'Yeah, I guess it would. Maybe I was selfish to have mine. I mean, it's not the greatest of worlds I've brought them into, is it?'

I squeeze Amy's hand. 'You are *not* selfish. You are the most selfless mother I've ever known. You give everything to those kids.'

'But I do resent it sometimes. And sometimes I wish I could be me again, the old me.'

'Surely that's totally normal. Being a mum doesn't mean you stop being human.'

Amy runs her hand through her hair. She's so pretty. I don't think she has any idea how pretty she is. 'Anyway, we're not supposed to be focusing on me. We're supposed to be sorting you and Jamie.'

'I'm not sure there is any sorting it. Perhaps I should just end it.'

'No. It's his choice, Luce. You've been honest.'

'But I'm scared he might leave me.'

It takes me by surprise but I suddenly burst into tears, my body shaking with the force of it. And Amy wraps her arms around me and holds me.

'I'm sorry for not understanding before,' she says, stroking my hair. 'You're so brave, and beautiful and self-*less*. I'm proud of you for not just following the crowd when it's not right for you.'

'Thank you.' I lean into her, enjoying the comfort of her arms and her words and feeling immediately stronger. And I realize that, however devastated I might be to lose him, if Jamie can't accept me as I am then he's just not right for me after all.

JAMIE

I feel bad for walking out of Lucy's place this morning without waking her up to say goodbye. It was a coward's excuse – that she was asleep – because I'm sure she felt like I'd abandoned her. And yet I just felt angry, that it was me making all the sacrifices, asking myself all the questions, whereas she just lay there, stubborn in her conviction. If I had woken her this morning, I'm not sure it would've helped, that either of us would've had anything useful to say to each other. But at the same time we have to overcome this stalemate one way or another.

I know I'm not being a good work colleague today. In fact, I'm being decidedly crap. And I know that Matt thinks it too because he keeps bringing me coffee and chocolate as if he thinks it might wake me up a bit and then looking a little dismayed when it doesn't work.

'Do we need a pub lunch?' Matt says, after I've been absent-mindedly staring at my screen and doing very little typing for at least an hour.

'Um, I don't know, I don't think so . . .'

I can't even answer this simple question coherently.

'Come on. It's on me.'

I don't need a lot of persuading and follow Matt out the office like a lamb following a shepherd. The pub is packed, mostly men in suits, and we struggle to find a table, but eventually spot a small one in the corner and I swoop in on it whilst Matt gets us a beer and two menus.

When he joins me, we both take a sip of our beers before starting a conversation.

'Let me guess, Lucy's realized what a total waste of space you are and decided she doesn't want to move in with you after all?'

'Not quite.'

'Well, it's definitely woman trouble. I can tell that a mile off.'

'How?'

'I don't know. Us men get a certain look when we've got woman trouble, a sort of sad-dog look, and you've had it all day.'

I laugh. 'I look like a sad dog?'

Matt laughs too. 'Yeah. Yeah, you do.'

I sigh, scanning the menu. I'm not sure why I'm even bothering to look. Whenever we come here, I always have the club sandwich and Matt has the ultimate burger. He might as well have ordered when he got the beers. 'Same as usual?' I ask, looking up at Matt, who nods. 'I'll go and order and then I'll tell you all about my woes.'

I order our food, having a quick chat with the barman, Ben, who we've sort of become friends with over the years, and then return to Matt, who looks at me as if to say 'spit it out'.

'All right, all right. Just let me sit down, will you?' I position myself back on the stool. 'It's Lucy. She doesn't want kids.'

It somehow manages to sound trivial as I say it.

'And you do?' Matt looks surprised. 'You've not even moved into the new house yet.'

I shake my head. 'I don't mean right now. She never wants kids. She thought it was only fair to tell me before we buy a place together and stuff. I mean, neither of us want to waste years on something that isn't going to last.'

'And she's one hundred percent sure?'

I nod.

'And you're one hundred percent sure you do want them?'

I nod again.

'I see. Tricky.'

'Exactly.'

We take elongated sips of our beer, as if the dilemma requires both time and alcohol.

'I don't know what to say,' Matt says, putting his beer back on the table. 'Something trite like "follow your heart"?'

'Super helpful, thanks, mate.'

'OK. I suppose my advice would be, do you think you could potentially meet someone as great as Lucy, who you feel the same about, who also wants kids?'

I shrug. 'Sadly haven't got my fortune teller qualification.'

Ben brings over our food and places it in front of us. 'Enjoy, fellas.'

We both thank him and take it in turns to squirt ketchup on to our plates.

'Look, I get that you can't predict the future and I

might be totally wrong, but in my experience, there are very few people in life we really connect with. Take you and me, for example.'

I smile and raise my glass. 'Cheers, mate.'

'It's true though, isn't it? How many friends do you have that you *really* connect with? And in the same way, how many girls have you been with that make you truly happy, where you don't have that niggling doubt in the back of your head that the relationship just isn't quite right?'

I sigh. Because he's right. In my entire thirty-three years of life, I've had one other really great friend, a lad I grew up with, but even we drifted apart, and I've never felt this way about a girl before. I know that if I leave Lucy, there is a really high chance I'll never find anyone that makes me as happy. And it'd be just my luck to then find out that I was infertile anyway – that I threw her away for nothing.

'It's a valid point.'

Matt offers a sad smile. 'Doesn't make it any easier though, does it? I'm sorry. But for what it's worth, I think you guys could have a really fantastic life together, even without kids. Think what an amazing time you had on your holiday. You never would've tried half that stuff without Lucy. I think she's really good for you.'

'She is. And you're right. Kids aren't everything, are they?'

'You don't sound convinced.'

I tuck into my sandwich, avoiding having to respond. Then once I've finished my mouthful, I say, 'Is it OK if we change the subject now? I'm pretty exhausted with the whole thing to be honest.'

'Sure, but I'm here any time, yeah?'

'Thanks, mate.'

We change the subject to safer topics, to work, and TV, and mortgage deals, and actually it feels nice to just talk about something normal, to take a break from the weight of making a decision. But when I get back to work, I feel like crap again, utterly torn, and I wish I had one of Lucy's jokey messages to cheer me up. But, all day, there's nothing.

On the way home, I stop off at the cemetery. I don't come here very often. I sometimes feel guilty about that, like Dad might think I haven't got the time. But I just find it so unremittingly bleak. Talking to a man who will never reply. His headstone just one of so many others. But this evening, something has drawn me here and I sit down on the grass in front of Dad's grave, brushing some stray leaves off the stone.

There's no one around but I still won't talk aloud. I never do. I don't know why. It just feels odd. But I talk to Dad in my head and I imagine him answering, fairly sure I know exactly what he'd say.

Me: I met this girl.

Dad: Sounds ominous.

Me: I think she might be 'the one'.

Dad: If she's 'the one' there's no 'I think', son.

Me: Fair point. She *is* the one.

Dad: So why do you look like you just stepped in shit wearing your best shoes?

Me: Because I'm not sure whether I should stay with her.

Dad: Are you wrong in the head, boy? Look at me, you could wake up seemingly healthy one morning and be dead of a heart attack by the afternoon. Grab the girl with both hands and don't let her go, do you hear me?

Me: I hear you, Dad.

Dad: You better bloody do. I'm watching you, you know? And I'll haunt you in a really horrible way if you cock this up.

Me: Got it.

Dad: Miss you, son.

Me: Not as much as I miss you, Dad.

I don't bother to go home, picking up a burger from the McDonald's drive-through on the way to Lucy's. When she answers the door, she's wearing a tiger onesie and looks seriously cute.

'You discovered my terrible secret,' she says, looking down at her outfit. 'On days when I'm not seeing anyone, I come straight home from work and put my onesie on.'

'Don't worry. My one's a crocodile.'

'No, it's not.'

I smile. 'You're right. I don't have a onesie. But I definitely want one now.'

Lucy opens the door wider and I follow her in, slipping

off my shoes in the hallway. She's got the TV on and, as I get closer, I see a bag of Kettle Chips and a packet of giant chocolate buttons open on the coffee table.

'It's been a taxing day.' She gestures at her little cozy hive of relaxation.

'Can I join you?'

'Sure. But I'm watching re-runs of *Ally McBeal* so you might want to find something else to put on.'

'Sounds perfect to me.'

I snuggle up with her on the sofa, wrapping the throw around us, and we eat junk and watch nineties TV. Unlike the past few weeks, the atmosphere between us is relaxed, the elephant in the room seemingly having a day off and hanging out elsewhere. It's really nice for things to feel normal again, if only for a little while, and I don't want the episode to end because then we'll have to start up a conversation and I know it'll inevitably turn to our future together.

And I'm right. As soon as the episode finishes, Lucy sits up, moves out from under the throw and looks me straight in the eye. 'I know you might think that my decision not to have children is impulsive or that it's because I'm damaged . . .'

'I never said that.'

Lucy holds up her hand. 'Just let me finish.'

'OK.'

'The thing is I've thought about it *a lot*. In every slightly serious relationship you get into as an adult, it's there, this kind of lingering question in the background. When my sister and my friends from school started having children, it felt like I was asked the question on a weekly basis, even by people I barely knew. So, unlike the majority of people who just fall into having children, who never have to ask themselves the difficult questions I have – like my mum's lovely "Do you want to die alone?" – I've had to go through the sort of painful self-examination that only people who don't follow the norm have to do.'

'I wouldn't just be *falling* into having children. I wouldn't just be doing the done thing.'

'I'm not saying *you* would. I'm saying lots of people do. And that's not even my point. My point is I've asked myself *all* the questions, and of course there are things I'll be sad to miss out on, and no, actually, I don't want to die alone. But I hope that I won't. That the person I love might be there. And who's to say if I had a kid they wouldn't end up disowning me anyway?'

'I'm sure that wouldn't happen.'

Lucy shakes her head, as if whether it would or not is ultimately irrelevant. 'None of us can predict the future like that. There are no assurances either way. But, on balance, I see more pros to not having children than to having them. And if I had a child for you, or for my mum, or my sister, that wouldn't be fair on the poor child who didn't ask to be brought into the world. A child I didn't want. I can't do that. I *won't* do that.'

I know that I can't argue with her. That she's thought it through carefully. That her not wanting kids is not a reaction to a troubled past. Lucy is, in fact, perfectly whole as she is. Perhaps I'm the one with the character flaw, for not being complete as I am.

'I understand if you don't want to be with me,' she continues. 'It'll break my heart, but I will get it completely. But I don't want to go through life with you constantly questioning me or trying to persuade me or being distant with me. I don't want to spend our lives having this argument on and off. Accept me as I am or let me go.'

I run my hands through my hair. 'I could never let you go.' I think about Dad, our 'conversation', because although it was imagined, I know it's exactly what he would've said. 'If I have to choose, Lucy, then I choose you.'

'You're sure?'

As sad as I am to give up on my dream of having children, I know that women like Lucy do not come along very often and that I couldn't be happy without her.

'I'm sure.'

There are tears in Lucy's eyes and I can see from the relief on her face the toll all of this has been taking on her. She sits down beside me again and kisses me and a feeling of contentment settles in my chest and my stomach. There can be no more questions, no more 'what ifs' – I've got everything I need to make me happy right here.

'I'll put in an offer on the house first thing tomorrow morning.'

LUCY

We're extremely lucky – everything goes smoothly and a couple of months later we're finishing packing up the last box before moving in the morning. I'm utterly exhausted. Jamie has been amazing, gently encouraging me to throw out some of the stuff I really don't need to be hanging on to – I'm a hoarder, what can I say? – and being patient when I ask him to pack things into boxes that will only ever live in the loft, never to be seen again, but that I can't bring myself to get rid of.

We lie on the lounge floor – the room suddenly feeling huge now that all the furniture is pushed to the side ready to be loaded on to the van – and I notice the cracks in the ceiling like some sort of road map.

'You OK about leaving this place?' Jamie asks.

I look around. I love this house. I'll always love this house. My first real home of my own. The place it felt like I became a woman instead of a girl. And all day I've been fighting this sort of underlying nausea, a feeling of nostalgia, of this being a significant moment in my life. One that I will look back on when I'm older. But lying here with Jamie now I actually feel more excited than sad. Because it feels like the start of an amazing journey. And I'm definitely ready.

'Yeah. Can't wait to get into the new place tomorrow.'

Jamie reaches over for my hand. 'Me neither. Although I'm slightly nervous about where we're going to put all your stuff.'

'You know this is just the start of finding out all the irritating things we don't yet know about each other.'

'When I shave, I tip the hair down the sink and it blocks.'

I laugh, taking the baton. 'I leave my clothes all over the floor.'

'I knew that one.' Jamie smiles. 'I have a certain way of stacking the dishwasher and it *really* annoys me if people don't follow it.'

'I eat in bed and then find the crumbs there when I'm trying to sleep.'

'I have forty-three pairs of trainers.'

'I fart sometimes. I'm sorry, I think you need to be prepared. I've been able to keep it in up to now but I can't do that twenty-four/seven.'

Jamie really laughs at this and then, seconds later, he lets out the most enormous fart and we both collapse into giggles. 'God, I'm so glad you said that.'

I punch him in the ribs. 'Bloody hell, you stink.'

'I'm sorry. I do. But I'll bring you snacks home every day after work. And I'll buy you flowers at least once a month. I'll take the bins out. I'll cook for you. I'll bring you breakfast in bed every weekend.'

'Sounds like a fair trade-off.'

Jamie kisses me on the cheek and then stands up. 'I'm starving. Fish and chips?'

'We've packed away all the plates and cutlery.'

'I think now that we've reached the farting openly stage of our relationship, we can eat with our fingers in front of each other.'

'Go on then. And curry sauce for me, please.'

'Curry sauce with your fish and chips? That might be a deal breaker.'

'Bugger off. I'm starving now you've started talking about it.'

'OK, OK, I'll be back in five.'

We eat fish and chips out of the paper with our fingers.

'Want to sleep here tonight? On the living room floor?' I ask.

'Yeah, cool. It'll be like camping out.'

I search through the piles of stuff and find the one labelled 'camping stuff' then grab a sleeping bag from the top of the box, unzip it and lay it over us, noticing Jamie suddenly looks serious.

'What's up?'

'Nothing. Just reminds me of camping with my dad.'

Jamie smiles but I can see the loss in his eyes, how much he misses his dad, and I wish there was something I could do or say to make it better, but I know that I can't. I dread the day I lose one of my parents. I don't know how I'll ever bounce back. It seems unthinkable that the world could go on turning without them, however much my mum does my head in half the time.

'Would some sex make you feel marginally better?'

At first, Jamie lifts his head and looks at me in shock and I wonder if he thinks I'm horribly insensitive, but then his face breaks into a huge smile and he starts laughing. 'Definitely worth a try.'

So we make love on the final night in my first ever home. And then we fall asleep, cuddled up close under my sleeping bag, and all that's missing is a campfire and marshmallows.

JAMIE

Lucy has a lot of stuff. And I mean, a lot. I'm not saying she's quite ready to be featured in one of those hoarder documentaries where the person can't actually get through their door any more, but she's easily got five times as much stuff as me and I'm not sure all of it is particularly *necessary*. Luckily, the new place has a fairly big loft so some of her boxes go straight in there without us even re-opening them.

'You regretting moving in with me yet?' Lucy asks as I bring in yet another pile of boxes.

'Not for a second.'

Lucy smiles as she starts unpacking several trinkets and putting them on the fireplace. And it's true. Being here, surrounded by all the little bits of Lucy, things that show different facets of her personality, like the bold pop art print ready to be hung on the wall, the ornaments and ceramics she's picked up on her many travels, the ten thousand cushions for the sofa – it feels like home. The most anywhere has felt like home since Dad died.

I pick up one of her ornaments, a laughing Buddha statue. 'Where did you get this one?'

'Oh, I stayed in this meditation retreat in Thailand. It's supposed to bring good luck and happiness to the home.'

'And that?' I nod my head towards the ornate china elephant in her hand.

'India. I volunteered on a Women Empowerment project and one of the women gave me this as a thank you.'

'Is there anything you haven't done?'

Lucy smiles. 'Lots of things.'

'Well, I'm looking forward to doing them with you.'

'Me too.'

After unpacking one van full of boxes, I leave Lucy to organize (or not) and drive the van back to her old house to collect the heavy furniture, meeting Matt there.

'Thanks for offering to help, mate,' I say, getting out of the van, Matt waiting for me on the pavement.

'No worries. You did the same for me, after all.'

'I think there's a bit more stuff this time.'

Matt laughs. 'It can be my workout for the day. An excuse for a curry tonight.'

'Absolutely. And a few beers. I was going to ask if you guys wanted to join us, actually.'

'Well, if you're sure you don't want to celebrate just the two of you?'

'Not at all. Lucy said she'd love you and Mia to christen our first night with us. Make the most of finally having a dining room, although we might have to all squish around the table.'

'OK, thanks, sounds good. Suppose we better get to work, then.'

We load all the heavy furniture into the van – sofas, beds, bookcases, wardrobes – both of us covered in sweat by the time we've finished despite the fact it's November and bitterly cold outside. So I pop to the local shop and buy us two ice-cold beers, and we sit in the back of the van to drink them.

'So, look at us. All grown up,' Matt says, clinking his beer bottle against mine.

'How's it going? You and Mia living together without me getting in your way?'

'Well, I obviously miss you, mate, but it's great. In fact, I've got something to tell you.'

'What is it?'

'I asked Mia to marry me. And she said yes.'

'Ah, that's great, Matt.' I slap him on the back. 'I'm so happy for you guys.'

'Thanks, buddy. It'll be you next, I reckon. Can you imagine us both, entering the world of the smug marrieds?'

I laugh. 'Perhaps I should be more concerned that you're quoting Bridget Jones.'

'Perhaps I should be concerned that you *know* I'm quoting Bridget Jones?'

We both take another large swig of our beers. 'God, what happened to those two cool badass blokes we once were?'

Matt raises his eyebrows. 'Let's be honest, we've never been all that badass.'

'Speak for yourself.'

Matt smiles. 'My lasting memory of you will always be when you brought that girl home on New Year's Eve and she clearly just wanted a shag and you sat her down on the sofa with a glass of water because she was wasted and said "Shouldn't we get to know each other a bit more first?" and she just walked out laughing.'

'She barely knew her own name. I couldn't have slept with her.'

Matt looks suddenly earnest. 'I'm glad I met you, you know? It's not always easy to find other blokes who, you know . . .'

He trails off, struggling to find the words.

'I know. I'm glad I met you too, mate.'

'I was going to ask you later but now's probably as good a time as any. Will you be my best man?'

I'm surprised how touched I am. I mean, I'm not saying I'm about to start blubbering, but there's definitely something resembling a lump in my throat.

'Of course. I'd be honoured.'

We hug, but soon release. Even us two metrosexual modern men can only cope with so much affection at one time.

'Great. Mia will be pleased. You're definitely her favourite out of my mates.'

'She's a wise girl.' We finish our beers at the same time and I take his bottle off him and shove them both in the corner of the van. 'Right, I suppose we should get this show on the road. Who knows what state the kitchen cupboards will be in with Lucy left in charge.'

'Mr Organized and Mrs Disorganized. It's a match made in heaven.'

'Well, they say opposites attract, don't they?'

*

When we get back to the house, it's worse than I feared. Lucy's just shoved things in cupboards, on surfaces. There is no continuity, no logic. Utensils like peelers and graters do not belong in a cupboard, they belong in a drawer. And why oh why would you put some pans in one cupboard with plates and other pans in another cupboard with pasta?

'I've nearly done the kitchen,' she says, looking up at us from her position on the tiles, putting mugs into a floor cupboard rather than a wall cupboard next to the kettle. But she looks so proud of herself I haven't got the heart to tell her we need to start again. I'll have to come down in the middle of the night and hope she doesn't notice in the morning that I've moved everything around.

'Looks great. Well done.'

Matt looks at me and stifles a smile.

'Oh, and thanks so much for helping, Matt,' Lucy says to him. 'You and Mia will join us for take-out later, won't you?'

'Yeah, of course, sounds good. And no problem about helping. Jamie is always a legend when it comes to helping me out.'

'Yeah, he's a good 'un, isn't he?' Lucy smiles at me and, after the doubts I experienced a couple of months ago, it's great to finally feel sure that this is exactly where I should be.

We sit around Lucy's dining table, which looks tiny in our new kitchen/diner, a range of Indian dishes squeezed in the centre for us to help ourselves to. We all tuck in, trying out a range of different things, passing dishes round and tearing off pieces of naan bread. I'm starving. I'd forgotten how exhausting it is moving house, how much energy you use up.

'So I suppose we should do a toast. To the happy couple in their amazing new home. May you have many wonderful years here together.' Matt raises his bottle of lager and we all do the same, chinking them together.

'Thanks, mate. And to you two on your engagement.'

'Oh, when did you find out this, Jamie? You didn't tell me,' Lucy says, slapping my arm.

'Matt just asked me to be his best man, when we were packing the stuff up to bring over.'

'Oh, that's amazing,' Lucy beams. 'Congratulations, guys.'

We chink our bottles together again.

'And I hope you said yes, Jamie,' Mia says, looking over at me questioningly.

'Of course I did. Wouldn't miss it for the world.'

Mia puts her hand on top of mine. 'Good. I couldn't have chosen a better bloke myself.'

I smile. 'Thank you. I'll try not to lose the rings or anything.'

'You'll be awesome. I know it.'

'So have you set a date?' Lucy asks.

'Nothing set in stone yet, but we were thinking probably May next year, weren't we, Matt?'

Matt nods, his mouth full of naan bread.

'Pretty soon then?' Lucy says.

'Yeah, well, we've been together a *long* time so now that he's finally asked me, I want to get on with it really.'

'It hasn't been *that* long,' Matt chips in.

'Maybe it just feels like a long time being with you, darling,' Mia teases and Matt gives her an affectionate smile. 'It'll be you two next, I reckon.'

I glance over at Lucy, wondering if Mia's comment will have freaked her out. It feels like she's already made a huge step selling her house and buying a place together, as I know how much she loved it. But I'm surprised to see a relaxed smile on her face and it makes me really happy.

Neither of us respond, but there's nothing awkward about it, and the conversation turns to our plans for the house and garden, Lucy's dream of getting a hot tub (I'm going to surprise her with one for Christmas), and the venues Mia and Matt have been looking at for the wedding. The conversation flows easily – Lucy gets on brilliantly with my best friends – and it's the perfect start to our new life in our new home.

Later, once Matt and Mia have gone, Lucy takes my hand and we go upstairs to our bedroom, which so far is empty other than the mattress on the floor. And as we lie there, under the light of a full moon, I don't think I could be happier if I tried.

The Day of the Break-Up

JAMIE

The sun's peeking out from behind the clouds so I force myself up and out into the garden. Lucy always said she felt better outside. If she was feeling down, she'd go out in the garden and when she returned, her face would always be brighter. I never really got the whole 'feeling better in nature' thing until I met her, but now I do. It's almost immediate. You take in a breath of fresh air, feel the sun on your face and suddenly everything seems easier. Not easy by any means, but easier.

I go back inside to get myself a beer out of the fridge, making an exception to my usual 'don't drink in the day' rule. And then I think I hear a knock on the door but I'm not sure because of the sound of my beer clanking, so I pause, the bottle in my hand. This time it's a clear knock. No one ever knocks on our door uninvited. I'm not expecting any deliveries unless Lucy ordered something without me knowing, but I think she would've mentioned it when she left. My heart starts to race – could it be her? But then she has a key – would she knock?

I leave the kitchen, looking at the mirror as I walk through the lounge, straightening my hair – a ridiculous desire to look my best as if it might convince Lucy to come back to me – and then I go to the door, taking a deep breath before opening it.

When I see it's Mum and not Lucy standing there, at first I feel deflated, but then I realize Mum's exactly who I need to see.

'What are you doing here?' I ask, my voice weaker than expected.

'When I got your message, I was going to give you a call and then I thought, why not just come and see you. So here I am. I hope you don't mind.'

I open the door wider and usher Mum in. 'Of course not. I'm really glad to see you.'

We stand awkwardly in the hallway for a minute and then suddenly Mum pulls me into a hug.

'I'm so sorry, Jamie. I know how much you love her.'

I don't say anything for a moment, just enjoying the comfort of Mum's arms, but then I pull away.

'I'll be fine,' I say, leading her towards the kitchen.

'I know you will,' she says from behind me. 'But it's OK to admit defeat for a while. And let someone in, let them help you – even if it's not me, if it's Matt instead, or whoever. Don't always put on a brave face.'

'I won't. Thanks, Mum.'

She sits down at the dining table whilst I make a cup of tea.

'I wish I'd let people in . . . when your dad died, I mean. And when Thomas . . .'

I focus on the kettle and the two mugs in front of me.

'Foolish pride, hey?' she continues, and when I quickly glance back at her, she's looking straight at me with a sad smile on her face.

I finish making the cups of tea and take them over and sit opposite Mum at the table.

'I know you won't want to hear this, and I hope you won't take it the wrong way,' she says, wrapping her hands around the mug. 'But I think it's probably for the best. I'm not sure you ever would've got past it . . . what happened, I mean.'

I shrug, unsure what to say, whether she's right or wrong. All I know is right now I can't envisage any sort of future, let alone a happy one.

'I'm sorry. Maybe that's a horrible thing to say.'

I shake my head and then I let it fall into my hands. 'It just hurts, Mum. It really hurts.'

Mum shuffles her chair closer to mine and puts her arm around my shoulder. 'Oh, I know it does, love. I know it does.'

Before

LUCY

Living with Jamie is more than I could've hoped for. We've had a few silly arguments – over what colour to paint the door (I wanted bright, he wanted dull and we finally settled on a beachy blue although Jamie blankly refused to rename the house 'Driftwood Cottage' – *we live over a hundred miles away from the sea, Luce*), over those little face wipes I leave out everywhere (*there's this thing called a bin*), and the ridiculous rules Jamie has about where to put things in the dishwasher – but mostly it's been great. I'm surprised how much I like sharing my space with someone, how much joy it gives me when I get back from work and find him there, or wake up in the morning to see him beside me.

Our first Christmas together passes – Jamie thinks it's hilarious how many decorations I put up, including a large light-up reindeer outside the front door. We manage to share the time amicably between both our families, and Jamie gets me a hot tub (best present ever), blindfolding me and guiding me out to it on Christmas morning, all set up with glasses of champagne. We spend the week between Christmas and New Year watching Christmas films and eating mince pies, drinking mulled wine in the hot tub each evening and then making love in front of the fire. And it's the best Christmas that I can remember.

Tonight, it's New Year's Eve, and whereas we planned to spend the night with Matt and Mia (they're having a party at their place), I'm sitting on the toilet feeling like death warmed up. Unpleasant liquid has been leaving me from every orifice for the past two hours and the worst thing of all is that Jamie is here, seeing the whole thing. At first, I kept trying to lock myself in the toilet, to hide my disgustingness from him, but now I've given up. I feel that bad.

'Do you think I'm going to die?' I ask Jamie from my now-permanent position on the toilet, while he sits on the bathroom floor. When I caught myself in the mirror a few minutes ago, my skin was grey, my eyes sunken, so I know it's not a pretty sight. Or smell for that matter.

'No, I think you're going to survive.'

'Quick, close your eyes. I need to wipe before I'm sick.'

Jamie covers his eyes with his hands, whilst I clean myself up and flush and then turn my body and kneel by the toilet. As I start being sick, Jamie shuffles over and holds back my hair, like my mum did when I was a child. And I empty my insides into the toilet bowl, my head starting to spin.

'It's OK, I'm here,' Jamie says softly.

I should be mortified, but I feel so poorly that I'm just glad I'm not on my own.

Once it feels like my body is temporarily empty (I've

already been fooled several times thinking it was over), I try to stand up, but I'm so weak that my knees buckle and I fall back on to my bottom.

'Do you want me to carry you into the lounge?'

I shake my head. 'I'm too scared that I might poo myself.'

Jamie laughs. 'Shall I go and buy you some nappies?'

I hit him, but I'm so weak it's not much more than a flick. 'I feel so terrible.'

'I know. I'm sorry. Come here.' He moves back, crosses his legs, and guides my head into his lap. And as he strokes my hair, I feel my eyes getting heavy until I can no longer keep them open and I must fall asleep.

When I wake up, it takes me a few seconds to realize where I am, then I see I'm on the sofa. Jamie must have carried me through. He's sitting by my feet, watching something on the television.

When he sees I've woken up, he picks up the remote control and pauses it. 'Hey you, how are you feeling?'

'Empty.'

He smiles. 'Yeah, I can't imagine there's much left inside that stomach of yours.'

'What time is it now?'

'It's eight o'clock. You went flat out so I thought I'd move you somewhere more comfortable. Bloody hell, you're heavy when you're asleep though. I think I might've put my back out.'

'Sorry. You should've just dragged me by the ankles.' I put my hand on his and then realize it's probably not the most appealing prospect – my contaminated hand on his clean skin – so move it away. 'Thank you for looking after me.'

'No problem. Just getting in practice for when you're old and grey and incontinent.'

'You'll be old and grey before me, you know.'

'True.'

'I'm just going to put you in a home and go off and travel the world.'

'Wouldn't surprise me.'

'Seriously though, will you ever want to have sex with me again?'

'Well, it's not the first thing on my mind right at this minute, but I'm sure my desire for you will slowly trickle back.'

I know he's joking, but there's something infantilizing about being so ill and I feel insecure. Despite how wonderful Jamie has been, I wonder if he'll ever be able to look at me in the same way. 'Are you sure?'

Jamie turns to look at me more intently. 'Are you being serious?'

I shrug. 'I'd understand if it had put you off.'

'It's going to take a lot more than that to put me off you. You even look beautiful now, pale and gaunt.'

'I look like crap.' All of a sudden, I feel the first pangs of hunger, my stomach starting to grumble in a way that doesn't mean I'm about to be sick. 'You know, I think I might try and eat something.'

Jamie stands up. 'I'll get you some toast.'

He goes into the kitchen and comes back with a tray. 'Just go slowly. Let your stomach get used to it.'

I take a bite of toast and a sip of water, then put the tray down on the floor beside the sofa. 'I might just go to bed. I'm sorry. You should go to the party. I'll probably be asleep in about five minutes so it won't make any difference to me.'

'I don't want to go without you. And anyway, I like watching you sleep.' Jamie furrows his eyebrows. 'Sorry, did that sound really creepy and stalkerish?'

'A little bit,' I joke and then I sit up, swinging my legs off the sofa and gingerly standing up, Jamie helping me up the stairs as you would someone who's sprained an ankle. When we get to our room, I just about manage to brush my teeth – still feeling faint – and then take off my clothes and put on a big baggy T-shirt and climb into bed. Jamie strips down to his boxers and joins me, sitting up against the headboard with his laptop on his knee.

'Sleep tight. I hope you feel better in the morning. If you need anything, just ask, OK?'

I look up at him, wondering what I did to deserve someone so perfect.

'Thank you. And happy new year. I promise the rest of the year will be better than this.'

He bends down and kisses me on my forehead. 'I have no doubt about that. Happy new year.'

JAMIE

When I wake up, I leave Lucy asleep in bed and go to the supermarket to get a few things to cheer her up. Of course I wouldn't wish her ill, but I actually like looking after her. She's so independent, it's nice to feel she needs me sometimes.

I get the food bits first – croissants and fry-up ingredients for breakfast, a variety of treats in case she's got that 'after being sick hunger' thing you sometimes get – plus some fizzy drinks to settle her stomach.

Then I go to the home decoration aisles, deciding it's time to turn the spare room into a writing room for Lucy. I know she's too proud to ever suggest it, but what better time than New Year for her to start taking her writing seriously – and, hopefully, a proper space will help her to do that. I've already got my old desk to put up in there (the only item of furniture I held on to) so I search for bits to make it cosier – a plant, a candle, some cushions and a throw for a little armchair she's got that I can put in the corner (in case she sometimes prefers to write in comfort than at a desk). I also get her some notebooks and a new pen, and a bunch of flowers because, well, every room looks better with a vase of flowers in it. Finally, I buy a pin board so she has somewhere to put up her ideas and she's got a great print at home – this inspirational quote about follow-ing your dreams but written in an untrite way – so that can go up in there too. I'm really excited about surpris-ing her. It'll be just my luck that she's all bright-eyed and bushy-tailed when I get home and I won't get the chance.

Luckily, when I do get home, she's still asleep. I put all the things I've bought into the little bedroom and then close the door and go back into our room, standing there and watching her for a few minutes before she starts to stir.

'What time is it?' she asks, her words a little slurred.

'It's eleven. Would you like some breakfast? I got croissants and fry-up stuff, so your choice. Or I can just do toast if you don't feel up to anything more.'

'You've been out?'

'Well, I know I'm always starving the day after I've been sick, so I wanted to get a few nice bits in just in case.'

'You're a legend. A croissant would be amazing, thanks.'

'Nutella?'

'Of course.'

'Coming right up.'

I go downstairs to make her breakfast and then put it on a tray with a single flower from the bunch I bought to go in her room and take it up.

'Breakfast in bed, madam,' I say, handing her the tray.

'A flower too?'

'There's a whole bunch downstairs, by the way, not

just the one. I figured flowers always cheer a girl up, don't they?'

'I'm going to ignore my slightly feminist objections to your assumption because yes, they do cheer me up.'

'Sorry, what an awful chauvinist I am.'

'You're forgiven.' She starts stuffing her face with the croissant. 'Perfect amount of Nutella. Well done.'

'Glad to have passed the test.'

'I'm sorry it's been such a shit New Year. I'd love to say I feel well enough to do something together today, but I think it's going to be another day on the sofa for me. Feel free to go out and leave me to it.'

'It's OK. I might do a few bits around the house. Start to put up some shelves and stuff,' I say, preparing my cover story for the banging.

'OK, but only if you want to. I'm happy to help you when I feel better.'

'It's fine. I'm better doing DIY on my own, what with being so anal about accuracy and stuff.'

'Yeah, I remember the interesting "debate" we had about the frames.'

I laugh and go downstairs to set Lucy up a comfy haven on the sofa so that I can keep her away from the spare room then nip out to the shed to get my toolbox and sneak it up. When I go back into our room, Lucy has finished her croissant and is pulling on some joggers.

'I've set up the sofa for you. I haven't got a bell, but if you need anything just buzz my phone and your servant will appear.'

Lucy smiles, but then her eyes turn serious. 'I love you.'

'I love you too. Now go on. Go and get yourself settled.'

She gives me a kiss on the cheek and heads downstairs. Once I can hear that she's installed on the sofa with the TV on, I find the pieces of my old desk. After a lot of sweating and a fair bit of swearing, I manage to put it back together and then carry in Lucy's little armchair, complete with new cushions and throw, and put up her large print and new notice board on the wall, struggling to get the buggers straight. Then I place the plant and the candle I bought on the windowsill and put the notebook and the pen on the desk. It's looking pretty good but there's something missing. To make it really inviting, it needs a rug.

Creeping downstairs, I'm pleased to see that Lucy is asleep again so I rush out (leaving a note to say I just needed to go and grab something for work from Matt's) and pop out to get a little rug. There's not a great deal of choice, but I find one with brightly coloured dots that's in stock in Argos so I grab that and hurry home. I check the coast is clear first then grab the rug from the car and bundle it upstairs, my heart racing when it sounds like Lucy's stirring as I'm only halfway up the stairs. But, after a sigh and what sounds like Lucy turning over, all is quiet again – so I take the rug into her new writing room and lay it out on the floor. It's exactly the finishing touch it needed and I'm pretty chuffed with myself as I survey the finished project. Finally, I place the vase of flowers on the desk and it's done.

I go back downstairs, now desperate for Lucy to wake up so I can show her the surprise, but she's still fast asleep, so I take up residence at the end of the sofa by her feet. Roughly ten minutes pass before she starts to rouse, moaning first and then slowly opening her eyes.

'Hey you. What are you doing down here?'

'I just came to check you were still breathing.'

She stretches. 'Hopefully I'm not speaking too soon but I actually feel loads better. I think that sleep, and my croissant of course, were exactly what I needed.'

'Good. Do you want anything else? I could make you some lunch?'

She stands up. 'I'll give you a hand.'

We make bacon sandwiches and eat them at the dining table, the winter sunshine pouring through the patio doors.

'I'm not sure I'll ever get over this view,' Lucy says, sandwich raised to her mouth.

'No, it is pretty spectacular.' I take in the trees, the little stream trickling along.

'I'm so glad we decided to sell my house and go for this place.'

'Me too.'

'I mean, I still want to travel loads, but this place definitely makes me want to be home more often, you know?'

'Isn't that the perfect combination? When you travel to amazing places but are always happy to come home?'

'Yeah, I guess it is.'

We finish our sandwiches and push our plates away. 'How are you feeling now?'

'Almost as good as new.'

'Good. Then I want to show you something.'

I stand up and hold out my hand. Lucy takes it, albeit with a sceptical look on her face. 'Where are you taking me?'

'You'll see.' I lead her through the lounge and up the stairs, pausing when we reach the door of the spare room. 'So, I figured that every writer needs a writing room.'

I open the door and gesture for Lucy to go in first, which she does. When she turns back to look at me, there are tears in her eyes, and I feel that huge rush of contentment you get when you've made someone else happy.

'I can't believe you did this. Did you do it all whilst I was asleep?'

I nod.

'And you got me all this stuff?' She starts picking up all the individual items in turn.

'Well, you can't have a writing room without stationery.'

'Or a pot plant or a candle, of course.'

'They seem like essential writerly items.'

Lucy smiles.

'And I put the chair there in case sometimes you need a bit more comfort to produce your masterpiece.'

Lucy looks at the chair and then looks back at me. 'Come here.'

I walk towards her and she puts her arms around my neck and kisses me. And then it becomes more intense and somehow we end up naked. And afterwards, we just lie there on the new spotty rug, tangled up in each other's limbs.

'You know, I've never loved anyone as much as I love you,' I say to the top of Lucy's head.

'Me neither,' she says, just quietly, and it makes me so happy that I know, with a certainty I don't think I've felt about anything else in my life, that this is the person I want to spend the rest of my life with. And I wonder if I should just tell her, propose whilst we lie here on the rug in her new writing room, but as much as I want to ask her right now, before anything changes, I want to do it properly. She deserves the best, most romantic proposal there is. Which now just poses the problem: how can I give her that?

LUCY

It's weird, but having a writing room really does make a huge difference to my productivity. After averaging about a hundred words a month for the past couple of years, I'm now pumping out pages like Jilly Cooper. I look at my pot plant and smile, then check the time. I'm due to meet Mia in about half an hour. She's going to try on wedding dresses and, touchingly, she's invited me to go with her. But I'm desperate to finish this chapter before I go, the scene where the two protagonists *finally* get together after all the obstacles that have been stopping them. I type as if my life depends on it, then rush out the door with minutes to go.

We're due to meet at The White Room and, when I get there, Mia is standing outside waiting for me. After a hug, I follow her in. It's a small shop – really cosy – and the staff are warm and friendly.

'Welcome back, Mia. We've got all your choices ready for you. Do you both want a drink first? Bubbles?'

'That'd be lovely,' Mia says. 'This is my friend, Lucy.'

'Nice to meet you, Lucy. She's been stuck on these four dresses for a while – haven't you, Mia? – so hopefully you might be able to help her decide.'

'I'll try my best,' I say, suddenly feeling the pressure.

'You're definitely the most stylish person I know, so I

trust your judgement,' Mia says, putting her hand on my arm.

I wave away her compliment and then the shop assistant, Zoe, goes off to get us a glass of bubbly. She brings our drinks out on a tray, then we follow her through to a walk-in changing room where I sit on the sofa while Mia goes off with Zoe behind the curtain.

'Now, I want total honesty,' Mia calls through. 'No being polite.'

'Ask Jamie. I don't really do being polite.'

I hear Mia laughing behind the curtain. 'Good.'

I sip my champagne while Zoe helps Mia into her dress. Then, she steps out. And she looks so beautiful it unexpectedly makes me want to cry. The dress is simple, elegant, made of white lace, thin shoulder straps and a V-neckline. It accentuates every part of Mia's lovely figure.

'It's beautiful.' My voice breaks and I feel slightly ridiculous. I haven't even known Mia long and yet it feels like such an intimate moment, and I'm so happy for her. She and Matt are one of those couples who seem made for each other.

'You're not just saying that?'

I shake my head. 'It's perfect.'

'Well, wait until you see the others before you make your mind up.'

'OK, but I can't see how anything is going to compete with that one.'

The corners of Mia's mouth turn up and I wonder if it's her frontrunner too, but she doesn't say anything, heading back behind the curtain to change into the next dress.

She shows me the others one by one, and they're stunning too — she'd look great in anything — but for me nothing compares to the first dress.

Once she's tried them all on, Zoe tops up our drinks and then leaves us to relax on the sofa and discuss.

'You sure about dress number one?'

'Absolutely. No question.'

'Truth be told it was my favourite too, so I'm really glad you've confirmed it for me.'

'I'm so happy for you. Matt is going to be blown away when he sees you.'

Mia smiles. 'I hope so. We're definitely at the "very comfortable" stage of our relationship. Neither of us even bothers to close the bathroom door any more, and there's something lovely about that type of intimacy, but I just hope it means we don't stop fancying each other, you know?'

I nod, thinking back to Jamie holding my hair as I flooded the toilet bowl with vomit.

'So how about you and Jamie? How's it been living together?' she asks.

'It's been amazing. I keep waiting for the hitch, the arguments, keep thinking I'm going to discover he's got some awful secret, but he's just so lovely.'

Mia nods, her mouth full of champagne.

'I was poorly the other day and he looked after me so well,' I continue. 'No one's ever taken care of me like that. And then he surprised me by turning the little bedroom into a writing room. He'd thought of every detail. I couldn't believe it.'

'Oh, you've definitely got a good one there, Luce. He's always been my favourite of Matt's friends by far. Trust me, I've searched and there are no secret flaws.'

'I'm not used to it, being treated so well, you know?'

'It's easy to think it's too good to be true, isn't it?'

'Exactly. That's exactly it. How can I have got so lucky?'

'Well, you're stunning and fun and lovely. Of course Jamie was going to end up with someone like you.'

'Thank you. But I'm not sure that's true.'

'It is. And I'm glad he's found you. He's been through a lot. And he's always wanted a family.' She pauses. 'Somebody to love, I mean.'

From the way she so quickly backtracks, I can tell she knows my 'dirty' secret and I can't help wondering what she thinks about it.

'So he told you about the kids thing then?'

'Matt might've mentioned it.'

'Lucy, the freak.'

Mia shakes her head vehemently. 'Not at all. There's nothing wrong with not wanting children. Trust me, the friends I have who've got kids mostly look like crap and are always moaning about the lack of "me time".'

I force a smile but I know Mia's only trying to make me feel better. 'Bet you want them though, don't you?'

She gives me a sympathetic look and nods.

'Sometimes I worry Jamie's giving up something he's always wanted for me.'

Mia takes a deep breath. 'It's how I knew how much he loved you.'

Her words hang between us, making me feel sick. I finish my drink and put it on the side. 'Actually, I forgot. I promised I'd pick my niece and nephew up from school. I better go.'

Mia gives me this look and I know that she can tell I'm lying. 'Luce, I didn't mean to upset you. I'm sorry if I said the wrong thing.'

I shake my head. 'You didn't. I just need to go, otherwise there'll be two kids crying at the school gates and I'll be the world's worst aunty. Thank you for inviting me. The dress is perfect.'

'Thanks.' Mia gives me a sad smile and I leave hurriedly, Zoe the sales assistant giving me an odd look as I do.

On the way back to the car, I call Amy. As soon as she answers, I can't stop the tears from coming, the sound of her voice causing something in me to unblock.

'Luce, what is it, lovely? Why are you crying?'

I can't speak, tears falling with every step I take along the pavement.

'It's not Mum or Dad, is it?'

I shake my head but then realize that she can't see me. 'No, it's nothing like that,' I manage to splutter.

'So what is it, darling? Tell me.'

I walk past a bench, stop, turn around and go back to it, sitting down. 'I can't do it.'

'Do what?'

'Can't ruin Jamie's life.'

I can hear Amy sigh on the other end of the line. 'That's not what you're doing. He loves you.'

'I know he does. That's why I have to end it.'

Amy doesn't respond and I know that she agrees with me, even though she'd never say it.

'I'm just scared. What if I never find anyone who loves me like he does?'

'You will.'

'Look, I have to go. If I don't do it now, I never will. I'll call you tomorrow, OK? I love you.'

'Love you too, Sis. You will be OK, I promise.'

'Thanks.'

I put the phone down, wipe my face with my sleeve and head back to the car.

JAMIE

I've suddenly realized that choosing an engagement ring is actually really hard. I borrowed one of Lucy's rings from her jewellery box to get an idea of size, feeling really clever at my ingenious plan, until I arrived at the jeweller's and realized there's about a thousand different designs of engagement ring and I have no idea which one Lucy would go for as we've never had the engagement discussion. I should've waited until we'd walked past a few windows and she'd pointed some out, a subtle hint for me to get my act into gear. But instead I'm jumping on this crazy idea of mine that I have to make her my fiancée, right now. It can't wait.

The girl behind the counter is really sweet. I've described Lucy's style to her and she's pulled me out a selection of rings that she thinks Lucy might like and been very patient as I keep picking them up one at a time, putting them on the end of my little finger, holding my hand out and then placing them back on the counter.

'I'm sorry. I'm a bit of a nightmare customer.'

The girl shakes her head. 'Not at all. It's a huge decision. It has to be right. She might say no otherwise.' I must look terrified because she quickly adds, 'I was only joking. I'm sure she won't say no.'

Up until this point, I hadn't even considered that she

might turn me down. I was so wrapped up in how sure *I* was I didn't stop to think that she might not be sure about me. I try to shake the thought away and focus again on the rings.

'It might sound a bit cheesy, but if I were you, I'd go with your gut. Which one do you picture getting down on one knee and holding out? Which one do you picture her having on her finger for the rest of her life?'

I take a deep breath and then pick one of the rings up. It's unusual, vintage, with a large blue stone. I might be getting it horribly wrong; she might actually want a traditional ring with a huge diamond that she can show off. But that's not how I see her. That's not the sort of ring I picture her wearing.

'I'm going to go for this one.'

'Perfect. Let me check the size for you.'

I pull Lucy's ring out of my pocket and give it to her and she holds it up against the engagement ring. 'Would you believe it? It's the perfect size.'

'Meant to be.' I smile.

'Definitely.' She gets a box and a posh bag from underneath the counter and slots the ring inside before passing it to me and then typing in the amount into the card reader. I put my card in and tap in my pin number, starting to feel a little sick with nerves.

'Well, good luck. Please bring her in after you've proposed. I'd love to meet her and see the ring on her finger.'

'Thank you. I will do. That's if she says yes.'

'I'm sure she will.'

I leave the shop and go to the flower seller on the street to pick up a large bunch of pink peonies. Then I go to Starbucks, grab a cappuccino and sit with a pen and paper and start to write the clues for the treasure hunt I've planned for the proposal. I'm going to hide clues around the house and garden (a flower attached to each one) that eventually lead her to the place where I'll be waiting, on one knee, holding out the ring. As I'm trying to think up clues, I soon realize that I am not a poet and that rhyming is actually really tricky. If only I could ask Lucy, she'd probably come up with all sorts of great lines, but as it is, it's just me, so I come up with classics like 'We made love here after you'd been sick, luckily it didn't itch' and 'Here I made my spaghetti bolognaise, don't pretend you weren't amazed.'

Despite the fact it's freezing, I've decided to be waiting out in the garden – let's hope the rain stays off – surrounded by candles, a bit like our meal in the olive groves when we were in Spain. When I've finished all the clues and numbered them to make sure I get them in the right order, I put them into my pocket, finish my coffee and head home.

Lucy is sitting at the dining table with a glass of wine and when she sees me, she smiles but it doesn't reach her eyes and I'm suddenly terrified that my great plan is going to be thwarted by her being in a bad mood.

'Good day?' I ask, hoping she doesn't give me too long an answer. The clues in my pocket feel like they're burning a hole.

'I went to see Mia's wedding dress.'

'Oh yeah, how was it?'

'She looked amazing.'

'Oh great.' I pat my pockets as if I've lost something. 'Oh shit, I've left my phone in the car. You couldn't do me a favour and go and grab it for me, could you? I'm whacked tonight.'

She looks at me oddly and I worry she's going to tell me to sod off and do it myself (which would be completely justified), but I can't think of a better way to get her out the house. Luckily, she nods. 'Give me your keys then.'

'Thanks, you're a superstar.' I hand her my car keys, wait until I hear the door close and then rush around the house like a mad man, following my plan and depositing the clues in their hiding places, grabbing the flowers from my bag (a little squashed) to accompany them. I parked as far away as I could so I'm expecting an earful when Lucy returns, but I needed to buy myself as much time as possible.

I put the last clue in place just in time as I hear the front door open and close and Lucy returns, looking flustered. 'I can see why you didn't want to go.' She hands me my phone and my car keys.

'Yeah, sorry, I couldn't get a space any closer.'

'Well, there's loads now. Must have been a mass exodus after you arrived.'

'Must have been. Anyway, I just need to make a business call. I'll go out in the garden.'

Lucy furrows her eyebrows. 'OK, but I can be quiet, you know?'

'It's fine.' I pull the first clue out of my pocket. 'Just read this for me whilst I'm gone, will you?'

Lucy takes the piece of paper. 'Is everything OK?'

'Yeah, just wondered if you could check this for me. It's a work thing.'

'OK.' She begins to open it so I rush outside and pretend to start my phone call. It's quiet inside and I can feel my heart in my chest as I wait for Lucy to appear. I get all of our outdoor candles and put them in a circle, light them and then kneel down inside the circle.

It seems to take Lucy ages and I picture her reading the clues, hoping they're obvious enough for her to decipher. It turns out they must be, because after about ten minutes, she appears at the back door, tears in her eyes and all the flowers and clues in her hands.

She walks towards me and I take the ring box out of my pocket and open it, holding it out to her.

'Lucy Maddison, would you do me the honour of being my wife?'

She stops just outside the circle and I suddenly have this terrible feeling that she is about to say no and it's as much as I can do not to faint. My hand's shaking and I can see that Lucy sees it too.

'Are you sure you want to marry me?'

'What does it look like?'

Lucy moves towards me, bends down and takes my empty hand in hers. 'But I mean *really* sure. Even though it means no family. Just us, for the rest of our lives. It would be OK for you not to be sure about that. I'd still love you.'

I put the ring box on the grass and take her hands in both of mine. 'I'm sure. And I've *really* thought about it. I've pictured my future without you, with a family with someone else. And I've pictured it with you, getting old together, just us. And I *know* that the picture that makes me the happiest is the one with you in it. I wouldn't ask you to marry me if I wasn't completely certain, I promise.'

Lucy releases her hand, picks up the ring and examines it. 'How did you get it so right?'

'You're sure you like it? I can get you a different one if you'd prefer something else.'

Lucy shakes her head and slides it on to her finger. It looks beautiful and I can't stop the tears from welling up. 'It's perfect. This whole thing. It's more than I could have ever hoped for. And if you're really sure then of course I'll marry you.'

I grab her face in my hands and we kiss amongst the candlelight. And just as we do, I feel the first drop of rain fall on my head.

'Just in time.' I laugh.

And then she takes my hand and pulls me up as we run inside, the rain putting out the candles one by one.

The Day of the Break-Up

LUCY

It feels strange being at Amy's. She takes me to the spare room to unload my bag and then says she needs to go and do something with the kids, but I think she's just giving me some space.

After a while, she comes up with a glass of rosé in one hand and a cup of tea in the other.

'I wasn't sure which one you'd be in need of.'

I smile at her and she comes and joins me on the bed and I take the cup of tea out of her hand.

'Great. That means I get the wine,' she says, taking a sip. 'So, how are you holding up?'

'I don't know. Feels like my life's over, I guess.'

'Oh, Luce.' Amy rubs my back. And then she stands up and reaches into her back pocket, pulling out an envelope. 'I wasn't sure whether to give you this yet. I found it on the doormat earlier. I'm guessing it's from Jamie.'

She hands me the envelope and I look at my name on the front in Jamie's handwriting.

'Do you want me to leave you alone to open it?'

I shake my head and then open the envelope, finding my engagement ring inside. Taking it out, the familiar feel of it between my fingers, hurtles me right back to the day Jamie proposed to me.

'You know, when he gave me this, I really believed I could be all he needed.'

Amy brushes my hair off my face. 'And are you definitely sure you're not?'

I look at the ring, how totally perfect it is, how it made me feel so *known*. How it felt like he loved me completely, for all that I am.

'Not any more.'

I can't tell her what happened. I'm scared if I do she'll never look at me in the same way. Just like Jamie didn't.

'Look, obviously I'm not in your relationship and the last thing I want is to encourage you to do something that doesn't make you happy. But if you're leaving Jamie because you don't think he loves you as you are then I think you're wrong. When you were here last night, the way he looked at you . . .'

I shake my head. 'I don't know. It doesn't always feel like that.'

I open the envelope, dropping the ring back in, and that's when I notice there's a little note. I pull it out and read it.

This ring will always belong to you x

I feel tears in my throat and hand the note to Amy. She reads it and then looks me in the eyes. 'Go get him, Luce.'

I nod, pick up my car keys from the bedside table and head straight for my car.

Before

LUCY

'So you're getting married?'

'Yes.'

'Not splitting up?'

'No.'

'Explanation?'

I tuck my phone between my ear and my shoulder and open one of the boxes of books in the stockroom, taking out a couple of copies to put on the shop floor.

'I mean it's amazing news, don't get me wrong,' Amy continues. 'Just a bit of a shock after our last conversation.'

'I know. It's hard to explain.' I put the books on the floor and take my phone in my hand again. 'I guess I realized that Jamie doesn't feel like I'm ruining his life after all.' I laugh, despite it being the truth.

'Of course you're not. That's great, Luce. I'm really happy for you.'

'Thank you. I'm really happy for me too.'

'Who'd have thought it, hey? My little sister finally getting married.'

'Hey, less of the finally, thank you very much. I'm not even in my thirties yet, unlike some people.'

'Twenty-nine next week though. You're not that far off.'

'All right, all right. I know I'm getting old.'

'Well, I'll always be older so I can't really talk. But seriously, I think it's brilliant. You and Jamie are meant to be. I can't wait to start planning the wedding. Can we go abroad? Somewhere hot and exotic?'

I laugh. 'We haven't started discussing any of that stuff yet, but I'll keep you posted. A wedding abroad *would* be amazing.'

'I'm actually quite envious of you having it all ahead of you. I loved mine and Dave's wedding day.'

'It *was* an amazing day. You guys could always renew your vows, do it all again?'

'Yeah, I guess. I'm not sure the level of romance between us is quite what it was though. You'll discover that after eight years of marriage. Although you two will probably still be at it like rabbits without kids draining all the life out of you.'

'I'll try not to rub your nose in it.'

Amy laughs. 'Right, you. Get back to work. And congratulations.'

'Thanks, Sis. Love you.'

'Love you too.'

When I get home, Jamie has got us take-out so we eat it at our new dining table (big enough for a family of six) and then he reaches into his rucksack and pulls out several wedding magazines.

'Inspiration,' he says, passing them to me.

'Shall we peruse them in the hot tub?'

'Sure. You go and turn it on and I'll bring some wine.'

I go out and start up the hot tub and then nip inside to get my bikini on. It's freezing as I run outside and I can hear Jamie laughing at my squeals. Then he appears in his trunks, tiptoeing over the patio slabs as if they're hot coals.

'Ah,' he says, as he slides in beside me, putting the wine glasses in the drinks holders. 'That's better.'

I hold out a magazine and he dries his hands by running them through his hair and then takes it off me. 'I'm looking at dresses, which obviously you're not allowed to be privy to. You look for theme inspiration.'

'Ooh, are we having a theme?' Jamie teases.

'You know what I mean – the favours and the table names, et cetera – they have to have some kind of connection.'

'How about places you've travelled to? Each table could be decorated in the style of a particular country you've visited?'

'That's a really lovely suggestion. But it's supposed to be about both of us, not just me.'

'Well, they're all the places you're going to take me to. So it is sort of about us too.'

I put my magazine down on the side and lean over and kiss him. 'I love you.'

'You too.' Jamie takes a sip of his wine and then continues flicking through his magazine. 'So I guess you want to get married abroad?'

'What do *you* want?'

'I don't know. I quite like the idea of a barn, lots of candles, somewhere all the guests can camp over. But I'm easy really. As long as you're happy.'

'Your idea sounds perfect. I'll get looking.'

'Are you sure?'

I nod. 'I've never been as happy at home as I am with you, so it seems fitting that we have it near here.'

Jamie drops his magazine over the edge of the hot tub and shuffles over and puts his arm around me. 'I can't wait to spend the rest of my life with you, you know?'

I lean into him. 'Me neither.'

JAMIE

It's Lucy's birthday and, after watching *In Bruges* a couple of months ago and both saying how much we fancied visiting, I've surprised her with a romantic weekend away in the Belgian city. As soon as she got home from work yesterday, I told her to pack her case and drove her down to the airport, a chilled bottle of champagne and flute in the car. Part of the appeal is that she's never been here – finding somewhere she hasn't visited is not an easy task.

The B&B is lovely, possibly a bit too ostentatious – the bedroom is a deep red, a bit brothel-like – though the owner is really welcoming. But now we are lost. Pounding the cobbled streets, starving and ten minutes late for our dinner reservation at the fancy restaurant I wanted to surprise Lucy with.

'Why didn't you bring your phone?' Lucy asks as we cross over the same bridge for the third time. 'We could've used Google Maps.'

'I have a map,' I say holding up the now slightly crumpled piece of paper the B&B owner gave us. 'I was being considerate by leaving my phone at the B&B, so that it didn't disturb our dinner. Why is your phone always dead anyway?'

Lucy reaches into her pocket and checks her phone

again as if she thinks it will somehow have magically recharged itself. 'You're supposed to be the organized one.'

'I *am* organized. That's why I have a map. I can't help that the map is wrong.'

'The map is wrong?' Lucy says with a wry smile.

'Yep, according to this map it should be on the right at the end of this road.'

'You can keep saying that as many times as you want, but we've walked up this road about twenty thousand times now and it's definitely not on the right. Have you got the map the wrong way round or something?'

'I'm not a total dunce.'

'Are you sure?'

'Here you go.' I hold the map out to her. 'See if you can do any better.'

She takes it from me and examines it then walks a little further along to find a road name. 'This is St Jacob's Avenue not St Jacob's Street,' she announces in an unbearably superior tone.

'Surely that's the same thing?'

She doesn't respond as she continues to study the map and then marches over to me and holds it up, tapping on it with her finger. 'We're there, on St Jacob's *Avenue* and we need to be there,' she moves her finger several centimetres to the right. 'On St Jacob's *Street.*'

She looks so smug that I can't find it in me to apologize. 'Better get walking then, I suppose.'

When we finally arrive at the restaurant, Lucy turns to me as if to say, 'See, here it is, stupid,' and then waits for me outside the door. I catch up with her, hold open the door for her and then we go in and wait for a waiter or waitress to come over and seat us.

A girl comes over, asking for our booking in perfect English (is it that obvious we're English?) and I give her my name. She checks on her computer screen and then looks at her watch.

'I'm sorry, but your booking was for forty-five minutes ago. We no longer have the table.'

'We got lost,' I say, feeling flustered and aware my forehead is covered in a layer of sweat. 'Are there no other tables?'

'I'm sorry, sir, but no. This is the most popular restaurant in Bruges. We don't have spare tables and we have to stick to a strict schedule.'

I know how popular it is. That's why I booked it a bloody month and a half ago. 'But it's her birthday,' I say a little desperately and Lucy glares at me, clearly mortified.

The young girl shifts from foot to foot. 'I'm really sorry. There is nothing I can do.' She turns to Lucy. 'Happy birthday, madam.' Then she walks away to close down any further begging on my part.

Once we're outside, Lucy goes and sits on a nearby post and I wander over, shoulders slumped. 'I'm sorry I messed up your birthday.'

Lucy looks up. 'You didn't mess up my birthday. I'm in Bruges with you, I wouldn't exactly call that messed up.'

'It was an understandable mistake to make, wasn't it? St Jacob's Street and St Jacob's Avenue. It's a bit silly having two nearly identical-sounding roads two miles apart in the same city, don't you think?'

Lucy smiles. 'No. I still think you're stupid. But I love you anyway.'

'I love you too.'

'And thank you for booking the most popular restaurant in Bruges for me, even if we didn't end up eating there. It can't have been easy getting a table.'

'I booked it a month and a half ago.' I let my head fall.

Lucy stands up and puts her hands on my cheeks, lifting my face up to look at her. 'Thank you. Now come on, let's find somewhere else to eat before I collapse.'

We head back in the direction of the B&B, hoping we find somewhere to eat on the way, and luckily we spot an 'all you can eat' ribs place, which is buzzing, but manages to squeeze us in.

'Is it seriously all you can eat?' Lucy asks, her eyes gleaming.

'Seems that way. I guess there's only so many racks of ribs you can manage in one night. It's probably quite a clever sales concept.'

'Until I came along. I'll be able to keep going all night.'

I laugh. 'Looks like I found the perfect place for you after all.'

Lucy looks around. 'You really did. This *is* perfect. Thank you. I bet the other place would've been pretty-pictures-on-a-plate sort of food anyway. And ten times the price.'

The waiter brings over the beers we ordered – huge, boot-shaped glasses full to the top.

'Wow, you really did mean large,' I say and the barman laughs.

'Wait until you see the ribs,' he jokes and then he leaves and Lucy and I just about manage to lift our glasses long enough to clink them together.

'Happy birthday to my gorgeous fiancée.'

She smiles. 'Still sounds funny but I like it.'

'Me too.'

We eat and drink until we are so full we both have to unbutton our jeans and then stumble back to the B&B, getting lost again but this time we don't care, enjoying the elongated tour of Bruges' beautiful streets. When we're nearly back, we stop on one of the many bridges and hold hands, looking out over the canal.

'You know, you were right. This no-kids life's not half bad.'

Lucy leans up and kisses me. 'And this is only the beginning.'

LUCY

It's Valentine's Day, and Jamie is supposed to be taking me out for dinner in an hour. But as I stand in the shower, I feel like I might faint and find myself starting to cry – the tears mingling in with the water plummeting from the showerhead. I've been feeling awful for the past couple of weeks, pretty much since we got back from Bruges, and, me being me, have put myself six feet under. Because life couldn't possibly just be this wonderful, could it? I'm too happy therefore I must be dying. I wondered for a while if it was some sort of residual aftermath of the sickness bug I had at New Year, but I've felt fine in between, and when I started googling symptoms I decided it had to be some sort of cancer, probably ovarian as some kind of bitter punishment for never having children. I haven't mentioned anything to Jamie because I don't want to worry him, but at the same time keeping it a secret makes me feel horribly distant from him.

I really don't want to let him down tonight, as I'm fairly sure from the secretive way he's been acting that he's booked somewhere special, but at the same time the thought of eating a big meal is making my stomach churn. I just about manage to finish my shower, get out and look in the wardrobe for something nice to wear but soon find I have to sit down on the bed.

Whilst I'm sitting there, trying to force myself to get back up, Jamie appears at the door having just got back from work.

'You OK?'

I try to look as well as I can. 'Yeah, just trying to decide what to wear.'

'You look exhausted. You know, I can always cancel the reservation if you're not feeling up to it.'

'I look like crap, don't I?'

Jamie sits down on the bed beside me. 'Never.'

I feel another wave of nausea coming over me.

'You know how much I appreciate you booking somewhere special for tonight, don't you?'

'But you'd rather not go? Sorry, I did wonder whether you'd be on board with the whole Valentine's Day thing or see it as a load of commercial nonsense.'

I shake my head but quickly stop when it makes me feel even sicker. 'I promise it's not that. I'm just not feeling great.'

'Shall I go and cook you something instead? Something light like a chicken salad?'

'I'm not really hungry. I might just have a little lie-down. I'm sorry. First I ruined New Year and now Valentine's Day. I'm a terrible fiancée.'

What if I never make it to the wedding? What if I've got something terminal?

'Don't worry about tonight. But do you think perhaps you should go to the doctor? You've been off your food for quite a while and that's definitely not like you.' He's treading gently, neither of us wanting to voice our fears.

'Yeah, I'll book an appointment tomorrow.'

'Hopefully they can give you something to help.'

I nod. 'Feel free to go ahead and eat. If you leave me some, I'm sure I'll feel more like it after a little nap.'

'It's OK. I'll wait for you. It is Valentine's Day after all. I don't want to sit down there on my own.' He picks up my book from the bedside table. 'Do you want me to read to you for a bit? Help you sleep?'

God, he really *is* too good to be true. I must be dying.

'You don't have to.'

'I know I don't have to. I want to. Find out what rubbish it is you're filling your head with.'

I force a smile. 'Better than that crap *you* normally read.'

I shuffle up the bed and lay my head on the pillow and he opens the book and tucks the bookmark into the back. Then he starts reading and I close my eyes, letting the rhythm of his voice soothe me until I fall asleep.

'So you had a sickness bug at New Year?'

'Yeah, I thought maybe it was just something I'd eaten but it hasn't really gone away. Well, it did for a while. I felt fine for about a month. But the past couple of weeks the nausea seems to have come back. I've lost my appetite and normally I have a huge appetite.' I pause and laugh, but the doctor just looks at me with a serious expression and I worry he's preparing to tell me I only have weeks to live.

'Any other symptoms? Pain? Diarrhoea? Headaches? Problems urinating?'

'I've had headaches and I've been feeling really exhausted and quite bloated. None of the others.'

He nods, taking notes on his computer. 'Normal periods?'

'Well, I'm on the pill – Lybrel – so I don't get periods.'

'Oh right, OK.' He reaches into his drawer and hands me a urine specimen pot. 'Do you think you could squeeze me out a sample?'

'Yeah, sure, I'll try.' I smile again. I get the sense he's not the type of doctor you can have a joke with, but maybe it's just because he knows he's soon going to have to impart devastating news.

I take the pot and go to the toilets, producing a sample and then wrapping the bottle in tissue, ridiculously, to disguise my wee. Then I wash my hands and take it back to him.

He takes it, removes the tissue and places it in the bin and then he opens the lid and puts various test sticks into my urine, removing them and laying them down on a little tray. 'It's probably worth us doing some blood tests as well if this doesn't show anything up.'

'OK,' I say, feeling nervous at how seriously he's taking it. I was hoping he was going to say I was just being silly and send me packing.

He looks again at the test strips. 'So you're on Lybrel? Do you ever miss a pill?'

I shake my head. 'I'm religious about it. Take it at the same time each day.' It's always the first thing I do when I wake up, as soon as the alarm goes off. Even at the weekends, it's like my body clock automatically wakes me, the fear of delaying my pill by even a few hours causing me to stir.

'When you were sick, did you have diarrhoea too? Was it very violent?'

'Yes, I don't think there was a lot left inside by the end. Why?'

He holds up the test stick showing a dark red line next to a more faded one. 'You're pregnant. My guess would be you conceived around the time of your sickness bug, which would make you roughly eight weeks.'

Suddenly, the memory of Jamie and me having sex on the new rug in my writing room hits me, and I feel sick, even sicker than I was feeling when I came in. I've always been so careful. Why hadn't I thought this could happen?

'When you're very violently ill, you can expel all of the pill,' the doctor continues. 'So if you have sex close to that time, it can result in pregnancy.'

I nod, my voice lost somewhere.

'Forgive me if I'm reading the situation wrong, but I'm guessing this pregnancy isn't a particularly positive surprise?'

'I was on the pill, wasn't I?' He looks a little taken aback by my bluntness so I add, 'Sorry, no. I don't want children.'

He nods slowly. 'Well, there are plenty of options to consider. Abortion. Adoption. Is the father in the picture?'

'Yes.'

'Well, maybe book another appointment when you

leave. We can discuss things further once you've had a chance to talk to him about it.'

'Thank you.'

He smiles, but it feels like it's laced with pity and I imagine how stupid he must think I am. 'No problem.'

I take a detour on the way home, driving around the countryside just to give myself some breathing space, to avoid having to go back to the house and see Jamie. I know he'll be full of questions about my appointment and I just don't feel ready to tell him about the pregnancy, knowing he'll want to accompany me to the abortion clinic, to hold my hand, all the while thinking I'm a monster. I've always wondered whether, if I did somehow accidentally fall pregnant, I'd feel any sort of bond with the being growing inside of me, whether it would change my perspective on things. But it doesn't feel real. Even feeling so poorly doesn't fill me with any sense of reality. If anything, I just want to remove it, to go back to feeling normal again. Part of me wonders if it'd be easier to just drive to the clinic now, beg someone to get it over and done with. Does Jamie really have to know? Wouldn't it just hurt him?

I drive around for a little longer, my music blaring out of the car speakers. For a while, I imagine I'm eighteen again, cruising around in my first car singing at the top of my voice and feeling on top of the world with my new-found freedom. But then it dawns on me that I can't avoid going home forever – Jamie will be getting worried. So I turn the car round, stopping off at a Tesco

Metro to buy a cheap pregnancy test, just to be sure, hoping beyond hope that the result in the doctor's office was a false positive. It must happen sometimes. Nothing is one hundred percent accurate. At the checkout, I hide the box under a loaf of bread in case anyone I know sees me, and then throw it in the car before removing all the packaging and shoving one of the tests in my pocket, hiding the other one in the glove compartment.

Jamie is already home when I get there and when I appear in the kitchen, I can see he's trying to play it cool but that he's desperate to know how it went at the doctor's. I decide to put him out of his misery before he asks.

'Some kind of strange bacteria in my stomach, it turns out. He told me the proper name for it but I can't remember. Anyway, he's given me antibiotics.' I can't look him in the eye so instead I dump the loaf of bread on the worktop and focus on pouring myself a glass of water.

'Oh, that's great. I mean, not that you've got an infection, but that it's an easy solution. Do you need me to go to the pharmacy for you and get your prescription?'

'Oh no, I left it in the car. I'll grab it later. Have to space them out every twelve hours so might as well wait until bedtime to take one now.'

Jamie comes up beside me, puts his arms around my waist and kisses my cheek. 'I'm so glad. I've been worried about you.'

'Yeah, me too.' I down the water, hoping to fill my bladder again so that I can do another test. 'I'm just going to go and have a shower actually. I've been a bit hot at work today.'

Jamie furrows his eyebrows. 'It's been raining all day. It's freezing out there.'

'I think it must be the infection giving me a bit of a temperature or something.'

'Yeah, probably,' Jamie says, but I can tell that he knows something's not right with me. That's the problem when you become as close as we have. The other person can sense the little shifts in your mood, when you're preoccupied, or not quite present.

'Do you want me to cook anything for dinner or are you still not feeling up to it?'

I've got this strange mix of starvation and nausea in my throat, but I'm really not sure what I could stomach. 'Don't worry. I'll come and make something in a bit. I'll probably just have a little snack, so feel free to get yourself something.'

'OK. Will do.'

I leave Jamie and go upstairs to our en suite, turning the shower on and then taking the pregnancy test out of my pocket, opening it and sitting on the toilet. Thankfully, the glass of water enables me to squeeze out enough wee to cover the stick for the suggested ten seconds, then I put the cap on and place it on the side. I'm not really going to have a shower. Jamie's right. I've been shivering all bloody day. I just wanted to buy myself enough time to do the test and be alone for a bit.

The pack says it can take about five minutes for a result to appear but my second line is there in seconds, blazing up at me. And it makes me surprisingly angry. I've taken my pill religiously since the day I started having sex. I've often used condoms as well, like putting a brick wall up against the sperm. A big fat 'no entry' sign. How could this have happened? That stupid bloody stomach bug.

I turn off the shower, open the en-suite door to check Jamie isn't in the bedroom and then sneak the pregnancy test into my bedside table drawer, hiding it under all the other crap I keep in there. Then I pretend to be drying off and getting dressed (instead I stare at the wall in despair) before heading downstairs to make myself some cheese on toast, the only thing that doesn't turn my stomach when I think of eating it.

JAMIE

I reckon Lucy is either dying or having an affair. I'm not sure which would be worse. I know that maybe I'm a bit sick in the head that her dying isn't automatically the worst outcome I can imagine, but at least that way it wouldn't be a betrayal. I could go through life knowing that I wasn't a total fool for believing that she loved me as much as I loved her. If she's having an affair then everything I'm basing my life on is a lie.

Evidence that she's dying: she feels poorly all the time, she looks exhausted and is constantly sleeping, I've seen no evidence of the antibiotics she supposedly got from the doctor last week and she doesn't seem to be getting any better.

Evidence that she's having an affair: showering when she got back from the 'doctor' with the terrible excuse that she'd been hot on what was probably the coldest day of the year. She *never* has a shower as soon as she gets home, even when she's been to an exercise class and is dripping with sweat. She waits until before she goes to bed as she says it's pointless putting clean clothes on when it's near the end of the day. Also, she can't look me in the eye, and I think if she really *was* dying, she'd break down and want me to comfort her, whereas she just seems to be avoiding my affection at all costs.

Like now. A Sunday morning and she's gone out for a 'walk' on her own. She never goes out for a walk on her own. She never goes out on a Sunday morning full stop. Sunday mornings are our time to lounge in bed, me bringing her breakfast, drifting in and out of sleep. Sometimes we'll have sex or she'll do some writing on her laptop and I'll surf random articles on the web. But today she was off like a shot at about nine o'clock, saying she thought the fresh air would help with her recovery, and when I offered to join her, she added the excuse that she needed the time to try to solve a tricky plot point in her novel.

So, like a terrible jealous and possessive boyfriend, I am searching the house for some kind of clue, some evidence for why Lucy's suddenly undergone a personality transplant, why the person I felt so very close to has become so painfully distant. I take her car keys off the hook and go out to her car, searching in the door pockets and under the seats, but there are only cereal bar wrappers, receipts and a random mass of biros. I'm not sure what I think I'm going to find, what would serve as incriminating evidence, but I'm just hoping for something. *Anything.* I'm just about to admit defeat when, I'm not sure why, but a word on one of the receipts jumps out at me and I feel sick to my stomach. I pick it up and read the two items, a loaf of bread and a pack of two pregnancy tests. The night she came back from the doctor, she'd had a loaf of bread in her hands. I check the date on the receipt, and sure enough, it's the date of her appointment. I look in the glove compartment, wondering if she might have hidden something in there, and there it is, the pregnancy test box. Inside, there's one unused test and the empty packet of another.

I run back inside and search the bathroom bin in case there's a used test in there – nothing. Then I look in Lucy's underwear drawer (isn't that where people hide things?). It's a mess, so I rifle through but there's nothing there either. Then I search in her bedside table drawer, pushing the overflowing junk aside frantically, and that's when I see it, upside down. Feeling nervous, I pick it up and turn it over, and am faced by two lines, one of them so dark it looks like someone's drawn it on with felt tip. I've seen enough pregnancy test adverts to know what it means.

The time seems to pass tortoise-slow until I hear the door open and shut downstairs. I put the pregnancy test back in her drawer and go down to greet her in the lounge.

'Feel better now?'

'Much. Thank you. And I might have solved the tricky plot point too. Double win.'

'Great.' I say it with absolutely no enthusiasm and I can tell by Lucy's face that she knows something's up. She suddenly looks nervous and it confirms for me that she has been purposefully lying to me all week, especially as she doesn't ask 'What's up?' Instead she says, 'I think I'm going to go and get my ideas down before I forget.'

'You don't want to say anything to me before you go?'

Lucy furrows her eyebrows, but I can tell it's in pretence. 'Like what?'

'I don't know. There's nothing happening in your life, in *our* life, that you feel you need to tell me?'

This stops her in her tracks and she goes over to sit down on the sofa and gestures for me to sit next to her. I do, but at a distance.

'How did you find out?'

'Find out what exactly?' I know I'm being a bit of an arsehole but I'm just so angry that she's been deceiving me about something so important.

'Have you been searching my stuff?' Of course she's trying to flip this so that she's the victim, but I won't let her.

'You've been acting really weird for days. I thought you were *dying*, Luce. I was worried about you.'

'So you invaded my privacy? Looked through my things?'

'Lucy, you're *pregnant*. And you didn't tell me.'

'I was waiting for the right time. I just wanted to get my head around it.'

'And when exactly was that going to be? What about *me* getting *my* head around it? That's if it's even mine? Have you been keeping it from me because it's Jude's?'

'Are you serious? Of course it's bloody yours. I'm not a cheat.'

'Just a liar.' I know it's harsh but I'm such a ball of emotions I can't help it.

'No. I'm not a liar either.' She looks like she's about to cry and I feel immediately guilty. 'I just needed some time. It's my body, you know?'

'But it's *my* baby. *Our* baby, Lucy. Did you not think I had a right to know?'

She puts her head in her hands. 'Of course you have a right to know and I was going to tell you. I just knew what your response would be and I wanted to tell you at the right time, to figure out how to hurt you the least.'

'What do you mean by that?'

'Well, obviously I'm not keeping it. So I wanted to sort out all the technical stuff first. To find out how it all works.'

'How *what* works? An abortion? I think it's fairly straightforward, Lucy. You just kill our baby.' When she doesn't speak, I can't help but continue. 'You were going to get rid of our baby and not even tell me, weren't you?'

Lucy shakes her head, but I get the sense that's exactly what she's been considering. 'Of course not. I just wanted to get a plan in place. So I could tell you more when I had it sorted.'

'So I don't get a say in this plan?'

She gives me a condescending look and it pisses me off. 'We agreed to not having children, Jamie. It's not like I haven't been clear with you about that.'

I clamp my teeth together and swallow hard. 'I agreed to not *trying* for a baby, Lucy. I didn't agree to killing our baby if we accidentally made one. Surely you see the difference?'

But as Lucy looks down at the floor and then back up at me, it's very clear that she doesn't. So I storm out of the house and get into my car.

At first I have no real idea where I'm heading, but then I find myself driving towards Matt's new place, pulling into the driveway and then walking down the path. It's Mia who answers the door, her hair wrapped in a towel.

'Hey, Jamie. You've literally just missed Matt. He's gone for a run. You OK?'

I shift uncomfortably from foot to foot. 'Yeah, sorry. I should've called. I'll go.'

'Don't be silly. Come in. I've just put the kettle on.'

I gesture to her hair. 'I didn't mean to disturb you.'

'Nonsense. I'd finished my bath. I was only going to sit and have a cuppa. It'll be nice to have the company.'

She sounds genuine enough and I realize that I can't face going home, and that actually Mia might be the perfect person to talk to. A female perspective. 'OK. If you're sure.'

'Of course.'

I follow her in and we go through to their lovely old country kitchen. I sit down at the round wooden table squished into the corner and Mia makes us tea and then brings it over with a jar full of biscuits, sitting down beside me.

'So I get the sense you weren't coming to see Matt to talk about work or football. I might not offer as good advice as him but I can give it a go if you want?'

I sigh, running my hand through my hair. 'Am I that transparent?'

Mia nods. 'Sorry.'

'It's Lucy. She's pregnant.' I come straight out with it, unable to hold the burden of it inside any longer.

'The fact you're not jumping up and down tells me it

wasn't planned? She hasn't had a huge change of heart about having children?'

'She didn't even tell me.'

'Well, when did she find out?'

'Last Monday. And she's just kept it to herself all this time. I'm not sure she was ever going to tell me. I found the test.'

Mia furrows her eyebrows. 'I'm sure she was going to tell you. Maybe she just needed a bit of time to get her head round it.'

'That's what she said.'

'Well, there you go then.'

I take a sip of my tea. It's still boiling and burns my mouth. 'She says she's not keeping it. That that is what we agreed and I don't get a say.'

Mia reaches over and puts her hand on top of mine. 'I'm sorry.'

'Can she even do that? Don't I have any rights?'

Mia shrugs. 'I'm not sure. I guess it's her body.'

'But it's my baby. It's part of me.' I feel like I'm about to cry so stop talking. I've known Mia for a long time and have grown very fond of her over the years, but I still don't feel comfortable breaking down in front of her.

'I know. I'm so sorry, Jamie. I don't know what to say.'

'There's nothing to say, is there? I can't exactly force her to have it. Like you said, she's the one that has to carry it.'

'But she should listen to your opinion too. It has to be a joint decision.'

I shake my head. 'But we will never ever agree on this. And she's right, I did agree to not having children for her. But *this*. After what happened with Thomas, I mean . . .'

Mia nods. 'I know. Does she know about what happened?'

I shake my head. 'I've never really found the right time to talk about it.'

'Maybe you should. It might help her understand your feelings about the whole thing.'

'Yeah, maybe. But what if she still wants to go ahead? I just don't know how she could do it. Could *you* do it?'

'I don't know. But I want children, Jamie, so I'm not a fair comparison.'

I sigh. 'I guess so. It just feels like it's a bit of us, you know? A part of her and a part of me. I don't know how I'm supposed to sit there and hold her hand whilst she destroys that.'

'I expect she'd understand if you couldn't face going with her.'

'I couldn't do that to her, make her go alone.'

Mia gives me a sad smile. 'You're one of the best blokes I know, Jamie, do you know that?'

I force a smile in return. 'I don't feel like it right now.'

Mia drinks some of her tea so I retry mine, which is now just the right temperature. Then she reaches into the biscuit jar and takes one out then holds the jar out to me. I hold up my hand to decline. I can't stomach anything. I'm not sure I'll ever feel like eating again.

'Do you want me to call Matt? I'm sure he wouldn't mind cutting his run short. He hates it anyway, but says he wants to get ripped for the wedding.' She rolls her eyes.

'No, it's OK. Actually, I should be getting back. I didn't exactly leave things on good terms with Lucy. Time to face the music and all that.'

'OK. Well, we're both here whenever you want to chat, you know that, don't you? And the spare room will always be reserved just for you.'

'Thank you.'

'We actually miss you sometimes. Can get a bit boring just the two of us.'

I smile. 'Tell Matt I said hi.'

'Will do.' She taps me on the arm and then seems to change her mind and pulls me into a hug. 'Tell her everything you feel, Jamie. Don't have any regrets from your side.'

I nod, give her a kiss on the cheek and head back to my car.

On the journey home, I think about what I'm going to say to Lucy. How to explain to her how much I want this baby, but as soon as I get through the door and Lucy looks up at me from her position on the sofa, I can tell by her eyes, the angle of her chin, her closed body language, that she's got her armour on and that any attempt at conversation is going to land badly.

'I'm going to go out and do some gardening.'

Lucy nods, her expression unchanging, so I head

towards the door, pausing for a moment and wondering whether I should stop and go and sit beside her, but then she stands up and stomps off upstairs so I go outside, grab a fork and start hacking away at the ground.

LUCY

'I have an appointment at the clinic next week if you would like it?'

'Next week? I didn't expect it to be so quick.'

The doctor gives me a sympathetic look. I expect it's well practised but it seems so genuine that I wonder whether he's been on my side of these decisions before. He certainly doesn't have the judgemental air you get from some health professionals with topics like this. 'There's one the following week too if you'd rather wait and think about it a bit more? I can organize a counsellor for you to see in the meantime if that would be something you might be interested in?'

I shake my head. 'It's not me, it's my boyfriend. My fiancé actually.' It now feels far too grown-up using that word and I wonder how I suddenly became an adult. I still don't feel ready. 'I'm sure about my decision. I don't need to talk about it. It's just he doesn't feel the same way.'

The doctor nods slowly. 'Ah, that's a tricky one. And unusual. Normally I have women in here being pressured into the decision by their partner, so I have to say I'm glad that's not the case here.'

'Except aren't I the one pressuring him into it?'

The doctor moves his head from side to side. 'You could look at it like that, I suppose. But for what it's worth, off the record of course, you seem like a sensible person. I get the feeling you've thought this decision through. That you're not just acting on impulse because a baby doesn't quite suit your lifestyle right now. That's very different from a lot of the people I see.'

It should be a comfort but I'm struggling to find any solace in what I'm planning to do. Although I'm totally certain about my decision, it's still so far from being easy. I know I will bear a lifelong emotional scar from terminating this baby.

'Thank you.'

'I'll book you the appointment for next week, provisionally. The earlier you do it, the easier it is physically. But go home and talk to your partner and if you need to cancel or postpone it, just give the surgery a call and I'll sort that out for you.'

'Thank you for being so kind to me. For not treating me like I'm evil like my partner does.'

He gives me a sympathetic smile and I pick up my bag and stand up.

As I put my hand on the door handle, he says, 'There are plenty of people who just have kids without even thinking about it, people who don't *really* want them if they actually thought about it. I spend a lot of my working life trying to help those children as they become adults.'

I nod, hoping he can see the gratitude on my face, and then leave and head back to work. Mandy keeps asking if I'm OK all day but I can't bear to tell her about what's going on with Jamie, especially as she thinks everything is so perfect. So I lose myself in mundane jobs like re-arranging the books on the table and stacking shelves. Although I really don't want to be here, I also don't want to go home, so when the clock strikes half-five and we're locking up, I feel a sinking in my stomach at the thought of facing Jamie.

When I get home, I'm glad he's not there yet and decide to cook him a curry. I'm not sure why; maybe I want him to see there are *some* good things about being with me. *Hey, I won't give you a baby but I can make a mean curry.* Or maybe it's just that I want it to feel like a normal evening, just this once, for things to be how they were before our little 'accident' ruined everything. I've had a wall up ever since he found the pregnancy test, which is probably not the best approach, but I haven't found the courage to allow myself to be vulnerable with him yet, scared of seeing the love slowly drain out of him whilst I sit there begging. But I know we can't carry on like this.

By the time Jamie gets back from work, the curry is nearly ready, just marinating in the pan, and when he comes into the kitchen he says, 'Smells good.' And I want to wrap my arms round him and never let him go. I want to hold on to this tiny moment of normality, of positivity, forever.

'You said it was one of your favourites. I thought it might be nice to sit down together to eat, as it's been a while. I'm not feeling so nauseous tonight.'

I see it in his eyes – the change as soon as I mention the nausea, because I've unwittingly marched the elephant back into the room, to stand between us and ruin our dinner.

'Sounds nice. Thanks. I'm just going to go and get changed and I'll be down.'

'Great. I'll put some rice on.'

I continue cooking but any hope or positivity I felt earlier has vanished. Of course I can't just gloss over everything with a nice meal. We need to have this discussion, to face our truths, however painful they may be.

When Jamie reappears, he's changed into his denim shorts and white Carhartt T-shirt, the one he wore on our first date, and he looks so gorgeous it makes me want to cry.

'You look nice.'

He rubs his hands down his T-shirt. 'This old thing.'

We both smile at his joke and, again, it feels for a moment that we might be able to find a way back. I really hope so, because I think that losing Jamie would be the greatest tragedy of my life.

He sits down at the dining table and I drain the rice and pour it into two bowls, spooning the curry over the top. Then I grab a packet of ready-to-eat poppadoms out the cupboard, open them up and put them on the table.

'This looks delicious. Thank you,' Jamie says politely, but there's a formality to it that cuts me.

It wasn't exactly true that the nausea has gone, but there's no way I'm going to show him that, so I tuck into my curry as zealously as I can muster. We don't speak, both using the excuse of our mouths being full as a get-out clause, but I'm well aware that it's just that we both have nothing to say. That until we've reached some kind of conclusion about the pregnancy, everything else will seem pointless, forced, like making small talk with a stranger.

I swallow down my food, and then force myself to be brave, even though I feel like a small child lost in a supermarket. 'I went back to the doctor's today.'

'Oh?' And I'm not certain, but I think I see a flicker of hope in Jamie's eyes and it makes me feel sick.

'There's an appointment at the clinic next week. You don't have to come with me. I'll understand if you don't want to, but I just wanted you to know.'

Jamie nods and then puts his fork down in his bowl. 'So that's it? Decision made?'

'I don't know what you want me to say. I'm sorry that it's come to this, that the accident happened, but it doesn't change anything for me. In fact, it just makes me even more sure that I feel the way I thought I did about having children.'

'So do you need my permission? Do I need to sign something?'

I shake my head.

'Right, your body, your choice.'

There's so much bitterness in his words, it feels like if they were liquid they'd burn straight through my skin.

'But I want you to be there with me. I do want us to come to this decision together.'

'As long as I come to the same decision as you.'

I get how much he's hurting, I understand that he feels helpless, but at the same time, this is what we agreed. These were the conditions under which we got engaged.

'We've been over this so many times, Jamie. I can't go over it again. I understand that the fact I actually got pregnant makes it feel different for you, but it doesn't for me. It's a collection of cells.'

'Our cells,' Jamie retorts and I sigh but he powers on. 'Do you know that everything is already decided? Whether it's a boy or girl? Eye colour? Hair colour? Whether he or she would look more like you or me? Whether our baby would have a natural ability at painting or writing or maths?'

'If you're trying to guilt me into keeping it, it's not going to work. Don't you think I already feel guilty? I know what I'm doing, Jamie. I know it's a really shitty thing and I wish to God I'd never got pregnant. But I did and I can't change that. Don't you think it'd be worse for me to have this baby and spend my life resenting it?'

Jamie reaches over for my hands and I know he's about to try to change my mind, that he's hoping a softer approach might be all it takes. 'But what if you didn't? What if you loved it? What if you found a joy you didn't even realize you were capable of?'

I pull my hands away and shake my head as forcefully as I can so he knows that I'm serious. 'I'm going to the clinic next week. Let me know if you want to come with me.'

And then I leave the table, storming through the patio doors and marching down to the end of the garden, where I break down, finally releasing all the tears I've been holding in all this time.

JAMIE

I'm not sure I'm going to find the answers to my sorrows at the bottom of a pint glass, but here I am sitting at the bar of our local pub on my own. I've never drunk alone before. It always seemed something that old men do, desperate for a bit of company, but when I thought about calling Matt to join me, I just couldn't face it. I don't want to see the sympathy on his face and, more than that, the relief, that Mia would never do something like that. That he has his future with his lovely family to look forward to and I have . . . well, I don't even know what I have any more.

It seems so strange that just a couple of weeks ago, I was completely at peace with our decision not to have children. That my future with Lucy seemed nothing but impenetrably rosy. And now it feels like this situation has left a big fat dirty blemish on our relationship that may never be able to be removed. And I'm so fucking angry about that, I can feel it leaking out of my pores, infusing every word I say to her with bile. And that makes me hate myself. And then I hate the world and, yes, occasionally Lucy. Our appointment at the clinic is tomorrow. In many ways, it's felt like the longest week, but now it feels like the time is speeding towards tomorrow morning at breakneck speed, like my life is on the verge of catastrophe and I don't know how to stop it.

I empty my glass and hold it up to the barman who nods and pours me another pint. In the corner of the pub, I notice a group of women, getting louder by the second. And then I notice one of them has a bride-to-be sash across her middle and they're all drinking their wine through willy straws. Although they're about the same age as me, I suddenly feel so much older. Like the weight of the last few days has encumbered me with a cynicism I didn't have before. *Oh, look at them, so naïve, so full of anticipation. It's all downhill from here, folks.*

One of the group comes over to the bar with her purse in her hand and, after the barman has put my pint down in front of me and I've instructed him to add it to the tab, she orders a round of shots.

'Bit too early for shots if you ask me, but apparently that's what you have to do on a hen night,' she says.

It takes me a minute to realize she's talking to me and therefore my response is an incoherent mumble.

'I'm Charlie by the way.' She holds out her hand and I shake it.

'Jamie.'

The barman fills a row of shot glasses and then she gives him her card to pay. 'Join us if you want. We could do with a bit of testosterone over there to balance things out. That's if you're not waiting for someone.'

I shake my head. 'Not waiting for someone. But I think my current mood might put a bit of a dampener on your friend's celebrations. So, thank you, but I won't inflict myself on you all.'

'To be honest, I find all the forced joviality makes me want to run into the canal with weights attached to my limbs.'

I find myself smiling. 'Well, don't do that.'

'I'll try to resist.'

'Maybe the shots will help.'

'Can't get much worse. I swear, when I get married, there better not be a willy straw in sight.'

'Really? I want the whole shebang. Strippers, nappy costume, dummy.'

She really laughs at this and it feels surprisingly nice. By contrast, with Lucy at the moment, everything I say seems to make her sad.

'So you're not married yet then?' She gives me a shy smile so there's no doubting what she's implying, and I'm flattered. I've not been approached in this way for a very long time, and it's nice to think I've still 'got it', because right now I feel like a washed-up old fool. But as messed up as things are with Lucy at the moment, there's no way I'd ever be unfaithful.

'Engaged,' I say, with a consolatory expression.

'Ah, all the best ones are.'

'Thanks, but I definitely don't feel like one of the best ones right now.'

She starts to pick up a few of the shot glasses. 'Well, I suppose I better get back to the festivities.'

'Have fun.'

'I'll try.' She takes some of the shot glasses over to the

333

table of hens and then returns to get the last few. She nods at my beer. 'I hope things improve.'

'Thank you. Me too.'

And then she smiles at me and returns to her friends and I suddenly realize that I need to go home, to be with Lucy, however much it hurts.

I walk back quickly, and when I get home all the lights are off so I go upstairs and find Lucy in bed. She's lying still in the dark, so I presume she's asleep, but when I slide in behind her, she says, 'Good night?'

I shake my head, which brushes noisily against the pillow. 'No. I missed you.'

I feel her whole body relaxing. 'I missed you too.'

And then I shuffle up closer to her and put my arm around her waist. 'I'll go to the clinic with you tomorrow.'

She turns around to face me. 'Are you sure? You don't have to.'

'I know. But I want to. You shouldn't have to go alone.'

She turns back to face the wall but I can hear the tears in her throat as she speaks. 'Thank you.'

After that, we don't talk for a while, but I suddenly realize I have to tell her everything before it's too late. I sit up and turn on the lamp and she turns towards me with a questioning look in her eyes.

'I had a brother,' I blurt out. 'He was called Thomas, but he died at birth.'

Lucy looks up at me and I can see how painful it is for her to hear, especially knowing what we're about to do tomorrow.

'I was eight,' I continue. 'I'd been hassling my mum to have a baby for ages. At the time, she kept saying, "If it's meant to be, it will be." Now I know that she had fertility issues for years. Her and Dad had conceived me pretty easily and the doctors couldn't understand it. Secondary infertility, they called it. Did all sorts of tests but couldn't find anything wrong. Then one day she came home with a scan picture and told me I was going to be a brother and I think that's the happiest I've ever felt.'

Lucy doesn't say a word, but she looks like she's about to cry.

'I used to talk to my mum's stomach all the time. She said then the baby would recognize my voice and find it comforting when it came out. I read it books and sang it songs. When they found out they were having a boy, I was over the moon. I would've been happy with a sister but I really wanted a brother. I imagined us being best friends for life. I helped them paint the nursery. Mum showed me how to use a stencil and let me help her paint rockets and spaceships on to the walls . . .'

I stop suddenly, aware that I'm waffling. 'Anyway, she started having contractions in the middle of the night and I remember waking up and finding my nan and grandad making breakfast. I knew it was because Mum was having the baby. She'd been talking about it for weeks, how my grandparents would look after me, and as soon as it was allowed, they'd take me to visit her and my new baby brother.' I feel my throat tightening and wonder if I can make it to the end of the story. 'When the phone rang, I could tell by my nan's face that something was wrong. It just crumpled. She crumpled all together, holding on to the dining room table and guiding herself on to a chair. And then she handed me the phone and I remember Mum saying something about Thomas being "born sleeping", something child-friendly like that, and I remember shouting at her, "Well, wake him up," and I could hear her burst into tears on the other end of the line, losing all the composure she'd been trying so hard to maintain.'

It's not until Lucy sits up, puts her hand to my cheek and wipes away a tear with her thumb that I realize I'm crying. 'I'm so sorry. Why didn't you tell me before?'

I shrug. 'It never seemed to be the right time. And sometimes it feels silly, to still be so cut up about it. I'm sure it happens to loads of people, but it felt like our family never recovered.'

I want to say, 'So that's why I can't bear to get rid of this baby,' but I'm pretty sure from the look on her face that she knows exactly why I'm finally telling her all this.

'Well, you shouldn't feel silly. And I'm really sorry.'

Lucy doesn't say any more, just settles back under the covers, so I turn off the light and rest my head on the pillow again. And although she lies behind me and wraps her arms around me, it doesn't feel like much of a comfort. And I just pray that she's thinking deeply about what I said. That she wakes up with a change of heart.

We sit at the dining table eating our cereal, the radio on in the background. I wonder if Lucy is going to bring up what I told her last night about Thomas or just avoid it.

So I wait, focusing on my bran flakes even though I can only manage one or two, but she doesn't say a word. So instead, I take the plunge, wondering how long it will take for us to meander our way through the small talk before we get to the important stuff.

'Did you sleep all right?'

I don't immediately mean it as a challenge but that's how it sounds. And the truth is it does piss me off that she seemed to sleep soundly while I tossed and turned, slipping in and out of a recurring nightmare where she'd just given birth to our beautiful baby – a boy, it turned out – and I was frantically searching the house and the baby was nowhere to be found, we'd lost him, and Lucy seemed no more concerned than if we'd mislaid an unimportant kitchen utensil. It doesn't take a rocket scientist to decipher my dreams – they're not exactly coded – but every time I woke up, I felt this sense of panic and struggled to drift off again. By contrast, every time I looked at Lucy, she looked totally peaceful and it made me want to prod her awake.

'Yeah, I slept OK, thanks.'

'All right for some. I'm exhausted.'

Lucy doesn't take the bait, just continues to shovel cereal into her mouth, and again it annoys me that she can eat when we're about to go and do what we're going to do.

'So what time do we need to be there?'

'The appointment's at ten but I guess we should get there a little earlier to fill out forms and stuff.'

She's talking about it like it's an appointment at the bank and I want to scream at her, to shake her.

'Is there parking?'

'I don't know. I've never been there before. Let's just leave plenty of time. It's not like we've got anything else to be doing this morning.'

I nod and then push my almost-still-full bowl of cereal across the table. 'So we're definitely still going?'

Lucy gives me a weary expression, as if she's so sick of me she can barely be bothered to respond. 'Yes, we're still going. Well, I am. It's up to you if you want to come with me or not.'

'Even after everything I told you about Thomas?'

It's a low blow, I know. But doesn't it make her realize how much some people would give to be where she is right now? And she's happy to just throw it all away.

She finishes her cereal and then takes her bowl and puts it in the dishwasher. 'I'm really sorry about what happened to your brother, Jamie. I can only imagine how devastating that was for you and your family. But I haven't changed my mind.'

She sounds so clinical, and I think it's probably the furthest apart I've ever felt from her.

I turn the radio off – needing the headspace of a quiet room – and then busy myself with cleaning the kitchen. I'm not sure where Lucy has gone but after about half an hour, she comes in and turns the radio back on and it irritates the shit out of me because she never *ever* considers what I want. It's all about her. And I'm about to go and smack the power button when she puts her hand on my back and says, 'I'm bleeding.'

At first, I'm not sure what she's talking about. Whether she's cut herself and is looking for my help or something. But then it hits me like a bus hurtling into me at speed. 'Oh.'

'I've been having a bit of spotting for the past few days, but I didn't think anything of it because it was only light. But it's pretty heavy now.'

'You're having a miscarriage.' I'm not sure if it's a question or a statement, but it feels like the most terrible word I've ever said. It's ridiculous. Only last night I agreed to going to the abortion clinic with her, but I can't help the intense feeling of devastation at the news that she is losing the baby. I think that maybe, in my heart of hearts, I thought she'd change her mind at the very last minute. 'Do we need to go to the hospital or something?'

She shakes her head. 'I've googled it. It says unless it gets ridiculously heavy or I start feeling really ill then I can just stay at home and let it take its course. I'll call the clinic and explain what's happened.'

'Oh right. OK.' I rub my eyes, which feel sore. 'And how are you feeling? Are you OK?'

I want her to say she's devastated, that the reality of losing the baby has made her see what I was talking about all along, but I can see it on her face, the relief, and it hits me that it's something I'm not sure we can ever come back from.

'I'm OK. Might just go for a lie-down.'

I just nod, knowing that anything I say I'll probably regret.

'You might as well go to work,' she continues. 'There's nothing you can do here.'

'Don't you want me to stay with you?'

'No, I'm fine. Honestly.'

'OK. Well, call me if you need me, if the bleeding gets worse or anything.'

'Of course. Will do.'

It feels wrong leaving her but I can tell she'd rather that I go, and to be honest I'm not sure how much longer I can be here, in this house, with her acting like nothing significant has happened.

She gets herself a biscuit and it fills me with an inexplicable rage. *How can she eat right now?* Then she pours a glass of water and turns to leave the kitchen.

'Have a good day at work. I'll see you later.'

A good day? A good day? How can she tell me to have a good day?

'Well, if you're sure?'

She nods.

'See you then.'

As she passes me, I want to reach out and grab her hand. For us to hold each other and sob into each other's shoulders until we're all dried out. But, although she falters for a second, she doesn't stop and I watch her leaving the room, an ache in my chest so raw I feel like I'm struggling for breath, and then I head out the door and go to work.

The Day of the Break-Up

JAMIE

Mum hands me the spade and I dig a hole about thirty centimetres deep as instructed.

'I'll just go and get it from the car.'

I nod and continue digging. Soon, Mum reappears, the little tree in her hand, and just the sight of her makes me want to cry again.

'This is such a lovely idea. Thanks, Mum.'

'I bought it a couple of weeks ago and I kept meaning to bring it over but then I didn't know how Lucy would react.'

I shrug. 'Yeah, I'm not sure if she would have wanted it here or not.'

'I mean, it's not going to take the pain away, but I think sometimes it can help a little, to commemorate them, to acknowledge the loss somehow. I think sometimes people think because they never lived in this world, you don't need to grieve in the same way you would if you lost a loved one you'd known for longer, but I don't think that's true. I think the grief is just as strong.'

I put my hand on Mum's back. 'Thank you. For understanding.'

'I wish I didn't.'

I smile sadly. 'Me too.'

'Right, let's get this thing planted.' She releases the

tree from its pot and hands it to me and I put it in the hole that I've dug and start to fill some of the soil back in, securing it around the roots, and then we sit at the table outside and survey our work.

'Sounds stupid, but sometimes I can picture him or her running around the garden, spotty wellies, a yellow raincoat,' I say as I pour us both a glass of wine.

'*You* used to have a yellow raincoat. I loved it so much I saved it for Thomas . . . I've still got it in the loft.'

I take a sip of my wine and then put it back on the table. 'Why didn't you ever try again? After Thomas, I mean?'

Mum shrugs. 'Your dad wanted to, but I just . . . I couldn't.'

I nod, reaching out and putting my hand on top of hers. 'You know, I used to hate the photos you had of Thomas. I always wondered why you kept them. But not having anything to remember our baby by . . .' I clear my throat so I can continue. 'Lucy never wanted to talk about it and it's almost felt like I've not been able to grieve. So the tree is perfect. Thank you.'

'You're very welcome. And you can always talk about it to me.'

'I know. I'm really glad that you and me, well . . . you know what I mean.'

'I do. And I'm glad too.'

There's a pause in the conversation and I listen to the birds. They're so loud here. It really surprised me when we moved in. I watch as a pretty songbird lands on the tree we just planted. 'Do you really think it's for the best?' I ask, not taking my eyes off the bird.

'I do.'

And as much as it hurts more than anything, as much as the thought of a world without Lucy right now feels empty and devoid of all colour, I start to wonder if perhaps she could be right.

Before

LUCY

When I first saw the blood, it startled me. Because of the pill I'm on, it's been years since I've had a period and it felt a bit like the first time, when I was twelve and went to the toilet at youth club only to find my pants stained with a smear of red. And then it dawned on me what it meant, and, as awful as it makes me feel to admit it, my overriding emotion was relief. That the whole thing was over and I didn't have to go through the ordeal of sitting in a waiting room knowing I was about to end my baby's life. I guess a part of me hoped Jamie would stop looking at me with such anger and disgust because the decision had been taken out of my hands. It was happening beyond my control.

But ever since it happened (well, it's still happening four days later, but ever since I told him), Jamie seems to have travelled to some distant land that I can't reach. He pretends like everything's OK and he doesn't want to talk about it, but he's been getting up super early, often leaving for work before I even wake up. He says he's got loads on, but I don't buy it. Then he gets home, we eat together but the conversation is always small talk (what happened at work that day, a story in the news), which wouldn't be too bad but there's none of our usual banter. And the worst bit is in bed where we would normally spoon, barely parting for long even in the middle of the night – now it feels like he must be hanging off the edge of the mattress because he's so far away from me. I'm surprised he hasn't fallen out.

It's strangely busy in the shop today and it's a relief. Whilst I'm chatting away to customers and recommending books, it's possible to forget that any of this is happening. For a while I can escape reality – getting totally lost in someone else's story instead of my own shitty one.

My phone buzzes in my pocket and I check it, hoping for a light-hearted message from Jamie, like we used to send to each other all the time, but it's a message from Mum.

Hello darling. Are you still alive? Or have you just disowned me at long last? x

I put my phone back in my pocket. I guess I *have* been avoiding Mum, but I just don't know how to look her in the eye. How can I ever tell her that I was pregnant and wasn't going to keep it? And if I skipped that part and just told her about the miscarriage, she'd make a huge fuss and shower me with sympathy and that would just make me feel guilty. I haven't even told Amy about it. I'm scared she might think less of me, even though she'd do her best to pretend she didn't.

'Fancy some drinks after we close?' Tilda asks after we finish serving a long row of customers. 'Aaron's away with work tonight and it feels odd going home to an empty house.'

I know I should probably go home and try to talk to

Jamie, but actually the thought of going for a few drinks, of chatting about nothing much, of laughing and not having to go straight home to a fiancé who can't even bear to look at me – it's exactly what I need. 'Sure. Let's do it.'

We quickly work our way through a bottle of wine and I go to the bar and order another, taking it back to our table and re-filling our glasses. I can tell I'm going to end the night very drunk but I no longer care. I feel younger and freer than I have done in a very long time.

'So how is married life treating you?' I ask, secretly hoping I'm not the only one whose relationship isn't picture perfect, even though I know that makes me a horrible person.

'It's really good, thanks.'

'Expect it'll be babies next.'

It's a very un-me thing to say. It's the sort of assumption I spend my life battling against, but I feel so desperate to offload, even though I know I'll regret it in the morning, that I'll feel uncomfortably exposed.

'Actually, we don't think we're going to have children.'

In my drunken haze, it feels like the most amazing news – that I've finally found a kindred spirit.

'Me neither,' I almost yell. 'I can't believe it. I just assumed because you'd got married so young that having a family would be a huge priority of yours.'

'No. I mean, Aaron and I talked about it but neither of us feels a passionate desire for a child. We're happy with things the way they are – just the two of us.'

The relief is replaced by a deep stabbing pain. 'I wish Jamie was like that. He thinks I'm evil because I like our life the way it is.' I down another glass of wine and immediately re-fill it.

Tilda looks at her hands. 'I'm sure he doesn't.'

'Sadly, he does. Trust me to end up with a bloke who can't see the benefits of a childfree existence.'

'Yeah, I guess it's unusual, isn't it? That way round, I mean. Usually it's the woman desperate to have kids and the man needing persuading.'

'Yep. Lucky me.'

When did I become so bitter?

'So what are you going to do about it?'

I wonder whether I should tell her about the pregnancy, the planned abortion, the miscarriage, but I still feel so much shame about it all, even though I hate that I feel that way.

'I don't know. We'll probably just spend our lives arguing about it.'

My phone buzzes in my pocket and I take it out to see it's a text from Jude.

I'm leaving for India next week. Sure you don't want to join me? x

I put my phone back in my pocket and, at the same time, 'Rhythm is a Dancer' starts blaring out of the stereo and because I'm drunk and sad and don't know what the hell to do about it, I grab Tilda's hand and lead her on to the dance floor. It's practically empty as it's a weeknight but there are a couple of leery men who stare at us and we play up to it, dancing with each other provocatively. The men gawp and we giggle, feeling drunk not just on the wine but on the power of being sexy, of knowing that we could ask those blokes for anything we wanted and they would give it to us. Although I'm a staunch feminist, sometimes you need to feel desired, in control.

At the end of the night, we stumble to the taxi rank and wait for one to arrive.

'I was pregnant.' It comes out almost beyond my control.

'What? When?'

'Last week. I had a miscarriage.'

'Oh, Lucy, I'm sorry.'

I shake my head. 'Don't be. I was going to have an abortion anyway. That's why Jamie hates me.'

Tilda puts her arm around me and I rest my head on her shoulder in a way we would never do if we were sober. 'I'm sure he doesn't hate you. But even if he does, it's not your fault. You've done nothing wrong. You do know that, don't you?'

I nod, even though deep down I hate myself for the decision I was about to make, and I feel the tears slipping down my cheeks, glad that Tilda can't see them. And then a taxi pulls up and we both jump in. We hold hands until we get to my place and then I hug Tilda, give her some money towards the fare and get out. When I finally get to the door, I can't manage to get my key into the lock so I have to knock and I can tell Jamie's fuming when he answers.

'Good night? Thanks for the text to let me know where you were.'

I take my phone out of my pocket. I've got another message from Mum but nothing from Jamie. 'You didn't bother to message me either, so you obviously weren't that worried.'

'I didn't think *I* should be the one to have to contact *you*.'

I push past Jamie and clumsily make my way to the kitchen where I get myself a glass of water in a feeble attempt to sober up a bit. 'I just went for a few drinks with Tilda. It's not a big deal. I'm still allowed to have fun, you know?'

Being drunk and full of emotional turmoil is not a good combination and I know I'm going to say things I regret, but I'm also well aware I can't stop myself.

'Well, I'm really glad you had fun.'

'Is it not allowed now we're settled down then? Does life have to become stagnant and boring?'

Jamie laughs but there's not an ounce of humour in it. 'Fuck off.'

'I will. That would make you happy, wouldn't it? So you can walk away with your conscience intact? Perfect Jamie. Not only did she suggest aborting your baby, she buggered off and left you too. What an evil bitch!'

'If that's what you want then do it, but it's not what I want.'

'No? You want to spend your life making me feel guilty, do you?'

'That's not my intention. I'm sorry that I'm here breaking my heart whilst you're off celebrating your freedom. I wish I could be more like you, trust me.'

'Oh yeah, it's so easy being a cold, heartless bitch like me. Poor you having emotions.'

Are all relationships destined to get to this point? No matter how amazingly they start out? Is it inevitable that people will grow resentful, start trying to score points against each other, almost subconsciously planning the best way to hurt one another with their words? I never thought it would happen to us.

'What do you want me to say, Lucy? Do you want me *not* to care?'

I sigh, suddenly feeling tired of the bravado. 'I don't know. I guess I just want things to go back to how they were before. Don't you think the miscarriage shows it wasn't meant to be?'

Jamie pauses, and I hope that perhaps my having been honest with him might help him to soften with me too, but then he gives me a look of utter contempt and storms off to the front door, slamming it on his way out. As soon as he's gone, my brave face well and truly falls off and I break down in tears. I think about texting Jude, about how amazing it would feel to just jet off to somewhere exotic, but I know that as crap as things are with Jamie right now, he's still the only person I want to be with. I find Jude in my contacts and delete him once and for all and then suddenly I find myself retching and am sick right there in the kitchen sink.

JAMIE

I'm not sure how I end up at Mum's house in the middle of the night. It's like my feet have carried me here without my full permission. And when she answers the door, she looks as surprised to see me as I am to be here.

'Whatever's the matter?' Mum asks, pulling me into a hug, and unexpectedly I find myself crying. And not just gentle crying but big, shoulder-shaking sobs. But as well as feeling embarrassed, there's actually a great sense of relief. Like for a moment, I can stop being an adult. I'm a child again, before we lost Thomas and Dad, back when Mum's cuddles could solve any problem in the world.

When we part, we both smile, a little sheepish, but I'm pleased that it doesn't actually feel that awkward. It feels like we've pulled down a screen that never needed to be there in the first place.

She guides me through to the lounge and I sit on the sofa whilst she goes through to the kitchen. When she comes back, she's carrying a bottle of beer, a glass of wine and a huge bowl of crisps.

'I didn't think tea would quite cut it tonight.'

'I think you might be right.' I drink some of the beer and take a handful of crisps, realizing I've not actually eaten anything since lunchtime. 'I'm sorry for turning up here so late.'

'Don't be silly. You're welcome here whenever you want. It's still your home, you know?'

'Thanks, Mum.'

'So are you going to tell me what the matter is? The last I spoke to you, you were on top of the world, making plans for the wedding and everything.'

'I know.' That time feels so long ago. It's hard to believe it's only been a couple of weeks.

'So what happened?'

'Lucy fell pregnant.'

'Oh.'

'She had an abortion booked, not my decision, but then just before we were about to leave for the appointment, she had a miscarriage. She thinks that shows it wasn't meant to be. That, fundamentally, she was right, I suppose.'

'I see. And what do you think?'

So many people said it to Mum after Thomas died. *Oh, it wasn't meant to be. There's a plan for all of us. It happened for a reason.* Bollocks. It was a shitty fucking thing that happened and absolutely no good came out of it. It didn't bring our family closer. It wasn't the 'wrong time'. It didn't teach us anything. Our lives didn't suddenly take some unexpected greater path. It just broke us.

'Do you think you losing Thomas was "meant to be"?'

Mum seems to contemplate it deeply for a minute. 'I don't know. I suppose I've never thought about it like that. I'm not sure I believe in fate or the whole "everything happens for a reason". But that's not to say she isn't right.'

'But the point is she was going to get rid of it anyway. This isn't just something that happened *to* us.'

'I get that. But you did agree to not having children, didn't you?'

'Yes. But I didn't agree to killing our child. Knowing everything that happened with Thomas, how it destroyed us all, how could she think that a life is just something you throw away? Doesn't she realize how special that is?'

'I don't know, Jamie. I don't know how anyone could throw away a life like that.'

A single tear forms in the corner of Mum's eye and then slides down the side of her nose.

'I'm sorry. I didn't mean to upset you.'

Mum shakes her head. 'Not at all. I should probably have a good old cry about it more often.' She smiles and takes a sip of her wine. 'You know, when I was pregnant with Thomas, one of my favourite things was how close you were to me. You wouldn't leave me alone, hugging and kissing my tummy all the time. For the first time ever, it was all about me instead of your dad. I remember when I got close to giving birth, I felt a bit sad about the prospect of losing our closeness, even though of course I was looking forward to having the baby. And then when I lost Thomas, it felt like I lost you too.'

'I'm sorry I made you feel like that.'

'Oh no, I'm not saying it to make you feel bad. Sorry, I'm not sure why I said anything at all.'

'I'm glad you did. It probably would've helped us both to be more honest over the years.'

'You might be right.' Mum takes a crisp out of the

bowl. 'Anyway, I'm really sorry you're going through this. You deserve more from life.'

'Thanks.'

'I hope it doesn't sound callous, but I guess the one good thing about the miscarriage is at least you didn't have to go through with the abortion. I can only imagine how horrendous that would've been for you.'

'I know. But it feels so final. It's ridiculous as we weren't going to have kids anyway, but now that one has been taken away from me, it feels like my life's over. Like I'll never recover.'

'You will.' And I hear the weight behind what she's saying – *look at me, I survived, didn't I?* But was she ever really the same again? Were any of us?

'And you know the very worst of it all? I don't know if I can love her any more, at least not in the same way, and I feel terrible for that. When she touches me, I feel myself flinch. When she looks at me, I can barely stand to look back at her.'

Mum offers a sad smile.

'She just seems so OK about it, you know?' I continue, as if suddenly unblocked. 'Like the miscarriage is one big relief. She's been out tonight with her friend as if nothing's happened.'

'Perhaps she's just putting on a brave face?'

'I don't want her to put on a brave face. I want her to show that this is affecting her, just slightly. That she actually gives a shit.'

'Talk to her, love. Tell her how you feel. You might be surprised. A miscarriage is a tricky thing for any woman to go through, even one that didn't want the baby. I would guess a lot of what you're seeing is an act, because she was the one to make the decision and because she knows how you feel about it all. There's probably an element of pride there.'

It occurs to me that Mum is actually very wise and I wish I'd listened to her more over the years. Made more of an effort to stay close to her instead of putting all my focus into Dad.

'You might be right. She is very proud.'

'Us women can be.' Mum smiles and it's nice to see she acknowledges it too. The way she's kept me at arm's length since she lost Thomas.

'You loved her enough before all this to sacrifice having a family,' she continues. 'And the hole caused by losing your child, that won't ever go, but it will start to close up a bit in time. The thing you need to decide is whether you still love her, knowing the choice she wanted to make. I mean, none of us are perfect, but it would also be OK if you couldn't accept it, you know? That wouldn't make you a bad person.'

I sigh. 'I thought I could, but I just don't know any more. I know that the thought of not being with her is heartbreaking, but at the moment the thought of being with her is heartbreaking too.'

'Talk to her. It's all you can do. Be totally honest. Lay it all out on the table and get her to as well. Only then will you know if you can move on together or whether you'd be better off apart.'

'You're right.' I down the rest of my beer and realize

that I need to see Lucy now. That we need to have this conversation.

Mum seems to sense my haste because she says, 'Go. I won't be offended.'

'Are you sure?'

'Of course.'

We both stand up and I wrap my arms tightly around her. All these years that we've not properly hugged each other, they feel like such a waste. 'I love you, Mum.'

'It's OK. I know if you could've chosen, I wouldn't be the one left behind.'

It hurts to hear her say that, because for a long time, although I'd never admit it, it was probably true. But it's not any more. I'd give anything to have Dad back, but I wouldn't swap their places.

'No way. That's not true, Mum.'

'It's OK.'

I put my hands on the tops of her arms and force her to look at me. 'It's not true.'

She's unable to hide the emotion on her face, even though she tries her best. 'Well, I love you too. And I am so proud of the man you've become. Your dad would be too.'

'Thank you,' I say, then kiss her on the cheek and leave.

When I get home, I'm surprised to see that Lucy is still up, sitting on the sofa drinking coffee. Looking up at me with tired eyes, she pats the seat beside her.

'Will you come and talk to me?'

I nod, going over and sitting down. 'I think we need

to start being totally honest if we're going to get through this.'

'I agree. I'll start. I'm sorry I said you needed to get over it, that it was obviously meant to be. That was wrong of me.'

And so we start listing our truths, instead of arguing with each other, instead of saying what we think the other one wants to hear.

'I hate that you're clearly relieved about the miscarriage. That you're not torn to pieces like I am.'

'I'm sad that all this has affected how you look at me. When you knew all along I didn't want children.'

'I'm angry and hurt that you don't see a difference between choosing not to have a child and getting rid of one we've made. That me telling you about Thomas didn't make a difference to your decision.'

'I feel like you agreed to marry me under false pretences – that you always secretly hoped I'd change my mind about the kids thing.'

'I feel like you don't care about how *I* feel. How it's always about what *you* want.'

Lucy sighs. 'Do you think this is getting us anywhere?'

'I don't know. I sort of feel better for saying how I feel. You?'

'Yeah, but I feel sad that you feel how you feel.'

I give her a melancholy smile. 'Yeah, me too.'

She reaches over and touches my hand, and for the first time in a while, I don't recoil. In fact, I welcome it being there.

'I'm not as OK as I might appear about all this, you

know? I feel guilty and sad every day. And of course there's a part of me that will always wonder what this baby would've been like.'

'Really?' It's such a huge comfort to hear her say that. I just really hope she means it, that she's not just saying it to make me feel better.

'Of course. I'm not a bloody ice queen. Just because I didn't want a child doesn't mean I don't feel any pain at losing the one we created. To think it would've been a part of you, a part of me, it hurts. And yes, maybe I am relieved about the miscarriage but only because then I didn't have to sit there and take some tablet that ended that little bit of us. I didn't have to be the one to make that horrible decision. It doesn't feel like it's my fault, if that makes any sense, and before it would've done.'

I put my other hand on top of hers. 'Thank you. For opening up to me.'

'Do you think you'll ever be able to forgive me?' She looks so fragile, so scared, that I feel terrible for how cold I've been to her through all this.

'You haven't done anything that needs forgiving.' It's true. She's been honest from the get-go, and yet I do feel like I need to find it in myself to forgive her. And then I feel guilty for feeling that way.

'So why do I feel this desperate need for you to say you don't hate me? That you still love me? Still see me in the same way as you did before all this?'

She starts crying and I can see how hard it is for her to be so honest, so vulnerable, so I wrap my arms around her and we lie back on the sofa together. 'I still love you.'

'Are you sure?'

'Of course.' And I do. It's the truth. And I desperately want to find a way back to what we had before.

'I love you too. So much.'

And then she kisses me, and we spend the night on the sofa, wrapped in each other's arms, as if we're scared that if we move it'll all fall apart again.

LUCY

We're on holiday in Copenhagen. It was my suggestion. A weekend away to take our minds off stuff, to remind ourselves of who we are as a couple. It's been just over a month since the miscarriage and, although we've both been trying our best and things have been much better between us, they've still been a little strained. So I'm hoping a holiday will help us to reset. Plus, it's the anniversary of our first date today, though neither of us has mentioned it so I'm not sure if Jamie's aware or not. I sneaked a card into my hand luggage just in case he has one for me, but I'm not going to bring it up otherwise as I don't want him to feel bad.

So far, our little break away is going great. We've done the usual tourist stuff – Nyhavn, the slightly insignificant statue of the Little Mermaid, Amalienborg – and now we're travelling out on a train to this modern art gallery by the sea that looks amazing in the photos.

'So it's not going to be all stuffed cows in formaldehyde, is it?' Jamie asks, tucking into a baguette we got from a little bakery on the waterside.

'No, and if you hate it, you can sit out in the sculpture garden and look at the sea.'

The weather's been a bit hit and miss so far. When the sun's out it's pretty warm considering it's only April, but then suddenly a huge rain cloud will come over and it absolutely hammers down. But looking out of the train window, it's currently gorgeous.

'So what do I get in return for the next few hours of pain?'

'I don't know. A blow job?'

Jamie spits out some of his baguette and a splatter of mayo lands on his chin so he wipes it off. 'In that case, let's start going to art galleries more often.'

I smile. 'Your choice tomorrow. I'll go wherever you want.'

'Another art gallery?'

I roll my eyes.

'Can we go to Tivoli? Spend the day riding the roller-coasters and eating candyfloss and hot dogs?'

'Of course. Sounds great.'

'Great.' Jamie leans over and kisses me on the cheek and the relief at having 'my' Jamie back is almost over-whelming. I suddenly realize how acutely I've missed him.

We reach our stop, getting off and following the crowds along the path to the art gallery. When we get there, it's amazing. Typical Scandi décor – tons of glass and wood panelling, and it's set in the most amazing grounds full of sculptures. It's the kind of place where you feel so calm that you want to stay there forever. We walk around the exhibitions first, Jamie feigning interest as we look at the different artwork. And then I put him out of his misery and we grab a coffee and take it out into the fresh air. There's this giant sculpture that's basically a pyramid of steps, with tons of people sat on all the different levels, and rather than just sitting beside them, Jamie points to the top.

'Race?'

He knows that with my competitive spirit I won't be able to resist, so we put our coffees down on the bottom step and then clamber up the steps. I'm beating him all the way – but, just as I start to tire, he sneaks past me and slaps the top of the pyramid. The elation on his face makes me laugh.

'I actually beat you.'

Everyone sitting on the statue stares at us like we're crazy and then a bunch of kids start copying us, much to the annoyance of their parents.

'Oh no, I think we might have started something.'

'Oops. Let's quietly sneak back down and get our coffees.'

We walk around the grounds. At one point, there's a slide buried into the hill, and we wait until the queue of children dies down and then I sit on Jamie's knee and we fly down together, speeding off the end with a bump.

'Ow. You're heavy.'

I slap him on the arm. 'I am not heavy.'

'You are when the full weight of you smashes me into the hard ground.' He stands up and wipes the mud off his shorts. 'I'm going to have a bruised bum after this.'

I lean over and stroke his bottom. 'There you go, rubbed it better for you.'

'Any excuse for a touch of this bad boy,' he teases. To be fair, he does have a great bum.

We stroll past a big glass-walled part of the gallery, noticing it looks like a studio or workshop.

I grab Jamie's hand and pull him along. 'Let's go and make some art.'

We navigate our way to the workshop, which we realize on closer inspection is aimed at children, the only adults being parents. We join the end of one of the tables (a mum, dad and little girl speaking in Danish) and the gallery assistant brings us over a lump of clay each. She gives us a second glance but doesn't seem annoyed to see us joining in.

'We're trying to make a pot like one of these in front of you,' she explains. 'There are instructions provided, but just ask if you need any help.'

'Great, thanks.'

Jamie meticulously follows the step-by-step guide on the table in front of us whilst I use a more intuitive approach, using my thumbs to make a hollow.

'That's not how you're supposed to do it,' Jamie says, nodding his head towards the instructions.

'Art is about being expressive, not following rules.'

'That little girl's looks better than yours.'

I kick Jamie under the table. 'Just wait and see. It's a work in progress.'

Annoyingly, when our pots are finished, Jamie's does look better, not that I'd admit it to him. Instead I say, 'Yours is a bit formulaic. Mine's more original.'

The mother in the family opposite gives us both a thumbs up and then the assistant comes over, gushing over the little girl's pot in her native tongue and then she turns to mine and Jamie's.

'Excellent,' she says to Jamie with a beaming smile and then she turns to me. 'And yours is very unusual.'

As she walks away, Jamie is unable to contain his amusement.

'Whatever,' I say to him. 'She probably just fancies you.'

'Well, it is a common problem.'

That evening, we go to the huge street food market by the river. It's a fantastic place, absolutely buzzing and full of every style of food you can imagine. Jamie decides on a Chinese place early on, but it takes me a good forty minutes to choose. For someone who loves food as much as I do, it's like Santa's Grotto, although there's almost too much choice and I know that whatever I order, I'll get food envy when I see someone else's. I eventually decide on an Indonesian curry and Jamie and I split up to get our dishes and then meet up again on a table outside, where he's also got us a beer each. The weather is perfect this evening, warm and sunny, and there's such a positive vibe you can't help but feel uplifted by it. We sit and people-watch, the sun glistening on the river, and we eat our delicious food (of course I have to steal some of Jamie's too, which luckily isn't quite as delicious as mine although pretty close) and I wish that we could stay here forever because it's the happiest I've felt in a very long time.

'Copenhagen was a good shout,' Jamie says, raising his beer to me.

'Thank you. It was, wasn't it? It's definitely one of my favourite holidays so far.'

'What else is up there?'

'I don't know. I've been to some pretty amazing places, but I'd say Thailand has to be near the top.'

'And what's left on the bucket list?'

'Oh, tons of places. But I think at the very top it would be Lapland. Bit random, I know, but I'm desperate to see the Northern Lights. Do you fancy it?'

'Absolutely. Husky rides, snowmobiles, and a visit to the real Father Christmas. What's not to like?'

'We could go this winter if we started saving. We could even spend Christmas out there.'

'Yeah, sounds like a plan.'

It feels good to be making plans, to be focusing on all the things that make this life we've chosen such a good one. It feels like the clouds that have been shrouding us have dispersed, like the edges have been sanded off all the words we speak to each other.

'Another beer?' Jamie asks, standing up and picking up our empty plastic glasses.

'Yes, please. It'd be a shame to turn our backs on this beautiful night.'

'Absolutely.'

He goes to the outdoor bar and comes back with two more beers. After he's sat down, he reaches into his bag and pulls something out.

'Tesco Finest cookies,' he says, putting them on the

table. 'Don't worry if you didn't realize, but it's a year since our first date. I thought we should celebrate.'

'You brought them all the way from home?'

Jamie nods. 'I'm sorry it's not much.'

I shake my head, feeling like I might cry, and take his hands in mine. 'Don't be silly. They're perfect.' Then I reach into my bag and pull out the anniversary card I bought him, which is a bit crumpled from being hidden at the bottom of my case. 'And I did remember. I just wasn't sure if you would.'

Jamie's face breaks into a huge smile then he suddenly looks more serious. 'How could I not remember? It was the best day of my life.'

I kiss him, then he opens my card and we chat until it gets dark, Jamie wrapping his arms around me to keep me warm as the sun goes down and the air begins to feel chilly.

JAMIE

After a late night, we sleep in. We're staying in this little apartment on the outskirts of Copenhagen and it's the kind of place that is so cool that it rubs off on you and makes you feel cooler just by association. It's like whilst we're staying here, we can imagine that we're this awesome Scandi couple – Lucy, a novelist and me a graphic designer or a photographer or something else equally creative – and we eat vegan food and subscribe to some kind of amazing design magazine that we sit and read on a Sunday morning, whilst drinking the best coffee from the barista just down the road.

I wake up first but Lucy isn't long after, and as soon as she stirs we start kissing and it's not long before she climbs on top of me, and of course the sex we have here is amazing because we're no longer Jamie and Lucy (not that our normal sex isn't amazing), but now we're Stefan and Freja and our sex life is part of our exercise routine so it's energetic and adventurous and we've probably achieved a good two-thousand calorie deficit before we've even got out of bed.

I'm looking forward to Tivoli. Apparently it inspired Walt Disney to create Disney World, so I figure it should be a pretty good place to spend a day. Plus I love anywhere like that, anywhere that feels like stepping back into your childhood. Before the world got complicated.

Talking of complicated, things feel a lot better between me and Lucy. As long as I don't think about what happened, it feels like before, when we were both really happy, which is a huge relief. Sometimes I worry it can only last so long, this avoidance of really facing up to it all, but it seems like the best solution for now.

After our mammoth sex session, we go to a local café and have Danish pastries and coffee, then we head on the bus into the city. When we arrive at the gates of Tivoli, it's as amazing as I imagined it to be. It's like walking into some sort of wonderland – paper lanterns and fairy lights zig-zagging across the sky over the paths, a huge outdoor stage showing some kind of fairytale re-enactment, giant fairground rides stretching up into the sky, large expanses of water dotted amongst beautiful gardens.

We pass a candyfloss stand and I buy us both large stickfuls, taking a photo of Lucy with hers. Even with the amazing colours and sparkling lights in the background, the bright pink candyfloss in her hand, it's Lucy's smile that steals the shot, and the twinkle in her eyes.

I put my phone back in my pocket and kiss her, full on the lips, and she tastes sweet.

'What was that for?' she asks coyly.

'Just because.'

She smiles and then we stroll hand in hand, eating our

candyfloss and taking in all the different areas of the park. When we get to the towering drop ride, we both crane our necks to look up at it.

'As soon as we've digested this, we're going up there, you know?' Lucy says.

'I'm not sure. Heights aren't really my thing.'

Lucy shakes her head. 'We paid an extortionate amount for full access to all the rides. We're doing every single one.'

'Even the teacups?'

'Especially the teacups.'

'I'll be sick on you. Don't say I didn't warn you.'

'I'll take that risk.'

We sit on a bench and finish our candyfloss and I find myself watching a family sitting on the grass eating ice cream. The two children, a boy of about six and a girl of about three, look like they couldn't be happier as they tuck into their treats, the ice cream topped with so much whipped cream that it is bigger than each of their heads. Their faces are covered in cream and chocolate sauce and their parents laugh at them and then start wiping their faces.

I suddenly realize that Lucy must have been talking because she puts her face in front of mine and says, 'So are you ready or not?'

She must follow my eyeline and realize what it is I've been staring at because her face suddenly falls and she quickly tries to paint on a smile. Then she takes my stick off me and wanders off to throw it in the bin. When she returns, she takes my hand, pulling me towards the giant drop ride. And we both pretend that everything's fine and I try to get the feeling back that I had before, the joy at just being here in this awesome place with the person I love.

The views from the top of the ride over the city of Copenhagen are amazing, and every time we're at the top we point out various sites before being terrified into silence as the ride drops and all we can focus on is continuing to breathe. Then we rise back up to the top and giggle because we know we're going to get cut off mid-sentence again.

After a few more terrifying rides and a go on the dreaded teacups (I actually have to lie down on the grass for half an hour afterwards, I feel that sick), the light begins to fade and Tivoli takes on an even more magical feel as all the lamps dotted around the park light up, reflecting on the water. We grab a couple of beers and sit in front of the outdoor theatre to watch a band. They're not amazing, but it doesn't matter. It feels great to be sitting outside, huddled together to keep warm, the alcohol running through our systems and the cosy feeling of being surrounded by all sorts of different people just having a good time. *Live in the moment* — isn't that supposed to be the key to happiness? If I can just stop myself from looking back or forward, if I can just stay right here, surely I can be happy?

'Thank you for suggesting we spend the day here,' Lucy says, looking up at me. 'I've had an amazing day.'

'Me too.'

*

But like all good things, our break has to come to an end, and the following morning, we board the plane home. There's a family in the row behind us; the toddler keeps kicking Lucy in the back and the baby is screaming its head off, probably because of the fluctuations in the air pressure hurting her ears.

'God, I don't know how people travel with kids.'

It's a throwaway remark, Lucy doesn't even look up from her magazine as she says it, but for some reason it makes me feel horribly alone. Because although I don't envy the poor parents trying to keep their two children quiet amongst all the other grumpy passengers tutting or giving them judgemental glares, I can't help thinking about the adventures they would've had in Copenhagen and how so many of the things we did would've been enriched by seeing it through our children's eyes. The visit to the zoo – the children's faces lighting up as they watched the polar bear swimming up to the screen, its body squashed up against the glass. The sights, sounds and smells of Tivoli – all new, all magical – how the rides would've all seemed impossibly big, the candyfloss that much sweeter. The boat trip along the river – the way all the children giggled and gasped when we had to duck under the low bridges. Their first ride on a train, maybe their first trip on an aeroplane – how we'd look out the window and to them the clouds would look like snow, or cotton wool, like you could jump out on to them and bounce back up as if you were on a trampoline.

I try to focus on my book. *The parents behind me can't read a book. They can barely utter a sentence to each other without*

376

it being interrupted. Lucy and I are so free. It's easy for us to jump on to a plane to anywhere, to book a last-minute hotel, to catch a show without having to plan it months in advance to ensure we can get a babysitter. We can focus solely on each other, and on ourselves. And yet I can't help wishing I was the one having to play endless games of eye-spy just to keep my little girl quiet. The one with my baby fast asleep on my shoulder.

'So, Lapland next then, yeah?' Lucy says, looking up from her magazine. 'Or shall we fit in another few city breaks? If we do it on the cheap?'

'Whatever we can afford. The more the merrier,' I say, and I force a smile so that she has no idea about what I'm really thinking: the gaping hole in my chest.

The Day of the Break-Up

LUCY

I drive towards our house, still not sure exactly what I'm going to say. *That I've realized all we ever have is right now? That in the end nothing else matters? That the thought of wearing anyone else's ring, of waking up to a face that isn't yours, of someone else bringing me breakfast and not understanding how I have to have the exact right amount of Nutella . . . it all makes the future seem so unbearable that I have absolutely no desire to experience it?*

I arrive too soon. Unprepared. Turning off the engine, I take a deep breath and then force myself up and out of the car, my legs weak. I make my way to the front door, letting myself in as if it's any other day and I've just been out for a bit. The lounge is empty and I can't hear any clattering in the kitchen so I wonder if Jamie has gone back to bed, or gone out, but then as I head towards the stairs I hear voices coming from the garden. I feel suddenly terrified that he's got another woman here even though I know that's ridiculous (Jamie is the epitome of loyal) so I sneak into the kitchen to see if I can hear more clearly. The patio door is open so I stand and listen, recognizing the second voice as belonging to Jamie's mum.

I'm unable to move, fascinated and terrified in equal measure by what I'm going to hear.

'I don't know. I just can't imagine ever being happy without her,' Jamie says and it makes me want to run outside and jump into his arms.

'That's how you feel right now and I totally understand that. But I really believe that one day you'll thank her.'

'That's what she said.'

'Well, I think she's right.'

'She'd love to hear you say that,' Jamie says and I can almost hear the slight smile in his voice.

'You know, you are going to make the best dad one day and I can't wait to see it.'

'Maybe. Thanks, Mum.' He pauses. 'Can you imagine it? Granny Bateman!'

'I am not being called Granny. Let's get that straight right away.'

They both laugh and I wish I could run and hide but my feet feel welded to the spot. Then I hear the movement of chairs and suddenly panic that they're going to come out and find me, that they'll know that I've been listening, so I rush back through the house and outside, trying not to make a sound. Once I get to the road, I run to my car, jump in and drive to Amy's on autopilot, tears flooding my vision like rain on the windscreen.

When Amy answers the door, I fall straight into her arms, my body shuddering as she holds me. I finally pull away and Amy takes my face in her hands. 'What happened?'

'He's better off without me, Amz. Like genuinely, truthfully better off.'

Amy rubs her thumbs down my cheeks and then pulls me back into a hug, speaking quietly into my ear. 'Oh, sweetheart. Then although it might not feel like it right now, that means you're better off without him too.'

Before

LUCY

I hate unpacking after a holiday. I always feel such an intense sadness. It's not that I don't like our home – I love our home. But it's like the reality of life hits me again – the monotony – unstacking dishwashers and putting the washing machine on and going to work and paying car tax and doing the Tesco order.

And particularly at the moment, the dynamic between Jamie and me is very fragile. The trip away definitely achieved what I intended it to. We are much closer, the future together much brighter. But I also get the sense that it's hanging on a knife edge, and I'm scared that being back in the place where we shared all the negativity, where we said all those painful things to each other, will taint things between us, send us back into shadow.

Jamie's pottering about in the kitchen, putting away the few bits of essential shopping we picked up on the way home, when his phone starts ringing on the bedside table beside me. I glance over at the screen.

'It's Matt calling,' I shout down the stairs.

'Thanks. Just coming.' I hear the fridge shut and then Jamie runs upstairs and answers the phone, walking in and out of the bedroom as he chats. He never stands still when he's on the phone. I wonder what he would've done before there were mobile phones. I expect he would've been a doodler, or a tapper. I catch bits of the conversation as he paces.

'Amazing place, mate. Yeah, I'd highly recommend it.'

And then Matt must start talking about work because Jamie says, 'Not looking forward to it at all. Back to reality with a bump, hey.' A pause. 'Yeah, no problem. I'll get it done, don't worry.'

And then Matt talks for quite a while and when Jamie wanders back into the lounge, he looks pale, like he's just heard some devastating news. But by contrast, he says, 'No, don't be silly. That's absolutely amazing, mate. I'm so happy for you.' And then, 'Yeah, well, you can delay the wedding a bit, it won't hurt,' and 'don't worry about that. Loads of people do things a different way round these days. Both your families know you're totally committed to each other. I mean, you might as well be married already.'

And I have a sinking sense of dread as I put two and two together and feel fairly sure that Mia is pregnant. And although of course I'm happy for her and Matt, the timing really couldn't be any worse. And if Jamie's face is anything to go by then this has just sent us spiralling backwards after all the progress we made on our trip.

I go back to my unpacking, preparing my face for when Jamie reappears – the forced happiness that I'm sure will be reflected in his own. And sure enough, when he comes in, he has a smile plastered on to his face that looks like it's been drawn on.

'How's Matt?' I ask.

'He's good.'

'Good.'

I wonder if he's going to tell me about Mia or whether we're going to go back to hiding our feelings from each other.

He takes some of the clothes he didn't wear out of the case and starts putting them away in his drawer.

'Actually, he had some news. Mia's pregnant.'

'Ah, that's amazing,' I say and I sense from his eyes that he knows we're both playing a very careful game.

'I know. They're going to delay the wedding until after the baby now. Mia apparently is desperate to fit into the dress she's chosen.'

'Well, she *does* look amazing in it.'

Jamie nods. 'Right, I better go and iron my shirts for work. Do you want me to iron anything for you?'

He knows my clothes have never seen an iron in their life, which makes his offer feel unnaturally polite, and confirms for me that this isn't going to be something we can just gloss over. That we might as well not have bothered with the trip away as we're right back to square one.

'No, I'm fine, thanks,' I say, trying to make it sound as upbeat as possible. 'Remember we've got Mum's birthday dinner at Amy's at five. I'm sorry, I know it's a bit much on top of a day's travelling, but if we don't all make a fuss on the exact day of her birth then Mum gets her knickers in a twist.'

'No problem. It'll be nice to see them all.' When he leaves the room, I feel the tension deflate like the air in a paddling pool when you've got a puncture. It's horrible really. How it suddenly feels easier to breathe when Jamie's not near me.

I decide the only thing to do is to try to carry on as we were, as if Matt and Mia's news has no bearing on our life (because to be honest it doesn't really, does it?), so I shake myself off, jump in the shower and put on a new outfit, ready to start the day afresh.

In a stereotypically gendered division of roles that I don't quite feel comfortable with, the men are gathered in the lounge drinking beer and probably talking about cars or sport (I actually have no idea what they're talking about) while us women are in the kitchen preparing the food and talking about my upcoming wedding.

'So you've booked the venue? I would've liked to have seen it *in person* really before you committed, but the photos look amazing,' Mum says, not attempting to hide the slight annoyance in her voice that we'd ever dare to make a big decision without her. We found this cute rustic barn that we liked and were all ready to book for next spring but then the whole pregnancy thing happened and neither of us has dared mention the wedding since.

'We haven't booked it just yet.'

'Oh, I thought you were going to book a couple of months ago.'

'We wanted to show you first,' I say, sickeningly sweet, deciding on an excuse that also wins me favour.

'Well, yes, I'd love to come and see.' The gratitude on Mum's face is actually quite touching and I try to imagine what it must be like to be a mum, being the centre of your child's world for so long and then gradually drifting to the outskirts.

'Great. I'll book an appointment.'

'But you're still aiming for the beginning of next year, yes? Nothing's changed between you and Jamie?'

I focus on cutting the spring onions for the duck pancakes. 'No, of course not. Nothing's changed.'

Mum smiles, a look of relief on her face, but when I look at Amy, I can tell that she spots something in my eyes, a reservation.

When we've finished preparing the salad bits and the duck is in the oven roasting, we take a bottle of wine to the dining room table and sit down. Then Mum gets up, nips into the lounge to get her bag and comes back with a load of bride magazines.

'Right, dresses. Come on, ladies, let's get looking.' She hands us each a magazine and we begin to flick through, Mum regularly showing me photos of dresses she likes and me rejecting them. And then Otto and Lauren run over with a pile of books in their hands.

'Story, story,' Otto whines.

'Sorry, darlings, but we are very busy finding the perfect dress for Aunty Lucy. She's *finally* getting married,' Mum says, as if I'm some middle-aged spinster. Then she looks at the men lounging on the sofa. 'One of the men will read you a story,' she says loudly enough for them to hear. 'They're not doing anything useful.'

I notice Jamie is the one to stand up and take the pile of books off the kids. 'Come on then, where shall we go?'

'To our den.' Otto points to the hallway. 'It's in the playroom.'

Jamie follows the children past us to the staircase.

'You'll probably just about squeeze in,' Amy says, laughing, as they walk past. 'You just have to curl up your legs a bit. There are some cushions in there to make it a bit more comfortable.'

'No problem.' Jamie smiles and Otto takes his hand and leads him upstairs, Lauren following behind.

We go back to looking at the bride magazines for about half an hour and then the oven beeps and Amy goes to check on the duck.

'I think I better go and see if Jamie's OK. He's been up there quite a while.'

'Just tell the kids to let him out, Luce. Sorry, I'd totally forgotten he was there. Food will be ready in about ten.'

I head upstairs and when I get closer to the playroom, I slow down and stand in the hallway, listening to Jamie reading a story. He's doing all these funny voices and the kids are giggling away. Then he finishes and I hear him close the book.

'When are you and Aunty Lucy going to have a baby?' Lauren asks and I feel a tightness in my chest at the thought of what Jamie's going to say.

'Well, we've decided we're not going to have any children, which means I'm just going to have to borrow you two lots instead.' I can hear Lauren and Otto giggling and imagine he's tickling them or something similar.

'But why aren't you going to have any children? We want a cousin to play with.' Lauren sounds so confused and I wonder whether I should be the one to step in and explain, but I don't want Jamie to know I've heard their conversation and I'm also quite intrigued to hear what excuse he's going to give.

'I guess not everyone wants children.'

'Why? Don't you like us?' The sadness in Otto's voice makes me want to cry.

'No way, it's not that at all. You two are the most awesome people I know. And I'm thirty-three so I've met a *lot* of people and you are the best by far. In fact, I think that's probably it. Your Aunty Lucy and I realized that no other child would ever be as good as you two so there's no point having one.'

It's a far better answer than I ever could've given them, and Lauren and Otto seem satisfied as they ask for another story, which Jamie quickly starts. I leave it a few moments and then peer in through the door and just watch them. They're in the tent I bought them one Christmas and Jamie's got a child under each arm, their heads resting on his chest, and he looks so content. I thought he'd be desperate for me to come and save him, but he looks like he never wants to leave. All of a sudden, he notices me standing there. And the look on his face says everything I've always feared – everything he tries so hard to keep hidden from me most days – and I feel so very sad.

I sleepwalk my way through the rest of the evening. We eat and drink and talk about Copenhagen and the upcoming wedding, despite the fact Jamie and I never talk about it when we're alone any more. And when we've finished our meal, Amy brings out a cake (of course she's made one, putting me to shame as usual) and Mum hugs her with such love and gratitude that I wish, not for the first time, that I was more like Amy and that I had what they have. We all sing 'Happy Birthday' and toast Mum, and Jamie is the perfect boyfriend, showering Mum with affection and compliments. To all intent and purposes, it's a very successful evening.

'Hot chocolate before bed?'

I nod and sit down at the dining table and Jamie makes us both a drink, neither of us speaking the entire time he does. It seems crazy to think this morning we woke up in Copenhagen feeling close, happy, and now it feels like the Berlin wall has been reinstated between us.

Jamie brings over our drinks and sits down at the table beside me. And I *could* just drink my hot chocolate and then go up to bed with Jamie. Maybe we'd have sex, more likely we'd just watch something on the laptop. And then we'd get up and do it all over again. And it would be fine. But then ten years would pass and I'm sure some of that time would be great but I also know that for a lot of it Jamie would be sad – like when we spent time with Matt or my sister or all our other friends yet to have kids – where Jamie would do his best to hide the fact that seeing them with their families was like a knife to his heart, but I'd be able to see it. I'd know. And he'd wake up one day and wonder why he'd wasted all those years when he could've been raising his own family, seeing them grow. He would realize that I really wasn't worth the sacrifice. That I wasn't that special. And he'd leave before it was too late. That's the thing. He'll leave one day anyway. Me leaving now is just a way to prevent all those wasted years. The outcome would be the same either way.

'That was an amazing cake Amy made,' Jamie says, taking a sip of his drink.

I let out a long sigh, unable to bear the small talk. 'I heard what you said to Otto and Lauren.'

'Oh, I was put on the spot a bit.'

I shake my head. 'It was the perfect thing to say. Even *I* almost believed you.'

Jamie stares into his cup as if he's trying to read tea leaves.

'I can't let you do this.'

'Do what?' He's playing dumb, but I can sense in his eyes that he knows exactly what I'm saying. That he's probably been expecting it. Maybe he's been waiting to start the same conversation himself.

'I love you too much to watch you give up everything for me.'

'I'm not giving up everything.'

'You're giving up too much. And I can't let you.'

He looks down again and I know that he knows it too. That one day he'll hate me if I let him do this for me.

'You'd be the best dad in the world, you know that? Seeing you with Otto and Lauren, the way you light up around them, it almost makes me want to have a child with you, just to see you so happy, so in love.'

A tiny flicker of hope appears across his face and

it just confirms for me that I'm making the right decision.

'You know I love you enough that I'd have a child for you,' I continue. 'I've realized that too.'

'But you wouldn't want it?'

I shake my head. It feels so heavy.

'But . . .' Jamie stops and hangs his head and although I should be relieved that he finally understands I'm not going to see things differently, it actually makes me sad that he's no longer bothering to put up a fight. That he's given up trying to convince me.

'I don't want to have this conversation for the next ten years at which point you decide to leave me anyway.'

'I wouldn't do that.'

'You don't know that, Jamie. And I'd want you to leave me.'

'Thanks.'

'Because I love you. Don't you get it?'

'But I made a commitment to you. You were open and honest with me and I chose *you*. So why this? Why now?'

I sigh, the sadness threatening to overwhelm me. 'I think maybe if I'd never got pregnant . . . I don't know. Maybe things would've been different. But you can't forgive me for what I was going to do. And I don't think we can come back from that.'

'I do forgive you. I never even mention it.'

'But it's there in everything you don't say, Jamie. In the way you've looked at me ever since. It's always there.'

'That's not fair.'

'I'm not blaming you. I get it. If things were the other way round, I'm sure I'd never be able to forgive you either.'

'I *do* love you.'

'I know you do. But I guess sometimes love isn't enough.'

'Do you really believe that? Surely it's always enough. More important than all the other stuff.'

I shake my head. 'It's not more important than this. Than your future. It doesn't mean we won't always love each other.'

Jamie stands up. 'I need some fresh air.'

'Can I come with you?'

I expect him to say no, that he needs his space, but instead he nods. So I take his hand and we walk through the patio doors into our garden, sitting at our outdoor table and taking in the view. For a while neither of us speaks and then I move towards him and rest my head on his shoulder and he puts his arm around me and I realize how I wish he'd never let me go.

JAMIE

Holding on to Lucy, I hope that this is just another one of our fights. That tomorrow we'll wake up and act as if it never happened. But deep down I can sense that it's not. Because we're not really arguing, no one is saying things just to score points, there are no angry remarks that we'll come to regret.

All of a sudden, the wind howls. It's unseasonably cold.

'Remember how hot it was last spring?' I say, shivering. 'We spent the whole time outside, didn't we?'

'The honeymoon period? God, how I miss it.'

'Was that all it was? The good bit everyone has at the start of a relationship before it all goes wrong?'

Lucy moves away a tiny bit so she can look up at me. 'Not to me.'

I reach out and hold her hand. 'Me neither.'

We stay there for a while then she sits up, wrapping her arms around herself. 'It's really cold. Can we go to bed, please? I don't mean like that. I just want you to hold me. To warm me up.'

'Of course.'

We head inside and Lucy leads me up to the bedroom. We undress and then climb under the covers and I lie behind her, wrapping my arms around her, her warm, soft skin against mine.

'Are you really saying what I think you're saying?'

Lucy turns towards me and nods, her eyes full of tears. 'But it's only because I love you.'

I want to argue with her, to tell her I'm not a child and I can make my own decisions, but there's a niggling feeling in the pit of my stomach that tells me that maybe she's right.

'What if I end up with the worst kid in the world? A "We Need to Talk about Kevin" situation?'

It's sort of a joke, but in a way it's a genuine fear. I could be losing her for something that doesn't make me happy anyway.

Lucy gives me a sad smile. 'I'll try not to gloat.'

'Oh, come on. You'd gloat big time.'

'You know me too well.'

It's true, I do, and it makes me so sad.

'I don't want to be without you.'

Lucy puts her hand on my cheek, stroking it gently with her thumb. 'Nor me you. But one day we'll look back on this and be so glad we made this decision.'

'Are you sure? Because I can only imagine looking back on it and still being as heartbroken as I am now.'

I'm on the verge of tears and I can see that Lucy is too but that she's trying to be strong and I want to say, *No, be weak. Let's both be too weak to do this and just stay here forever.*

'Shall we try to get some sleep?' she asks and I nod because I'm not sure how much more of this conversation I can take, even though I know I'm not going to sleep a wink tonight.

She kisses me on the cheek and then turns so she is facing away from me again and, again, I wrap my arms around her.

After a short while of lying in silence, our breathing naturally falling in line with each other, she says, 'Do you regret it? Meeting me, I mean.'

The vulnerability in her voice makes me hold her tighter and I kiss her lightly on the shoulder. 'Never. You're the love of my life, Lucy Maddison.'

I sense her tears, the way she lifts her hand to her face to wipe them away, the sound of her breathing changing. 'And you mine.'

After

LUCY

'If you're going to live under my roof, Lucy, then you need to pull your weight. It's only fair.'

I'm sitting in my childhood bedroom, surrounded by bowls of half-eaten food on the verge of rotting, endless mugs, glasses, my clothes strewn all over the floor. After a couple of months living with Amy, I realized that it wasn't fair to inflict my chaos on her so I reluctantly moved home.

'It's my room, Mum. Why don't you just stay out of it then it won't bother you?'

I feel like a kid again, the constant arguments.

'Or how about you get a grip and employ basic hygiene measures.'

'Lyn,' Dad calls from the corridor. 'Give her a break.'

'Have you seen the state of it in here?' Mum calls back and then she turns to me. 'Look, I know you're having a hard time, but just clean up after yourself a bit, yeah?'

'I'm sorry I'm such a disappointment to you.'

I know I sound like a petulant teenager, but I'm at my lowest ebb and the last thing I need is more judgement from Mum.

'Oh, come on. Is it always going to come back to that? Will that always be your get-out whenever anything is asked of you? You're nearly thirty, Lucy.'

'And single, no house of my own and working in a crappy bookshop. I don't know how you can even bear looking at me.'

Mum lets out a pained breath. 'Just put your plates and cups in the dishwasher.' Then after a pause, she adds, 'Please.'

I desperately want her to say she *can* bear looking at me, that she doesn't see my life as one big fat failure, but one thing Mum is not is a liar. She's not the type of person to sugar-coat things just to make you feel better, so I know her 'please' is about all the softness I'm going to get.

'I'll do it now.'

'Thank you.' She leaves the room and I feel a desperate desire to text Jamie, to laugh about the situation with him, how I've ended up transported back fifteen years in time, how my mum gets even more annoyed with my messiness than he did, but I know that I can't. So instead, I gather all the dirty crockery lying around my room and take it through to the kitchen, depositing it into the dishwasher.

Later that night, I sit with my dad drinking whisky. I never drink whisky. It reminds me of my grandad. He used to have a glass with Dad every time we visited, only ever one, and the smell of it always takes me back to being a little girl sitting in his lounge. But Dad says it's the only cure for a broken heart, so I'm giving it a go. I have to try something. Because it's been a few months now and I don't feel any better. Time has not been a healer.

'He had a slightly strange jawline,' Dad says, trying to muster a smile out of me.

I manage a small one. 'Almost too chiselled.'

'Exactly that.'

I take another sip of my whisky and it makes me wince. 'Thanks, Dad.'

'Any time, darling, you know that.'

'Do you think Mum will ever forgive me?'

'Oh, God, no. I think she loved Jamie more than you did.'

I laugh but then feel my face fall. 'I never meant to be a disappointment to her. You know, I used to be jealous of Amy, but now I'm glad Mum's got her. Imagine if she'd just had me. How terrible her life would've been.'

Dad shakes his head. 'She adores you. She just worries about you, that's all. I mean, we both do. Of course we do, we're your parents, that's basically what being a parent is. But she doesn't always have the best way of showing it.'

'I adore her too. I hope she knows that.'

'I'm sure she does, but you know your mum, you can never tell her too many times.'

I nod and we sit in silence for a bit. I've always liked that about Dad. Mum would need to fill the gaps in conversation, but Dad's perfectly happy to just sit here, drinking and both lost in our own thoughts.

After a while, I put my empty glass down on the side. 'Do you think I'll ever feel happy again, Dad?'

'I do. These things just take time.'

'How much time, do you think?' I feel my voice

cracking and then tears fill my eyes and Dad immediately stands up and comes towards me.

'Come here.' He holds out his arms and I stand up and let him hold me. There's no safer place than in the arms of your father and for a short while I enjoy the comfort, but then it dawns on me that I'm no longer a child and Dad's not able to solve this one for me.

We let each other go, but this time when I sit down on the sofa, Dad sits beside me.

'You know, there was a girl I loved before I met your mum. Broke me in two, she really did.'

'You've never said.'

'It's not the sort of thing you talk to your children about, I suppose. And if your mum heard me, she'd kill me,' he says, his voice low.

I smile. 'So what happened?'

'We were together at high school. Then she went off to university and I didn't. She wanted me to go with her but I said I'd rather stay at home, work my way up through Dad's company. She was gutted but she said she'd stay faithful, that we'd manage to keep it going long distance, but the very first time I went to visit her, it was clear something was going on with one of the lads in her halls. She denied it to start with but I could see it a mile off.'

'But that's different. She was obviously never right for you or she wouldn't have gone off with someone else.'

Dad shrugs. 'I don't know. Maybe if I'd gone with her like she wanted me to . . . It wasn't all her fault. Anyway, my point is, I thought I'd never mend, cried in my bedroom every night for months and then one day I walked into a pub and saw your mum and, well, as they say, the rest is history.'

I smile. 'Do you ever wonder what would've happened if you'd followed the other girl to university? Ended up with her instead?'

Dad shakes his head. 'Never. Your mum is like a thorn in my side sometimes, but I've had the best life. Well, I hope I've still got a fair bit of it to go.' He laughs. 'And she gave me you and Amy. How lucky does that make me?'

I give my dad a kiss on the cheek. 'I'm the lucky one to have you.' Then I stand up. 'I'm going to hit the sack. Thanks again, Dad. For everything.'

'You're very welcome.'

When I get into bed, I can't help thinking of Jamie. How I wish he was here beside me. I know the point of Dad's story was to show me I'll get over this, that there's someone else waiting around the corner. But when Dad talked about Mum, that look of love in his eyes – that's how I feel about Jamie.

JAMIE

'We've had an offer. It's the full asking price.' The estate agent is unable to hide her elation. Our place has only been on the market for a week. I just couldn't face it any sooner. I can't face it now, but I know it's not fair on Lucy to hold on to it. She deserves her half of the money, and I can't afford this place on my own, not that I'd really want to live here without her. I guess I keep hoping she'll come back, walk through the front door and say it was all a big mistake. Even though I know that can't happen. That this is supposedly 'for the best'.

'That was quick.'

'Well, it's a great place.'

'I know it is.'

'Right, well, I guess you're going to accept?'

'Of course. I'll let Lucy know. Thank you.'

'No problem. I'll be in touch.'

I put the phone down, stupidly excited to have an excuse to call Lucy. We've spoken a few times since she left, the conversation always starting off as house stuff and then soon drifting into silence, neither of us knowing what to say. It's been a week or so since I called her to finalize details before putting the house on the market and I've missed her so much. Every day I don't speak to her feels like a decade. My life's so fucking empty without her. I only eat to stay alive. I go to work. Come home. Try to sleep and mostly fail. And repeat. The only thing keeping me going is the phone calls and I'm terrified about when the house sale is completed, because I know I'll have no more reason to ring her. And then what am I going to have to look forward to?

I pick up the phone and press on her name. She's still at the top of my call log. I've got no one else to speak to. It rings for quite a long time and I start to panic that she isn't going to pick up, that maybe she's decided to cut off from me completely. But then, thank God, she answers, and the sound of her voice is like a medicine (albeit in reality more like a drug because really it's making me sicker, not better).

'You OK?'

No.

'Yeah, I was just ringing to say we got an offer on the house. Full asking price.'

'Ah, that's great.' She sounds genuinely pleased and it feels like a smack to the stomach. 'I mean, that we got the full asking price,' she qualifies, maybe because I don't respond.

'Yeah, I know. Guess I'll have to start looking for places. You found anywhere yet?'

'No. I'm staying with Mum and Dad for a bit. Amy said I could stay there for as long as I wanted but it didn't seem fair. I'll start looking soon.'

I wonder if she feels how I feel. That once she starts looking, it means it's properly over.

'So, how's your week been?' I ask. I don't know what I want her to say. Catastrophic?

'Same as all the others.'

'I know what you mean.'

'They'll get better, won't they?'

'I hope so.'

'Yeah, me too.' I hear a voice calling her. 'Look, sorry, I've got to go. Mum's calling me to say dinner's ready. It's like being fourteen again.'

I smile. 'No worries. I'll keep you posted with the house stuff. Let you know when I need you to sign things.'

'Of course. Thank you for sorting it all.'

'Anytime.'

'Bye, Jamie.'

'Bye,' I say, even though I desperately don't want her to go.

It's ten o'clock and I *should* just go to bed but instead I get in my car and drive. When I arrive at Matt and Mia's, I hold up my hand to knock on the door and then drop it back to my side and start to walk back down their path. Just before I get to the gate, I hear the door open and Matt's face appears.

'The spare room is just as you left it. You're very welcome to stay.'

'No, I'm fine. Sorry. I was coming to talk work, but then I realized it could wait until the morning.'

Matt gives me a sympathetic smile. 'Truth be told, we miss you when you're not here. Come on.'

I know I have to stop turning up on their doorstep at night like this, that I should continue walking back to my car and go home, but I just can't bring myself to. 'You sure?'

'Hundred percent.'

'Thanks, mate. I owe you one.'

'Not at all.'

I go in and take my shoes off in the hall.

'Mia's asleep so we'll just have to keep the noise down. She's knackered all the time since being pregnant.'

It's still always there, the little stab of pain when anyone utters that word.

'All-night party's off, then?'

'Afraid so. But I can stay up with you for a bit. I've got a couple of beers in the fridge.'

I shake my head. 'Thanks, mate. But I'm actually pretty tired.'

'No problem. Well, if you change your mind, the offer's here. If not, I'll see you in the morning. I expect a full English.'

I smile. 'Of course. In bed?'

'No, that'd just be weird. Plus, I think seeing me without my top on might give you an inferiority complex.'

'Quite possibly.'

I get myself a glass of water and then retreat to the spare room, just thankful to be out of the bed that I shared with Lucy. That house is a hive of constant painful reminders. Sometimes, I even think I see her there, making a cup of tea in the kitchen or standing at the bathroom mirror doing her make-up in the morning.

And then the ache of her not being there feels unbearable, the lack of the sound of the radio blaring out when I go downstairs, being able to watch exactly what I want on the television, the dishwasher never being stacked the wrong way – I hate every moment of it.

LUCY

Walking along a tropical beach with the sun on your face and the sea air blowing your hair should be on the treatment lists for a wealth of illnesses and disorders. It's the first time I've felt vaguely human in the past eight months. Antigua had never really been on my hit list, but then this couple came into the bookshop and were going on about how peaceful and relaxing it was and that night, almost beyond my control, I found myself booking a week at an all-inclusive beach resort. Ironically, Jamie probably would've jumped at it, instead of the 'adventures' I forced upon him. And I was right – it is exactly what I needed. A pile of books, cocktails on tap, the sea on my doorstep, my own personal hammock on the beach outside my apartment, yoga classes each morning, aqua aerobics of an afternoon.

It's my thirtieth birthday today. Mum was fuming when I told her I wasn't going to be at home for it. She wanted us to have a proper party, all the family together, and I think she took it quite personally that I didn't want to spend my 'special' day with her. I did try to explain to her that I didn't want to spend it with *anyone*, but I'm not sure it did much to alleviate her hurt. But I'm still glad I came. I can think of worse places to spend my thirtieth birthday. Jamie texted me this morning. It was only brief, a standard 'Happy birthday. Hope you have a wonderful day', but I was touched that he'd remembered and that he bothered to get in contact.

After my late afternoon stroll on the beach, I head to the pool bar for one of my all-inclusive cocktails. Over the past few nights, I've got a few funny looks, sitting at the bar completely on my own, but it's a small price to pay for the escape, the headspace, the peace and quiet.

'The beautiful Lucy is back.' The barman greets me with a wide smile. I expect he feels sorry for the sad heading-towards-middle-age woman sitting on her own every evening (I expect he'd feel particularly sorry for me this evening if he knew it was my birthday, and a big one at that), but he always makes me feel special and I enjoy his company, even if he *has* just been told to charm me in order to get the resort a good review on Tripadvisor. He must be in his early twenties, dreadlocks that nearly touch his bum, and the brightest smile you've ever seen.

'A Ruby Sunset, yes?' he asks, automatically getting the necessary bottles off the shelf.

'Am I that boring and predictable?'

'You just know what you like. I like that in a woman.'

I smile. 'Ruby Sunset it is.'

He pours multi-coloured liquids from the various bottles into a cocktail shaker and then dances with it to the music behind the bar, shaking it to the beat and making me laugh, before pouring it into a fancy glass and putting an umbrella and a cherry in it.

'There you go. Almost as gorgeous as you are.'

I roll my eyes. 'You know I'm going to give you a ten

out of ten on the feedback form regardless. You can drop the act.'

It surprises me that he actually looks really offended. 'It's not an act.'

'Sorry, that sounded rude. I just mean you don't have to be so complimentary. I'm going to write in my comments that you were the stand-out member of staff anyway.'

'Well, thank you. But I actually do think you're beautiful.'

I push a loose strand of hair behind my ear, feeling suddenly self-conscious.

'And I think it's a tragedy you're here on the most romantic island in the world on your own.'

'I like being on my own.'

He shakes his head. 'No one really likes being on their own. Not all the time.'

'I do have friends and family, you know? Just not here.'

'Well, I could be your friend whilst you're here if you want? My name's Alban by the way, as you've never asked.'

I suddenly feel really rude as he asked me my name on my first night here, but I'd just presumed it was something the staff were told to do.

'I'm sorry I haven't asked.'

'It's OK. No one ever does.'

I can imagine that's true with the typical clientele they get here. Mostly superior businessmen with their trophy brides.

'Well, I'm not like those other people and I'm sorry.'

'Make it up to me with a walk along the beach later? We could watch the real ruby sunset?'

'Wouldn't it be breaking the rules to socialize with a customer?'

Alban laughs. 'Well, sex is probably off the cards. But I think we'd be allowed a walk along the beach.'

I nearly spit out my drink. 'Who said anything about sex?'

'Come on, it crossed your mind, just for a second,' he teases.

I smile. 'Not once.'

He puts his hand on his chest. 'You're a harsh one, aren't you?'

I sip my cocktail, enjoying the warm, heady feeling it gives me. 'Sometimes. Sorry again.'

'It's OK. I like it. I find you interesting.'

I laugh. 'So what time do you finish here then?'

'About ten o'clock. Can you stay up that late?'

'I'm not that old and boring, thank you very much.'

'No. Not old or boring. Definitely not.'

I pick up my cocktail. 'Well, I might see you back here at ten. See if I get any better offers in the meantime.'

Alban laughs and then another customer wanders over so I take my drink back to my apartment and lie in my hammock and read my book. The temperature is perfect now. It was a bit too hot in the day, humid and stormy. But it's rained since then and the air finally feels fresher. There's a gentle breeze and it's so relaxing lying in the hammock, swinging gently, the sound of the waves crashing up against the shore, that I must doze off for a bit because when I wake up it's a quarter past ten. *Shit*. Alban. I go inside and slap some water on my face, then freshen up my mascara and head along the beach towards the bar, when suddenly Alban appears walking in the other direction towards me.

'Got a better offer, did you?'

I shake my head. 'I fell asleep. I blame the extra shots you put in my cocktail.'

Alban laughs.

'But the sunset you promised me was about three hours ago.'

'True. It was a . . . what do you call them in England? A chat-up line.'

'Well, it worked.'

'I could offer you the stars instead? I know the best spot on the beach to watch them from.'

'Sounds good to me.'

'OK, follow me.'

He takes my hand and guides me around the corner to a clearing where there aren't any beach apartments, and because there's no ambient light, Alban's right, the stars here are absolutely amazing.

'Wow. I didn't realize I only had to walk ten minutes to see this.'

'You need to hang out with me more often.'

We sit in silence for a while and then Alban pulls out a hip flask and takes a swig. 'Want some of one of my amazing cocktails?'

I put out my hand. 'Now that is an offer too good to refuse.' I take a large gulp, wincing slightly at how heavy it is on the alcohol. 'Blimey, are you trying to get me wasted?'

'What's wasted?'

'Drunk. Very drunk.'

He laughs. 'Oh right. Is it too strong?'

I take another sip. 'It's quite strong.'

I hand it back to him and he knocks back a large amount and then looks at me for an extended amount of time, a smile slowly creeping on to his face.

'What?'

'Nothing. I just find it hard not to look at you.'

'You're a charmer, you really are.'

'I'm just being honest.'

Gazing up at the stars, listening to the sea lapping up against the shore, the warmth of the alcohol in my tummy, it's impossible not to get swept up in it, to feel the romantic haze over everything.

'Can I kiss you?' he asks, looking directly into my eyes again, and I notice how beautiful his eyes are, such a rich, deep brown.

'Couldn't you get into trouble?'

'I think we're safe out here in the dark.'

'OK then.'

And so he kisses me, and whilst his lips are on mine it's possible to forget the pain of the past eight months, and for a short time I feel special and beautiful. I've not felt that way for so long. And it makes me realize that the future isn't entirely bleak. That there will be lots more wonderful moments like this, that hopefully in time they'll become more frequent. And that, more importantly than anything, I can learn to like myself again.

JAMIE

I've never been a fan of stag dos. It's pretty much everything I hate about being a man put together in some seedy, drunken concoction. Luckily, Matt's is a very quiet affair, just me, Matt, a couple of his mates from university and one of the lads he plays football with. I've met them all before a couple of times and they're decent enough blokes. His footie mate, Seb, is the loudest and most annoying of the lot but even he's not too bad really. We've spent the day snowboarding at the local dry slope and we are now at our local pub for a few drinks. No fancy dress. As I'm the best man, unless one of the others has gone rogue and organized one, there will be no stripper. The conversation is pretty tame, bordering on boring, and although we are on our fifth round and I'm feeling relatively drunk, at least it's just been pints rather than shots, plus no inane drinking games.

Of course my mind drifts to Lucy (when doesn't it?) and the fact *I* should have been having a stag do like this. I should be the one feeling nervous about whether I've got all the suits ordered, the rings safe, whether I've made it clear enough in my speech how much I adore my wife, how happy she makes me. Have I got the wedding cars ordered? Booked for the right time? Does the venue have the correct numbers? Is everyone going to be happy with the table plan? Instead, I'm supporting Matt with all that. And I'm so happy for him, I really am, but I can't pretend tonight's not tinged with more than a bit of sadness. The wedding isn't for about six months yet but now that Matt and Mia have had the baby, a beautiful little girl called Talia, it's been harder for them both to find a convenient time for their pre-wedding celebrations whilst the other one babysits.

I go to the bar – it's my round again – and order a tray of pints. And then I feel a hand on my back and for a moment my heart skips a beat at the thought that it might be Lucy, but when I turn around, there's an entirely different woman standing in front of me.

'I thought it was you. Fancy seeing you here again.'

It takes me a minute to place her, her long dark hair with a natural kink, pretty brown eyes, slightly ironic smile. But then I remember. The girl who was on the hen do in here when I was drowning my sorrows about Lucy not wanting to keep the baby.

'Oh, hi. You're not going to believe this, but I'm actually on a stag do.'

'No way! Not your own, I hope?' She follows her flirty comment with a shy smile and I can't help but find it endearing – this mix of surface confidence and obvious vulnerability.

'No, not my own. I'm the best man.'

She looks over at our table where Matt and the others are huddled. 'Indeed, it would appear you are.'

I smile. 'And how about you? Coming to prop the bar up on your own like I was last time?'

'Actually, no. I'm on a date. Or supposed to be. He's not turned up yet. Maybe he won't. Now that would be a bit embarrassing, wouldn't it?'

Again, there's that flash of vulnerability in her eyes and I can't help but feel drawn to it. Her honesty. Her openness. I joined Tinder a few weeks ago (pressured by Matt), and it feels like the whole world is so full of pretence these days, it's impossible to really get to know anyone. I look at people's profiles and I want to scream, 'But who are you really?', but it feels like no one wants to show you.

'Do you want me to sit with you until he turns up so you don't look like a sad loner?' I ask. 'Plus, it might make him think he's got some competition if he turns up and sees you with me. Nothing better than a bit of competition to encourage a bloke to make more effort.'

'Yes, you are stupid, screwed-up creatures, aren't you?'

I laugh. 'So, do you want me to sit with you or not? I'd just need to take these over to the boys first,' I say, gesturing towards the tray of pints.

'Oh, I don't want you missing out on the stag do. It looks riotous,' she mocks.

'Would you be more impressed if we were doing shots off women's breasts?'

She smiles. 'Fair point.' Then she sits down at the bar and orders a drink, looking back at the door presumably to see if her date is here yet. 'Go on then. But as soon as my hot date comes, I'm getting rid of you.'

'Deal.'

I take the tray of drinks over to the boys and Matt

wiggles his eyebrows at me when I tell him I'm just going to go and chat to the girl at the bar. It's fair enough, I'd be the same with him, but I feel a bit sad to see the happiness on his face at the thought that I'm actually having a conversation with a woman that isn't Lucy. That his best mate, who has become a shadow of himself over the past eleven months or so might finally be emerging from the gloom. I wish that were true, but sadly I don't think it's the case. And yet it does feel nice to be walking towards a pretty girl who makes me laugh and seems to think I'm all right.

I put my pint on the bar in front of me and sit down beside her.

'So, Jamie. Tell me a bit more about yourself.'

Shit. Last time she told me her name too and I can't remember it for the life of me.

'Well, what do you want to know?' I ask, somewhat distracted trying to remember what she was called. I'm sure it was one of those unisex names. George? Sam?

'I don't know. Something standard. What do you do?'

'I work in event management. How about you?' I hold on to the 'you' for a bit too long and she laughs.

'It's OK if you don't remember my name.'

'I'm sorry. I was in a bad headspace at the time. I couldn't focus on anything much.'

'And now?'

'Well, I promise I'll remember your name this time.'

'It's Charlie.'

I was nearly there.

'But I was meaning more are you still in a bad head-space?' she continues with a tilt of the head.

I contemplate whether to lie or not. I'm not really in the habit of spilling my soul to strangers, but at the same time, there's something about her that makes me feel I can be myself and she's not going to judge me.

'Better than I was, I guess. But if I'm honest, not perfect.'

She drinks a little more of her wine. 'Surely no one in the world is in a perfect headspace? I'm certainly not. Don't think I ever have been.'

'True. Think I might be a bit lower down the scale than most, though.'

'Bad break-up?'

I nod. 'Well, amicable, but sometimes I think that's worse.'

'Oooh, amicable break-ups mean unfinished business to me. Maybe I should be keeping my distance.'

'Why? Are we meeting up again then?'

That shy smile again. 'I kind of hoped so.'

'I'd like that.' My response surprises me.

'But are you sure this other relationship is really over?'

'Yes.' It may be the first time I've really admitted it to myself, but it's true. I know there's no going back for Lucy and me, however much I miss her. 'We want different things.'

'Such as? Just checking, you know, in case I'm in her camp.'

'She didn't want children and I do. I mean, not right now, but eventually.'

Charlie raises her eyebrows. 'I wasn't expecting you to say *that*.'

'I'm full of surprises.'

Charlie finishes her wine and plonks her glass down on the bar. 'Well, I do. Want kids, I mean. Not with you, of course. But when I meet the right person.'

'Like your hot date, perhaps?'

She looks at her watch. 'He's twenty minutes late and hasn't messaged me to apologize. It's not looking very hopeful.'

'Maybe he's got no reception.'

'You're not supposed to stick up for him. You're supposed to tell me he's an idiot and you're much better.'

I take a sip of my beer. 'I'm not sure I'd be being honest if I said that.'

'So you're going to stand me up if we arrange to meet up after this?'

'No way. I'd never stand you up. I'm just a bit broken, that's all. Possibly not the most attractive option right now. I'd run pretty fast in the opposite direction if I was you.'

She looks down at the floor and then up at me from under her wavy fringe. 'I don't know. I think we all need a bit of mending, don't we?'

I look into her pretty eyes. 'I guess so.'

Suddenly, a bloke comes blustering through the door, eyeing us up as if he's not sure whether Charlie is the person he thinks she is or not. Then, tentatively, he makes his way over.

'I'm so sorry I'm late.' He puts his hand on Charlie's

shoulder and then looks me up and down, a confused expression on his face. 'I didn't have any phone reception.'

I give her a sneaky look to say 'told you so' and she smiles and then turns to her date. 'Luckily, I just bumped into my friend Jamie here, so I wasn't too lonely waiting for you.'

The bloke looks immediately relieved and I almost feel a little bit sorry for him, because although it sounds a bit cocky, I'm fairly sure it's me she'll be contacting at the end of the night. I might be wrong, and I'm sure she'd be better off calling him. He's a good-looking bloke – dark hair, stubble, a strong jaw. And he doesn't appear to be nursing a severely broken heart. But I get the sense from the way she looks at him that she's not feeling it; that really she'd rather stay here and talk to me. And, it surprises me, but I realize I'd rather she didn't have to leave either. That we could stay and chat a little longer.

'Right, I'll just get myself a drink,' the bloke says. 'Do you want another glass of wine?'

'White, thanks,' Charlie says and her date heads down the bar to get the attention of the barman.

'So, should we quickly exchange numbers? Just in case we decide we're feeling desperate enough one day to want to see each other again?' she says, taking out her phone.

'Ah, I'm not sure I'll ever be that desperate.'

The barman pours their drinks and her date takes out his card to pay.

'Come on, quickly. It doesn't look great to be exchanging numbers with someone else on a date.'

'OK.'

I give her my number and she types it in and then quickly puts her phone in her pocket. As her date rejoins us, she climbs down off the barstool and takes her glass of wine from him. 'Well, it was nice bumping into you again, Jamie. See you soon.'

'You too. Take care.'

'Nice to meet you, mate,' the bloke says, and then he puts his arm around Charlie and guides her to a table in the corner, and just before she sits down, she glances back at me and gives me a cheeky wink, and I can't help but smile, a feeling a little like optimism coursing through my veins for the first time in a very long while.

LUCY

It's the day I've been both dreading and longing for in equal measure since I received the invitation. It's been over a year since I last saw Jamie (when we did one last clean of the house before handing over the keys to the new owner). It was horrible precisely because it wasn't horrible at all. We tidied and cleaned and joked and got on just as well as when we first met. And with the distance of time between us and the whole pregnancy thing, it was harder to remember why things hadn't worked out. So when we handed over the keys to the estate agent, it felt almost stupid, like someone was shouting at me, 'Why are you giving away this fabulous house and this wonderful man? Are you insane?'

Once the estate agent had got into her car we were just left, standing side by side on the pavement, me holding Sharky in a plastic bag full of water, looking back at the house we'd once called a home. And then we looked at each other and the question of whether we should hug or not hung in the air between us. For a moment I thought Jamie was going to lean in so I stepped a little closer towards him, but then he turned away and I realized he'd never had any intention of hugging me and I felt like a fool so I said coldly, 'Well, I guess this is goodbye then,' and Jamie muttered something about a plant but then stopped and just nodded. And ever since, I've wondered what he was going to say. That maybe if I'd said something different, he would've said what he really wanted to say too. But the truth is, none of it would've changed the outcome, the hard truth that we aren't destined to be together.

Anyway, the phone calls stopped after that. I guess neither of us had the excuse of house organization to call the other any more and so it would've felt loaded to get in touch. Today will be the first time we've spoken since that day. And as hard as it's been, it was probably for the best. There was no way I could've started to heal if we'd still been in contact. I never would've been able to let go. And, a year on, I'm in a good place. Since Antigua, I've fitted in city breaks to Stockholm, Rome and Prague, and I finally made that long-desired trip to Lapland, which was everything I'd hoped it would be and more. I've dated a little bit, nothing serious, but that's been through choice. I've needed the time to forgive myself, and as cheesy as it sounds, to learn to love myself again. To feel secure with who I am and my life choices.

And perhaps that's why I'm so scared to see Jamie. The fear of going backwards. And yet, at the same time, I can't help but feel excited. I always think it's strange how you can be in a relationship with someone, best friends, closer perhaps than even family, and then suddenly they're gone and you never see them again. It's unnatural.

When I get to the church, it's busy. Lots of faces I don't know. And then I see him, standing in the doorway greeting people and handing out the orders of service, and God, he looks gorgeous in his morning suit – charcoal grey with a purple cravat. He hasn't noticed me yet and I use the time to calm my racing heart, to try to prepare myself with something clever to say, but I've got nothing. I follow the crowd towards him, and just before I reach the door, he looks up and notices me, the forced polite smile falling from his face replaced by a different sort of smile. A smile that you can only give someone you've once loved intensely. I give him a similar smile back, trying to push back the tears threatening to fill my eyes.

The people in front of me disperse, going to find their seats, and suddenly Jamie is less than a metre away and I have no idea what to say.

He holds out an order of service. 'Hi.'

'Hi.'

'You can sit on either side. Mia's is that one.' He gestures to the left-hand side of the church. 'But I don't think it really matters.'

'Thank you.' I take the paper off him, our fingers lightly brushing as I do, and it's like sparks shooting off in every direction. I wonder if it'll always be like this between us. I expect so. 'You look very smart.'

Jamie runs his hand down his suit. 'Thanks. I feel a bit silly.'

'Well, you look lovely.' He gives me a sad smile and I sense the people behind us, waiting to come in. 'I guess I better go and sit down. Catch up later, I hope.'

'Of course.'

I sit down on my own, feeling exceptionally lonely, while the last few remaining guests arrive. Once everyone is in, Jamie walks down the aisle and as soon as he sits down, I search the pew next to him and behind him for a potential partner, but after close inspection, I'm fairly sure he's here on his own – and the extent of relief I feel is ridiculous as it's not like it makes any difference.

The service is beautiful. The deep and wonderful love between Matt and Mia is apparent in their every gesture, every word. Jamie does a great job as best man. About halfway through he climbs up to the pulpit and reads a poem and, at the line about once-in-a-lifetime love, he glances up at me and I feel a sharp pain in my chest and have to look down at the floor. When he sits back down, an older gentleman hands him a baby and for a second it feels like I'm having a panic attack, but then I realize that it's Matt and Mia's little girl. I haven't seen her since she was born and she already looks so much more grown-up. She looks just like Mia, the same jet-black hair and beautiful brown eyes. Jamie holds her on his shoulder, her little face peering back at all of us in the crowd, and then he kisses the top of her head, just softly.

After a few minutes, a woman takes the baby off him (I'm guessing it's Matt's mum) and Jamie fulfils his role of handing over the rings and then going to the back of the church to sign the registers. He poses for all the photographs and I can tell he's uncomfortable with the attention, it was never his thing, but he handles it with his typical poise.

Once the service is finished, people gather outside

whilst they take a few more photos of Matt and Mia inside the church and I feel a bit lost because I don't know anyone, and part of me wonders if I should have come. But Mia begged me and she's someone I have a lot of time for. She easily could've cut me off when I broke Jamie's heart, but she kept in touch and, if anything, we've become closer since Jamie and I split up. When we see each other, we consciously avoid talking about him but he's always there in the air between us.

I take my phone out, using it as a social shield, when suddenly Jamie appears and makes a beeline for me.

'All right there, loner?'

I push him gently in the chest and drop my phone back into my bag. 'Sod off.'

'I think we put you on a good table for the reception. Nobody too annoying. Even by your standards.'

'Well, you know how fussy I am.'

'I do indeed.'

'Speech prepared?'

Jamie nods. 'I'm shitting myself. Just want to get to the venue and have a few drinks to calm my nerves.'

'I'm sure it'll be brilliant. I know you'll have the room in tears.'

'Hopefully not tears of boredom.'

Before I can reply, Matt and Mia emerge and everyone cheers, then the crowd parts to form a tunnel and we all throw the confetti we've been handed over the happy couple. Jamie wolf-whistles and Matt turns to him and laughs, and then Mia catches my eye and blows me a kiss so I blow one back and mouth, 'You look beautiful,' and she mouths, 'Thank you.'

Once they've passed and got into their wedding car, Jamie says, 'I think my car will be waiting too. I better go.'

'See you later. Good luck with the speech if I don't see you before.'

'I'll try to come and keep you company when I can. I didn't realize what a big job being a best man was.'

'It's fine. You know me. I'll be best friends with everyone after a few drinks and some canapés.'

'I expect your blood sugar's getting low, isn't it?'

'Seriously hangry.'

Jamie laughs. 'The canapés are pretty good. I'll make sure they get them out quickly so you don't get too violent.'

'Thanks.'

He smiles and then heads off down the path and I leave the churchyard behind him.

Jamie's right. The canapés are amazing, so I slyly position myself near to the trays whenever they're heading remotely in my direction. I get chatting to another woman on her own, similar age. She says her boyfriend couldn't make it because he had a stag do, rolling her eyes to show she's not happy about him choosing to go to that over joining her. I tell her I'm single and she gives me the look most people do when I tell them, a look of pity, and like so many others she accompanies it with a faux, 'Lucky you. They're more hassle than they're worth most the time.'

'So how do you know Matt and Mia?' I bring out my typical wedding chatter to fill the slightly awkward silence.

'I used to work with Matt so I met Mia through him and we all became friends. How about you?'

'We met through Jamie. We dated for a while.' It's such an insignificant description for something that changed my entire life.

'Oh, you're not Lucy, are you?'

'Yes,' I say, raising an eyebrow. 'Do you know Jamie, then? Whatever terrible things you've heard about me, they're not true.'

She smiles, but there's a trace of pity in it. 'I worked with Jamie and Matt a while back. And no, nothing terrible at all.'

I can tell she's holding back and can't help wanting to know what has been said about me. 'Don't worry. I won't be offended.'

'No, honestly. I mean, I don't even see Jamie any more, but Mia said you were pretty serious. You were engaged, weren't you?'

I nod. 'I expect she told you why we split up?'

'She mentioned it. I mean, it's none of my business. I just know he was pretty cut up about it.'

'Yeah, I think we both were for a while. But at least it was amicable. We're still friends.'

'Yeah, that's great. And he seems happy with Charlie.'

I nod and paint on a smile, pretending this news isn't a terrible and painful shock. 'Yeah, I'm really happy for him.' I finish my drink. 'Right, I just need the ladies and then I'm going to hunt down some more champagne.'

The woman smiles. 'Good idea. Probably see you later.'

I practically run through the crowds to the bathroom, going into one of the cubicles, putting the lid down on the toilet and sitting down. There's no point trying to stop the ambush of tears. It feels like I've been sitting on my emotions all day as it is, and after hearing that Jamie is with someone new, I know that if I don't release the pain somehow I'm going to burst. I wipe my tears away as soon as they fall in a futile attempt to save my make-up, but every time I think they've subsided, they return with force, until it feels like I'm completely dried up and empty.

I feel my phone vibrating in my bag and rifle through all my crap to find it, planning on rejecting the call, but then I see that it's Mum and surprisingly feel the desire to talk to her.

I clear my throat before answering, hoping Mum won't be able to tell I've been crying. 'Hi, Mum. You OK?'

'Yeah, I just wanted to call to see how the wedding was going. Is he there?'

'Of course he's here. He's the best man.'

'OK, OK. I just meant, how is it? Seeing him?'

I realize she's actually calling to check I'm OK and feel suddenly guilty for being a bit short with her. 'I'm sorry. It's OK. I mean . . .' And then, beyond my control, it all comes flooding out. 'He's met someone else, Mum.'

'Oh, love. Is she pretty? Not that it matters but . . .'

'She's not here. I'm not sure why.'

'So how did you find out? Did he tell you?'

'No, some random I got chatting to. One of his friends.'

'Oh, I'm sorry, darling. That must have been a horrible way to find out.'

I suddenly wish Mum was here, holding me and stroking my hair.

'I bet she's perfect and beautiful. And she'll probably have hundreds of his babies and be the perfect mother.'

'Well, she won't be a patch on you.'

'I know you're just saying that. That you think I'm deeply flawed.'

Mum laughs, but then her voice takes on a serious tone. 'I'm sorry I've made you feel that way. But it's not how I see you. I think you're perfect just as you are, I really do.'

The tears are back but then I find myself laughing. 'God, I'm going to look such a mess after all this crying.'

'Where are you?'

'In a toilet cubicle.'

'Classy.'

I smile. 'Thank you so much for calling, Mum. You know I love you, don't you?'

'And I you. More than you could possibly know.'

'I suppose I better go and face the music. I'm probably missing the starters.'

'Oh, well, you don't want that. The free food is the best thing about a wedding.'

I laugh. 'Like mother, like daughter.'

'Now sort your make-up out and go back out there as the beautiful strong woman you are with your head held high, OK?'

'I'll try.'

'And when you get home, we'll sit in our PJs and eat Ben & Jerry's, yeah? I'll even put your bowl in the dishwasher for you.'

'Sounds perfect. Thanks, Mum.'

'See you later, darling.'

And then she puts the phone down and it feels like my first day at school, having to let go of Mum's hand and go out into the world on my own. But I definitely feel better knowing she'll be there waiting when I get back.

JAMIE

The speech isn't too terrifying, helped in large part by the glasses of champagne I've consumed. I was conscious not to get drunk – there's nothing worse than a drunken, incoherent speech at a wedding – but I've had enough to take the edge off my nerves. The only part where I falter is when I'm talking about Matt and Mia being that rare sort of couple where you know without doubt that they are completely made for each other, that they were put on this earth to complete each other, and, as I'm saying it, I accidentally catch Lucy's eye and have to quickly look away.

Charlie was supposed to be here with me today but she went down with a stomach bug at the last minute and I'm ashamed to say I experienced a moment of relief. It's not that I didn't want to spend the wedding with her, but more that I worried how Lucy would react, how Charlie would react to her. It already felt like a lot to be seeing Lucy again after all this time. Having Charlie beside me when I did would've taken it to a whole new level of challenging. But I also feel bad because I know how desperate she was to come. She said it was because she 'loves a good wedding' but we both know it was more than that – that she wanted to assess the girl that broke my heart. And I get that she's nervous about me seeing Lucy again without her here. I do understand. And although Charlie has nothing to worry about, when I saw Lucy arriving at the church, looking beautiful in her stripy dress, I can't lie, it was like hurtling back in time and I felt my heart thumping in my chest at the sight of her, that fragile vulnerability she always tries so hard to hide. When her hand brushed mine as I handed her the order of service, there was a part of me that wanted to grab on to it, to pull her towards me and hold her until our bodies ached. It's not great and I wish I could say I felt absolutely nothing when I saw her, but I can't. All I know is I'm committed to Charlie, and that's as good as I can give right now.

Once the speeches are done, my phone starts vibrating in my pocket. It's Charlie so I excuse myself and take my phone outside. It's cold and I sit on a bench and shiver whilst answering the phone.

'Hey, you. How did the speech go?' she asks and I can tell that she really cares, that she's genuinely interested, and it makes me feel guilty.

'It went well. Mia cried. Happy tears, I think.'

'Ah, you realize you get twenty bonus points if you make the bride cry? Well done.'

'Thanks. How are you feeling anyway?'

'Like death. Wish you were here to bring me grapes and mop my brow.'

Suddenly, I have an image of Lucy lying on the bathroom floor. That fateful occasion: the beginning of the end. Sometimes I wonder if she hadn't got pregnant, if the prospect of us having a child together hadn't been so harshly put in front of me and then snatched away, whether our relationship would've survived. But I guess there's no way of knowing.

'I'll be back in the morning. I'll try not to be late.'

'Don't be silly. You enjoy yourself. I'm not exactly an exciting prospect to rush home to.'

We moved in together a month ago. Well, I moved into her place. She suggested it when the contract ended on the flat I'd been renting since Lucy and I sold our house and it seemed like the sensible choice. And it's going really well. I'm not sure we're quite ready to commit to buying a place together yet, we've only been together about six months, but it definitely feels like it's heading in that direction.

'I miss you, though,' she continues.

'You too.' And listening to her voice on the other end of the phone, I mean it. I do miss her. I never thought it would happen after Lucy but I've definitely fallen in love with Charlie. And yet there's always that slight something holding me back from *fully* handing over my whole heart to her. And now that 'something' is inside the building I'm sitting outside of. Which makes for a real head fuck, that's for sure.

'Make sure you tear up that dance floor, OK? I want to see the videos.'

'Will do.'

'Well, I suppose I should let you go.' I can tell she wants to ask about Lucy, that she's trying so hard not to play the jealous girlfriend, and I know that I should reassure her but I'm not sure what to say.

'I'll see you in the morning. Sleep tight. At least you won't have to fight over the cover with me.'

'Bliss,' she says, but she sounds sad. And then she adds as nonchalantly as she can manage, 'Is she there?'

I wonder if I should play dumb, 'Who? Oh, Lucy,' but she knows that I know exactly who she's talking about. 'Yes.'

'Has she aged horribly?'

I laugh, feeling a sudden desire to give Charlie a reassuring hug. 'Terribly.' Then, after a pause, I say, 'You have nothing to worry about.'

'Of course I don't. I mean, I'm a goddess, right? No one could compete with me.'

'You are.' Matt's mum comes out and mouths 'first dance' and I nod. 'It's the first dance. I better go.'

'Oh, OK. Have a good night. I love you.'

'Love you too. Hope you feel better in the morning.'

I put the phone down and head inside.

I know I can't avoid Lucy all evening, and what's more I don't want to. I noticed she's been chatting to the people she was on a table with so I wait until she's on her own, eventually spotting her at the bar, and head over under the pretence of getting myself a drink.

When I stand next to her, she looks up from fiddling with something in her bag. 'Oh, hi. Great speech by the way.'

'Thank you.'

'And you were right about the table. They're a good bunch.'

'I'm glad. I told Mia to put you with them.'

Lucy looks genuinely touched. 'Thanks for thinking of me.'

I want to say, 'I'm always thinking of you', but I don't because I know it's an inappropriate thing to say and I'm not even sure if it's true any more. It was for a long time after we split, but since meeting Charlie, I think about Lucy less and less. Maybe only once a day if I'm lucky.

'No problem. I was tempted to stick you with the fuddy-duddies, but I resisted.'

'Punishment?'

'Something like that.'

Lucy smiles and then her face changes, as if she's looking at me from behind a screen. 'I hear you've met someone new?' She says it in as casual a way as possible, but I can see the emotional impact resting on my answer and feel guilty that I have to confirm that it's true, even though I don't really have anything to feel guilty for.

I nod, rather than having to say the words.

'I'm happy for you.'

'Thank you. You?'

She shakes her head and then pushes a strand of hair that falls across her face behind her ear. 'I've been travelling a lot. I haven't really had the chance to develop anything serious.'

I can't help the relief that surges through my veins and feel immediately guilty for it. It's not even that I don't want her to find happiness. I do. I'm just not yet ready for that happiness to be with somebody else, which I'm well aware is totally hypocritical. 'Been any-where nice?'

'I finally went to Lapland.'

It hits me in the chest, the fact we'd planned to go together. 'Wow. And did it live up to your expectations?'

'Exceeded them. It was amazing. I cried on the coach back to the airport.'

'I'm really glad you got to go. I'll put it on the bucket list.'

'Maybe you could take your new partner. What's she called?'

'Charlie. She's called Charlie.'

Lucy nods, and she looks so sad it makes me want to rewind the clock and pretend Charlie doesn't exist and that makes me feel horrible.

Then some soppy love song I've never heard before comes on and without really thinking, I hold out my hand.

'May I have this dance? For old times' sake.'

Lucy looks at my hand as if she's not sure whether to take it or run away and then she glances up at my face and nods. I lead her on to the dance floor amongst all the other couples, young and old, locked in embraces and swaying slowly to the music, and she puts her hands on my shoulders and I rest mine lightly on her waist. Then we move from side to side, at first avoiding eye contact, but then looking into each other's eyes and it feels just like the time we danced at Tilda's wedding before every-thing became so broken.

'I think I'll always be a little bit sad about how things

went down between us,' I say, because I need her to know that just because I've 'moved on', it doesn't mean I'm over what happened, or that she won't always be a significant part of my life.

'Me too.'

'And I'll always love you. That's OK, isn't it? It doesn't mean we can't love someone new as well, does it?' I'm not sure where my sudden rush of honesty is coming from. Maybe it's the alcohol I've consumed over the day, or the fact that this feels like my last chance to say how I feel. That I realize this is ultimately goodbye. Perhaps you could call it closure.

'I hope not, because I will too. Always love you, I mean.'

'Maybe we could be friends?' I offer, even though I know that realistically it would slowly ruin my relationship with Charlie, ruin all the progress I've made.

'I think it might be too hard, don't you?'

'Probably. And yet the thought of never seeing you again . . .' I trail off, scared of the emotion in my throat spilling out into tears.

'I know.'

She moves her hands to around my neck and rests her head against my shoulder and I place my hands on the small of her back, breathing her in one last time, trying to bottle this moment. And then the song ends, all too soon, and the next song is upbeat and everyone starts flinging themselves around enthusiastically, but I can't find it in myself to join them. It seems Lucy feels the same as she suggests we leave the dance floor so I follow her through the crowds, back to one of the tables around the side of the room where she left her bag.

She glances at her watch. 'My taxi will be here soon. I better go outside and wait for it. You staying the night?'

'Yeah, I booked a room.'

'Well, enjoy the rest of the wedding.'

'I'll try. Do you want me to come and wait outside with you?'

Lucy shakes her head. 'I'll be fine. You go and show everyone else up on the dance floor.'

I force a smile, but every part of me feels so heavy, it's hard to make my mouth turn upwards. 'I don't want to say goodbye.'

Lucy looks like she's about to cry. 'Me neither.' She checks her watch again. 'How about we just don't? Let's just pretend this isn't a hugely momentous event. That it's just "see you later". Yeah?' Although she's trying to make light of it, I can see this is hurting her just as much as it is me.

'Sounds like a plan.'

She holds out her arms. 'Quick hug then. And then I'm just going to turn around and head outside, OK?'

'OK.'

'It's just "see you later", right?'

'Right.'

She wraps her arms around me and I squeeze her tightly before she releases herself and then, as ever so much stronger than me, she does just as she said she would – turns around and walks out, never looking back. And I force myself to just watch her go.

LUCY

Amy and Dave have gone away for the weekend to celebrate their fifteen-year wedding anniversary so Aunty Lucy is on duty. I think I'm doing an all right job so far. The children are alive. They've been fed (OK, it was pancakes with lashings of Nutella, but the kids enjoyed it and their tummies are full), I remembered to brush their teeth and even made them do it until the little light on their toothbrushes started flashing even though they argued that Amy doesn't make them do it for a specified amount of time.

Now we're at the park even though the weather is a bit drizzly because I figured it was best to try to tire them out before we're stuck inside all afternoon if the forecast of torrential rain is to be believed. I forgot their raincoats, but they don't seem to mind getting damp as they dart across the apparatus and push each other on the swings. The park is empty except for a little boy playing in the sand, dressed in a full-on head-to-toe rain suit, his dad building sandcastles for him to knock down, him giggling away every time he does as his dad feigns annoyance.

I sit on a bench reading a book, Otto and Lauren having reached ages that mean they don't require me to help lift them on to stuff or hold their hand as they track along like I used to when they were little. When I look up, I notice the little boy running over to the swings, where Lauren is pushing Otto, and for a second I'm terrified he's going to run right into the path of Otto's flying legs so I stand up and shout, 'Watch out,' but his dad swoops in just in time to grab him and then picks him up and plonks him on the swing next to Otto before standing behind the swing to push him.

And suddenly, now that he's facing me, I see who it is and I feel my breath catch in my chest. His hair is shorter, but other than that he looks just the same. It's a few minutes before he clocks me and when he does he just stares, his mouth falling open slightly, and then it's like he has a word with himself and waves. I wave back and wonder if I should go over and speak to him, or stay sitting here. And I'm so focused on the logistics of it all that it takes a while for it to hit me. Jamie has a son. And even though three years have passed since I last saw him at Matt and Mia's wedding and so much has changed, that fact still feels impossible.

Jamie obviously notices it's Lauren standing beside him and Otto on the swing as he starts chatting to them animatedly and I imagine what he's saying, about how he barely recognized them, how much they've grown, and then Otto jumps off the swing and starts talking to Jamie's little boy (he loves younger children and is desperate for Amy to have a baby even though she's adamant that she's done at two). Then Otto takes over pushing Jamie's son on the swing and Lauren stands in front of him pulling funny faces when he gets near to her, and the little boy's face lights up and he giggles every time they get close.

Now that Jamie's been freed from the responsibility of pushing his son, he's got no excuse but to come over, but before he does he seems to check with him that that's OK, the little boy barely acknowledging him, evidently too excited about being surrounded and entertained by other children. When Jamie gets closer, my heart rate quickens (will that ever change?) and I try to deep-breathe away my nerves. And then suddenly he's there, sitting beside me, and it feels almost surreal. In many ways, it's as if Matt and Mia's wedding was yesterday, when we danced in each other's arms, and at the same time, it feels like it was a completely different lifetime.

'Hello, Stranger,' he says, as he takes his rucksack off his back and places it underneath the bench. 'Long time, no see.'

'Indeed.' I smile.

'I can't believe how grown-up Lauren is.'

'I know, it's scary, isn't it?'

'It's nice to see them though.'

'Them? Not me, though, hey?' I try a little humour, hoping it might break the tension between us, that strange awkwardness when you haven't seen someone for years, especially someone you were once so close to.

'Oh no, it's horrible seeing you.' It's such a relief to see the cheeky twinkle back in his eyes, the Jamie I knew and loved all those years ago.

'So, you've been busy?' I nod my head towards the little boy who is still giggling away every time his face nears Lauren's.

Jamie looks a little uncomfortable, but at the same time, there's an unmistakable pride on his face. 'Yeah.'

'What's his name?'

'Leo. He's just turned one.'

'He's gorgeous.'

'Thank you. We think so.'

I suddenly wonder who the other part of the 'we' is. Was it the girl he was dating when I saw him at the wedding? Or was it someone new who swept him off his feet, a whirlwind romance where they were so sure about each other they decided to have a child immediately? I don't know why, but it feels like it matters.

And maybe it matters to Jamie too because he says, 'His mum's Charlie, the one I was seeing when I saw you at the wedding.' It almost comes across as an explanation, an 'I didn't rush into it' plea, not that he owes me anything.

'And you're still together?'

Jamie nods.

'That's great. I'm so happy for you, Jamie. He looks just like you, by the way. A real "mini me".'

'I know. It really pisses Charlie off.'

In a way, I'm glad to hear she has a little fire. But at the same time, I wish she was the total opposite to me. 'I can imagine.'

'How about you? Any big news from your side?'

I hold out my left hand, showing him my engagement

ring. It's a single diamond. Very simple. Unlike with Jamie, Elijah and I chose it together, casually deciding to get married over breakfast one day on a beach in Thailand.

'Congratulations. That's great news. I bet he's one of those wild adventurous types. Let me guess, a free runner? Trapeze artist?'

I laugh. 'He owns an adventure travel company.'

'Seriously? Wow, he's perfect.'

'Well, he actually has to work a lot more than either of us would like, but we do get cheap holidays.'

'So where's the wedding? Let me guess, Bali or somewhere equally exotic?'

I smile. 'Costa Rica.'

'Well, the weather's got to be a bit better than here.' He looks up at the dismal grey sky. 'Oh, and talking of holidays, I went to Lapland. You were right. It was amazing.'

I imagine he went with Charlie and am surprised that I don't feel too jealous.

'And I've kept up the paddle boarding. I'm pretty good now.'

'You were always a natural.'

'And you? How's the novel going?'

'I finished it.'

'Wow. That's amazing. Well done.'

'I wouldn't have done. You know, if it wasn't for you, I mean.'

Jamie waves my comment away. 'I'm sure you would've done. So, when am I going to see it in the shops?'

I shrug, a little self-conscious to admit that I've had a few requests for the full manuscript, because I know it's still very unlikely it will come to anything. 'It's with a couple of agents at the moment. I'm sure they'll hate it.'

'Come off it. What I read was amazing,' Jamie says, looking over to check on his son, who is giggling away happily. 'I'm guessing it's the one you were working on before?'

'Yeah. Although it didn't quite have the ending I thought it was going to.'

Jamie looks at his feet and then back up at me. 'Yeah, I guess that happens sometimes. Some of the best stories don't end how you expected them to.'

I turn away, unable to cope with the intensity of his eyes.

'Well, I'll be first in line to buy it when it comes out,' he continues.

'I'll give you your own signed copy.'

'I'll hold you to that.'

Jamie smiles but I can't help feeling sad that we might never see each other again after today.

Then suddenly, his little boy starts crying and he jumps up, some sort of parental instinct, and runs over to a worried-looking Otto and Lauren. I follow Jamie over to check that everything is OK.

'He just started crying. We didn't do anything,' Lauren says.

Jamie picks him up out of the swing and immediately he stops crying. 'Don't worry. He always does it when he wants to get off the swing. His only real words are

"Mama" and "no" at the moment so we still get a lot of crying to tell us what he wants, don't we, monkey?' He kisses the top of his son's head with such tenderness it makes my heart both hurt and swell.

The little boy reaches up and grips Jamie's cheeks and Jamie moves his head and kisses his son's fingers. 'Hey, you, don't rip my skin off.'

Otto and Lauren laugh and so Leo does it again and this time Jamie holds him up into the sky so it looks like he's flying. As he does, a long string of dribble falls from Leo's mouth and lands on Jamie's forehead.

'Ah, nice. Thanks, bud.' Otto and Lauren laugh again and Jamie puts his little boy back on to his hip. 'We're heading back along the canal to the car. How about you guys?'

'Yeah, that's the way we came, didn't we, Aunty Lucy?'

Jamie smiles at me as if to say, 'You don't have to join me if you don't want to,' but I nod and say, 'We did. Let's walk together.'

'Great.' Jamie looks genuinely pleased and I'm glad that there doesn't seem to be any resentment on his part after everything that happened. In fact, he looks really content and for a moment I have to remind myself that I'm content too. That it's OK that we're both no longer broken.

He puts Leo in the pram and Otto and Lauren fight over who gets to push him, Jamie calmly sorting it so that they can both hold on to part of the handle, and then they walk off down the canal path pushing Leo while Jamie and I follow on behind.

JAMIE

It's a little surreal walking alongside Lucy, my son in the pram in front of us. She looks beautiful, her skin glowing from what I guess is one of her recent adventures.

'It's like our first date,' I say and then wonder if it's a stupid thing to say.

Luckily, Lucy laughs. 'I guess it is.'

'Feels like a long time ago, doesn't it?'

'In some ways yes, in some ways no.'

'Yeah, I know what you mean.'

Being so near to Lucy again, it's easy to wipe away the years that have come between, but at the same time it feels like looking back on a different person. Being a father has changed me so much, it's hard to imagine who I was before, what I thought about every waking moment, because now so much of every day is focused on Leo.

'Those were good cookies, weren't they?' Lucy says and I'm grateful to her for it, for her making this so much easier than it could be.

'Almost as good as that street food in Copenhagen.'

'Oh, God, yeah, that *was* good.'

An elderly couple walk past, smiling at us broadly, probably thinking what a lovely family we are.

'That was a great trip, wasn't it?' Lucy continues.

gone. And I look at my son and feel the sudden urge to take him out of his pram, to squeeze him tight. So I do. After standing there for a few minutes, Leo starts to wriggle so I put my beautiful boy back in the pram, kiss his forehead and then take him back to the car ready to go home – taking one last glance back down the road before I do.

Acknowledgements

I've been working on this book in a very strange time in my life. Last February, I was diagnosed with aggressive triple-negative breast cancer six months after the birth of my third child. What followed was a terrifying, exhausting and grueling year of chemo, surgery and radiotherapy, and learning about lots of stuff I wish I'd never had to learn about. Writing and editing this book has been both a challenge and a huge comfort. Sometimes, I couldn't even bear to look at it. I wanted to shout at the characters, 'Get over yourselves. Your problems are stupid and you're not even *real.*' Other times, getting lost in their lives was one of the only escapes from my racing negative thoughts and fears. And for that reason, Jamie and Lucy and this book will always have a special place in my heart.

I couldn't have done any of it (the book or dealing with cancer) without some very special people who I would like to take this time to thank. To Alice Lutyens, my agent, and Clio Cornish, my editor, for being so patient and understanding with me during this time and for helping to make this book something I feel really proud of. Thank you to Olivia Thomas for believing in my book and shouting about it, to Sarah Bance for copy-editing and all those at MJ for working so hard to support me as an author.

To the lovely readers of my previous two books. So often, messages from you about my words brightened a chemo session when I was stuck with a tube in my arm and a freezing cold cap on my head. It still feels unbelievable to me that strangers are reading my books, so to have positive messages from you is the absolute best part of the job.

To all the wonderful friends who supported me – sent me cards, thoughtful gifts and just checked in on me. I've never felt more loved than I did during that time. A special mention to Sarah, for keeping me and the family fed for all those months with your delicious home-cooked meals so that the little time I did have where I felt energized enough, I could spend it working on this book.

To my parents for helping out every single day without having to be asked. For enduring the pain of homeschooling with me when we couldn't risk sending the kids to school as I was so vulnerable. I know it wasn't easy, but we did it and I don't think they fell too far behind! Without you both, I would never have had time to write a book, let alone three! And more importantly, I wouldn't have had the confidence to follow my dream of being an author so thank you. To my brother and sister for giving me strength, love and support through such a difficult time – I really believe we are lucky to have the family we do.

To my boys – for making so many sacrifices in order to keep me safe and for loving me so fiercely. One day, when I'm a bestseller (!), I'm going to take you on the trip of an absolute lifetime to pay you back for all that you missed out on and to thank you for always giving me a reason to fight.

To Carl – I know you had to wait until book three, but I couldn't think of a better book to dedicate to you. I couldn't have finished it without you. I couldn't have done any of last year without you. You are truly one in a million and I am so blessed to call you my husband and my best friend. We might have had some rotten luck recently, but this is our time – I feel it! And thank you for loving this book as much as you do (and even shedding a tear when reading it – I know, I know, you had something in your eye . . .)

And last but not least – to my baby girl – I truly believe that having you saved my life. I hope that you will read my books one day and that they will inspire you. And I hope that, like Lucy, you will always have the strength to follow your heart wherever it is that it leads you.

Turn over for an extract from
Rachel's new novel
One December Day

LAURA

The crowd is packed so close that we have to fight our way towards the stage. I struggle to keep hold of Sarah's hand and pull at the neck of the Christmas jumper I had to wear to gain entry. I struggle out of my jacket as we move through the room, the change in temperature from the icy wind outside to this tiny club causing my face to burn.

'I think we might get a bottle smashed over our heads in a minute,' I shout into Sarah's ear as we reach the front, acutely aware of the hundreds of eyes boring into the back of my skull.

'It's fine, it's fine. We're VIPs,' Sarah says, waving up at Luke on the stage. He smiles and nods his head in acknowledgement, his hands glued to his guitar, his mouth up against a microphone that's wrapped in tinsel.

And then, he sings – his gorgeous raspy voice filling the room, his deep brown eyes fixed on me. And I'm ashamed to admit it but my knees actually feel *weak* – a properly 'Bambi learning to walk' level of unstable.

'They're really good, aren't they?' Sarah shouts over the top of the music.

They are. I've read the articles online. 'University Band Bursts on to the Music Scene After Being Featured on Radio One'. They're picking up rave reviews, becomi the talk of the town. But I was still worried that they v going to be crap. That I was going to have to lie to Luke when he asked me at the end of the gig what I thought of it.

I nod in response to Sarah, embarrassingly lost for words and unable to break eye contact with Luke. The fact that he is wearing glasses with two reindeer waving out the top of them should make him less appealing, but, worryingly, it doesn't.

'God, you two.' Sarah moves her head in front of mine and points two fingers into her mouth.

I elbow her and then we turn back to the band to listen to the music. We watch the whole set – a mixture of beautiful lyrical ballads where it feels like the room falls silent except for the sound of Luke's voice coming out of the speakers, and rousing guitar-heavy numbers where everyone seems to move in time with the music, no longer aware of where they are. When they end on 'Last Christmas', there's such a joyful festive atmosphere that even *I'm* nearly swept up in it.

Eventually, to the sound of hysterical screaming, the band leave the stage and, along with the rest of the crowd, Sarah and I head to the bar. When we finally get to the front, both of us order two drinks so we won't have to rejoin the queue for a while – Sarah going for the 'Scrooge-Driver' while I opt for the 'Mistletoe Margarita' (because of course drinks must have cringey Christmas names throughout the month of December).

'I'm surprised you didn't go for a "Bah Humbug Highball"', Sarah teases as we take our cocktails (adorned with Christmas tree straws) over to a corner of the club. There are no free seats, so we lean up against the wall, finally able to hear each other talk without shouting quite so loud.

'So, what did you think?' Sarah asks.

'Yeah, they were pretty good, weren't they?'

She laughs. 'I reckon if Picasso had asked for an appraisal, you'd have said, "not bad".'

I roll my eyes. 'The last song was a bit of a low point. Plus having to wear this.' I run my hands over my jumper, accidentally causing Rudolph's nose to start flashing.

'I saw you singing along.'

'Never.' I smile. 'Must've been a twitchy nerve in my lips.'

'Ah, so that's what it was.' Sarah scans the room. 'God, I'm going to miss all this. The course, I mean.'

She's doing a masters in music performance at the local university – it's how she met Luke – and she's only got just over a month left.

'Still the best thing you ever did?'

'Composing all day? It's felt like a bit of an indulgence, to be honest. I mean, what's the likelihood of finding a career off the back of it? But I've loved every minute.'

'It's not an indulgence. You've been following your passion. I'm jealous.'

Sarah started playing the piano aged three. By the time I met her in primary school, it was already clear that she was hugely talented. And not only can she play, she writes the most beautiful scores. When she's sitting at the piano, her fingers like ballet dancers on the keys, it's like she travels somewhere else.

'You'll find your passion, too.'

I wrap a strand of hair around my finger, a habit my mum loves to berate me for.

'Hmmm. I hope so. It's certainly not working in Thomas Cook.'

'You do get us the best holiday deals, though.'

'True.'

'So, come on then, make me sick with jealousy.' She nods towards the stage. 'Is the sex still "out of this world"?'

I smile. 'Never tell him I said that. His ego's big enough as it is.'

'Oh, to be back in those heady early days again.'

'We're only twenty-two,' I laugh. 'You sound like an old married woman.'

'Well, Tom and I *have* been together since we were fourteen. It does feel like a lifetime. We're certainly not at the "at it like rabbits" stage any more. More the "leaving the toilet door open whilst he has a crap" stage.'

'You know you wouldn't change it really.'

Sarah shrugs and I can tell she's trying not to smile. Her and Tom are perfect together. I've been jealous of their connection since the moment they met. But, at the same time, he's the only bloke I know who does actually pass the "good enough for my best friend" test.

There's a sudden cheer as the band come out from backstage and start to mingle with the crowd. Within seconds, Luke is surrounded, and he starts chatting animatedly to a stunning blonde wearing a skin-tight glittery jumper, with boobs so full and round they make mine feel like cushions where the stuffing's fallen out. Luke keeps putting his hand on his stomach, his (almost stylish) reindeer Fair Isle jumper creeping up, the girls he's with practically fainting at the sight of his washboard abs. Perfect Boobs whispers something in his ear and he laughs and whispers something